To Grab
with

April

The Day God Met Father
and Other Fables

The Day God Met Father
and Other Fables

Ieuan M Pugh

ATHENA PRESS
LONDON

ISBN 10-digit: 1 84748 144 2
ISBN 13-digit: 978 1 84748 144 3

First Published 2007 by
ATHENA PRESS
Queen's House, 2 Holly Road
Twickenham TW1 4EG
United Kingdom

Printed for Athena Press

Contents

Introduction

The theme running through these three short fables is time. Patterns of inflated delusion unite the harrow of time in its physical, metaphysical and psychological manifestations. I avoid the territory of the theoretical physicist, for whom I hold enormous respect; but as my fables will as fables do, they often venture into time's enigmatic playground.

Without time everything would happen at once: no looking forward; no reminiscing. Our grasp of time remains tenuous. A comment on time by St Augustine of Hippo sums up the enigma: he knew what time was until asked to describe it, whereupon it ran away through his mind's fingers.

Einstein discovered that motion space and time are relative. This is a massive counter-intuitive leap for our everyday experiences. More mind-stretching experiences are to come, for today's quantum physicists are claiming that the interaction between two quantum states through the phenomenon of quantum entanglement is instantaneous; in other words, time reversal. Woosh! Even so, scientific advance has not divined a lucid reflection on the phenomenon of time, which remains an enigma. These fables dwell in the realm between tangible experience and the enigma of time's elusive shadows. Time has got to be one of God's cleverer inventions.

In *The Virtual School of Art Affair* all events are experienced through Johannes Taliesin, a research student at the school. Characters and scenes cooperate unknowingly with his time frame. His friend Rees Bowen possesses a critical, if long-suffering, attitude to what he assumes to be Johannes's simple eccentricities. Michelle Hastings, however, is guided by a deeper female intuition that all is not right with Johannes. Sensing something sinister – yet unable to identify its genesis – she expresses her suspicions through irritation with his gauche mannerisms. Johannes justifies the ever-increasing fractures in his timeline by treating matters as everyday experiences at the Virtual School of Art. Of the many surreal events, one in particular unifies the physical with the psychological.

The Mandelbrot Dilemma demonstrates time's elasticity. I am an artist; during a moment of temporary insanity I climb into my painting to join its characters. I experience a world in the painting that is alarmingly different to that which I had intended when applying brush to canvas. My greatest challenge is to comprehend the painting's many simultaneously occurring time zones. At Heaven's Gate I discover an exquisite animated three-dimensional model of the Mandelbrot Set, its myriad points scintillating rhythmically. Concentrating my attention on a specific moving incident, it knowingly freezes for closer inspection. The metaphors elude logical explanation, inviting deeper collaboration with the experience in order to justify the superimposed time zones as isolated events spaced in linear time. But Heaven's Gate is far from being what at first it appears to be: as the painting's time decays, the images and characters around me elaborate yet more sinister metaphors.

In *The Day God Met Father*, I am in thrall to my older brother Bobby. The linear experience is suspended at a time when I was a boy. All events are witnessed contemporaneously through my twelve-year-old eyes; time for all characters is anchored to mine and they dutifully conform to the illusion. Bobby mediates the experience through time's refraction. Father's death is accordingly brought down in time to become an experience of my boyhood; relatives respond to my childhood fixations in their usual idiosyncratic matter-of-fact ways. Bobby projects the time-shift imagery on his television: he closely monitors God accompanying Father's ghost on a visit from heaven to our farm at Troed-yr-Henrhiw. We are enthralled, as the images on the screen are redolent with scenes we need to experience.

I trust these fables will compound the enigma of time. The harrow of time divines a lucid reflection on matters best embraced, but it plays games with all of us. Time's effluxion demonstrates that the greatest challenges occur within our minds.

Ieuan M Pugh
Drenewydd, Powys. 2007

The Day God Met Father

Paradox

Nothing about Father was normal. In my early years I took the cue from brother Bobby who accepted Father's eccentricity without a by-your-leave, so I assumed nothing of it. A few years later I suspected something odd about other men because none of them was like Father. Eventually reality sank home and the scales in my little head swung in the direction of reality: it dawned on me nothing about Father was normal. Occupying an orbit of his own, he was the most extraordinary character I have ever known.

My brother and I cultivated an ability to see the funny side of Father's eccentricity. We devised scenarios in which Bobby was Father and I was someone, anyone, else. These always ended in the same way: whatever part I played I always lost, and too much giggling interrupted the flow. One such scenario involved Father meeting God; more daringly we reversed the confrontation where God was obliged to meet Father. Bobby and I swapped roles and as usual my giggling spoilt proceedings.

Having read chunks of the Bible, Bobby acted the role of God with amazing conviction. If I pestered him for my turn to play God, I was invariably useless. Unfortunately, my role as Father was no great improvement because my little voice was far too weak to reach the lower registers necessary for the part. On the rare occasions I acted a small part just about right I spoilt the scene by laughing at the moment I was supposed to be acting outrageously cross in some trivial incident. Father's all-pervasive personality had that effect on me. My enthusiasm for older brother's productions was rewarded by his patience with my slow development.

We persisted with our theatre and began to develop the scenes to a fine art. On one occasion we tested our best rehearsal on Mother. She was not amused. Mother was a devout Quaker and implored us to cease the blasphemy. From that time onward our scenarios were played clandestinely, provoking a level of giggling measurable on a scale the medical profession uses for severe cases of hysteria.

Other people's reactions to Father were informative: they were either struck dumb by the sheer voluminous noise and torrent of words, or they adroitly shied away from his permanent bad temper. Eating the carpet was nothing for Father, except we didn't have carpets at the farm. During our early scenario days we yearned to witness the Great Confrontation in reality. How would the Master of Infinite Patience cope with him? I remember Bobby telling me he had read of Winston Churchill's seventy-fifth birthday speech: 'I am ready to meet my Maker,' said Mr Churchill, 'but whether my Maker is ready for the ordeal of meeting me is another matter.'

We laughed and laughed. This resonated with the little scenes we had constructed when God would eventually meet Father.

Time and again over the years we revisited and updated that scenario, and each time God had to cope with an ever-burgeoning basket of complexities in the form of Father's bewildering eccentricities and incandescent temperament. When we were sure Mother was safely out of hearing we would stray into the zone of blasphemy by having Father lecturing God concerning flaws and discrepancies he had discovered in the creation of our wonderful universe. This was bending the moment to breaking point, a piece of pure magic. Happy days!

My brother possessed the knack of identifying the funny side of Father's personality. Unfortunately, my only knack was giggling helplessly at his revelations, a condition he classified as a 'turn', which was soon utilised for all of my untoward actions. However, there were occasions when Bobby experienced difficulty in locating the comedy in Father's outbursts, exhausting even his enormous reserves of humour and patience.

Bobby was four years older than me. Up to my early teens he played a dominant role in my life, often adopting the parental role. This came naturally. At sixteen Bobby was six foot three, broad shouldered and mature, while at the same time my twelve years returned a child of such short stature that he affectionately renamed me 'Stunted Runt'. Incidentally, the name stuck until much later in my teens when we each adopted the name 'Hen' in order to confuse Mother. This worked, but it has to be said Mother was easily confused. We were blessed with an adorable little sister, Francesca, who was bright but mostly quiet. Like all little sisters she was quite capable of being a brat at times. On Bobby's behest she was allowed to be involved in most of our projects and escapades. Unfortunately, due to the girl thing, Francesca was devoid of our intellectual humour.

Both of Father's parents were illegitimate. His father was abandoned in the street in Dolgellau when only a few days old and he never knew his parents. His mother knew only her mother. Both parents grew up in dire rural poverty and their lack of domestic discipline, education and money conspired to sow the seeds of bitter frustration in Father, from which he never escaped. Father's uncontrollable temper shouted volumes, regardless of his protestations that he cared not a damn. The storm raging within him never abated, and he never escaped its malign influence – not that he strove too hard, to be sure, for Father enjoyed the indulgence of rage. His internal battles were ferocious stalemates, indefatigable armies defending his natural lethargy battling with the invading forces of conscience. Father's internal pressures caused violent eruptions, always it seemed, at the least convenient of moments – during a happy children's tea party, or whenever strangers were present, or just for the cussedness of it when the world was innocent of provocation.

To the outsider Father appeared as a wild misfit whose behaviour delivered humorous eccentricities. But to those who lived with him, his violent rages and his oblique eccentricity were perceived more as dark caprice than any other diversion. His roaring voice would echo around the hills, seemingly endeavouring to stir his guilty ancestors from their slumbers. In fairness to our father the die had been cast long before he was born. When he was eleven the Devil's disciple granted him a transient privilege to squander his few natural assets.

Father's reticence to discuss his early years was legendary. The frequent enquiries we made always elicited the same status of unintelligible growl, followed by 'and that's the end of it' signalling our return to the zone of burning curiosity. It was obvious even to our little minds that Father's unconstructive approach to our researching his history was all to do with his wishing to keep it buried, which of course inflamed our curiosity even more.

Mother professed to know next to nothing about Father's past, but we suspected her Trappist disposition camouflaged matters she preferred to remain hidden. That which could not be observed through direct experience seemed taboo at Troed-yr-Henrhiw Farm. Fortunately one of God's cleverer arrangements was to oblige our Uncle Maldwyn to live with us on the farm.

Uncle Maldwyn was Father's only sibling. Father was seven years the senior, but in reality looked a good deal more. Physically the two brothers were similar – very tall, large-framed and raw-boned, wide forehead, clumsy gait, knees and elbows knocking all and sundry. But their personalities were as different as could be imagined. Father was permanently angry at the world; Maldwyn laughed at life and, like Bobby, saw its funny side. Father generated quarrels over minutiae; Maldwyn was devoid of anger and easy-going. Both Uncle Maldwyn and Father possessed very deep voices. Discussions between them were hilarious, Father growling at him in a large, deep voice, Maldwyn singing his responses in mellifluous bass tones. We three children adored our uncle and he reciprocated our affection in equal measure. Regarding matters Father, Maldwyn was a mine of information provided we persisted in the 'pack of three versus one' formula.

'Questions, questions!' he play-acted his protests in response to our persistent questioning about Father on an occasion we had cornered him indoors due to rain. 'Just bear in mind, children,' he said, wagging a huge finger, 'some of the answers I give may be to questions the angels have asked me, so I deny all responsibility for the adjudication. Also, I don't intend exciting your little imaginations by relating scurrilous stories about your father because, when I return to God's counting house, God will have my name next to your father's in the final audit.'

This was a typical Uncle Maldwyn perambulation before revealing facts of gold from baskets of silver, a pattern of prologue to which we had grown accustomed. Asking our uncle the time of day elicited a sworn affidavit exonerating him of blame for the sun's marches through the heavens. So, with the absolver clause in place, I think he set off.

'My knowledge of your father's early years is surprisingly limited,' Uncle Maldwyn apologised while scratching his head, 'considering he is my brother. You must remember he is eight years older than me—'

'Eight years? Mammy said you were seven years older,' interrupted Bobby, getting the working of the information mine off to a bad start.

'There you are, arguing straight away. What you should have heard me say was seven years older for three months of the year, eight years older for the rest. It depends which way your pencil thinks out its sums, and whether you have sharpened it since your birthday or not,' reasoned Uncle Maldwyn. 'Anyway, your father was keen to point out the eight years part to me whenever I pestered to join his expeditions and, as every mathematician knows, an eight-year gap is far more demonstrative a put-down to one's little brother than seven when you are planning an under-cover operation to hijack the local hostelry with your nincompoop acolytes.'

This was to be one of our uncle's circumlocutory excursions into the Land of Maybe, where his fantasies were tangled with our tenuous grasp of reality. By 'reality' I mean a relative matter dependent upon the phases of the moon and his being a 'mine of information' is more to do with puddling the galena spoil to skim it from the ore.

'Both of us were born in fields – Ifan when late potatoes were being planted, and I when the sheep were lambing.'

We gasped. Born in a field of all things. How spectacular a start in life!

'Was it the same field?' Bobby asked, ever the rational one.

Uncle Maldwyn looked confused.

'My mother was a tough turnip and thought nothing of it,' he continued. 'It had happened before but almost certainly will not happen again. You are fortunate your father was not mistaken for a potato otherwise he would have been planted by any of the yokels. Fortunately for him he made an enormous noise of it, a declaration he has continued to this day. Anyway, by the time the curtains were drawn back from the windows of my little mind your father was already looking and acting the grown-up man he thought he was. As a child I was so ill that at times my parents thought I was going to die. My mother prepared for my inevitable death by digging a grave behind the barns where animals that had died of reportable diseases were secretly buried owing to absent-minded lack of reporting.'

We looked at each other; this could not have been true. Bobby shook his head. 'Nain would not have buried you with the swine fever pigs, would she?' he asked in a tone that implied being buried with swine fever pigs was worse than being buried.

'Nain was not particular, no grading according to disease for her, because dogs shot for persistent barking were also buried behind the barns. Even a horse, but there was a lot of singing in those days,' Uncle Maldwyn affirmed.

'Really! Uncle Maldwyn!' Francesca screwed up her little face in horror.

'Really, you have to believe me,' he said, 'every village had its own choir.'

'But as time went on and I survived one crisis after another,' he continued, 'Mother's endemic characteristic to do as little work as possible rebelled against the task of lengthening the grave by increments. The point of this digression is that my sickliness was a defence against my brother, although I didn't realise it at the time. Ifan was embroiled with matters concerning the spittoon of uncouth village youths he was leading on forays into lawless-ness—'

'Surely you mean a platoon, Uncle Maldwyn,' interrupted Bobby.

'Do I? Your logic impales me!' our uncle exclaimed in a loud voice, then, 'No, I don't think his gang was as big as a platoon. Anyway, he had no time for his sickly infant brother. To attract Ifan's attention during those critical years of leadership generally meant a bleeding nose. Fortunately my nose was mostly ignored.'

'He ignores us as well,' I contributed.

'Yes,' Uncle Maldwyn agreed.

'Unless Daddy is cross with us, then he doesn't ignore us,' piped Francesca.

'Which is most of the time,' Bobby added ruefully.

'When your father was eleven,' Uncle Maldwyn continued,

bringing us back to his narrative, 'our father, your Taid, met with a dreadful accident at Penrhiwceiber mine in South Wales.'

We settled down, realising that an epic was unfolding.

'Taid was the mine's fireman, which status implied an expert knowledge of explosives. I use the word "implied" with gravitas and the term "knowledge of explosives" very loosely.'

'Crumbs! Explosives!' squeaked Francesca.

'Explosives,' repeated Uncle Maldwyn. 'However, when defusing a charge that had failed to ignite – BOOM!' and our uncle's huge bass voice resonated to the rafters. 'Your grandfather's expertise had deserted him, and almost his life as well. He sustained horrendous injuries – blinded, a mangled leg, a mutilated arm and multiple shrapnel wounds together with extensive burns – didn't your father tell you about this?'

'No,' answered Bobby, 'only to say he was injured down a mine doing silly things with dynamite and that's the end of it.'

'That sounds right. Our father's survival was without doubt due to his enormous physical and psychological strength,' Uncle Maldwyn continued.

'What's psychological?' Francesca asked the question I needed to ask but didn't in order to avoid showing my ignorance.

'Psychological,' said Uncle Maldwyn, 'psychological is… is—'

'The mind and its control of behaviour,' interrupted Bobby, who was good at words.

'Yes,' continued Uncle Maldwyn, 'our father's mind and the control of his behaviour were strong. Well, he lived for another sixteen years as a blind cripple.

'From the moment of the accident, my father lost control of Ifan the wilful. Before that, control had been a tenuous armistice having complex rules of engagement, which in a nutshell meant Ifan did what he liked and our father was powerless to stop him. Mother was oblivious to it all, which taking everything into account was for her a positive frame of mind. She was more concerned with digging graves, bullfighting and looking at comics,' at which Uncle Maldwyn stopped talking, looked through the window at the pouring rain and smiled wistfully.

'I was three or four at the time,' he continued, 'not fully aware of goings on, but I later surmised from predicaments of family tensions and the way Ifan ignored our parents' orders that all was not right. One would have thought a big strapping boy the size of a man would have assumed the necessary responsibility for the circumstances misfortune had delivered on the family! Although Ifan is my brother I must say nothing of the sort occurred. He had more important things to do.' Uncle Maldwyn was unusually serious about this matter, talking in grave tones. If he criticised Father, it was normally in the form of a joke, so our uncle was indeed saying something seriously special. I believed in my immature way it was information Uncle Maldwyn decided we should know.

'I have put a lot of thought to this over the years, a lot of thought for me that is,' he added with a grave nod, 'and I cannot come up with an answer, so don't ask me for one,' he warned, wagging his finger. 'Contrarily, your father manifested an altogether opposite geometry to the one expected of him: he became detached from us and resentful of his circumstances. It caused a good deal of unhappiness in our home, if you were adventurous enough to call it a home, that is. To this day I don't understand the underlying reasons. It could have been a throwback to Taid's rumbustious days. I'm sure deep down Ifan harbours his reasons, but I very much doubt anyone else would know. Certainly your mother knows nothing, and she of all persons should be the likeliest.

'Your father began demanding his own comforts,' continued Uncle Maldwyn, pouring forth as if for the first time being able to offload his thoughts on the matter. What a story this was becoming. I was glad it was raining and Father was miles away visiting Jones Waungrug.

'Our father's incapacity brought about the lack of discipline that suited Ifan's intrinsic elements of indolence and rebellion. Diawl, there's wordiness for you! I don't know which comic I got it from! Your father grasped the opportunity with alacrity to indulge his hobbies of mitching school, smoking, drinking, fighting and generally acting the waster. Mind you, I'm a hypocrite, for I wished to join them but was prevented from doing so for several legitimate reasons: I was too young, too small and too frail.'

'You are not now, Uncle Maldwyn,' I said.

'No, I'm not now, true. Neither would I want to join Ifan's gang now. Ha! Ha! Anyway, the real reason I was *persona non grata* was for fear I would let slip their state secrets. So I was banned, even from the planning stage.'

'What's that?' piped Francesca.

'Not welcome in the gang,' Bobby answered, and, 'What state secrets, Uncle Maldwyn?'

'Oh, important logistical constructions regarding gaining access to the chosen pub of the night – they were underage, you see – which orchard to visit, the source of their budget, who needed inculcating into the gang. You know, complex war cabinet strategies like that. They swaggered the grown-up and after all I was a sickly infant.'

'How old was Daddy at this time?' asked Bobby.

'Twelvish, I would say,' replied Uncle Maldwyn.

'Twelve! What about school?' I asked.

'Off the agenda. I'm disclosing too many secrets of your father's youth, and I am doing your father a disservice.'

'Oh, come on Uncle Maldwyn, don't stop now!'

'I believe too much information will give you indigestion.'

'Please?'

'Your father was expelled on his thirteenth birthday,' he promptly replied.

'Expelled!' Bobby exclaimed.

'Expelled!' I piped.

'Didn't you know?' Uncle Maldwyn asked, innocently.

The three of us shook our heads. Learning of Father's expulsion from school came as a bit of a shock and we registered the surprise with obvious emphasis. No wonder our uncle was showing reticence, for he quickly added, with a finger to his mouth indicating the requisite level of secrecy, 'Now don't go blabbing this information all over the place! I'm beginning to think I'm letting out too many confidentialities and I shall suffer for this. No doubt I will be tied to the great yew for three nights until the crows peck my tongue out for telling stories.'

'Uncle Maldwyn!' cried Francesca.

'Oh, all right. Two nights, then.'

'We wouldn't dream of blabbing on you!' Bobby pledged and, turning to us, 'would we?'

'No, never!' we chimed, 'we swear if God strikes us dead.'

'Oh dear, tempting the Lord! No need to go that far!' said Uncle Maldwyn.

Our blatant swearing of secrecy set Uncle Maldwyn's mind at a reasonable level of rest, appropriate enough to allow him to continue.

'Hitherto your father was enjoying a privileged education at Dr Ellis's, showing great promise in his early years, top of the class with ease. There is no doubt your father has a brilliant brain, but the workforce inside his cranium would much prefer to down tools and take a reclining posture at the slightest provocation!'

Our mother frequently fretted that our father was bone idle, so Uncle Maldwyn's humorous description corroborating his laziness was refreshing.

'The discipline maintained by both my father and the school had kept Ifan on the straight and narrow. He matured to physical manhood at a precociously early age so the teachers at his school elected him as the official school flogger, regardless of the damage to Ifan's psychology. Permission to inflict pain on others with impunity engendered a sense of invincibility in your father that has remained for ever. Punching the life out of some little dimwit who had got his sums wrong brassed up your father's knuckles no end for future conflicts,' whereupon our uncle burst into ironic laughter.

'But it was hell for my father. I remember him complaining to my mother that Ifan was out of control and every night he prayed that God would grant him five minutes of his former self in order to give his son the lesson of his life. You see, your father and I are tall, but our father was a giant. You know the horse story.'

We knew the story of Taid lifting a horse on to his shoulders; Uncle Maldwyn had the photograph to prove it.

'Tell us the story of Taid and the horse again, Uncle Maldwyn,' Francesca requested.

'Not now, sweetheart,' ordered Bobby, 'don't sidetrack Uncle Maldwyn.'

Fortunately our uncle was not going to be sidetracked.

'After his expulsion from school,' he continued, 'your father's chrysalis metamorphosed with commensurate ease into an uncouth hoodlum. At thirteen he passed for twenty-something – moustachioed, muscular and coarse-voiced, a wild horse devoid of discipline possessing six hooves. This was the time I was convinced our family comprised three adults and me. Ifan's perspective however was different: two lame ducks, a sickly child at death's gateway whose grave was being incrementally processed and him, the untouchable man of the house. Unfortunately Ifan's teenage years were extirpated – diawl, there's a big word for you! I learnt it only yesterday when reading the *Beano*,' said Uncle Maldwyn, with a broad, toothy grin.

'You've got this week's *Beano* already?' we two lesser ones squeaked.

'No, no. It's from last week,' Uncle Maldwyn quickly corrected.

'I don't remember seeing "extirpated" in last week's *Beano*,' said Bobby.

'It must have been in the *Dandy*, then.'

Bobby and I fell about laughing. Uncle Maldwyn looked very serious.

'Daddy doesn't do those things now,' said Francesca protectively.

'This is indeed true,' replied Uncle Maldwyn seriously, 'as your father is now a holder of Quaker beliefs his little eccentricities come out in different ways.'

'Like his long greasy hair?' asked Bobby, giggling again.

'And his greasy clothes?' I added, convulsed in giggles.

'And his wanting to lie in bed all day.'

'And his terrible tempers.'

'And his eating with a cigarette in his mouth!' Bobby exclaimed.

'And talking to the pigs,' Francesca said, at last grasping the idea, 'I caught him talking to Voroshilov!'

'Exactly! He's a horse whisperer who dislikes horses, so he practises on the sheep and pigs, without the necessary authorisation,' said Bobby.

'But he's a God-fearing, honest, law-abiding, fair-playing,

horse-whispering, non-swearing, chain-smoking, no-longer-drinking, anti-social, non-washing, roaring, bad-tempered, slugabed, toothless, converted Quaker. And a card-carrying Communist,' sang Uncle Maldwyn, bursting into Gilbert and Sullivan style.

We laughed heartily, albeit not maliciously, because underneath all the gossip we loved our Father dearly. Without him there would be nothing to talk about on a wet day at Troed-yr-Henrhiw Farm. Suddenly the narrative took us down a dark road.

'When your father was about twenty he saw the Light, and God spoke to him.'

'Wow! I didn't know Daddy had seen the Light!' exclaimed Bobby in amazement.

'Daddy always talks about the Almighty,' I put in.

'Well, seriously, the Almighty talked to your father. Your father termed it a strange experience owing to his head having struck the road with great velocity,' averred our uncle. 'It certainly wasn't the aura of a spirit descending from heaven to show him the straight and narrow. But from the story he told me, all the evidence points to an awakening.'

'How did it happen?' Bobby asked.

'The occasion was his last motorbike accident.'

'Which one was the last one?'

'I thought you knew his last crash was at Bwlch Nant-yr-Arian.'

'I know of the Bwlch Nant-yr-Arian crash,' Bobby replied, 'but he had so many crashes.'

'It is significant that the Bwlch Nant-yr-Arian crash was the last of them. The other crashes like the Wall of Death crash, the Isle of Man crash, the one into the ice-cream parlour and the one through the front door of Y Bwthyn in Goginan were just crashes. Nothing was like his experience at Bwlch Nant-yr-Arian, for something deeply divine happened.'

'All on the AJS, leading link, I bet,' said Bobby, knowingly.

'No. The first was on a BSA, then a Brough Superior on the Wall of Death, then he had a Vincent. Only the Bwlch Nant-yr-Arian accident was on an AJS,' said Uncle Maldwyn. 'But you are missing the point of what I am saying,' he added firmly. 'The circumstances are difficult to believe without the assistance of a mountain of salt. Having been reprimanded by the Almighty your father looked for loopholes, making just enough concessions that would enable eligibility for his return to the human herd.'

'Daddy always puts a lot of salt on his dinner,' Francesca said.

'Your Father was returning from a motorcycle race meeting at Fan, Llanidloes, where his best place was second in the all-comers race. It was a night of broken cloud with a fitful moon. The lights on his motorbike did not adequately illuminate the road. Near Bwlch Nant-yr-Arian the road winds treacherously, clinging to the perilous slopes, as you know. An old cow had strayed on to the road and Ifan ran into her full pelt. He should not have been going full pelt on that road with poor lights, but he was. The impact embedded the bike in the cow and both cow and motorbike fell on top of him. Your father's head struck the road with great velocity and he temporarily lost consciousness. You know about this accident. I was present at the time your father retold of events up to that point. But he omitted to tell you the part where he was subject to a weird experience.

'Coming round from unconsciousness he discovered he was in the midst of a nightmare. He was pinned to the road, as the ancient Celts pinned their sacrificial corpses in the bogs to prevent their spirits from escaping. The dying cow was on top of the motorbike and Ifan was pinned beneath them both. Although his left leg was broken he recalls feeling no pain. The right leg was pressed against the hot exhaust pipe and was being fried.'

'Ugh!' cried Francesca.

'It gets worse,' Uncle Maldwyn warned. 'He was unable to move and was bleeding furiously from a head wound – hence the big scar on the left side of his forehead. The cow's entrails had poured over him, blood everywhere, cooking on the hot exhaust. The poor old cow was near death. Her great head with its wide horns was near your father's head. His situation was serious – if no one came along that lonely road soon he would perish. Then a strange event came to pass.'

Having spoken thus, our uncle reached his arms above us and spread his huge hands.

'Dark clouds had been spearing the night sky, allowing fitful shafts of moonlight to illuminate the scene. Suddenly, the clouds parted and the strange dance was bathed in bright moonlight. In her death throes the cow turned her large head and looked Ifan in the eye. He froze – it was a strange look, serene yet riven with anguish. The look penetrated your father's soul, at which he forgot his wounds and burning limb. Then, contradicting the moment and to your father's horror, the cow spoke to him!

'She spoke in a slow and deliberate manner: "God arranges his lessons in unlikely circumstances," the cow said. "Before I die I shall advise you on your redemption." Your father was horrified. He glanced nervously around as best he could to see if someone had happed on the scene unbeknownst and was talking the religious mantle. But no: the cow it was that spoke.

' "You are a sinful man, Ifan Pugh. Your sins have drained your soul empty of any worth. Your spirit is exhausted and almost departed. You have committed many ills for you have no feelings for any being but yourself. You have always assumed animals do not feel pain because they cannot talk. I am inflicted with this dreadful pain because I was the chosen messenger. Think on these things."

'Your father recalled the strange events with awe. He became very dizzy. Above him the moon vibrated in the sky and stars whirled around. He swore the fence posts between the road and the steep slope stood out as gravestones. Several names were carved on the gravestones, one of which was his. The road with winding tarmac held shadows in its curve, your father folded nondescript, snared in the lesson, convinced he had been struck insane.

' "I hope this moment haunts you," the dying cow continued. "You have done nothing in the past nine years to cloister a thimble of worth, yet you have amassed a conflagration of worthlessness and dismay. The sins of your father are registered, but you are undoubtedly a vile body, too much so for them to be delivered unto you. As my head jerks in death's final spasm, my horn will pass through your skull like a pitchfork through mud. Your worthless contributions to this world will end." '

We gasped, speechless.

'I have never seen my brother so humble. He told me he saw for the first time his ugly past looming like ragged clouds before his eyes. "What do I do? What do you suggest I do?" he heard himself imploring the dying cow, but she did not answer as her eyes were slowly fading. "Don't die yet, tell me what to do!"

'Terrified, your father winced in readiness for the cow's final death spasm. Unable to take avoiding action, he recognised for the first time the smell of terror. His thoughts scrambled to the times he and his hoodlum friends had held weaklings in similar circumstances of entrapment. They must have felt as terrified as he was at that moment.

'Then the cow opened her eyes and again looked at him. "Help me! Help me before you die," your father whispered in fear at the dying cow, "make a last effort to move off me." But the cow had almost completed her mission to deliver a lesson; helping your father was not part of that mission.

' "What does it feel like to be trapped?"

' "Something I have never experienced before," your humbled father replied.

' "Think on this circumstance, Ifan Pugh." '

Uncle Maldwyn lowered his arms.

'With this terrifying preoccupation your father had not noticed three strangers arrive on the scene. In silence they frantically heaved at the dead cow, lifted the motorbike and pulled your father clear. He struggled to the side of the road, hobbling as best he could with a broken leg. Turning to his rescuers to register his gratitude, he was astonished to discover they had gone.'

A Unique Entity

Mother described Father in various expressions of embarrassment. It was an easy task to pick Father out from a crowd, to separate him from the rest, to differentiate his persona against a spectrum of normal images.

Father was a unique entity. Decades before it became fashionable he wore his red hair shoulder length, greasy and unwashed. It hung in rats' tails over a greasy collar to dangle uncomfortably on his greasy shoulders. A greasy cloth cap that defied colour analysis was pulled at a perilous angle over his left ear. The cap was a fixture, whether he was attending to the animals, taking fifty winks, eating at table or in bed. Mother suspected creatures more adventurous than common lice nested in the abundantly tangled pastures of Father's scalp. We never cornered the animals, but evidence of strange fauna often fell out following a period of vigorous scratching. On one occasion a pencil stub of mine that I had lost for days fell out, but Father denied all knowledge of how it had got into the thickets. Our cat, Cog, watched expectantly.

When gripped by itch, location was irrelevant to our cussed father as his scalp rebelled the noxious creatures roaming the greasy plains: they were ejected over the dinner table, in the new milking parlour before it was washed away in the flood, in the pantry. On one unforgettable occasion he set about scratching his head over the open fire, a part of the world we had been forbidden to approach. The fireplace was broad and cavernous, possessing side ovens and a hob on which the crochan stood filled with Mother's best cawl. Scratch, scratch. The fire was no respecter of pecking order and readily flung its flames at Father's hair. Ablaze, Father staggered back. But the flames leapt from his hair to the soot hanging in robes from the gaping chimney aperture. With an explosion that drowned Father's roaring the chimney was ablaze, and we were in for one of those historic 'when the chimney caught fire' days.

Father quickly dowsed his flaming hair, but the inferno in the soot-filled chimney had a mind of its own. Black smoke belching from the chimney filled the farmyard and the surrounding forest. Smoke poured from cracks in the chimney walls, and oozed from beneath the eaves and slates.

'Oh-oh,' signalled Bobby, 'we'll have bats everywhere.'

It appeared as if the house was on fire. Sure enough, Bobby's prophecy came true, as bats by the hundred fled their smoke-filled bedrooms in the cloisters of the farmhouse roof. We all responded to the chimney fire in our separate ways.

'The house is going up,' said Mother.

'My scalp is burned,' growled Father.

'I knew we had bats in the attic, but not in these numbers,' said Bobby.

Francesca and I said nothing; instead, I ran around fruitlessly, plain scared. Spot barked at the belching black smoke.

'What on earth possessed you to set light to the chimney?' enquired Mother, as the conflagration subsided. 'Just look at the mess. If you had to scratch, why couldn't you go out into the barn to do it?'

'What, and ruin the hay?' chirped irrepressible Bobby.

It took us ages to clean up the mess. Father stood by, nursing his burned scalp. The cawl was spoiled, and we went hungry.

Apart from the large diagonal scar on the left side of his forehead that for ever betrayed his propensity for propelling his motorcycle in a manner unbefitting to the road conditions, several smaller facial scars – gained through prizefighting – competed for attention. His large blue eyes applied a transfixing stare at anyone who got in the way. His bright red bushy eyebrows interfered with his sight until he took scissors to their meddlesome habit. With elbows knocking doorposts and people at yards' radius, he walked with the lateral stagger characteristic of Pugh males.

His clothes were shabby and greasy, and stank of a kaleidoscope of aromas. Bobby attempted teaching me to differentiate one odour from the others in order to draw worthwhile information regarding Father's travelling plans. I was a poor pupil, my excuse being that Father prohibited me from getting close enough to glean a good sample of smell. Bobby insisted this was more to do with my stupidity than proximity, as he could detect the spectrum from the next room. Spot, talking of nose power, could detect Father approaching two miles away, downwind.

Father wore an old brown overcoat that resembled a multicoloured patchwork quilt, twisted nails doubling as buttons, belted with red baler twine. Considering the uniqueness of his attire, it was odd that he never took to wearing a potato sack over his shoulders in wet weather, the beloved uniform of farmers in wet west Wales. His boots were shabby, caked in years of mud and dung, their heels long since worn away revealing protruding nails, but the laces of baler twine were always neatly tied. From any perspective Father presented a sad sight.

From the age of eleven Father drank heavily. This makeshift oblivion continued until he experienced the life-changing event around the time of his twentieth birthday. Thereafter he rarely drank alcohol. His favourite tipple became milky tea, over-sugared to a critical specificity where the tealeaves would float atop like Dead Sea scrolls. In later years the tea concoction was carried in a vacuum flask that became his constant companion.

However, his life-changing experience did not oblige him to cease smoking. Father was born with a chimney standing through the thicket of his hair. Once a Rizla roll-your-own cigarette was placed in position, it would remain there until the cindered butt burned his lips; only then was it removed to pass the light on to the next generation. He had a good line in blowing off the ash, regardless of his environment or activity. He talked and even shouted with the cigarette still at ease; he ate and even drank without removing the smouldering fixture. The only concession Father's ever-present cigarette made to the interruptions of eating and drinking was to shuffle from a central position in his mouth to a corner, where it would loiter for the duration of the tiresome process of food consumption. If Mother had the temerity to suggest he removed it before eating he looked at her daft.

Apart from the farm and tractor smells that hung like flies around Father, stale tobacco smoke was especially prominent. He had no intention of abandoning decades of determined effort by stopping, or even slackening off, the altogether necessary process of smoking. Regardless, Mother Nature persisted in reminding him through the emissary of a constant bronchial sluice gate that his lungs could benefit from a gulp of fresh air on occasion, but Father decided to blame the cellulose vapours he had inhaled on the one occasion he sprayed the farm implements, together with the barns and sheds, all bright red. Even the spraying was cussed. The cellulose was not being used as a protective coating; we were informed it was in celebration of the Welsh Communist Party having at last drawn up a constitution that adhered to the main thrust of the world communist revolution.

Although the overall presentation of Father's face was bearded, he was adamant he was beardless, because he removed it at albeit irregular intervals according to religious and social orthodoxies. Father bathed less than once a year, no exaggeration. On the rare occasion this event occurred, a great production was set in motion with roared commands, boiled kettles and locked doors. Towels were placed at the ready, mostly to ensure his head remained dry. The farmhouse possessed no bathroom, this appellation being rendered to any room that could embrace the portable zinc bath. Father dragged the thing into the parlour; a sacred, musty room reserved for occasions when bigwigs visited the farm or when it was descended upon briefly by the family at Christmas. Nevertheless, the great palaver occurred in the parlour, behind drawn curtains and locked door.

Regardless of the bathing commotion, the lines of black grease around Father's neck hardly abandoned their stations, and in any event had consolidated their return within the week, back to competing for attention with fresh flea blows. Both flea blows and grease streams were worn with pejorative pride. My little imagination would yearn for the ownership of a magnifying glass in order to observe flea vegetables planted in the linear gardens. I believed Father resisted our childish advances to prevent our adopting his fleas, notwithstanding the adventurous nature of the flea, until I learnt it was down to his dislike of children, and altruism was out of the window.

Stubble around Father's mouth assumed nicotine yellowness. By comparison this was an endearing feature, for he possessed no teeth except for black root stumps flush with the gums. It is doubtful a toothbrush had ever entered Father's mouth, as the root stumps were the result of neglect, poor diet and the inevitable decay. As a consequence Bobby described Father's breath as like 'a gust from hell on a sultry day'.

Unsure of what hell smelt like, I requested elucidation, both for information and a giggle. 'Like Daddy's breath, of course,' came the matter-of-fact reply, 'which is a combination of stenches from the ash pit when the kettle has toppled off a smouldering log, the pigsties that have not been cleaned for a whole season, two sacks of rotting rats behind the barns and the stench when a free-ranger has hidden her eggs and forgotten about them. All these are emollients in a moist balm shrouded in cigarette smoke when Daddy uses newspaper because his Rizla has run out.'

My memory of Bobby's descriptions would be sealed with the endorsement of giggle.

Father used his deep bass voice to great effect in constantly shouted conversations. Even on occasions when he was merely talking, strangers believed he was shouting. Uncle Maldwyn described Father's voice as 'having a two-way switch: Loud and Louder'. Any alteration Father made to the ample volume would be in an upward direction. We were used to it. It goes matter of course that Dylan Thomas modelled Farmer Utah Walkins of Salt Lake Farm on Father. Why Dylan Thomas did not go the whole Pugh Troed-yr-Henrhiw hog I don't know, unless it was something to do with the overall balance of his play for voices.

Being mentally idle, Father's high intelligence was never used for learning, inventing, creating – that sort of thing. Rather, his intelligence was utilised in emergency only, such as calculating a way out of a muddle that bone idleness had allowed to grow around him. Otherwise his brain had a quiet time in life. Father was riddled with prejudices: his greatest dictum was to never allow facts to come between him and his made-up mind. The task of reassessment required brainwork, which of course was off the agenda for the duration. Father was never wrong; he never lost an argument, never admitted to being in error and never apologised. This philosophy guided him with unprincipled fervour. He could unfailingly articulate a winning viewpoint simply by raising his ample voice, which sent civilised people scurrying for sane havens.

Father dressed like a ruffian, his whole body's disposition looked the ruffian and indeed he acted the ruffian, especially if it could cause greater embarrassment to his family. Over the years he nurtured his social graces to match this stunning medley.

Having been born into it we were used to the apparition, but strangers happening upon it for the first time stared aghast. Children ran behind their mothers' skirts for protection and babes in cradles screamed. Grown men found it difficult to look him straight in the eye, occasioning to study their boots or the clouds.

Father was the first hippy, thirty-five or more years before the second, much-publicised hippy coming in California. During the second wave of the animal vegetation, they wore flowers in their hair and preached love – elements bearing no meaning in Father's vocabulary. Instead, he wore detritus and entanglements in his hair and preached pure scorn for his fellow being. Father was indeed an apparition apart, a unique entity.

Father was fearless. Refusing to carry his cross in life he peremptorily cast the thing off at the foot of Calvary and fearlessly goaded the Roman Guard to finish him off there and then. An attitude pervaded his psyche whereby death was a more desirable alternative to conformity. Were we confusing fearlessness with an indifference to life itself?

As the event of despatch by the Roman Guard never transpired he spent his life protesting a justification for his non-compliance by metaphysically preaching to the centurions specifically, and the populace generally, that he had devised a simpler way for the transportation of the burden of life. The mechanical aspect paled into trivial detail aside the psychological terrain that occupied Father's mind. Yet he would demonstrate the technical as though it possessed elements of the life force. This involved cutting the burden of life into manageable pieces at the start of Calvary, giving each hypocritical participator in the event a piece to carry to the top. Eventually each shall participate in reassembling the confounded thing.

Following this method, Father ingeniously contrived that everyone in the crowd should suffer the consequences of the crowd's insanity. His solution departed radically from the scriptures of self-effacement, or suffering on behalf of others' sins, and all the rest of the cant that drove him into a frenzy regarding the superficiality of it all.

While the crowd was busy attempting to reconstruct the pieces to form a cross, Father would lope away under the fog of babbling, securing his escape from such an avoidable event.

The conflict that raged within Father's life galleries was the utter contempt for humanity, its pictures being of weakness as mendacity, duplicity and perfidy. Set against this was the unavoidable nuisance of having to be part of the throng. Father never enacted any of these sins but possessed a sublime indifference to confessing his own weaknesses, exhibiting however, a similar nonchalance in doing nothing about them. The lone wolf tolerated at best the company of people, although he had been witnessed acting the gregarious politician in order to gain a desired end. This was not a contradiction; it was simply an expedient strategy when all other avenues were blocked by the cussed order of things.

He loathed the imbroglio of crowds, becoming louder and more awkward in behaviour when deluged by them. He saw it as an act of God's ultimate mischievousness in obliging people to gather in crowds before they felt at liberty to come to the wrong decision. This fatal flaw in mankind's frail mental construct was God pulling wool over sheep's eyes. The human sheep would agree to anything, Father preached, in order to detract from the cerebral responsibility of emancipation. If one challenged his view, his examples of blunderous decisions taken by the crowd through history were encyclopaedic.

'A tent to camouflage the acts of hypocrites,' was Father's description of democracy. 'The iniquities of a system that allowed guttersnipes and layabouts to vote,' he harangued.

Mother was sanguine, being aware Father's bone idleness doubled as layabout any time of the day. Sanguinity failed to penetrate the outer defences of insensitivity.

'Democracy sees the not-quite-mediocre of society manipulating the plain mediocre into believing they had freedom of choice in voting for the manipulator,' he harangued. 'After that?' He threw down the challenge. 'After that the hypocrites would crow that democracy was seen to be working.'

Father's ideal model of government was a form of benevolent communist tyranny where voting would be pointless, as pointless as in a democracy. Asked where he saw himself in such a government, he would chime, 'As a dutiful member of the proletariat working for the good of the ideology.'

When I asked Bobby for clarification of Father's ideologies he shook his head in dismay. 'His ideology is all rubbish. I believe Daddy does not believe in what he hears himself saying. You know as well as I that Daddy is incapable of being dutiful, not even in exceptional circumstances. As Daddy is a loner he considers himself apart from the proletariat. Working for the good? When did you see Daddy working, leave alone working for the good? Daddy goes to great lengths to avoid work. Listen, stupid, you seem to be getting more gullible the older you get. Daddy is saying all that for effect in case some card-carrying member of the Welsh Communist Party should be in earshot and would report him back to Moscow.'

'Why Moscow?'

'Don't you know anything? Moscow is the capital of world communism.'

'Why not the local communist representative he visits in Goginan?'

'Oh, he has only one leg and could not possibly uphold the ideologies of world communism as rigorously as they do in Moscow,' Bobby replied.

'But he could report back.'

'Believe me, that communist in Goginan wishes to hold on to his remaining leg. No, I mean some able-bodied snitch who doesn't like Daddy,' he muttered.

Which, to my way of thinking, covered nearly everybody in Wales, but I left it at that because my brother seemed to be losing his legendary patience.

Father was mentally and physically bone idle by gene, cussed in independency, awkward by intent, nonconformist in strategy, aggressive by instinct, loud in habit, indiscreet for effect, lupine by logistics. He had no respect for status, name tags and authority. He intensely disliked officers of authority, unless when requesting help from them, when he could cultivate embarrassing sycophantic grovelling. This *modus operandi* prevailed for the duration and, although he never united us with his strategies, we were expected to understand the purpose of the grovelling without question. Having acquired the desired objective from authority, he resorted to the status quo, i.e., his distaste for its officers. These Pavlovian tricks came naturally, and groomed us for our lives of semi-detached indifference.

Father reserved his quintessential prussic acid hatred for 'the toffs'. Toffs to Father were any persons owning more than he did, which was almost everybody. Yet he patronised these people and imbued us with the erroneous notion that grovelling was a requisite condition that we, born of low birth, were obliged to perform. It was all so horribly embarrassing and its tenets trail like entangled ivy crosses throughout our lives.

To exacerbate his aura of undivinity, Father passionately disliked stylish or even orthodox ways of doing things and would go miles out of his way to end up performing the ordinary in an extraordinary way. As children we assumed this was normal and stared abstractly at conformist fathers performing their duties in a conformist manner. Many a time during my childhood I would be addressed by observers who, in shocked whispers, enquired 'Is that your father?' and upon my timidly replying 'Yes' they would shake their heads and stare at me with compassion.

At primary school, children were delighted if their parents attended an event such as the summer sports day. I, on the other hand, would be delighted if my parents stayed away. If ever they arrived on the scene unexpectedly I would cringe in embarrassment due to Father's strange appearance and unorthodox behaviour. To compound the embarrassment, he would invariably say something out of place in his usual ample voice, so everyone within half a mile could hear him, which prompted all the teachers and my classmates to look at me, as if I were responsible for my father.

On the occasion of this visit an innocent school sports day was in progress. Only God knows why Father turned up because he detested all sports. As fate would have its way, Father arrived on the field at the beginning of the 100 yards race. At first sight of him I moved as surreptitiously as possible to the far side of the field, where a gaggle of gossiping girls was gathered. Upon seeing me approach, they warned me away with their glares, not wanting a smelly country bumpkin eavesdropping on their private grown-up conversation. On the far side of the field, competitors were lined up for the start of the race. Suddenly, Father spoke and several runners spurted off down the field, mistaking his bark for the starter pistol. The harassed teacher in charge shot his pistol twice to denote return to start, but the bewildered rest set off instead. There followed a deal of head shaking and tut-tutting from the mass of ordinary parents.

'Is that your father shouting over there?' one of the gossiping girls asked, as if she didn't know. Heavens! The whole of Wales knew who that strangely dressed ruffian shouting in conversation was. Father was obtusely unorthodox, rampantly eccentric and downright antisocial. He was tactless in the extreme, which I erroneously believed to be absent-mindedness until later in life I discovered it to be a deliberate ploy.

Yet Father was a paradox. Notwithstanding all his laziness and vulgar temper, his indiscretions and embarrassing idiosyncrasies, his antisocial eccentricities and off-hand dismissal of family and humanity at large, he nevertheless ploughed a furrow of genuine righteousness, never once asking for recognition of his piety. Following his great awakening he became a devout Christian of the Quaker calling. He never embarked on sorties into illegality – whether they were spiritual, natural or constitutional – and took great care not to contravene matters in accordance with what he believed to be the Almighty's wishes. The notion of greed was beyond his personal vocabulary.

He was scrupulously honest and truthful to an embarrassing fault. Father's sense of fair play recruited an army of followers in his lifetime. He never swore, and never took the Almighty's name in vain, regardless of his uncontrollable temper. Father never stole. He never incurred an indictment, nor was he summonsed for an offence. He never borrowed money, whether in the form of petty cash, mortgages or bank loans. If Father did not have the money in his pocket, he refused to borrow any and we were obliged to go hungry. He refused on principle to borrow material objects.

These principles incurred hard times for us all, and we were very, very poor. Rural poverty is far more debilitating than its urban cousin, for there are no handouts and shelters, no soup kitchens to slake the ravages of hunger, no volunteers to smooth the path when grime, cold and all-embracing hunger are eating into one's soul, damaging the fabric of one's psyche for the duration. Often Spot humped his bony back, tucked his tail, and whimpered for food but we had nothing to give the poor thing. Our chickens stopped laying due to hunger and malnutrition. We were visited regularly by such organisations as NSPCC and RSPCA, concerned for the welfare of child and beast. We were very, very hungry. Notwithstanding, Father would not beg, borrow or steal to alleviate the circumstances of our hunger.

Father was the raw quintessence of an entity best described as a storm about to break. The meteorology was familiar: foaming of mouth, roar of voice, veins of neck, beetroot of face, white knuckle of hand, glare of eye. But the ingredients never cooked anything original. Sure enough the lightning and thunder rolling about threatened devastation, but nothing came of it. We grew accustomed to the theatre.

Regardless of storms threatening, Bobby's gallows humour prevailed. We laughed a lot upon first viewing Sir Lancelot Spatt on film, agreeing he was the epitome of cuddlesome charm in comparison with Father. Some of the naturally bad-tempered farm animals reminded us of Father. This being too good an opportunity to let pass, it naturally followed they would gain the name 'Dad' for their duration. A Rhode Island Red cockerel so monumentally bad tempered that he danced with rage while plucking out his tail very quickly became 'Dad'. A young boar, vying with Father for the gold medallion was hastily tagged 'Dad' before being carted off for bacon.

Gastric the goat fully deserved the renaming, for its temper almost equalled Father's. Fortunately, Father never realised, although Mother cottoned on and admonished us, complaining that it was an insult to Gastric renaming him after Father.

'He has been dyspeptic towards me only once,' she said, 'which moderation I cannot accord to your father.'

Bobby turned around the quotation 'Beware – if attacked this animal has a bad habit of defending itself' to fit Father, becoming 'Beware – this animal doesn't need to be attacked and the habit is permanent'. I giggled silly. Father's intense dislike of giggling seemed to have the adverse effect; time and again Bobby's expert deadpan descriptions of different animals queuing for the rechristening event caused me to pee myself. Father warned me in growling gravitas that my 'uncontrollable hysteria', as he labelled it, would get me into deep trouble one day. He was right. When I transferred to the county grammar school I plunged into deep trouble, for there kindred spirits pursued giggling as a grown-up, businesslike product, light years ahead of me.

My brother and I founded an imaginary company called 'Rent-a-Storm Ltd'. The company's marketable commodity was Father, his explosive temper being the unique selling point. Truth was it was Bobby's idea, but I embraced the notion so enthusiastically that he patronised me by allowing my name to be attached as a co-founder. Bobby was already an expert at spreading risk and hedging his future insurances against Father taking a jaundiced view of our constructions. I vaguely contributed to the formulation of the marketing slogan:

'For hire: unique weapon of awesome potential. Capacity to solve any problem, however colossal. Can render national leaders to a state of mesmerised compliance within minutes. No problem too great. Catastrophes felled. Entity has global reach. This once-in-a-lifetime offer cannot last indefinitely. For further details and bookings please contact Rent-a-Storm Ltd, Troed-yr-Henrhiw Farm, Wales.'

Almost all of the words belonged to Bobby, my only contribution being the catastrophe phrase, which Bobby felt was somewhat contradictive, but he left it in as catastrophe was my favourite word for that week. It was fortunate we had not written the marketing blurb on the previous week; my favourite term then was 'suspension bridges'. My suggestion we add 'please enclose SAE' was dismissed by my brother on the grounds that it betrayed our lack of capital. 'Rent a Storm' epitomised the theatre of our early lives, but the driving force was the subject of our elaboration. Bobby pondered with all seriousness, means by which we could persuade Father in the unlikely chance we would obtain a customer.

Father joined the Welsh Communist Party having deserted an ultra-Left brotherhood that ploughed a lonely furrow on the fringes of Welsh society. His justification for abandoning his fringe party was their inability to guarantee funding for the intrinsically lethargic who, according to Father's thesis, played an enormous part in the economic infrastructure of Wales. Father complained he had had to move to the right of his political ideology in joining the Welsh Communist Party but, he conceded, at least they were able to supply the necessary infrastructure for transporting dead beasts from the farm.

Father believed throughout his life that Winston Churchill was a warmonger, and if Hitler had been left alone to undertake an overdue revision of Europe's borders, our country would have continued in its insular tranquillity. When the Attlee Government replaced Churchill's in 1945, Father performed such a hearty victory dance that his down-at-heel boots gouged marks on the living-room flagstones, pointed out to us years later by Mother.

Much to Father's disappointment, his farming lifestyle continued to accelerate southwards under the new Labour Government. He became adept at utilising his high intelligence to muster excuses for Labour's ineptitude, though most of his bile was reserved for leftover conservatism and the toffs of empire that entangled the new socialist way. He praised and congratulated the nationalising of the country's utilities, and forbade his brain to think beyond the consequences. He could not explain how West Germany overtook Britain as an economic power just six years after the war. When Attlee lost the 1951 election to Churchill, the shock Father suffered was fundamental. Socialism had not delivered the nirvana he had dreamed of and he loathed the Tory ideology of throwing responsibility back at the individual. So, between bouts of melancholia he enjoyed unrealistic highs when the Soviets showed signs of challenging Western capitalism.

One day Father mastered the art of horse whispering. It came about so suddenly and with such astonishing ease that we were convinced he had had private tutoring from Enoch Pant Gwyn, on the occasions he was supposedly searching for lost sheep on the Disgwylfa Fawr grazing keeps. As Father hated effort of any calibre something must have lit the touchpaper. We soon learnt.

Once the art of horse whispering was mastered he became inseparable from the farm animals, a spectre previously only alluded to, for it was my brother and I who hitherto had been cast to them: older brother to the sheep and I to the swine. I didn't mind. Father would have long political debates with the animals until it dawned on Mother this political haranguing was having a deleterious effect on their appetites.

'Their appetites are of paramount importance in the process of growing big and marketable,' she said, 'and are a key contribution to our livelihood. You must decide whether to allow us to sink with skinny animals conversant with Marxism, or swim with fat creatures happily ignorant of political undercurrents in Wales.'

It was ironic that the animals so enthralled with political discussions with Father were the sheep and pigs, the very ones needing bouncy appetites. This however did not curb Father's enthusiasm for horse whispering, especially when it became clear that Voroshilov, the breeding Large White sow, shared his devotion to communism. Bobby had often voiced his doubts about Voroshilov's sanity, even in the days when it was my duty to feed her, especially when she persisted in eating the runt of the litter. This last comment hurt because, due to my extremely diminished stature, my brother would never allow a day to pass without reminding me: 'As you are such a little runt, if you had been born a pig Voroshilov would have eaten you for breakfast.' This comment succeeded in putting me off my brother, pigs and breakfast in one sweep.

On the occasion that the Welsh Communist Party went to the dogs Father demanded hell to pay the compensation. What with Labour having lost the last election and the Conservatives back in power, he was apoplectic with anger and roared for three days until he temporarily lost his voice. 'What party was worth joining now?' he attempted to roar in a hoarse whisper. It was ironic, really, and Mother was the first to see the joke. Hoarse whispering, she explained to little Francesca and me. We got the joke.

But Father was serious. He accused Voroshilov of complicity, which to my unscientific reasoning accorded with Bobby's suspicions. The upshot of this was Bobby cautioning me regarding Father's next political port of call, on which he would lay bets with me if I were a little more conversant with national politics. When I protested my deep knowledge in such matters, he dismissed the notion. This fired me and, girding my loins, with my heart thumping where it should not have been, I asked Father what was to be his next political party. His reply was: 'Never you mind, you are too young, you would not understand,' and then he added after a moment's thought, 'Go and ask your brother, he seems to know more about my politics than I do.'

'Did you ask Daddy that?' was Bobby's incredulous reaction on being informed of my dramatic mission. 'To have done that you have to be either brave or stupid. As you are not brave, I can only assume the alternative.'

Francesca as usual supported Bobby: 'That means you are stupid,' she deduced, shaking her head. Happy days!

Following the demise of the Welsh Communist Party Father sank into another of his melancholic mollycoddle periods, taking to bed for three weeks. Horse whispering had gone the way of all fads. The peace around the farm was shattering. Mother was happier and Francesca's nervous shake subsided. At some stage during the three-week sojourn Bobby cautioned me on Father's inability to retain firm references, and in my early years I had difficulty in tying all these loose parts together to form an understandable basket.

Father's Difficulty with Punctuality

Father's death changed everybody's viewpoint. Suddenly he was a 'good old stick'. People who normally smirked behind his back heaped praise of him to Mother's face. Those who were used to whispering came out of the shadows and spoke openly. Friendliness and generosity of spirit crowded in through the dark apertures of our farm. Even the literati socialists laid claim to his acquaintance, ignoring the reality that Father's communism was light years from their squeaky practice of polished slip-ons. The world lurched out of kilter and suddenly almost everything appeared to me as false. It was at this time I realised the division between chattering socialists and doing socialists – not that Father was a doer, due to his bone-idleness.

Mother continued her quiet little life as before. She was a lovable little mouse before the storm was rented out, and she was the same lovable little mouse afterwards, save a few signally variant determinations. Bobby was as logical as ever, Francesca was quieter still; I missed the noise. None of us giggled for a day or two 'in deference to the dead' as Bobby whispered. Uncle Maldwyn made a gallant effort to adjust but failed, as he was unable to modify his singing.

Bobby acted a little peculiarly at first, but the reason soon came to light and all was explained. Trouble was, Father had never done anything in a normal way. He always ignored complex operations, which were left to others to be sorted out, but unfortunately he readily made an enormous production of simple ones. His dying was no exception. It was not so much the passing away but what followed that made it unusual. To this day I have not entirely solved the riddle of how Bobby managed things.

When Father died he went to heaven. This canto carries the burden of Quaker guilt, the celestial Registrar of time, so according to Bobby the particle should read: he eventually went to heaven. On that fulcrum the contradictions that constituted

Father were finely balanced against the tangled acres of matters untouched; touched but unresolved; resolved but devoid of satisfaction.

As Father had elevated lassitude to a fine art that had become legendary in his lifetime, his being late for his interview with God did not surprise us in the least. We were more taken aback by the silent hole being filled by sycophants than by the occasion itself. For the silence was almost unbearable. We missed the thunderous roar of distemper. 'Rent-a-Storm' had gone; our company had lost its unique marketable commodity, even though the contractual commitment had been one-sided, abstract and tenuous. But that is how it always was with Father.

Throughout our lives we had witnessed Father's consistent unpunctuality all the way from high events to low eventualities, so we were inured to embarrassments that had their genesis in his bone-idleness. Our casual response regarding Father's late arrival at Heaven's Gate was read amiss only by the uninitiated. Those who possessed insight into the obtuse machinations of his unique character numbered very few in Wales.

One of the few was Recorded Minister Cynfelin Jenkins of Pentreglanowen Friends who set off on a wrong foot with Mother and Bobby. Francesca and I were too inexperienced to recognise what was going on. Our uncle's approach was preordained oblivion, even for serious matters. Father had never publicised his Quaker beliefs, although regardless of the frothing surface of anger and tempest, his applications to the art of piety were unequalled. Recorded Minister Jenkins was no hero of conscience, otherwise he would have known better and would not have clucked like a hen. It was he who first picked up the notion of Father's non-arrival in heaven. I asked Bobby why Pentreglanowen Friends Meeting House should pick on a notion of this unlikelihood. He was as mystified as I was and clearly did not know. We asked Mother who, although never losing the balance of her mind, uttered a historical malapropism in reply, one best left alone.

The only occasion Father ventured into a Friends Meeting House was at Dolgellau, miles from Pentreglanowen. His visit was unintentional; his head was in the clouds and he had mistaken the establishment for a chemist's shop. Recorded Minister Jenkins impressed upon us the need for maintaining the decorum of punctuality in such matters as death, as if we were unaware, but he was playing on rumour. He was met by a wall of polite indifference from Mother, for in her he was confronted by a proper Heroine of Conscience. He should have known better: ours was not the gift to have a say in such matters. Even if we had been so inclined to intervene, we would have proceeded with caution knowing Father would have devised some method of raising his objections. Obviously the reality of Father's life-long dedication to designed awkwardness had somehow eluded Recorded Minister Jenkins.

Officiating a great distance from Troed-yr-Henrhiw Farm was no excuse. But Recorded Minister Jenkins was not involved in the land, so he had never experienced the displeasure of having dealings with Pugh Troed-yr-Henrhiw. Truth is, this had hidden blessings, and those wringing their wrists missed the point. Bobby believed Recorded Minister Jenkins' problem was that he could not leave well alone, his disadvantage being he had not been privy to Father's legendary lassitude. Clearly, Bobby did not approve of Recorded Minister Jenkins meddling in our affairs.

We had always assumed Father, although not playing any part in the matter of his destination, would ignore the non-negotiable nature of the decision and would attempt negotiation in some other form. Bobby had impressed upon me the universal law that instantaneous contractual compliance was the duty of the soul at the moment of death, but this decree failed to take Father into account. We were going through a semblance of learning, for Mother displayed surprise when Recorded Minister clucked the news two days before the funeral.

'I'm sure he has good reasons,' was Mother's only public remark on the matter, which meant mountains to us. Her surprise was theatrical for the sake of appearances. She later confided in measured whispers that Father's unorthodoxy would not end with his non-arrival at the place of judgement. Francesca and I took this very seriously indeed, while Bobby nodded sagely. The only person content with his awareness of Father's awkwardness was Bobby, who reminded us our father had had insight into the harps of heaven at the age of twenty. Obviously there was something mysterious afoot.

Although Mother was deeply aggrieved at Father's untimely death she was quite businesslike regarding the funeral arrangements, insisting on commissioning Jones Waungrug with his two black shires to haul the hay cart on which the coffin would be borne. What a fitting end! Father disliked horses intensely and Jones Waungrug disliked Father to the same degree.

The context of the hypotheses regarding Father's remiss nonconformism amused my brother no end, which meant they amused little sister and me no end also, as we were of an age not yet to have learnt the correct protocols of amusement. Among the prime instigators of our brother's scorn were the niggling men in frocks who corrupted the innocence of religious genuflection with first-class admission tickets straight into heaven.

'This is sour grapes,' averred Bobby, 'coming from people who knew Father at a superficial level only.'

'I don't understand what you mean,' I protested.

With a toss of his head, Bobby patiently explained.

'Father was the architect of an elaborate disguise,' Bobby explained showing some surprise I had not realised it, 'for he possessed a shaft of absurd genius—'

'Oh, absurd genius, I know that,' I interrupted.

'For he possessed a shaft of absurd genius,' Bobby repeated firmly, realising I did not know, 'that enabled him to expound on superficial details and false trails about himself to lull half the world and their dog into thinking they thoroughly understood him.'

I grasped Bobby's point, and felt a little guilty for interrupting. Mother, Francesca and I possessed half the knowledge at best. So we took our cue from Bobby and thereon did not attach much credence to the petulance of the men in frocks.

My brother's philosophy prompted me to recall Father's views on the Almighty. Father the born non-practising Quaker declared the whole universe was the Almighty's church so there was no need to build little structures to gesticulate the deference. But he took it further. Father reckoned God was in seeds and acorns and raindrops and mountains. He said every atom was a zealot of the faith so that when we breathed or drank or jumped over a gate we were consuming God at the essential level.

'Cleave the wood and God is there,' was another of Father's sayings. 'The essential level,' he contended, 'is pure energy, as it is the only indestructible entity. As living organisms we are constituted through pure energy, so we are all God at one and the same. When we mere mortals find a way of undertaking reciprocating correspondence with energy then, and only then, can we attempt to communicate with God.'

Father took it further yet by advocating that factories and farms and lead mines and dog kennels were the only structures necessary to appreciate the existence of God. Notwithstanding, Father contended elastically, God was far too busy spreading himself in an expanding universe to sit down with mere humans to celebrate his existence, and who was I to dispute this? My greatest problem was squaring Father's convictions with the contradictions poured daily into my ears at school.

Time was elastic, Father had expounded as a devotee of Einstein's special relativity where time's perception was individualised, ironically contradicting another of his over-used quotations – that a little knowledge was a dangerous thing. Father's quotations for convenience regularly clashed with what he was up to. His preaching was of little use now, as it seemed he had somehow triangulated with time. The concern expressed by Mother and Bobby centred on what reason, if any, Father could give for arriving late this time of all times.

'The time lapse between passing away here and arriving there implies his soul has been somewhere else in the meantime,' said a worried Mother.

'Well, you know Daddy,' said Bobby dismissively.

Precisely. Who could expect otherwise from Father? Where his soul was remained a mystery, even for those who were in a position to know better, like clucking Jenkins, or even my brother. But secretly, it all worried me.

Then there were the men in frocks, who swore: 'Your Father will not end up in hell because although he was a morphologically constructed storm about to break, he had not been wicked enough and would have been spared the everlasting task of shovelling the coal to generate the sun's fires.'

Although they were correct in their assessment of Father, they were hopelessly out of date regarding the sun's fuel because we all knew, right down to little Francesca, that the sun did not burn coal. At that time, none of us was sure what the sun burned but we were positive about the coal part because Bobby had calculated on the basis of the rate of consumption of the coal-fired back boiler in the pig swill shed that the sun's weight would have been consumed entirely before we were born, and we would have been done for.

'And if we had been done for,' he reasoned, 'proof of the correctness of my calculations would have resulted in us not ever being here to ponder the riddle.'

We were amazed at this without grasping the significance of what he had said.

'Anyway,' I piped, missing the nihilism of his reasoning, 'where would God have put all the ash?'

'Quite,' said my brother, shaking his head in dismay at my stupidity and acting as if he had already thought about the refuse matter.

'Quite,' echoed Francesca, shaking her head in dismay.

So much for the hypothesis held by the men in frocks.

Father Takes Leave of His Coffin

'I cannot believe we have heard the last of him,' Uncle Maldwyn said in his usual say-singing bass. 'He'll rise again from the dead, mark my words.'

'What on earth are you singing about, Maldwyn?' Mother asked.

'Ifan,' sang Uncle Maldwyn, knowingly. 'I cannot imagine Ifan remaining dead and dutifully reporting at the Golden Gate and obediently putting on a gown and letting the angels fit wings and being allocated a predetermined task by Archangel Gabriel to which he has to apply himself thereafter for everlasting eternity. Can you? Can you imagine Ifan proceeding to his allotted cloud and commencing his tasks punctually in an orderly manner? I cannot imagine it. Come on, now. He'll rise again from the dead as sure as God made little children.'

Francesca gasped.

'You have peculiar ways of looking at things admittedly,' said Mother, 'but this view is beyond. The Lord has ways of obliging members of his flock to undertake duties marked out for them in the order of things,' she added biblically.

'The Lord may have ways of obliging members of his flock to undertake duties marked out for them in the order of things, Fran, but the Lord has not yet confronted a member of his flock who is as confoundedly procrastinating, obtusely diffident and evanescent as Ifan. He'll rise again. He'll be back, mark my words.' Uncle Maldwyn nodded his head to accentuate his conviction.

'I would prefer you didn't talk like this in front of the children, Mal. You should not say such things, especially at this time,' Mother gently admonished.

'It was they who were discussing the matter long before I voiced it,' Uncle Maldwyn protested.

Bobby looked sheepishly like a member of the flock. Mother darted us an accusatorial glance.

'You have to agree, it has happened before,' Bobby said by way of admitting his guilt.

'Well,' said Mother, sighing, 'the occurrence of rising from the dead on the previous occasion was for the specific purpose of getting the Lord's message across. I cannot for the life of me imagine your father volunteering a role that would involve a good deal of unpaid work carried out in the self-effacing manner necessary for goodwill and love to all mankind, only to be crucified at the end of it. There are too many improbabilities and contradictions to consider your father for that role. Anyway, I would prefer this subject was not discussed in front of the younger children.'

Bobby looked surprised. 'Ieuan was compliant,' he said.

Mother sighed yet again; the conspiracy was broadening. She looked at little sister, who looked back innocently.

'What does compliant mean?' I asked.

'Yielding to my ideas. Pliant,' replied Bobby, 'and, by the way, Uncle Maldwyn, do you really mean Daddy is evanescent?'

'Did I say evanescent? Surely not!' a surprised Uncle Maldwyn responded. 'My brain department meant to say everlasting. Your brain department should have heard me say everlasting.'

'As you are all guilty except the little one of discussing such blasphemous matters,' ruled Mother, who was just beginning to appreciate the peace and quiet around the farm, 'I think we should all have more faith in the ways of the Lord. Let that be the end of it.'

Conversations between Mother and Uncle Maldwyn invariably got nowhere, both of them talking in circular riddles: Mother's riddle was biblically clockwise and our uncle's reasoning followed a surrealistically anticlockwise deviation. Usually Bobby strongly interrupted by affirming the logic missing from both parties, but on this occasion he was fairly quiet as he was planning something altogether different.

On the day before the funeral Mother double-checked the agenda. People who mattered had been notified. Welsh cakes by the ton had been baked. The black shires and hay wain had been ordered, and Jones Waungrug would arrive at ten thirty next morning. When told of the horses with Jones Waungrug Uncle

Maldwyn laughed outrageously. He excused himself and went outside, sitting down on the old bench beneath the giant yew tree and, putting his face in his hands, continued laughing. It looked as if he was weeping the death of his brother, but now and again he put his head back and roared with laughter. We could not help but see his theatre through the living room window. Mother shook her head.

'Losing his only sibling so young has unbalanced him. He's much more level-headed normally,' she said, 'but now I'm having my doubts. The gene must be all-pervasive.'

The laughter rippling from the yew tree coerced Mother into wondering whether to continue with the shires or perhaps to cancel them, even at this late stage. But Bobby, who in the last few days had taken a more sanguine view of the whole mess of our existence, stamped his foot and said firmly that the status quo obtains.

'It will be a fitting tribute to Father's obtuse personality – to be towed by animals he detested that are owned by a farmer who detested him in turn. There can be no telling the wonderful message of reconciliation this will signal to the congregation,' he said with newly-acquired authority.

'And Daddy was a proficient horse whisperer, as well,' I added helpfully; both Mother and Bobby looked at me as if the stress of the occasion had prised the little reason I possessed away.

'God knows the congregation will need messages of recon-ciliation where Father is concerned,' Bobby continued. 'Mind you, if Father were alive he would prefer to be dead than to be towed in the intended fashion.' Then, after a moment's reflection, he said firmly, 'No. The commission remains, even if it is giving Uncle Maldwyn great cause for mirth. After all, it is the widow's right to choose the mode of transport. The coffin could be put on a wheelbarrow if the widow so wishes. Some societies would give their right arms for wheelbarrows—'

'Then they couldn't drive the wheelbarrows,' I suggested, which brought me very close to receiving a smack from brother for having trespassed into the zone of cleverness, but I was rescued from the punishment by Mother.

'Both of you!' she said. 'All of you are manifesting this gene this morning. What I want to know is what is so funny about it?' she asked, still not getting it.

'It is all to do with Father not having a say in the matter,' reasoned Bobby, 'and having to look up the backsides of two giant shire horses from his wooden box and not being able to do anything about it. Also, it appears Uncle Maldwyn is invested with the same hysteria gene that afflicts Ieuan,' he added, endeavouring to distance himself from the levity. 'Come to think of it, I can see his point of view. I would laugh myself if I was certain it wouldn't be taken the wrong way.'

'What if the horses poo on the coffin?' Francesca suddenly piped. Until that moment she had been a wide-eyed and quiet observer of the goings-on. Her remark hit Mother like a bolt from the blue. The idea of it, horses pooing on Father's coffin, coming from the little one of all children – me, yes, but from Francesca! It stunned her into silence. Then, collecting her wits, Mother said, 'Obviously the shock of your father's sudden death has caused you to temporarily lose the balance of your mind as well, little sweetheart. Don't worry. You'll come back to normal when this is all over. Ignore the rest of them.'

'We'll take a shovel along in case,' suggested a straight-faced Bobby, helpfully.

'Bags I do the shovelling,' I said, and collapsed in a bout of giggling, quite unbefitting for the occasion. This was all too much for Mother.

'Now *stop* it, the three of you!' she exclaimed at the top of her little voice, glaring especially at me.

'Quite,' said Bobby, getting into line. 'A sense of decorum, please.'

'Quite,' agreed Francesca. 'A sense of decorum, please.'

I was of course isolated, giggling alone, struggling to dismiss the mental images of great dollops of steaming horse poo covering Father's coffin, with me trying discreetly to shovel it off, Jones Waungrug leading at the front oblivious, the horses with their ears pointing forward plodding on regardless, Mother weeping, Uncle Maldwyn looking up to heaven humming *Land of my Fathers*, Bobby looking at me straight-faced goading me to giggle, the congregation shaking their heads whispering their 'well I nevers',

Francesca squeaking 'I warned you, I warned you', Spot darting around trying to round up everybody, and Father's ghost hammering on the coffin lid, raging apoplectically about the large dollops of steaming poo on his coffin. I had to fight back the hysteria.

'Is Ieuan all right?' Bobby asked Mother. 'He's turned that funny colour again.'

'Oh dear,' said Mother, 'we're in enough of a pickle already without Ieuan having one of his turns.'

The day of the funeral was cold and sleety, as they are. I thought it would be more fitting if God had sent a thunderstorm as accompaniment, but you don't get everything you pray for these days. Actually, I had prayed for snow: two shires struggling up the mountain through huge snowdrifts to Soar-y-Mynydd; the coffin sliding off into the blizzard without anyone noticing and sledding back down the hill; the procession arriving with a hay cart heaped only with snow, everyone assuming the coffin was under the snow load; the shires as indifferent as ever, Jones Waungrug beside himself; the coffin lost in the drifts not appearing until after the thaw three weeks later, Bobby saying it was the best element to lose a coffin in, what a hell of a to-do. But, to avoid that tactic, God delivered a halfway house instead: sleet. The failure to produce a thunderstorm convinced me Father had not yet reached heaven. I explained my theory to Mother who persisted in fretting enormously regarding the actual location of his soul. Bobby said he had fixed things so we would find out soon; as I said, he had been acting mysteriously for a day or so.

So accustomed were we to Father's shouting that we were at a loss when the raging stopped. The farm was grey in the silence of his death. We longed for his noise again. When the wind whined through the high spruces I fancied Father was up them complaining about the weather. But against the normal cacophony of our farm – of a barking Spot telling lies about ghost wolves gobbling up the sheep, Voroshilov complaining because her latest litter had gone to market, the runs of chickens (Black Leghorns, Rhode Island Reds, Plymouth Rocks and White Leghorns) all clucking simultaneously that they had laid eggs, the bantams high in the yew trees crowing that they too had laid eggs but couldn't find them, the cows bellowing to be milked, Gastric attacking – against all of this commotion the hugely prominent foreground furore of Father in a rage would have been heard. His foghorn noise drowned everything; but now we missed it dreadfully.

Father's coffin had been placed on the Christmas table in the parlour, now declared a 'Parlour of Rest' by Bobby. It was draped in Father's favourite buttonless, ragged coat – his only coat – which Bobby had aptly tied down with red bailer twine. It was a clever touch, because it mostly camouflaged the cheap coffin. Uncle Maldwyn placed a little book, *A Father in Seion* by Caradoc Evans, on top of the coat. None of us apart from Bobby cared to go near the coffin.

For the duration I had persisted in hallucinating the coffin lid to be slowly opening and Father's hands silently feeling along its sides; my hallucination never got any further as I shook my head and started doing something, any something to take my mind off it. I told no one of my hallucinations. Since the coffin had arrived we all slept nights on the floor in Mother's bedroom, apart from Uncle Maldwyn of course who snored as usual in his own room. We had invaded Mother's room ostensibly to keep her company, but in reality she was keeping *us* company. The little one climbed into Mother's bed. At night my hallucinations turned into dreams.

Even as the coffin lay in the Parlour of Rest Uncle Maldwyn continued his usual sleep-singing, although his repertoire became Welsh hymns exclusively, frequently repeating *Calon Lan*, which was not his favourite Welsh hymn when awake because his deep voice could not comfortably reach the high notes. In happier times it amused us greatly listening to sung renditions of his somniloquisms.

We were all up early, fed the animals and poultry, left the eggs, milked the cows, had our porridge, dressed spick and span in our school clothes, and waited. Presently Mother said, 'Let's have a cup of tea.'

At the sound of tea being made Uncle Maldwyn joined us. He was wearing Taid's pinstripe wedding suit that was several sizes too large for him. Uncle Maldwyn was six foot four inches tall, broad shouldered and barrel-chested, so goodness knows what a giant Taid was on his wedding day.

We all stared. We stared and stared. We had never had occasion to see him in Taid's wedding suit before. Beneath the excess layers of flapping jacket hung a waistcoat as loose as an empty sack. The coat sleeves reached straight down to his fingernails and the shoulders pads drooped over his broad shoulders. The trousers were far too long, sitting in several folds on the top of his boots. The boots were his farm boots vaguely polished. We continued to stare.

'What?' Uncle Maldwyn righteously demanded.

'The suit,' said Bobby.

'What about the suit?' Uncle Maldwyn demanded again, shuffling uncomfortably from one foot to the other.

We waited. What would Bobby say? What could he say? How could he tell our uncle the suit was too big for him?

'Er… the suit… looks good,' he chickened.

'He means it looks too big!' blurted little Francesca.

'Yes, I know it's too big,' replied Uncle Maldwyn, addressing all of us, the note of righteousness gone, 'but I have nothing else suitable to wear for a funeral. I have my choir suit, but that's red as you know. I'll wear it if you want, Ifan wouldn't mind. Unless of course you want me to wear my working overalls, which I will gladly change into as they are much more comfortable.'

'No, no,' said Mother quickly, 'no one will notice. Anyway, I hope they will all be admiring the horses.'

'Yes, you are right, Fran,' said Uncle Maldwyn with relief, 'they will be admiring the horses all right,' and he smiled with relief.

'No, don't start laughing again, Uncle Maldwyn, it was bad enough yesterday,' Bobby reprimanded.

'Yes,' piped Francesca, remembering, 'decorum, and all that.'

'I'm not laughing,' said Uncle Maldwyn; but we all laughed, and for a moment forgot it was the day of Father's funeral.

Spot began to bark. 'Too late to cancel the horses,' said Mother with relief, 'Spot says they are coming.'

We all ran out. Sure enough, winding up the grey road through the sad spruces that waved their fronds so forlornly in the north-easterly wind appeared two monstrous black shires pulling a hay wain on which stood Jones Waungrug, loosely holding the reins.

'Gosh, I didn't realise they were so big,' fretted Mother.

The whole outfit came to a stop in the yard. The huge shires were magnificently bridled and blinkered. They had been brushed to a shine and their huge hooves were sparkling. On the first one's brass forehead plate read the name 'Dylan'; on the second, 'Thomas'. They dwarfed the farmyard. Spot spluttered a mini bark, recognised he had met his match, and took up a cowering position behind Bobby, head peering out.

As a touch of political irony Jones Waungrug had plaited blue ribbons into the shires' manes. Blue ribbons, would you believe! What a touch.

'Blue ribbons, notice,' said Mother, relaxing her fret, 'what a touch!'

'Daddy will be pleased,' said Francesca.

'Daddy will be pleased no half.'

'Morning, Mrs Pugh,' said Jones Waungrug, creaking down from the wain, sloshing across to Mother and shaking her by the hand. 'On this sad occasion, please accept my most sincere... er... comminsterations.'

He wore black knee-length gaiters polished to a mirror, and a long black coat over a buckled tweedy suit. He was a large man, most of which avoirdupois resided around the midriff zone. His round bucolic face reflected a lifestyle of pleasant enjoyment.

'Good morning and thank you, I'm sure, Mr Jones,' replied Mother, coyly, her eyes flooding with tears. 'Your shires are magnificent and you have done Ifan proud.'

'I have done you proud, Mrs Pugh,' replied Jones Waungrug, avoiding an admission that he had done Pugh Troed-yr-Henrhiw any proud at all, and turning to us: 'Good morning, children.'

'Good morning Mr Jones,' we piped in unison, except Francesca, who had addressed him as Mr Waungrug. He had already turned to Uncle Maldwyn.

'Good morning, Mal— good God! Maldwyn, I hardly recognised you inside that suit. You look attenuated if I may venture the description. Attenuated. Isn't it a little... er...?'

'Too big,' prompted Bobby.

'Too big,' echoed Francesca.

'Too big?'

'Well yes, indeed' Uncle Maldwyn said with a smile. 'I could say your horses are too big for the farmyard, Jones,' retorted Uncle Maldwyn. They were old friends so I supposed they could say what the heck to each other.

'Yes, fair play, Mal, though they are here for a purpose.'

'I am inside this suit for a purpose as well,' replied Uncle Maldwyn, smiling wickedly, 'but beware, the suit could have been bigger; I was going to wear my overalls, but they are not quite black enough for this wonderful occasion. Circumstances therefore obliged me to clamber inside this suit for the sake of Mr Decorum. I'm repairing the Massey Ferguson up the right sleeve.'

'And Spot's kennel is in a pocket,' I said, getting carried away. They all turned and scowled at me.

'Mr Decorum, heh? Who is Mr Decorum?' Jones Waungrug asked, coming back to sensible business.

'Mr Decorum is someone who will be with us during this ritual. Mr Decorum dislikes horses, especially shire horses, but will not have a say in the matter until he rises again, then we will all be sorry for carting him away on a hay wain,' replied Uncle Maldwyn.

'Diawl, Maldwyn, you have imagination!' said Jones Waungrug.

Uncle Maldwyn looked set for a lengthy conversation, but in the nick of time remembered the occasion.

'I meant the undertaken,' replied Uncle Maldwyn.

'Well, well!' said Jones Waungrug. 'Shall we get on with it? Where do you want the cart, Mrs Pugh?'

'Your shires are magnificent, Mr Jones,' said Bobby politely. 'They must eat loads of hay,' he added, mischievously glancing at Francesca.

'Oh, they eat loads of hay, all right, and loads come out the other end,' replied Jones Waungrug, obligingly.

We all looked at Francesca, who crinkled her little nose at Bobby.

'Round by the front door, please, Mr Jones. Ianto is in the

Parlour of Rest,' said Mother, guiding our attention back to the matter of the day.

'Parlour of Rest? Goodness, Mrs Pugh, you know how to do things in style. Round by the front door is no problem at all. Dylan and Thomas are as nimble as kittens.'

At this moment the undertakers arrived in their large black Humber Super Snipe and slithered to a halt in the mud, the driver realising the monster shires were manoeuvring into front door position. They wisely elected to keep the car a safe distance from the giant hooves. One blam and the car would be a write-off with its occupants on the way to hospital. Behind the Super Snipe Recorded Minister Jenkins buzzed up in his little Austin Ruby.

'Oh God, I forgot. Out-of-Touch Jenkins is here,' muttered Bobby *sotto voce*. 'I hope he doesn't say anything to start Uncle Maldwyn off.'

'Uncle Maldwyn's already started off,' said Francesca, not so *sotto voce*. 'What about Mr Decorum rising from the dead?'

'Now don't go nagging everyone's head off today of all days, sweetheart. I've set up a wonderful surprise for us later,' said Bobby with a wink, adopting an avuncular approach to the proceedings.

We all piled into the Parlour of Rest and crowded around the large coffin that lay on the Christmas table. Recorded Minister Jenkins uttered a few words of prayer. He had a large wart on the side of his forehead, which moved as he talked. I could not take my eyes off it. We all said 'amen'. The smell of Father coming off his old coat filled the parlour. Mother was weeping. Uncle Maldwyn wore a very sad face, and little sister began to cry. I had a huge lump in my throat that pained unbearably. The truth of the occasion floated out of the window, across the grey laurels, past the black shires standing silently in the sleet, and disappeared past Father's favourite spruce trees as they waved their arms goodbye, goodbye in the north-easterly wind. Father's noise had gone for ever. It was the saddest day in the world.

The two undertakers with the assistance of Jones Waungrug, Uncle Maldwyn and Bobby carried the coffin, still draped in Father's old coat tied on with baler twine, out of the house and placed it gently on the hay wain. Dylan hurrumphed.

'Don't you start,' said Jones Waungrug.

'Nice touch the coat, Mrs Pugh,' whispered Recorded Minister Jenkins, and the wart agreed.

'Bobby's,' muttered a tearful Mother.

'*A Father in Seion*, nice touch also, Mrs Pugh.'

'Maldwyn's,' muttered tearful Mother.

'The shovel?'

'The little one,' muttered Mother, having lost her bearings, and then, 'Shut the doors, someone.'

'Spot, into your kennel, guard the farm. Guard!' commanded Bobby in muffled tones.

From what I knew of Spot, he may as well have commanded the kennel to guard the farm. From what I knew of the kennel, it was in Uncle Maldwyn's pocket.

'Shall we ride behind in the Massey Ferguson?' suggested Uncle Maldwyn. I leapt at his inspired suggestion, but it was apropos his overlong trousers dragging in the farmyard mud, really.

'Good idea,' said Bobby, 'better than the Austin 7. We'll ask Mammy.'

'What's wrong with the Austin 7?' Mother asked. We had no logical answer; it just seemed an insensitive thing to do, driving Father's Austin 7 at his funeral, so we persisted with our unreasonable nagging. Mother relented. 'OK,' she said resignedly, 'so long as it doesn't backfire and frighten the shires.'

Starting it would be a miracle, leave alone backfiring.

Thomas hurrumphed.

'Don't you start,' said Jones Waungrug.

But the Massey Ferguson started and we all set off – Jones Waungrug leading the shires at a steady pace, the wain wheels grinding over the grey gravel lane; the purring Super Snipe containing the undertakers with weeping Mother and Francesca; the Austin Ruby with Recorded Minister Jenkins; the Massey Ferguson taking up the tail, belching smoke, driven stoically by Uncle Maldwyn, Bobby sitting on one mudguard and me sitting on the other; the cold sleet driving down, all the way up the Old Road to Capel Soar-y-Mynydd. Now and again Mother would look anxiously through the rear window of the Snipe, and Uncle

Maldwyn would solemnly wave everyone on. It was a great comfort to be with Uncle Maldwyn at this time; even his gesture waving everyone on was filled with unintended humour.

Spot deserted his post and came belting after us. Filled with excitement, he rounded up the lot, although he wisely elected to give Thomas and Dylan a wide girth. Up to the front, down to the back, back up to the front.

'One word from you, Bobby, and Spot guards the farm as courageously as the dog on the Dutch dyke,' sang Uncle Maldwyn. 'I'm proud of your masterly control over the animal. It's only to be regretted you did not enter him for the Bala sheepdog trials this autumn.'

'He's left the kennel guarding the farm,' I quipped and they looked at me and tossed their heads.

'Diawl, I completely forgot,' Bobby muttered. 'I hope he doesn't start his singing at the sound of the organ. Remember him at Eurfyl Llechwedd's wedding?'

'He hasn't got a clue about key,' said Uncle Maldwyn. 'Better tether him when we get there.'

'And so long as he doesn't take a bite out of one of the shire's fetlocks beforehand – they would probably stampede, and the coffin is not tied down,' I added.

'They are too big to stampede,' said Uncle Maldwyn in a reassuring voice. 'Shires don't stampede. They carry on walking at the same pace but instead go crashing through the trees and farms and mountains, Jones Waungrug holding on for his life, leaving a broad swathe that would be classified as the Disgwylfa Fawr bypass in next to no time. The Super Snipe would follow; they are daft enough,' said Uncle Maldwyn in pessimistic mode.

'Who? The shires or the Super Snipe driver?' asked Bobby.

'Oh, the shires, every time.'

Now and again the Massey Ferguson coughed and spluttered, emitting huge clouds of black smoke that enveloped us. Uncle Maldwyn began wheezing and tapped his chest.

'I'm singing at the service,' he reminded us, 'but at this rate they will be lucky to get a croak.'

'What are you singing, Uncle Maldwyn?' I asked. At that time we did not appreciate the great bass singer he would become.

'Sarastro's aria from Act Two of Mozart's *Die Zauberflöte*, better known in Welsh as *The Magic Flute*. Mozart designed the opera to lift the most downtrodden of spirits, hence my singing it. I hope to be a paragon of a Sarastro. I'm also the Tsar in Mussorgsky's *Boris Godunov* tomorrow. I don't think Mr Ferguson is helping the strings, though. I'll never reach the high notes.'

'Uncle Maldwyn, when do you reach the high notes?' I asked.

He then rehearsed a small part, just for us, conducting with both hands off the steering wheel. Fortunately the throttle, a hand-organised contraption beneath the steering column, was on a fixed ratchet and thus not subject to his tapping feet. The tractor, obeying a chronic defect in the front wheel alignment from which it had been suffering for years, lurched to the right once Uncle Maldwyn's restraining hold on the steering wheel was released. Following its nose, the Massey Ferguson was about to head for the wilderness. Mother gesticulated through the back window of the Snipe and Bobby grabbed the steering wheel; Mother made a gesture to heaven. Uncle Maldwyn continued singing, unperturbed.

Crowds awaited our arrival at Soar-y-Mynydd. Relatives with their best-tailored funeral suits and squeaking shoes swaggered. Overcoats, hats, gloves and scarves dominated. Wafts of camphor floated over.

'God, look how they're dressed,' whispered a horrified Bobby, mindful of our threadbare garments and Uncle Maldwyn's wedding suit.

It was freezing cold; although I was shivering all I could dwell on was how cold Father must be feeling in his coffin. But he had a coat on, except it was on the wrong side of the lid.

'I'm cold,' I complained, 'but Daddy must be colder.'

'It is cold, but not that cold,' Bobby said sympathetically.

'Fair play,' sang Uncle Maldwyn. 'Ieuan is a wimp, after all said and done, and yet he thinks of his father's comfort. Believe me, Ieuan, your father is not feeling the cold. Probably where he has ended up he's feeling the heat.'

'Uncle Mal!' Bobby burst out.

The sight of the shires hauling a hay wain as a hearse elicited a little ripple of applause from the congregation. A couple of tut-

tuts about Father's coat made me feel ashamed. Bobby said he felt proud of Father's coat. People stared at the Massey Ferguson, but forgot about the tractor when they saw Uncle Maldwyn's suit.

'Fashion parade now, boys, watch this,' Uncle Maldwyn whispered to us in his best *sotto voce* and, climbing off the tractor, he walked up to the crowd and twirled a full circle, his turn-ups dragging on the gravel.

'Either the cold or the tractor fumes have got to Uncle Maldwyn,' Bobby said in a weary tone.

We walked into the chapel, which felt colder than outside. A candle burned at the pulpit and I tried to estimate how long it would take to heat the chapel. The coffin, coat and all, was wheeled in on a trolley, the sort of thing we could do with when collecting firewood for the farm, and was left beneath the pulpit.

Silence fell over the congregation. Uncle Maldwyn mounted the pulpit, his six-foot-four frame appearing diminutive in Taid's wedding suit. His tie had gone askew and his face was smudged with tractor soot. The plaintive piano struck a chord and Uncle Maldwyn began Sarastro's aria. All the women were weeping. Recorded Minister Jenkins followed and issued words of atonement, reconciliation and redemption, his wart agreeing with every biblical sanctimony. But it was mostly lost on me. The wind howled and joined in the service. Its eerie whistling sounded like the voices of little girls squealing.

Once again, Uncle Maldwyn mounted the steps of the pulpit. This time he would read the lesson. Mother's face was arranged in elements of grief and concern, no doubt the latter due to Uncle Maldwyn's outburst of laughter regarding the shire horses, and my attack of hysteria that it had prompted, but I tried not to dwell too much on the proceedings. He glowered solemnly at the congregation, putting on his best theatricals.

'Verily,' he boomed, 'verily I yesterday partook of a discussion of momentous significance for the whole of this congregation.' His voice rose to a frightening volume. He spread his arms and Taid's giant jacket assumed ominous proportions. 'Verily, I spoke with the Lord!' he declared.

'Pobl anwyl!' came from the back.

Then Uncle Maldwyn careered southwards off the script.

'The harrow of time divines a lucid reflection on matters best left alone. Patterns of inflated delusion meander on well-exercised pathways. Dear people, we are fascinated by the impossible. We are convinced, erroneously as it transpires, that impossibility is an entity that can never muster danger.'

Uncle Maldwyn paused and solemnly looked about the silent congregation filling the little chapel. I did not understand his lesson.

'But the impossible is there for the conquering,' he continued, 'for the taking, the spoils laid out in a coffin for display. In the ways of the Lord, understanding is communicated by way of a process no more sophisticated than a series of monosyllabic grunts, except in Ivan's case they were monosyllabic roars.'

A ripple of murmur ran through the congregation.

'But in spite of no preordained agenda, the series of monosyllables cohered logically within the finite possibilities of his unique mind. Even when impossible to divine, the entity of impossibility existed for his unique way of thinking, and he conquered it. Dear people, Ifan Troed-yr-Henrhiw conquered it!'

He again paused for effect and it certainly worked. I avoided his eyes.

'I spoke in tongues regarding Ifan's untimely death. And the Lord spake thus: "I advise thee," the Lord spake, "I advise thee that thy brother Ifan's admission to the Kingdom of Heaven demands preconditions recorded in thy Great Book, in imprints of Mother Nature, in the stars of all the Heavens from the far reaches of Galactic beginnings to the near intimacies of the Rod of Nimbus." '

Uncle Maldwyn again paused and swept the congregation with a beetle brow. This was hair-raising stuff, and it was not only the cold that caused me to shake.

'The Lord Almighty spake: "Preconditions of thy brother's admission to the Kingdom of Heaven are subject to his substantiating the myriad spiritual implications he utilised when weighing upon my gladsome shoulders the responsibility for inventing everything, for which I, the Lord Almighty, am obliged to accept responsibility." '

A gasp rippled through the congregation. We of family alone knew Uncle Maldwyn was up to his usual word games. The rest were trying to fathom out what he was talking about. Capel Soar-y-Mynydd rocked its little slates. The wind squeaked its girlie noises. Uncle Maldwyn had taken leave of the lesson and was in his element. Those of us familiar with his circumlocutions knew he would reach the subject if left alone, in a quiet corner, by and by. The rest were clueless.

'The reality of those responsibilities was always apparent to Ifan, inasmuch as his grasp of abstract concepts never succeeded in evading his best efforts.'

Now I was totally lost. Glancing at Mother and Bobby I saw their faces reflecting the same incomprehension that had smitten the rest of the congregation.

'The harrow of time tolls the knell beyond daybreak, beyond renaissance, but only during Man's brief visit to these shores. As a consequence you may take for granted that challenging the impossible will be a normal procedure for Ifan, who will rise again! Verily, the realisation of this divinity obliges time to harrow its lines across your foreheads. Ifan will rise again!' he boomed in a colossal voice.

My wandering eye alighted on Father's coffin. In spite of Bobby's baler twine anchoring the old coat, it had slipped its moorings and was sailing past the christening font in the strong wind, well on its way westwards on the nine-o-nine to nowhere. The further away, so the larger it became; right up near me it became a speck. The coat transfixed me, and I followed its wanderings about the chapel. Distantly, I heard Uncle Maldwyn renew his assault on what must have been the remnants of the congregation's grasp.

'I am in a better position to divulge the full text of my meeting with God,' he said in a suddenly different voice. Gone was the booming of Uncle Maldwyn's mellifluous bass tones; they were replaced by Father's rasping harsher bass. This clever imitation of Father's voice brought my attention back to the pulpit, and I momentarily lost interest in Father's coat.

Father was standing at the pulpit, arms outstretched, wearing his old coat tied with baler twine, side by side with Uncle Maldwyn, still lost in Taid's wedding suit. I glanced elsewhere for the coat, but it was on Father, which explained why it had visited us in the congregation. Father standing beside Uncle Maldwyn at the pulpit seemed perfectly normal and, indeed, the congregation agreed. A burst of applause was followed by *For He's a Jolly Good Fellow!* and then more cheering.

Uncle Maldwyn had been right all along; Father had returned. It was a very clever act, and I admired Uncle Maldwyn's complicity, although I had not understood most of his lesson.

'Daddy!' squeaked Francesca, clapping her little hands for joy, 'you're back! I knew you would come back!'

'Ifan is back, I tried to warn you,' Uncle Maldwyn sang. 'Don't question the Lord's ways too deeply! A gift of two pennies is as profound as one of two thousand pounds in the Lord's eyes.'

'I have always preached that!' declared Father, 'especially when I had no money.'

'Which was most of the time, praise the Lord!' the congregation chanted in prayer of thanksgiving.

Mother was not happy at all at Father's return; she still looked sad and perplexed. Bobby was deep in thought. I tugged at his sleeve.

'Is it real?' I asked, hardly daring to look away from Father in case he should die again.

'Shhh, not now,' Bobby whispered, 'not during the service.'

'But Bobby, is Daddy really here?'

'Of course Daddy's really there, now hush,' he whispered.

'How many days have I been away, Ieuan?' Father asked as he walked past me.

'Since you died, Dad.'

'How many days, nincompoop?' And he nailed me with a glare. It was then I noticed his irises were dark hollows and I could see straight into nothing.

'Er... um... Bobby, how many days has Daddy been gone?'

'Shhh, not now, I said!' he hissed.

'Daddy wants to know.'

'Take him out, Bobby... please,' Mother whispered anxiously through her sobs.

So I joined the throng pouring out of Capel Soar-y-Mynydd, Bobby firmly gripping my elbow. Outside were streamers blowing in the sleet, and some were already leaving for Troed-yr-Henrhiw. Inside, Uncle Maldwyn was leading the final hymn, *Efengyl Tangnefedd O Rhed Dros y Byd*.

'Why is Uncle Maldwyn still singing inside?'

'More like why have you gone off the rails at this moment, of all times? Uncle Maldwyn is still singing because the service is in full flow,' hissed Bobby.

'Where has Daddy gone? I saw him coming out.'

'Daddy hasn't come out. He is about to be buried in the grave – that one recently dug over there,' he said, pointing.

'But why was he walking about?' I asked, seemingly unable to get a straight answer.

'Daddy has gone to heaven. You are hallucinating. I'm going to give you such a thump if you don't pull yourself together!'

'I've pulled myself together,' I was intimidated into saying, not believing my own words.

That was the moment, and I saw it. Bobby looked at me long and hard.

'Can you be trusted to behave yourself if we go back in? It's cold out here, and Mammy will be most upset with us if we miss the rest of the service. Remember now, I am a man of my word – a good thump, any more of your nonsense,' warned Bobby, whereupon he gripped my arm to breaking point and marched me back in. 'Though I still find Recorded Minister Jenkins's story hard to believe,' he whispered in consolation as we entered the chapel.

'You mean Uncle Maldwyn's story, and Daddy's story,' I whispered back, 'but I won't interrupt proceedings, I promise. Daddy did talk to me, honest. Did you notice his eyes? Must be due to the darkness of the coffin all these days.'

'Oh dear,' said Bobby. 'Now hush – remember my promise.'

'WHERE HAVE YOU BEEN?' Father roared at me. He was standing halfway down the aisle. I froze. Bobby tugged at my arm without speaking. But my legs would not walk.

'Come on,' he hissed.

'YOU! IEUAN, I'M ASKING YOU, WHERE HAVE YOU BEEN?' Father roared again, louder still.

'I've been outside with Bobby,' I whimpered.

'WHAT?' Father roared so loud the chapel rattled.

'Shut up,' said Bobby. 'You said you would behave.'

Mother shook her head and continued sobbing. Little sister gave me an accusatorial look implying it was my fault Mother was crying. Bobby dug me hard in the ribs. But I was transfixed and even the shire horses would not have dragged me past Father, blocking the aisle.

Then amazingly Bobby walked through Father. Straight through. Father was an apparition! So I plucked up what little courage I had, squinted my eyes and walked straight at Father, and crashed into something solid.

'LOOK OUT, NINCOMPOOP!'

Many people were fussing about me.

'Is he all right?'

'Passed out like a light.'

'What a time to pass out!'

'And a place.'

'One of his turns again.' Bobby's voice rang above the others.

'Has Daddy gone?' I asked.

'Buried,' said Bobby, solemnly.

I had been asleep on the back seat of the Super Snipe and had missed the graveside ceremony.

'You'll come back with us,' Mother said.

'No, I'm all right now, honest. Let me go back on the tractor, please.'

'Look after him, Bobby.'

At that moment a well-tailored gentleman distantly related to the family came up to Bobby.

'Well, Robert,' he said, always calling Bobby by his correct name, 'you are the male of the household now.'

'Uncle Maldwyn lives with us,' said Bobby, honest to the full stop.

'Oh yes, Robert, and a fine person is Maldwyn. But you are the official head of the family, and I shall watch with interest your ability to cope. What an immense character was your father! I daresay all of you will be lost in his shadow. And that little snivel over there,' he said, pointing at me, 'would be lost in the shadow of one of your father's glances.'

'Thank you for saying those kind words about Father. As for Ieuan, apart from his hallucinations, he looks after the chickens fine,' said Bobby. 'Daddy couldn't stand his imaginations at all, but the rest of us are able to put up with them most of the time, except today, of course.'

As we walked away towards the tractor I said: 'Thank you, Robert, for those supportive words.'

'I wasn't supporting you. He's right, you are a snivel, but I wasn't going to let him say it about anybody in the family and get away with it, even about you.'

'Loyalty to your brother, Robert. Daddy would be proud of you,' I said, taking advantage of the drifting congregation to safeguard being thumped.

Droves passed the Massey Ferguson back to Troed-yr-Hen-rhiw. Spot assumed a precarious perch on the bonnet, a trick of which he had had plenty of practice. He had been surprisingly well behaved considering the distractions. The only blot on his mark sheet was rounding up a group of little girls and herding them into a dark corner at the rear of the chapel. He must have kept them prisoner for the duration. I wondered why the wind sounded like little girls squealing; Bobby wondered why Spot had been so quiet the whole service. One child's father demanded Spot be shot for taking the children prisoner, which elicited a ferocious growl from Uncle Maldwyn, whereupon the demand was modified to a request he be left at home 'next time'. I ask you, some people are so insensitive; what next time could there be?

Uncle Maldwyn broached the subject. 'What came over you in the chapel of all places, Ieuan?'

I had been dreading this moment.

'He had one of his confounded turns again,' Bobby answered for me.

'Daddy came up and spoke to me after he had been standing with you at the pulpit.' I began my story to Uncle Maldwyn. But it travelled no further.

'Only you saw that,' Uncle Maldwyn said in deep confidential tones. 'Your father said nothing to me.'

'But he said he had had a full meeting with God, something like that,' I countered feebly.

'It might have been nothing like that – sounds play tricks in the vast auditorium of a tiny chapel like Soar-y-Mynydd, especially on an exceptional day such as your father's funeral,' reasoned Uncle Maldwyn.

'But he spoke to me,' I protested.

'I don't know whether you are intelligent with a highly developed imagination or stupid with a mind that plays tricks on you,' Uncle Maldwyn said thoughtfully.

'He's got to be stupid. Daddy was convinced,' Bobby contributed. 'But don't try to get sense out of him, Uncle Maldwyn. Ieuan is a liability even when ordinary events occur, so let alone the extraordinary situation of Daddy's funeral.'

'Nothing ordinary in Daddy rising from the dead to talk with me. Nothing ordinary with his eyes that allow you to see the back of his brain,' I protested, 'Oh, no!'

'Nothing that psychic wavelengths cannot explain, upside down behind a star, tucked away in the graveyard of Soar-y-Mynydd,' answered Uncle Maldwyn, and he winked at me.

'You two!' Bobby exclaimed.

'One and the same,' replied Uncle Maldwyn with strained joviality. 'Your mother is convinced it's the same gene.'

'Daddy used to say it comes from the Crees side, and Mammy says it comes from the Pugh side,' said Bobby.

'Pugh pot calling Crees kettle black,' sang Uncle Maldwyn, to the tune of *Cwm Rhondda*.

To cheer us up Uncle Maldwyn allowed Bobby to drive the tractor back to Troed-yr-Henrhiw. Father was back again, flying alongside us. I nudged Uncle Maldwyn and nodded surreptitiously in Father's direction. Uncle Maldwyn looked at the cloud-strewn hillside, the dark leaning hawthorns and driving sleet; he looked at me and nodded sagely.

'Apply the kerosene full blast Bobby, otherwise pneumonia will take over our souls and we will be sorting the stars tonight with your father.'

I fell into deep thought about Father and the burial that I missed, but was brought back to the cold sleet of day when Bobby lost control of the Massey Ferguson and we temporarily took to the wilderness. Fair play to Bobby, the weather was closing in and we were all suffering from the biting north-easterly sleet. From then on I forgot sombre thoughts as the tractor hurtled down off the mountainside at breakneck speed, Spot leaning into the bends like an ace, squinting into the wind. I wanted this feverish driving to go on and on as I was dreading our arrival at the Troed-yr-Henrhiw. There was something unreal about Father's appearances; I had fleeting glimpses of a dream that said it was the end of Father and the place would never be the same again. But those were fleeting dreams, although the place could never be the same again without Father.

The farm was overrun by relatives, friends and strangers alike, which was just as well. Crowds of people temporarily hid the grime and mess that was our lot, but unfortunately could not disguise the general squalor of Troed-yr-Henrhiw. Mother was in the middle with hills of aunts rallying to the cause, carrying piles of food from their cars. Apart from the food, we were best out of the way. Strangers came up to me, saying, 'You all right now, little boy?' and, 'No wonder your father was at his wit's end with the likes of you about the farm – one wonders how he coped.'

I wondered how wrong they could be. I wanted to say, 'Father coped very well, considering he lay in bed until eleven every morning and when he finally arose all the morning chores had been attended to.' But I was far too shy and anxiety-ridden to contemplate giving them an answer, whereupon my silence was interpreted as insolence. A strong characteristic of the Welsh is to be a bully. I was mindful if one stood up to Father, he burst into laughter and enjoyed it; if one cowered, he was scornful. Similarly with these visitors: if I had been six feet four inches tall they would have acclaimed my silence as being heroic. At least Father classified my silence as a victory of his logic over my idiocy.

Mother caught my eye and crossed over to me. She recognised my look of despair.

'When this is all over,' she said with big tears in her eyes, 'we will go up to Uncle George's Hafod Las farm for a holiday, otherwise cups will keep jumping out of your little cupboard.'

I was embarrassed and kept my council, save to say 'Good idea'.

Everyone was pleased to see Uncle Maldwyn and he as usual was big-hearted and welcoming. Grabbing a sandwich and two

Welsh cakes I hared upstairs, followed by Bobby. I turned the corner on to the landing and Father was waiting, but he must have been preoccupied for he did not speak. I had an ache somewhere but was unable to identify its engine. Evidently Bobby had not seen Father. Uncle Maldwyn had given us permission to use his room during the reception, and we gladly availed ourselves of the offer because it was the most interesting room in the whole farmhouse.

'I cannot believe the story Recorded Minister Jenkins is going on about, telling everybody. What business is it of his that Daddy hasn't arrived in heaven yet?' queried a very serious Bobby. And then, 'Did you really see Daddy in Soar-y-Mynydd?'

'Yes, he spoke to me. He asked how long had he been gone. He's here now, outside on the landing.'

Bobby took a quick look on the landing, but said nothing.

'He's there, isn't he?'

'Were you answering Daddy in the chapel? Were you answering his questions when you talked?' Bobby asked; clearly he had not seen Father.

'Yes, of course. He asked "How many days have I been away, Ieuan?" and I said, "Since you died". And he said: "How many days, nincompoop?" but at that moment I noticed the irises of his eyes were dark hollows and I could see straight to the back of his head. It was horrible.'

'OK, that's enough, stop talking about it,' Bobby said abruptly. 'Perhaps after all Recorded Minister Jenkins has a point.'

'Perhaps he has.' I reluctantly acceded to my brother's good logic.

'I hope he has a point now I have heard your story,' said Bobby gravely, 'but we will find out for ourselves. I believe we should investigate the events concerning Daddy arriving at the Gate.'

'Cripes.'

'Cripes, indeed. But you must stop hallucinating, for your own sake,' replied Bobby, firmly.

I certainly wanted to stop seeing things, but did not have a clue how to stop.

Uncle Maldwyn's room contained many interesting objects: an

upright piano; a portrait of Taid as Mine Captain of a coalmine in New Zealand; a picture of Taid with a horse on his shoulders; a photograph of Uncle Maldwyn in the Royal Engineers; and a photograph of him in a field hospital in Belgium. Best object of all was a television set standing on the floor next to the little fireplace. It worked sporadically, which reminded me of Father. Its aerial comprised of complicated rods and wired paraphernalia at the top of a spruce tree, and it failed when the wind played its games.

'I hope Mammy is all right with that crowd downstairs,' I said with worry, meaning I hope Mother isn't seeing apparitions of Father.

'Stop fretting! Since Daddy died you've done nothing but fret. It's either fretting or having attacks of hysteria. Neither fretting nor hysteria will bring Daddy back. And to make matters worse you are now hallucinating, although I suppose that is another form of hysteria. I don't know – not only are you small in stature, but you are weak in the mind as well!' Brother Bobby was losing patience with me, but fortunately he had not forgone his immense humour.

'It is time to be bold,' he continued. 'After all, you are the second in line to the throne of this great palace now, so be bold about it! All you have to do is bump me off by cutting the brakes of the Massey Ferguson and all this would be yours,' he said expansively with a swish of his arms.

This was Bobby at his best; his optimism and positive thinking were infectious. But then he had an afterthought: 'Not too bold, mind, we've got a million guests swarming around downstairs, and they wouldn't know how to cope with your hysteria.'

'Spot will keep them in order. He fully understands my hysteria,' I said, and we laughed.

'And the seat of our rule is a slummy hovel where all the cows limp because of their foot rot,' said Bobby.

'And the water system is muddy in winter and dries up in summer,' I added.

'And Voroshilov always eats the runt of the litter, except in your case. And this is the only palace in the world where a goat spends his days butting people,' said Bobby.

'And butting Spot down the water well,' I reciprocated. 'I hope he butts that distant relative down the well who said nasty things about me.'

'And the only palace in the world where bantam hens fly up into the yew trees to lay.'

'And then crow afterwards,' I added.

'And our rats are infected with Weil's Disease.'

'I thought it was wheel's decease,' I queried.

'Weil's Disease' Bobby repeated, 'as in Leptospirosis.'

'And the rabbits have Myxomatosis.'

'We don't keep rabbits. Spot wouldn't hesitate to eat them,' said Bobby.

'OK, then all the chickens have foul pest.'

'And the pigs have foot and mouth disease.'

'And we shoot farm inspectors.'

'Now, don't get carried away,' admonished Bobby.

'OK, Gastric butts farm inspectors down the well.'

'That's better, but still harsh,' he said. 'And Uncle Maldwyn is the only one who has a television set in the palace,' said Bobby.

'And Uncle Maldwyn says he has got squatters' rights in the palace,' I added.

We laughed and laughed. I laughed too much, to the degree where my hysteria began to return, so Bobby snapped to work on the new scenario.

'You play the part of Archangel Gabriel because he manifests certain weaknesses of which you have the gift,' declared Bobby. 'I shall be God.'

'Is that because Archangel Gabriel is short in stature?'

'No. It is more the spiritual weakness I was referring to,' replied Bobby.

'What is Archangel Gabriel's job?'

'In heaven's reality he is God's Messenger. But in this particular case concerning Daddy all the angels have complained to Archangel Gabriel that the new applicant at the Golden Gate is acting in an outrageous manner never before experienced in heaven. They find he has closed his mind to their imploring and is making unreasonable demands in his usual outrageously loud voice, and is altogether impossible to deal with. In other words he is just the normal father we knew him to be. As a result Archangel Gabriel has to deal with Daddy personally. But Daddy is so awkward that soon Archangel Gabriel flies into a tantrum of exasperation—'

I interrupted his flow with a fiendish bout of giggling.

'Don't interrupt! Listen and take note, because you are going to be Archangel Gabriel... So, Archangel Gabriel reports to God saying he cannot cope with Daddy.' Bobby concluded his summary, which did not seem to adhere to the scriptures at all. Fortunately Mother was preoccupied downstairs. Bobby cleared his throat and changed his voice to a God voice.

'What brings you to the Overseers Hall with that look of immense concern, Gabe?'

'Gabe? Is that the way God addresses Archangel Gabriel?' I questioned.

'Stop procrastinating and answer the question, Gabe,' said the God voice.

Obviously that was the way God addressed Archangel Gabriel, so I hesitantly joined the swing of the scenario.

'I wish to tender my resignation,' said Archangel Gabriel.

God roared with laughter. He laughed and laughed. I was unable to ascertain whether it was Bobby or God roaring with laughter. 'Archangels cannot tender their resignation, Ieuan.'

Obviously it was Bobby roaring with laughter.

'There has got to be a first time for everything,' I said.

'Not necessarily so,' said the God voice. 'Look at the chicken and egg conundrum, which has tied humans in knots for aeons. Anyway, what has brought about this unconstitutional thinking? Sit down and retell your concerns. You are so short it makes me uncomfortable.'

My Archangel Gabriel cleared his throat. 'I was obliged to deal with a recalcitrant newcomer name of Pugh Troed-yr-Henrhiw Farm, who was giving my angels a weight of grief at the Gate, flirting with the girl angels but roaring abuse at the boy angels. Unfortunately, Pugh's talent to irritate surpasses everything previously experienced this side of the Great Wall, and I soon enjoyed the unusual sensation of becoming irritated myself. When I realised I was transgressing the heavenly protocols by operating in the zone of infringement regarding self-effacement and all that, it became apparent I needed to see you urgently,' said Archangel Gabriel, 'or take a fishing holiday,' he added.

'Take a fishing holiday? This is heaven, you prat. You know

there is no such thing as a fishing holiday in heaven,' an exasperated Bobby voice preached.

'You cannot call Archangel Gabriel a prat. The inner council of ex-Gods disallows such insults in their articles of government,' I retorted in Archangel Gabriel voice, experiencing difficulty in keeping a straight face.

'Ex-Gods? What's got into you?' Bobby demanded. 'Take the scenario seriously. Anybody would think—'

'I am! You started it with the Gabe thing and roaring with laughter,' I said. 'If I were God I would be able to circumvent these testing trivia, and proceed with the narrative of the scenario,' I added in Archangel tone.

'OK, OK, you are quite right, Archie. Beware, I might bowl you a Godly googly.'

'Archie? Now who's not taking the scenario seriously?'

'I meant Gabe,' the God voice replied. 'Beware the Godly googly, Gabe.'

I fought back the convulsions. 'Anyway, I wish to tender my resignation,' I replied in Archangel Gabriel mode.

'Now you are fully aware that your job is for eternity,' God returned. 'Resignation is not in your contract. Before we have a more in-depth conversation regarding your in-service development, I will need to see this recalcitrant Pugh of Troed-yr-Henrhiw myself.'

'It is not in my remit to warn you, Boss, but beware this character. He is quite impossible,' warned Archangel Gabriel.

'Impossible is not in my vocabulary, Gabe – as indeed resignation is not in yours,' declared God. 'I will see him at the next Aeon Review before I submit my accounts. Arrange a suitable venue that befits this recalcitrant character.'

'Would the Great Hall of Mirrors be a suitable venue?'

'Heavens no!' expressed a surprised God. 'That would multiply his already multiplied personality. No, no. Find somewhere antipathetic to his peace of mind: crowds of people, children squabbling, cars not starting, wind tugging at his hair – that sort of thing.'

'And being nagged by his wife to get up from bed because there is work to be done on the farm,' added Archangel Gabriel.

'That sort of thing,' said God, 'and Gastric has just butted the bucket of milk over.'

'And on the table before him are piles of agricultural forms he should have filled in and returned weeks ago,' Archangel Gabriel continued.

'Yes, that sort of thing,' replied God. 'And two large shire horses are walking back and fore as I am interrogating him.'

'And they keep pooing on his agricultural forms.'

'Now, don't get carried away again, Gabe,' said God.

Whereupon I could stand it no longer and burst into profuse giggling.

'I shall undertake the magic television show now,' said Bobby. 'While I'm setting it up, pop downstairs, run the gauntlet of the aunts, and tell Francesca the magic television show is about to begin. Ask her to come up.'

Downstairs it was difficult finding Francesca among the crush of adults. Uncle Maldwyn's booming voice could be heard above all others. As I pushed my way through, various aunts grabbed the opportunity to pounce and command of me, now that my father had passed away, to grow up and assume some responsibility. I was already under the impression that contributing daily to feeding the chickens, cleaning the pigsties, collecting firewood and fetching drinking water was pretty grown up for a twelve-year-old but, regardless of the contribution I made, they persisted in holding a negative image of me. God knows who supplied them with such false information.

I eventually found little sister in the scullery hiding away from it all.

'Bobby is setting up a magic television show in Uncle Maldwyn's room and he wants you to join us.'

Her face lit up. 'Come on, then, let's go,' she said, darting for the stairs.

Mother caught sight of us. A look of fluster hummed about her face. 'Where are you two going?'

'Bobby is putting on a magic television show in Uncle Maldwyn's room, and he has invited Francesca.'

'Oh, all right, good. Bobby and his magic television shows!

Don't touch anything belonging to your uncle. Take some Welsh cakes before they are all gone,' said Mother, and we were on our way. Father was no longer on the landing.

Heaven

'This is entitled *The Day God Met Father* and it's an epic of the Lord's quintessential patience being tested to the absolute utmost,' Bobby began by way of introduction once we were seated on the floor before Uncle Maldwyn's huge television set. He had been tinkering around in his bedroom for some days following Father's death. He explained he had devised a magical method by which we could witness Father entering the Kingdom of Heaven, but cautioned he had never performed this type of magic before, so connection with heaven could be lost at any moment, especially as the strong north-easterly wind was catching the spruce trees a dance. Nevertheless, we were entranced.

The three of us were snug and private in Uncle Maldwyn's room. The room was warm as it sat above the scullery boiler, which fire was never allowed to go out. Outside, the November weather darkened with thickening sleet. I wondered where Father was. Although I had not witnessed the coffin being lowered into the grave at Capel Soar-y-Mynydd, I had seen Father several times since. As Bobby had said, my hysteria took some convincing. A clock beside Uncle Maldwyn's bed went tock-tock, tock-tock. I ate one of my Welsh cakes and gave the others to Francesca and Bobby. Little sister munched sadly, her eyes staring down at the threadbare carpet in Uncle Maldwyn's room. I was overcome by a feeling of compassion for her but could not translate it into words. Unlike me, if she had experienced hallucinations, she was courageous enough not to mention them. My mood soared to the height of enjoyment with my brother's scenarios, but immediately plunged to the depths when I was left with my own thoughts. This day particularly my mind was all over the place.

Bobby fetched a strange contraption from his bedroom. At last I could see what had been preoccupying him in the days following Father's death. It resembled a large crystal set modified by many additional features. This typical of Bobby, always tinkering with gadgets, never allowing anyone in his den when his contraptions were under construction.

'What's that?'

He did not reply, but proceeded methodically to balance it on top of Uncle Maldwyn's television set before connecting wires to points at the back that were unknown to me. Francesca and I watched transfixed, momentarily forgetting the sadness of the occasion.

Bobby turned from his gadgets to lecture us. He emphasised the need for us to believe. 'You must believe beyond believing. You must believe beyond endurance of believing for the experiment to work. If you don't believe, it will not work. It's as simple as that.'

'Will it half work if I half believe?' asked Francesca.

'No. It's all or nothing. You must believe beyond believing,' he replied as he twiddled some unconvincing knobs on his contraption. Then he twiddled the knobs on Uncle Maldwyn's television set. A blaze of snow filled the screen accompanied by a hissing sound that dimmed to a gentle hum.

'That's the hum of angels strumming the harps of heaven,' he said in an expressionless tone. 'Listen carefully, and you will pick out their words... listen!'

We listened. Bobby continued speaking in a monotonous manner, declaring repeatedly that if we genuinely believed in God and sincerely wanted to see Father enter the Kingdom of Heaven, the whole event would appear on the screen.

'Watch the screen carefully,' he said in monotone, 'keep listening and keep believing.'

The harps of heaven continued to hum.

The first thing to appear, dimly through the blaze of snow, was a little classroom. Its windows gradually became distinct and showed the ecclesiastical curve of Victorian school architecture. Small infant-sized desks appeared, cast-iron framed, seat and desk integral, lift-up lids. Francesca was matter of fact about the image.

'That looks like my classroom. Miss Williams teaches me. I'm going to Miss Thomas's class after Christmas.'

'Doesn't look like heaven to me,' I said cynically, 'looks like Penparcau Infants School.'

'Watch the screen carefully,' Bobby said in a low monotone voice, 'and if you genuinely believe in God, Daddy will be there. Remember, cynical little brother, heaven comes in many guises. Believe in heaven, not Penparcau Infants School.'

'There's a man coming into my classroom. Who is he?'

'Concentrate,' said Bobby, in a strange voice. 'Concentrate on believing for all you are worth.'

'The man is getting clearer,' I said, trying not to be so cynical.

'Yes, the man is getting clearer,' said Bobby.

'Who is he?' Francesca persisted.

'He is God, just like you know him in the paintings,' said Bobby. 'Continue to concentrate on believing.'

'That's God!' squeaked Francesca.

'Take a good look. That is God, but I didn't expect him to be in that old classroom.'

'It's Penparcau Infants School, I keep telling you,' I said, more in amazement than petulance.

'I said that! It's Miss Williams's classroom. That's my desk in the front,' protested the little one.

'You said that, sweetheart, perhaps Ieuan didn't hear you. Heaven comes in many guises.'

'Magic!' declared Francesca. 'God in my classroom! Magic! Wait till I tell Miss Williams!'

God was just how we had expected him to look. He appeared very old, even older than Madam Powell. His hair and beard were long and grey, just as clever artists had painted him long ago, except he had no halo. He possessed the air of great intelligence. By the expression on his face it was impossible to ascertain what was going on in his mind. A student teacher at school said God did not have a mind, just a centre of pure energy that went on and on for ever.

'Notice God's face!' Bobby declared, 'this is most remarkable! We are more privileged than Moses. God did not allow Moses of all people to see his face. We are very privileged. This means something – it means you are believing.'

God allowing his face to be seen was for me part of the whole exciting occasion, but Bobby, who was well read in biblical issues, interpreted it as possessing a greater significance than the whole.

'God has never been known before to assume anthropomorphic features,' he buzzed on excitedly, but Francesca and I were more amazed by the picture on the screen than historical details.

'What does anthrop-something mean?' I asked.

'Anthropomorphic features. Human features, features like us,' he answered quickly, anxious not to interrupt the flow of proceedings.

God did not walk between the little desks, but shimmered through them. That convinced me; that was the evidence that proved to me he was God. His face resembled that of any old man, but shimmering through the desks was the clincher.

'Look! God can walk through the desks, and he shimmers as he does so,' I exclaimed.

'I saw that too,' claimed little Francesca, 'but I thought I was seeing things.'

'You are seeing things, sweetheart,' said Bobby in the same hypnotic tone. 'You are seeing a miracle, the miracle of God's face, and heaven is represented as Penparcau Infants School, because Penparcau Infants School is heaven.'

'God in my classroom,' little sister proudly repeated.

'It's a mystery. I'm baffled. Where do these pictures come from?' I asked Bobby. Whatever he was doing, it was very clever, and completely beyond my understanding.

'We must all be reverent from now on,' warned Bobby, avoiding my question but clearly in command of the scene. 'Reverence means we should not blaspheme before God. I daresay God can see and hear us all the time. We are in his hands – watch him carefully. If you genuinely believe in God, Daddy will appear.' He gently turned a knob and we witnessed the picture becoming clearer.

'Magic!' cried Francesca.

A title printed clearly over the noticeboard on the far wall read: 'Department of Special Needs for Recalcitrants, Calvary Section'. To its right hung a large picture of two black shire horses pulling a plough. Beneath it the notice ran, 'Today's Lesson: list all the tasks shire horses can undertake'; next to that another notice read: 'The Obsidian Readings of Querulous Agents', which I did not understand. A swing ticket hanging from the blackboard easel read: 'Today's teacher is—' and scrawled in white chalk half-uncial script the name 'GOD' was clearly shown. A chalked notice on the board read: 'Weather forecast for today: cold north-easterly wind; sleet turning to snow'.

'Look at the notices,' I piped in excitement.

'Apt,' Bobby responded.

'Shire horses, pulling a plough,' said Francesca.

'We plough the fields and scatter,' said Bobby in monotone.

'The good seed on the land,' sang Francesca.

Meanwhile, God stood silently beneath the old Victorian windows, waiting with towering patience. The classroom had the air of predetermination and the excitement of the occasion was tantalising. Francesca and I held our breath.

'It's like an old film. That shimmering effect is the lighting of olden days and is used by heaven whenever the archangels are putting on a show,' said Bobby very calmly, very authoritatively. 'It's wonderful and all very real, like it's happening at this minute.'

'But it is, isn't it?' asked little sister.

'Of course it is, sweetheart, if you believe strongly enough.'

'I believe strong,' she said.

'Keep concentrating and think of Daddy arriving in heaven.'

'But why are all those notices saying things about lessons and shire horses?'

'Related to Daddy but only indirectly! Think of them as being there by the divine will of heaven,' replied Bobby in his flat hypnotic voice.

Suddenly a clattering and banging shattered the beautiful silence, and to the bottom left of the screen a door opened. Father burst through huffing and puffing, knocking his elbows on the doorposts and as usual looking extremely annoyed.

'It's Daddy!' squeaked Francesca, clapping her hands with glee, 'Daddy, see? I knew Daddy hadn't gone.'

'I told you he talked to me in the chapel!' I said, giving Bobby a hard look.

We all looked at each other, stunned. It really was Father entering Miss Williams's classroom. I think Bobby was more stunned than I that the heaven show was working. Little sister took it for granted.

'Let's tell Mammy,' she squeaked, 'quick, let's call Mammy!'

'Not yet,' said Bobby quickly, 'let the story get established first.'

'Yes suppose,' she said, 'but let's call Daddy, then.'

'Not yet,' forbade Bobby gently, 'he won't hear you just yet because I believe he has just arrived in heaven. Remember, your classroom is heaven. Besides, let's hear what God has to say to him before we call anybody.'

'Quite,' I said.

'Quite,' Francesca said.

'I wonder what will happen now?'

'Well,' Bobby began carefully, 'this is heaven, so anything in the universe could happen. Whatever happens, we must respect it, because it is heaven. Remember, for the time being it is best for this to remain a secret between just the three of us. We'll let the rest know if all goes well. In the meantime, we must continue believing like we never believed before.'

We could not take our eyes off the screen. God remained impassive, but Father as usual continued to bluster.

'Daddy's wearing his old coat in heaven,' said little sister.

'Tied with baler twine,' I said. 'I saw him wearing it in Soar-y-Mynydd.'

'And he's got his battered briefcase with him,' Bobby added.

Sure enough, Father had his battered briefcase with him. He used it to carry a vacuum flask of over-sweetened tea and an Oxo box full of freshly baked Welsh cakes, provision of which was one of Mother's daily tasks.

'I wonder if he's allowed to take tea into heaven?' I asked, and Father turned and looked at us. On the other hand, he could have been surveying the classroom, and coincidentally looked in our direction.

'And I wonder if there are any Welsh cakes left in the Oxo box,' Bobby said. 'The scriptures say we cannot take anything with us into the Kingdom of Heaven. It's easier to get a camel through the eye of a needle and all that.'

'Yes,' agreed little sister, 'eye of a needle and all that.' Then she must have had second thoughts: 'What does eye of a needle and all that mean?'

'Shhh! I'll tell you later.'

'Anyway,' she said, not shushing, 'Daddy is an excepted person.'

'Exceptional,' Bobby corrected, 'but we learn from the Bible that God makes no exception, exceptional person or not.'

God studied Father impassively. Father, seemingly unaware of God's presence, made a beeline for the picture of the shire horses. He was growling. As he closely scrutinised the picture he growled ferociously and muttered something that we could not pick up.

'That's too much of a coincidence, the two shire horses,' I said. 'They look the spitting image of Dylan and Thomas. No wonder Daddy's muttering something.'

'Daddy wouldn't know about Dylan and Thomas.' Bobby snuffled a giggle and looked at the little one.

'What? Of course Daddy would know all about them. He saw them. Uncle Maldwyn said we would be sorry,' Francesca corrected with conviction.

'You are quite right, sweetheart,' said Bobby.

'Does Daddy know Jones Waungrug was commissioned by Mammy?' I asked.

'Of course he does!' snapped Francesca. 'No wonder he's cross.'

'Sit down,' God spoke in a grave tone.

Francesca jumped and we clutched at each other. Bobby stirred.

God's voice was so deep it appeared to come from inside the lowest note on the school organ. It possessed a chilling certainty that defied contradiction. Father glanced about, evidently striving to locate the source of the voice.

'Sit down,' God said again.

'God's voice is ten times deeper than Uncle Maldwyn's,' I said in awe.

'Eleven times deeper,' said little sister.

'I believe Daddy can't see God,' Bobby whispered. 'This is very interesting.'

Father was already in a high state of irritation upon entering Miss Williams's classroom. Clearly the funeral arrangements had upset him; Jones Waungrug of all people! Being commanded to sit down by a person he could not locate did not improve his mood.

'Are you talking to me?' asked Father, looking around more earnestly.

'Sit down!' God commanded more strongly.

'Where are you?' asked Father.

'Sit down!'

'Where can I sit?' asked Father, relenting.

'Sit down!' God commanded yet again, in the same deep voice.

Father showed every sign of becoming angrier. His free hand clenched into a fist and he performed a little tap dance, which clattered noisily on the bare boards of the classroom floor. He would always dance in a childish tantrum when he was really angry.

'Uh-oh,' said Bobby quietly, 'Daddy's getting into one of his real tempers. This should be interesting.'

'Sit down!' God commanded again.

'All God says is "sit down",' said Francesca. 'I wonder if he is doing it on purpose?'

'Good thinking, little one,' said Bobby.

The sound of laughter wafted in from somewhere beyond the classroom. Father swivelled about, looking for its source. At the same time the shire horses grew larger and began plodding on the spot, neighing and hurrumping the while.

'This must be torture for Daddy, laughter and horses at the same time,' said Bobby.

'All we need now is wind,' I suggested.

'Or for the horses to poo,' said Francesca, quite matter of fact.

'Francesca sweetheart! Don't start that again – you are looking into heaven, don't forget,' Bobby reprimanded.

With that a huge wind swept through the classroom, flapping Father's clothes and tugging at his hair, but around God all was serene and quiet. Then the shire horses pooed in the picture, so much so that the excess spilled out of the frame on to the floor of the classroom.

Francesca looked on with fear and dismay.

'Oh no! This is more like hell than heaven for Daddy,' I blurted.

'Ieuan! Now we are for it,' warned Bobby.

'I only meant it was hell for Daddy, not hell we are looking at,' I said.

God looked straight at us. I gave a start and Francesca emitted a little shriek.

'Shhh!' said Bobby, 'that lot downstairs will be up here. You two, watch what you say from now on. You might spoil the whole magic.'

'Sorry,' I said, directing my apology at God.

God averted his gaze, and resumed watching Father. I was immensely relieved.

'Sit down!' God boomed more authoritatively still.

Father was reaching a climax of anger and exasperation. The smooth transition from docility to ferocity usually happened rapidly, and his display in heaven was no exception. He looked demented, striving to locate the voice's source, glaring at the plodding shires, tossing his head at the piles of poo, hating the laughter. Throughout this time the gale nagged at his intolerance.

'Poor Daddy,' said Francesca, her voice breaking, 'he didn't die to suffer all the things he hated.'

'Out of the mouths of babes truth springs eternal,' muttered Bobby. 'But Daddy hated a lot more than just those irritants,' he added.

At that the gale ceased as suddenly as it had begun. The shires galloped back into the leaf and resumed their two-dimensional stillness; their dollops promptly disappeared and silence prevailed but did not cast a shadow. Father stopped his wild searching, for his eyes had alighted upon God.

'Gosh, magic – it's all stopped!'

'That was God's little test of Daddy's forbearance,' was Bobby's explanation.

'Do you think Daddy passed the test?' I asked.

'Of course he did,' said Francesca.

'Well, from what we witnessed, Daddy certainly did not pass his test,' said Bobby.

'Sit down!' said God, for the umpteenth time, and he pointed to one of the little desks.

'I can't sit in that!' declared Father, 'it's far too small for me.'

'It reflects your maturity exactly,' said God.

'I'll have you know—' began Father.

'Don't waste your spiritual energy, I already know,' said God, delicately exercising his omnipotence.

Little sister took a sharp intake of breath. 'What does God mean, he already knows?'

'Good question, little one. God means he knows everything about everybody, all the time, including us,' Bobby explained.

Father stood silently by, a sad, forlorn figure. I found it difficult to measure the distance he had travelled from Wales to heaven. Perhaps it was a distance measuring for ever, or no further than our memories. Certainly, physical miles unbalance the equation, as they are both too big and too small. My little head could not get around the notion of timelessness and zero dimension, and measuring distance in minutes, periods of time in miles, and there being here all the time that it is being there at the same time. I found it very difficult to keep such abstract thoughts under control, and felt very proud of Father's having achieved the physicality of such expedients. Father had always disliked holidays and travel. He ignored those baying at the gates of his emotions with their solutions to his travelling plans, as he never availed himself of them. Other people's already limited perspectives missed Father's by at least a century, meaningless to all except God. Father's nirvana was always the hedge at the bottom of the garden. God waited for me to stop contemplating on a shire hobby horse.

'I was wondering whether to ask God how to measure the distance Daddy had travelled between Wales and heaven, but it can wait,' I said.

'Don't start your hallucinating meditations now of all times.'

I did not know what my brother meant by that comment, but nevertheless immediately came back to concentrating on the screen.

'Will God ask Daddy about Taid?'

'If he does, Daddy will have to answer. God won't allow him to simply growl and refuse to impart information,' said Bobby.

'Will secrets come out?' wondered Francesca.

'God has no secrets, but I don't know if they will come out of Daddy. Perhaps Daddy never knew, and his growling was more at his ignorance than anything else.'

'God will know anyway, so he doesn't have to ask Daddy,' I suggested.

'Surely,' said Bobby, 'God knows everything.'

'Sit down,' said God. 'You will realise at some point in your fixation that you are obliged to obey my instruction, either ultimately or now.'

'I will sit down when there is a proper chair to sit on,' said Father.

'This is a battle of wits between Daddy and God,' I said.

'Nothing of the sort,' said Bobby. 'Daddy is up against God, who is the Force of Nature. You wouldn't dream of saying Daddy was defying the call of nature by not breathing. You wouldn't call it a battle of wits between Daddy and the call of nature, would you?'

'No, I see what you mean, but I bet Daddy will try because he is resolute.'

'You may call it resolute, but I call it stubborn,' said Bobby, whereupon God looked directly at us.

'You notice if we say something strong, God looks at us.'

'Yes, I noticed that.'

'What does that mean? Does it mean God can hear us?' asked Francesca.

'Yes, of course God can hear us,' said Bobby. 'God knows everything we are saying or thinking all the time. That's why God is God. If Daddy looks in our direction I think it is coincidental, but with God I think it's deliberate.'

'Wow, magic!'

'Yes, magic. We are very privileged. We must make the most of this magic.'

'Sit down,' said God yet again.

With no further procrastination Father sat down in one of the tiny infant desks. No adjustment could be made to the rigid design so Father squeezed in until his knees came about his chin, his battered briefcase covered the top of the little desk and his arms hung over both. He looked most uncomfortable. I could not decide whence Father's compliance had sprung. As Bobby had said, the Force of Nature is infinitely stronger than Father's resolution. Be that as it may, I could not help seeing the funny side of it.

'Daddy looks funny squeezed into that tiny desk,' I said.

'Don't say that,' warned Bobby, 'he has only just begun to comply with God's command.'

'But it does look funny,' said Francesca, 'Daddy sitting in one of our desks.'

'Yes, sweetheart,' said Bobby, obviously experiencing difficulty in keeping a serious face, 'but let's think positively about it: Daddy's compliance is contributing to his happier entry into the Kingdom of Heaven.'

'Not a very happy entry into the Kingdom of Heaven squeezed into a tiny desk. The desk is so small it makes Daddy look foolish.'

'And the wind and the horses,' added Francesca.

'And the laughter and the pooing,' I added for good measure.

'Hmm,' thought Bobby, 'I think it's better if you two concentrate on believing.'

With Father's knees up to his chin we could see how dirty and ragged his trousers were. They were splashed with many different colours of farm. Years ago he had repaired his wristwatch strap with gum-tape and there was strong evidence it had grown used to the watch. His overcoat was ragged at elbows and cuffs, but showed much of Mother's stitch-work repair. The baler twine belt was unravelling at each end. A moth-eaten jumper had metamorphosed into Father, for we knew him in nothing else.

'When we see him like that it reminds us how unbelievably scruffy he is,' Bobby said.

'No wonder Mammy refused to go to town with him,' said little sister.

'And he had all those new jumpers as Christmas presents that are still in the drawers,' I said, amazed at the realisation.

'But after all the anguish I wonder if his appearance matters one jot to God?' reasoned Bobby.

'Can we call him yet?' asked Francesca.

'Not just yet, sweetheart, let's hear what God has to say first,' Bobby replied in soothing tones.

'Now you are seated we can proceed with your processing,' said God.

'I believe the interesting part is about to begin,' said Bobby excitedly, 'so concentrate you two for all you are worth.'

'There are a number of outstanding issues you left unresolved,' said God.

'Nobody's business,' said Father, 'I left no debts, no criminal record, no skeletons in the cupboard—'

'What skeletons in cupboards?' shuddered Francesca.

'Shhh! Tell you later.'

'But it is my business, therefore as you know it is everyone's business,' replied God, having paused for the interruption.

Father tossed his head. He muttered inaudibly, but whatever he said was not lost on God, who approached him with awesome deliberation. Simultaneously as if by a hidden signal the shires became animated again.

'You realise your children are curious regarding your ancestry. Should they be informed?'

'It's too late.'

'It is not too late. Should they be informed?'

'No.'

'Good. Then they shall be informed,' said God.

'I said no!' Father roared in an enormous voice, and he added, 'You will not intimidate me!'

'Yes, I know you said no and I have no need to intimidate you,' replied God calmly, adding, 'No does not exist in heaven, that is why they shall be informed.'

'How?' Father growled. 'It is too late even if I were to concede.'

'Concessions are irrelevant,' said God. 'In heaven new arrivals quickly learn that things and spirits concede, regardless of obstinacy, obduracy, procrastination, strong-mindedness or call it what you please. Holding out for years or even for an eternity is immaterial as time does not exist in heaven; so concessions simply hang in abeyance until new arrivals learn the art of conceding.'

'How shall they be informed?' Father asked in sullen tone.

'You shall inform them,' said God, as calmly as ever.

'Me?' roared Father.

'Yes, you.'

'How?'

'You will speak to them,' said God, still matter of fact.

We clutched at each other. God must have known we were watching! Father became silent, and sullenly glanced around the classroom while God calmly waited.

'Look up there,' said God, pointing at us, 'look where I am pointing, between the Rod of Nimbus and Galileo, the second nebula on the right. No, look at the second nebula on the right. There, you have located it. Humans call that smudge the Milky Way. Your children are watching from near one of the stars you glibly called the sun, amid the billions of stars that constitute the Milky Way galaxy, lost in the vastness of space and myriads of other galaxies far away for you, so far away. They can see you but fortunately, according to one of my laws that cannot be broken, you shall not see them again.'

'Astonishing!' said Bobby, 'but I don't understand. From here we are looking in on Miss Williams's classroom at Penparcau Infants School, so near.'

'Your children believe you are in Penparcau Infants School, so near,' said God. 'We have put you in Miss Williams's classroom which, at the time of your death, was the class your little daughter was attending at the time of your arrival here.'

'I'm attending class, Mr God!' corrected the little one. 'What does God mean?'

'I think God is saying heaven has no time, sweetheart,' Bobby said soothingly.

'They see you as you normally appeared at the time you arrived here,' continued God, 'in your transient body and shabby clothes. To them you look and sound perfectly realistic. It is a simple heavenly artifice for manufacturing the illusion of reality. Even your children cannot see beyond the superficial imagery. One of my laws that cannot be broken disallows their experiencing you as dissipated subatomic particles of energy.'

'Superficial imagery!' exclaimed Bobby, shaking his head, 'Well, I'm blessed!'

'Desiccated atom particles,' I said, 'Well, I'm blessed!'

'What's everyone talking about, well I'm blessed?' asked Francesca.

'Dissipated subatomic particles,' Bobby replied.

'Crumbs.'

'You can easily reach that distance. It is only a few nanoseconds wide, by earthly measurement,' continued God. 'Go on. If you make the attempt you may touch your children.'

Father hesitantly reached towards us, but his face disclosed his conviction that it was a silly exercise.

'Not far enough,' said God.

Father strained further. He expressed his dissatisfaction with the exercise by uttering one of his favourite expletives, 'Raswyd fawr!'

'Aeons short,' said God, shaking his head slowly, 'and yet you assumed you could decide the postulation of your narrow life! Please cease all this straining. It is hilarious to witness and besides, it will be to no avail. All you have measured are a few imaginary moments of space. So inconclusive, so negligible! A few sentences ago you were advising me you would not concede! Dear, dear, Ifan Pugh Troed-yr-Henrhiw.'

It appeared as though God was mocking Father, but surely that could not be so.

Bobby plucked up the courage to whisper, 'I'm getting lost in our magic game. I think Daddy is learning how insignificant he is against God's immense power. You two all right?'

'Yes,' we whispered breathlessly.

'I don't begin to understand. We can see them, but all they see is the Milky Way as a smudge! That which I thought was small is vast,' whispered Bobby.

'And that which is vast is so very small,' chimed God.

'Oh dear, I've started something,' said a worried Bobby.

'You are looking through a window at events that will start tomorrow,' said God.

'I'm frightened,' said Francesca. 'What's going to happen tomorrow?'

'Don't be frightened, little child,' said God, 'your father has already experienced tomorrow's events, yet these will occur long after you have grown old and have gone. I am attending to you simultaneously, on a similar plane which one of my laws disallows me to reveal. Remember, timelessness dwells in the realm of pure energy-speed. I am everywhere at once.'

'God is talking to us!' Francesca squeaked the tiniest of squeaks.

'Yes, we are very privileged,' whispered Bobby. 'I think I've started something much bigger than I had planned. I read somewhere in one of Fred Hoyle's books about parallel universes. But God is talking in riddles. I knew God is everywhere at once, but this timelessness thing baffles me.'

'It baffles me, too,' I said.

'Have faith, children,' said God reassuringly. 'It doesn't baffle me.'

'There! Nothing baffles God,' said Bobby.

'What is God going to do with us?' I asked in a hissed whisper.

'I'm sure God is not going to do anything with us,' replied Bobby with more hope than confidence. 'What have we done? I'm sure God will remember this magic trick and ask us about it when our time comes,' he continued, as if gripped by a greater truth. 'All we have to do is say the truth, and continue to believe.'

'Your time came far away, so far away; all steps are simultaneous,' said God.

'Is God talking to Daddy or to us?' I asked.

'Daddy, I think. I hope.'

'I hope so, because I don't understand any more,' I said.

'I'm frightened,' said the little one.

'How can I experience events before they occur?' growled Father, ever the cynic.

'You believed your life-bound events occurred in a linear time frame specific to you, but this is anthropomorphic self-centredness. Sentient beings believe there to be experiential sequence. However, while sequence is not disallowed, it is not necessary. Heaven allows simultaneity, as in all steps at once. Remember, you are henceforward processed as all stages simultaneously,' God explained with tireless patience.

'Hmm. Sequence is not disallowed, but it is not necessary,' Bobby pondered, and then: 'In that case Daddy should ask God, "Why bother with sequence?", as he was obviously fascinated by matters far deeper than I could grasp.

'In that case why bother with sequence?' Father asked on perfect prompt.

Little sister and I clutched each other.

'Sentient beings are permitted many peripheral activities that do not necessarily influence events in the final outcome,' God replied.

I was completely baffled. The conversation was now operating in several ways simultaneously and I hardly had time to think what a wonderful experience we were having. Bobby seemed far more controlled than I; Francesca was scared. Obviously there were many matters I was failing to grasp, like the surprising length of time God was prepared to spend on Father, considering he had the whole universe to look after at the same time.

'All steps are simultaneous; I am everywhere at once,' God repeated, as if reading my thoughts. 'Now,' God's voice assumed a greater resonance, 'we must make haste for your children's sake. You and I embrace eternity, while your children possess a finite module, as you are well aware. If you continue to procrastinate they could be watching until the next funeral.'

'Whose next funeral is God—' I began.

'The next funeral,' God interrupted. 'Now let us move on, and I shall have no further interruptions!'

'This is the film show heaven plays, like the harps of heaven you hear when you fall down stairs,' Bobby whispered almost inaudibly. He was very knowledgeable in such matters, having avidly studied the Bible since first he could read. At this precarious moment I was enormously glad he had done so, and regretted not having studied it myself.

'You are early.' God began a new phase.

'Believe me, I tried every trick to be late,' Father responded.

'Daddy admits it!'

'Unsuccessfully, as you are not late enough.'

'You think I don't know that? I was just about to lift the autumn late potatoes and this went and happened. Now who is going to do it?'

'Me,' said Bobby, 'like I did last year.'

'I helped.'

'You miss the point. You are several autumns early,' God said, persisting.

'I get the point all very well, but this particular punctuality was beyond my control.' And in a puerile attempt at changing the subject Father added: 'Back there the tears are falling like an autumn of crocodiles.'

'How dare you make assumptions of those to whom you never extended love?' God remonstrated. 'Besides, back there has not yet happened.'

Father stared at God in uncomprehending silence, shaking his head in a characteristic fashion that implied he was right and God was wrong.

'What does Daddy mean by tears are falling like crocodiles?' Francesca asked.

'No, it's—' I began, but I was cut off by Bobby.

'Tears fall like an autumn of crocodiles was one of Daddy's sayings. He used to say it a lot once. It's his way of telling God we won't miss him.'

'I miss him,' snuffled Francesca.

'So do I,' I agreed.

'Well, Daddy said to God we are shedding crocodile tears over his death. It's a most unfair thing to say. I wonder if God knows it's not true?' wondered my ever-patient brother.

'Why crocodile tears?' asked Francesca.

'Crocodiles only pretend to cry,' I said.

'How do you know what crocodiles pretend?' said Bobby. 'Their eyes don't possess tear ducts like ours do, that's what it is about.'

'But Uncle Maldwyn warned us,' I slipped in.

God waited with great patience until we had stopped our little debate. The expression on God's face painted a measure of resolution coloured with great forbearance. It was clear to us Father's time had come.

'Of course, your little saying bears no witness and your children refute its implication, and that is the end of the matter,' said God firmly. 'Now, before you are given your wings there are two matters that need clarifying—'

'I don't want wings,' Father rudely interrupted. 'I've already told that Gabriel clerk out there I don't want wings. I think they are a silly illusion.'

'Of course they are a silly illusion,' said God, 'that is why you will be given them, and you will wear them, regardless of your childish procrastinations. Incidentally, Archangel Gabriel is not a clerk.'

'I believed they were the inventions of Renaissance Paternosters, but now that I am being obliged to carry wings here I realise where the silly idea came from in the first place,' growled Father, continuing to procrastinate.

'Yes, yes,' said God as if addressing a child, 'your profound ignorance of history leaves you no alternative but to resort to dogmatism, although you always pretended otherwise by avoiding the company of those able to challenge your dogma.'

'What are you talking about?' Father demanded, apparently unaware he was sliding into a mode in which he was displaying his worst attributes. God had become more resolute and was pursuing Father's life view. Even I could see God was setting a trap for Father.

'Your rudeness is a minor symptom of that dogmatism,' continued God, seemingly heedless of Father's ill-tempered procrastinations, 'where dogmatism is a symptom of ignorance, and ignorance is due to a lack of education.'

'If you wish to disclose this information, then you well know I went to Dr Ellis's School.' Father was procrastinating yet more, to what end I began to doubt.

'A matter you were better advised to conceal from your children,' said God calmly, 'because you refuted an excellent educational opportunity in favour of nihilistic and self-centred behaviour among a group of young male ne'er-do-wells who did not possess the cerebral wherewithal to benefit from education and among whom, due to your higher intelligence, you appeared as the know-all of the pack.'

'That is not the complete story!' roared Father, utilising his narrow gift of anger as defence, 'and besides, are my children hearing every word of this?'

'You are so right it is not the complete story!' God proclaimed in measured tones, 'for unfortunately all you ever achieved was to be acclaimed as a big frog in a squalid little puddle. They hear every word of this conversation, as it is being stretched from heaven's compactified form to the normal tempo they know and understand.'

'Crumbs,' Francesca muttered.

'Crumbs, indeed, sweetheart,' replied Bobby.

Each time Father angrily objected, it appeared he simply instigated a deeper dissolution of his character. Father's intellect described the narrowness of a rain's road, and we were at a loss. All the crows were coming home to their rookery.

'It is not my purpose to change your elaboration – that was too late at the moment of your conception and besides, interference contradicts one of my laws,' continued God before an increasingly silent Father. 'Rather, I intend exposing your character to a mirror, for you alone were blind to the images it said. It was easier to cavort with beings of lesser intelligence, for those on a higher plane would have demanded effort by you to keep abreast of them. Due to your lazy character, striving, whether mental or physical, was off your agenda. The wastrel phase exhibited early in your life became a mask that assumed the man in lifelong habit. Your outward behaviour was a mask for your intrinsic bone-idleness. All of those wasted opportunities! Incidentally, wings were not the invention of Renaissance Paternosters,' God added dismissively.

'Gosh,' whispered Bobby, 'Daddy's receiving a proper telling-off. I have never witnessed anything of the sort before.'

'Wow!' the little one exclaimed. 'Only God dares to tell Daddy off.'

'You are right; no one else ever dared,' agreed Bobby, 'but I don't know whether this is good or bad for Daddy. It's probably all too late, anyway.'

God continued his lesson: 'The observer, even the half-educated observer, would discern a profound ambiguity in your psyche. That which determines fair play in the motives of man was stifled by a veneer of hate for all matters animate and inanimate.'

Father sat compliantly. Bobby was right, we had never witnessed Father being reprimanded before, it was always the other way round. Now he was sitting quietly and accepting it.

'You wrestled with psychological conflicts – nothing original in the phenomenon, per se; most individuals endeavour to clarify the dominant element at one stage or another. Fortunately for the majority this fluctuation occurs at an early age. Other people enjoyed the assistance of an applied discipline, which you lacked from an early age. A vacuum of self-discipline formed in your early life that unfortunately you chose to exploit at liberty. You chose the route to lethargy, hence the conflict. Endowed with the inherited physical attribute of a strong voice you soon discovered the ability to win in debate was not dependent upon adherence to fact and logic, or the application of thought, but simply to parcel your prejudice inside that voice.

'If you felt you were being enveloped by a stray wave of compassion you would immediately initiate a manual override to subdue the emotion – never allow outward signs that would have undermined your carefully cultivated theatrical image of aggressive manliness. So you quickly matured into an indecorous blackguard! Incidentally, the cow did not talk to you on the road at Bwlch Nant-yr-Arian. She was killed instantly on impact. Neither did she fall on you. Your mental state was such that your strong imagination worked the conversation when the floodgates of your guilt burst.'

'Wow!' Bobby exclaimed.

But I was hopelessly lost. Certainly I could understand the individual words – most of them. God was recalling examples of Father's recalcitrant character that were well-known to us, events that Bobby and I knew. It was the spectre of God reprimanding Father in a venue we knew that was supposedly heaven that lost me. The meaning behind the event, as well as the event itself, swamped me. It was clear brother Bobby, so much cleverer than I in matters of the Bible, God and electronics, had orchestrated the whole occasion. But his control over the direction in which events were going was another debate, although he did not outwardly express it. Instead he was deeply engrossed, for ever twiddling with the television knobs. Little Francesca was in thrall, and seemed to absorb the experience quite nobly. My fretting tendency insisted on getting in the way, which made my little head buzz.

For his part Father sat silently in his little desk. It was obvious God was determined to deliver strong messages as a natural process.

'The next point I need to clarify is the matter of your father,' said God.

'Would you please keep my father out of this?' Father requested.

'No,' said God. 'A myth abounds regarding your father and a certain strong-man act with a horse. Your children believe this story. Why did you not dispel the myth?'

'Because it is true.'

'I am analysing it now,' said God. 'What if I were to say it is nothing more than a photograph of a two-dimensional cardboard cut-out horse, curved to represent three dimensions, resting on your father's shoulders. Many circuses employed the device in those times.'

'My father gave us a photograph, which my brother now has.'

We automatically turned our heads to check the photograph in question standing on the sideboard behind us.

'Probably digitally modified to resemble reality.'

'Digitally modified?' asked Father, incredulously. 'What does digitally modified mean?'

'What does digitally modified mean?' I repeated Father's question.

'I think it's manually touched-up with the fingers, which are the digits, as in by hand. I think,' said Bobby.

'Digitally modified,' repeated God, matter of fact.

'Nonsense, my brother Maldwyn has the photograph in his room at Troed-yr-Henrhiw.'

We turned to check the photograph again. It did not appear modified in the least.

'Come along,' said God, 'let us go and see for ourselves.'

The three of us jumped with alarm. This was the biggest shock so far. We jumped and froze simultaneously. Whatever Bobby had started was now getting serious.

'God is coming here!' blurted Bobby, alarm in his voice. If Bobby was alarmed, then it was serious enough for me to have one of my turns.

'Is Daddy bringing God home?' squeaked the little one.

'It seems like,' Bobby whispered through his teeth, 'but I rather think it is God who is bringing Daddy home.'

'What about Mammy and Uncle Maldwyn?' she asked absent-mindedly.

We watched the screen. God and Father began moving out of Miss Williams's classroom; then the picture blurred and snow filled the screen.

'The picture is going – perhaps they are not coming here after all,' Bobby said with relief. 'Perhaps it's a God trick to denote the end of the miracle show.'

The picture quickly reappeared and to our surprise Miss Williams's classroom had gone. In its place was our farmyard. The picture was wobbling about as if seen through the eyes of God or Father, weaving through the mourners' cars and tractors towards the back door of the farmhouse.

Francesca ran to the back window and looked down.

'No one there,' she said. 'They've gone in, but the sleet has turned to snow.'

'We can see it's snowing on the television. I'm glad we cleaned the mess up for the funeral,' hissed Bobby.

'And Dylan and Thomas have gone. What would Daddy say?' I asked.

'And the bills on the mantelshelf,' Francesca added, coming back to the fold of her brothers.

'Sit down, sweetheart. Let's keep together. Anyway, Mammy hid the bills,' Bobby said; then he hissed in alarm, 'Look! They are coming through the lobby! Oh God – I mean, oh dear! What will the guests think? Something huge is going to happen.'

We held our breaths. Bobby never took his eyes off the screen. The reception hubbub downstairs did not alter in tone. The screen blurred again: figures moving and merging. We distinctly heard the voices of the mourners come from the television speaker. Uncle Maldwyn was heard saying,

'I don't know, don't ask me,' he boomed. 'They're up in my room doing something.'

'It's a God trick,' said Bobby. 'If they come up here, let me do the talking.'

'Look at the screen,' I hissed in fright, 'look at the screen!'

'Oh my G—' Bobby began in amazement.

On the screen God and Father were standing before the sideboard, their backs to us, examining the photograph of Taid lifting the horse, the one we were all greatly used to. They had silently entered Uncle Maldwyn's room. Whirling around we saw no one there, just the sideboard as before. We were rooted to our positions, switching from screen to sideboard and from sideboard to screen. The image of Uncle Maldwyn's sideboard was on the screen, superimposed by the unmistakeable figures of Father in his old coat belted with baler twine and still clutching his battered briefcase, and beside him was God. He could have been anybody, except we knew he was God.

'There's a shimmering light,' whispered Bobby, 'look carefully.'

I could not see any difference until Bobby whispered excitedly, 'Look! On the screen you can just make out the sideboard through Daddy and God!' and he touched the screen with a finger to mark the moment of his discovery.

Sure enough, God and Father were not in solid tones. Francesca got up and ran towards Father. Just as with the God and the desks event, Francesca ran through Father.

'Dad!' she called. Her voice dimmed as she reached the other side.

There was no reply.

'Dad?' she asked again.

'Dad, can you see us?' asked Bobby.

No reply. God and Father were engrossed in the old photograph.

Francesca did not appear on the screen, just God and Father shimmering before the sideboard. When I turned and looked, Francesca was standing alone as bright as ever in front of the sideboard. I could not pluck up the courage to do the same as she did, not trusting what could happen.

'Francesca! Come and sit down, sweetheart.' Bobby's persuading voice restrained alarm.

'So this is the photograph,' said God. 'Hmm, looks authentic to me,' and he picked it up, but we noted that the picture was still standing on the sideboard.

'Let's take it over to the light,' said God, carrying the picture over. The screen showed both God and Father walk over to the back window, with the photograph firmly in God's hands. But the photograph stood on the sideboard, as ever, untouched.

'I wonder where the cine camera is?' whispered Bobby, completely amazed by the events.

'I'm telling you it is authentic, although it was taken before we were born,' Father said.

'How does God do that trick?' I asked.

'Their voices are coming from the speaker,' whispered Bobby. He and I were frozen still, but little Francesca was jiggling about with excitement.

'All right, back to the classroom,' said God.

'No, wait!' called Bobby, looking around the room. 'Can we talk to Daddy now he's here…? Please?'

'Yes. Please?' pleaded Francesca, running over to the sideboard.

'Don't go yet, please,' I said, running to the door in a futile effort to bar their way.

But they left the room through me as if I were not there. God turned and looked out at us from the television screen.

They were gone, and the television screen showed them back in Miss Williams's classroom at Penparcau Infants School, in their positions as before.

'What do you make of that?' asked Bobby. 'God and Daddy here in Uncle Maldwyn's room! What do you make of that? Will anyone believe us?'

'I told you I saw Daddy in the Chapel and here upstairs,' I said hurriedly. 'I also saw him beside the Massey Ferguson when you were driving, and I pointed him out to Uncle Maldwyn.'

'I think God was demonstrating something profound to us,' continued Bobby, ignoring my claims, 'something that we will think deeply about in future.'

'Like what?' squeaked Francesca.

'Like God must have known the photograph was authentic. Surely he must have seen it being taken before Daddy was born?' was Bobby's logical reply. 'No, I'm sure God took the opportunity to deliver a message to us, rather than to Daddy. God demonstrated that Daddy is not part of our world any more. God doesn't miss opportunities. Remember, he said time does not exist for him.'

'Like he can come into the house, just like that?' I enquired, mystified.

'Just like that, all the way from heaven and back in less than a wink,' Bobby replied, showing obvious satisfaction with his explanation.

Little Francesca gasped and we looked at her.

'Are you OK, sweetheart?'

'Yes, I'm OK,' she replied timorously, 'but Daddy is not part of our world any more.'

Back in the classroom God and Father were commencing their discussion again.

'Why didn't you ask my father these questions for authenticity?' asked Father.

'There you are!' Bobby suddenly started, 'Daddy's thinking along the same lines. Hsst now, you two.'

'He's not here,' God replied.

'What do you mean he's not here? Where is he?'

'In the other place,' replied God.

'Hell? Do you mean my father is in hell?'

'What? This is getting weirder,' Bobby spluttered. 'Taid in hell? Never!'

'No. I said the other place,' said God, 'where the jury is still out.'

'All these years?' Father was exasperated.

'No time at all,' said God.

'Are you saying there are some souls you have no account of?' asked Father with an air that suggested he was on to something.

'No.'

'What, then?'

'Expediency,' God said enigmatically, which lost us all.

'Expediency? What is the point? Could you explain?' said Father.

'You are not able to understand.'

'I will understand if you give me more information!' Father shouted angrily.

'No, you will not,' said God, evading the subject of Taid's disappearance. 'Sentient beings turn their minds on a spurious algorithm of the fourth dimension when, lacking immediate comprehension of a phenomenon, they assume an understanding is there to be found; that an understanding will evolve following a little time and exploration. Sentient beings eventually grasp their physical and conceptual limitations. There are matters according to several of my laws, the phenomenon of time's effluxion being one of them, which will never be understood. Even I have occasionally to think hard about the time phenomenon. Be assured, I am saying this for the benefit of your children, because for you it is all too late.'

'All too late,' Father echoed.

'All too late,' Francesca echoed again.

'I don't understand God's explanation, or the reason for it,' Bobby whispered.

'You will understand,' said God, obviously addressing both Father and Bobby. 'For example, when we visited your brother's room at Troed-yr-Henrhiw Farm, although your children were sitting around the television watching the event in their real time, you did not see them. Of course, they could see both of us on the screen. Your little daughter ran through you with bewilderment. She called out to you, but obviously you neither felt nor heard anything. You were oblivious to her. They asked if they could speak to you. Your younger son ran to the door in a futile effort to bar our exit. You can only speculate on the number of times I have witnessed events of that nature.'

'You must take vicarious pleasure in setting up such events,' Father growled sonorously.

'But alas my law on the effluxion of time disallows communication during such events,' God continued, unimpeded, 'otherwise every Tom, Dick and Harry would want to speak to their dead relatives, most of them using the occasion to demand of the dead relative where they had hidden the money. The administration could cope with that detail but I created time for a more important reason than that triviality.'

'I cannot think of a more important reason,' said Father.

'Dear me, for a human endowed with a high intelligence you are strangely lacking in the common touch,' mocked God.

'Daddy isn't all that lacking!' retorted Bobby, protectively.

'I decided that the enabling of the universe's manifestation from a block state of uneventfulness,' God continued in magisterial tones, 'was sufficient reason to create time. Although the concept of time is simple, at the moment of physical definition it becomes one of the more difficult technicalities for sentient beings – even for me – to resolve.'

Father sat quiet and impassive, a state we had learnt was the harbinger of explosive moments.

'Sentient beings fully comprehend time until they have to explain it,' God continued, 'whereupon the meaning runs through their fingers like water. Imagine the difficulties in knowing the concept of time, then realising all endeavours to describe the thought come to nought.'

'What is time?' Father blandly asked, taking the opportunity to ask the obvious question.

'That is the most popular question that sentient beings ask upon entering the Kingdom of Heaven. I can only give the same explanation to all, but no one understands.'

'Try me!' challenged Father.

'You will not understand, but regardless. Time cannot be explained in words and symbols, as the concept of time exists as an abstraction in the mind, thus it can never escape to become substance. Neither can it escape from matter, space or energy, and the substance of the analogy loses the concept of time.

'Imagine travelling to the North Pole,' God continued, 'and, upon reaching it, taking one more step to ensure you really are at the northiest position of the North Pole. Unfortunately in so doing you have stepped away from the north and are now heading south. Did you feel any change in your mind? No. You have changed direction from north to south without a physical register. Just one of a myriad of subtle paradoxes. The consecration of the arrow of time is similar, which affords matter linearity instead of block existence.'

I could tell from Francesca's face that she was as lost as I was. Bobby as usual seemed engrossed in God's explanations, and was enormously entertained. But I for one was pleased to witness the magic heaven show rather than attend the reception downstairs. I felt sure Francesca felt similarly, in her own little way, but she was becoming fidgety. As for God, I believe it is a pretext that he does not understand time, to get Father to use his brain, or something like that. I was quite baffled at the intent of it all.

'I asked to visit Maldwyn's room for you to show me the photograph of your father holding a horse aloft,' God continued after I had stopped reflecting, 'precisely to illustrate: one, the fractal entanglement of time travel after death; two, the necessity for you to have to visit an object before seeing it; three, your inability to visit any object in real time that obtains in history after your death; and four, the subject of this conversation concerning your mental limitations. Knowing the photograph's authenticity before our visit additionally illustrates my ability to experience an object there simultaneously with duties here.'

'There we are! Worth waiting for,' Bobby loudly declared, but both Francesca and I were none the wiser.

'But if we transcend the arrow of time, then surely there is no differentiation between there and here,' said Father, at last showing signs that he was using his faculty for thinking.

'Correct,' God replied. 'Dimension is a mere illusion in order that I could facilitate the development of transient beings.'

'Which in itself is a contradiction, development being unnecessary in a timeless entity,' responded Father.

'Obviously you were not listening,' was God's contribution.

'I'm listening to every word you say, so long as each word makes sense,' snapped Father.

'This conversation is getting very complicated,' said Bobby. 'Daddy must be using his brain properly for the first time in his life.'

'But he died and is in heaven,' was my reply, which elicited a glare of contempt from Bobby.

'What's everyone talking about?' complained the little one, still upset over Father's fleeting visit.

'So, let me see if I grasp this: you set up the visit in readiness to illustrate a subsequent discussion?' suggested Father.

'Subsequent only in your understanding,' said God quietly. 'In reality we are having this conversation before the visit to your brother's room. Time can be used to generate illusions of sequence; you will quickly learn to occasion the phenomenon.'

'Before the visit to Maldwyn's room?' bellowed Father, losing his patience, 'before the visit? What's the point?'

It was unusual it took so long for Father to lose his patience, but it certainly appeared he was now getting to the point.

'Before,' replied God calmly.

'What is the point of keeping that facility privy to yourself?' demanded Father.

'You have had that matter explained once: every Tom, Dick and Harry, etc.,' answered God as patient as ever. 'But it demonstrates *more* than that. It also demonstrates the limitations of sentient beings subject perforce to my law governing the arrow of time. Sentient beings are slaves to the concept of sequential events. Experience beyond that horizon is impossible, just as one step more towards the North Pole takes you away from it.'

'You have already admitted heaven possesses the administrative capacity to cope without the need for a time dimension. You are not answering my question,' roared Father, pointing his finger threateningly at God.

'Well, I never,' said Bobby. 'Most of this is beyond me, though I must say of what I understand, I think Daddy has a point.'

'I agree, I think. Daddy is pointing out something important to God,' I contributed, comprehending even less than my brother.

'I agree,' said Francesca, wishing not to be out of the general agreement, 'Daddy's just like Daddy.'

'Daddy is pointing out an innate contradiction in God's explanation of our time and God's timeless dimension. We all think Daddy is right,' said Bobby inclusively.

Then something happened, something eminently more alarming than had already happened. We had become somewhat accustomed to looking into heaven on Uncle Maldwyn's television set, and to the related heavenly events. I, and especially Francesca, had been frightened most of the time, but then something really frightening happened.

A fleeting quiver flicked across the television screen, as if the generator in the back shed had hiccupped and power had momentarily dropped. But no sooner was the interruption there than it had gone. When the picture settled we saw God staring at us, as if we were the cause of the interruption. Father remained seated and unmoved, waiting for God's answer. But God's attention had been drawn to us for reasons far more profound than time's mere technicality, as we were about to learn in the most frightening of manners. Something indeed had happened. God continued to stare at us.

'Why is God staring at us?' squeaked Francesca in the tiniest whisper.

'God thinks we caused that flickering interruption on the television,' I whispered.

'No, nothing so straightforward, I'm afraid,' said Bobby in a barely audible whisper. 'It's probably because I said I thought Daddy was right.'

'What's going to happen?' breathed the little one.

'I don't know,' whispered Bobby, his whisper laden with foreboding. 'I think we should switch the television off and forget about this miracle show and go downstairs. We have seen enough, anyway.'

It was the threat to switch off the television that clinched it! God walked through the classroom furniture towards us, coming right up so his head filled the screen. His mouth was quivering in anger. His eyes were dark holes, like Father's in Soar-y-Mynydd Chapel. Stars twinkled in the distant night sky beyond the holes, or it could have been poor reception on the television screen. Regardless, it was alarming. God was angry with us. We were frozen with fear. Goose bumps crawled over me and my hair climbed high. I was shaking all over. Glancing at Francesca I saw she was convulsing in fright; her face was very pale, her lips white. Bobby was also transfixed and pale. We were all too shocked to speak. Something very strange was happening. The miracle show had flown out of Bobby's control.

'You should not draw conclusions on half-truths!' God bellowed at us angrily. 'I have not yet completed the lesson yet you erroneously pontificate rights and wrongs. You will *not* switch off the television. As you began this interference so you must suffer the consequences, and listen to the end of the lesson!'

God was very angry, angry like Father at his worst. He was behaving just as Father had always acted towards us. He bellowed just like Father had always bellowed. Over the years, we had grown more or less immune to Father's anger; but God's anger was a different matter.

God returned to his original station in the classroom, and upon reaching that point turned and again glared at is. At a distance it appeared his eyes had returned. Father had not moved during God's outburst, continuing to sit as still as a stage prop.

'Did you see God's eyes?' I whispered.

'Shush!' Bobby hissed, 'don't say anything,' and he made a calming action to us with his hand.

'Your tantrum is frightening my children, yet you have the reckless indifference to play causality.' It was Father who spoke, his voice uncharacteristically quiet and gentle. 'They are innocent of my conundrums and do not deserve such treatment from anyone, least of all from God.'

'Innocent!' roared God, waving his fists about in rage, his gown spreading large in the space of the classroom, 'innocent indeed! They are interfering busybodies! They should not have been born!'

Time and again throughout our lives we had experienced Father, while in an ecstasy of rage, declaring that we should not have been born. We had grown used to it, and the dismay had long since lost its currency. But coming from God this was terrifying. From God with all the unknown connotations!

'Come, come,' said Father, 'your disposition is most un-God-like. My children are mere sentient transitions utilising energy and matter in accordance—'

'Interfering!' God rudely heckled: 'How dare they spy on my admission procedures?'

'Oh dear,' said Father, soothingly. 'The matter revolves around the propriety of simple procedures – so you frighten my children because of their insightful advantages. Come, come now, I am sure we can arrive at an accommodating *modus operandi*.'

'Aha!' whispered Bobby, who had been as alarmed as Francesca and me. 'Now I'm beginning to understand what has happened. God's wrath is an imitation of Daddy's rage, but at the same time I can't believe Daddy's calmness is real, unless God has initiated a clever trick in character transfer.'

'Daddy is defending us,' said the little one, hopefully.

'Daddy is indeed defending us,' reassured Bobby.

'They shall suffer for their interference!' God's voice rose so high that it distorted and buzzed the speaker. God was challenging Bobby's reassurances.

'I don't like this any more, I'm going down to Mammy,' cried Francesca, and she got up to leave.

'You will NOT go down to your Mother, Francesca!' God bellowed, once again rushing up to the screen foreground. 'Sit down again with your brothers and you will learn more. SIT DOWN or else I shall freeze you to the floor for ever!'

Francesca yelped 'Mum!' then promptly sat down and began sobbing.

'Bobby, what's going on? Please stop it,' I pleaded.

'I can't stop it. I thought you realised I'm not doing anything any more. The magic show is out of my control. I think we had better obey God's commands,' he replied, as worried as we were.

'You have made my little daughter Francesca cry. You are a bully frightening an innocent little lamb. You will do none of your threats to my children,' said Father, remaining extraordinarily calm in the face of God's wrath, 'and my children will not be terrorised by you. They have committed no sin in my eyes and that is good enough for me, and if it is good enough for me then it will have to be good enough for you.' Father addressed God in a most extraordinary manner. 'To watch their father enter the Kingdom of Heaven through a clumsy little gadget set up by the oldest is no sin.'

'There's so much going on,' said Bobby in confusion, 'so much going on.'

'Daddy's lecturing God like he lectured us,' I ventured.

'They did not ask me for permission to watch,' God sulkily responded.

'Permission?' asked Father. 'What about the iniquities of your laws, the arbitrariness of natural selection, the perversity of survival of the fittest, the obtuseness of creating one part to be destroyed by another, the cussedness of your little games?'

'Think about it,' said God, calming.

'Of wasps stinging and snakes biting,' Father continued.

'Think about it,' God repeated.

'Do they have to seek your permission to go about their profligate ways?'

'Think about it, comrade,' God insisted.

'Of hypocrisy, corruption and exploding supernovae.'

'You and your children are products of exploding supernovae; think about it,' said God, calming.

'I am afraid you need a holiday or something like that,' Father declared.

'Now you know I cannot take a holiday,' said God.

'Obviously you must be very bored after fourteen billion years playing with the same old supply of toys.'

'Can't say I am, really,' God responded.

'Now we are both touching the stars. I am at one with the entity of pure energy. How dare you act out of character! Return to the character of the Almighty,' Father lectured.

'But I am God omnipotent. I have no need to act within or without character! Your children play partisan condescension, spying on a private process,' God said, but with the anger subsiding.

'Their little gadget would not have worked if they had not believed in you body and soul – if they had not believed beyond believing,' said Father gently.

'That's what I said,' whispered a startled Bobby.

'Of course you said it, Bobby. That is why I am saying it,' said Father, turning to look at us. 'And by the way, the three of you – Bobby, Ieuan, Francesca – never be afraid of God. He deliberately demonstrated flaws in his perfect countenance by expressing my character that has now been assimilated. Without you God would not exist.'

'That's magic,' I said.

'That's magic,' said the little one, greatly comforted.

'It might be magic,' said Father, 'but it is very obvious magic. Whatever you do, don't be afraid of God. Simply be afraid of your own consciences.'

'They were fools to have believed in me,' said God.

Father burst out laughing. He laughed and laughed. We had not witnessed Father laughing so heartily. Bobby's magic heaven show was growing stranger.

'Daddy's mocking God!' Bobby said, 'he's not intimidated at all. That's what he meant by never being afraid of God.'

'My children are not fools for believing in you. Believing in you means they believe in themselves – that explains why the gadget works. You blame them for implicit inspiration. Who knows what my children will achieve next? Let me penetrate the veil of myth. You are using reason as a tool of the moment in order to mask the unreasonable. By playing your timelessness card you are unfolding another dimension which you know sentient beings can never perceive, unnecessarily frightening little children.'

'Daddy calls us little children,' said Bobby. 'You two might be, but I'm certainly not, taller than he was. I suppose he means it in the context of innocence, as he is still emulating God.'

'In prayers Miss Williams said we are all sinners,' Francesca volunteered.

'And you are only innocent before you are born,' I added.

'Suffer your silly teachers not being here to witness a proper heavenly debate,' Bobby sighed.

'By playing timelessness you behave thus,' Father continued, having waited for us to stop our little discussion. 'Long after they have gone they touch the stars in no time at all. For us the Milky Way is a smudge between the Rod of Nimbus and Galileo, but is a line across Francesca's forehead.'

'What?' asked Francesca, rubbing her little forehead.

'In such behaviour you demonstrate fallibilities and flaws in your perfection,' continued Father in suppressed God-like tones. 'In so doing you have unnecessarily frightened the children. Children do not deserve such treatment, yet by your laws they suffer. I never cared a single damn for that "the Lord is testing you" hypocrisy!'

'Yes, Daddy often said that!' Bobby exclaimed.

'Why test arbitrarily?' Father continued. 'Conduct your laws in a proper universal manner, otherwise I do not wish to enter the Kingdom of Heaven. I shall be obliged to invoke the decree of rejection, and I care not if I burn in damnation.'

'Huh!' exclaimed Bobby, 'wait until we tell Mammy.'

'What does Daddy mean by that?' asked Francesca.

'Daddy means he would prefer to go to hell than exist for eternity in a heaven that practises hypocrisy. This is baffling but very exciting,' Bobby replied.

It certainly was exciting. Father's threat stunned God.

'Revocation of acceptance into the Kingdom of Heaven is not an option,' muttered God, his stormy act now faded.

'It happens to be immaterial,' said Father, 'as I am aware there is no option, the irreversible effluxion of time and all that. But now I will do the testing whereby I will revoke acceptance whenever I deem it necessary. Shortly I shall give my children permission to switch off the television and join my funeral wake downstairs. Either that or their mother will fetch them.'

'If that is your will,' said God, reverting to his normal role.

'God and Daddy must have reversed roles when the television flickered,' said Bobby, 'but although God has reverted to his normal role, Daddy has retained the God role. Now they are both God. Fancy Daddy becoming God! Astonishing! They are one and the same. Who would have believed it? Wait till I tell Enoch Pant Gwyn.'

Suddenly Bobby interrupted his own train of thought.

'Eureka! I get it!' he shouted. 'When people die they all become God! Everybody, the animals, trees, they all become God. Daddy has become God! He is Daddy-God. Why didn't I think of that before? How stupid of me!'

'Daddy-God?' I asked.

'Of course. Daddy has become God, so he's Daddy-God,' affirmed Bobby, full of confidence.

'Daddy-God. Daddy-God,' chanted Francesca, enjoying the sound.

'Do you think we should call Uncle Maldwyn?' I suggested, meekly.

'God told us to sit here,' Francesca said, remembering.

'God-God told us to sit here,' Bobby corrected, and we all laughed.

'Following the theatricals I am taking advantage of this inter-regnum in heaven's administration,' Father-God explained carefully, 'to explore a few items that should give future guidance to my children.'

'I'm astonished,' I said, picking up Bobby's word.

'Notice now that Daddy-God's English is perfect. It was never perfect like that here,' pondered Bobby, ever mindful of intellectual variations. For my part the events were moving at a puzzling pace, and I imagined little sister's emotions must have been dazzled beyond the mystery.

'I never dreamed God-God played the role reversal trick when people entered the Kingdom of Heaven. It has certainly had a beneficial effect upon Daddy-God,' said Bobby.

'Do you think God-God uses role reversal all the time?' I asked.

'Must do.'

'No, only for important people like Daddy-God,' piped the little one.

'I believe everyone is important in God-God's eyes. If all people are destined to become Somebody-God, then some part of God-God will welcome all people, even vagabonds,' said Bobby.

'Even Dai Snatch the cattle rustler?' I asked.

'Even Dai Snatch,' replied Bobby.

'Dai Snatch-God,' said Francesca.

None of the scriptures told us God played role reversal for people to enter the Kingdom of Heaven. It was all so very baffling to me, and shows how wrong the scriptures are.

'This is all so very exciting,' our older brother said encouragingly.

'Daddy-God wasn't frightened of God-God shouting, most probably because he knew he had become God when the television flickered,' I said.

'But Daddy-God was always brave even when he was Daddy,' Bobby replied.

Father-God looked at us, but momentarily.

'Notice they both go silent whenever we are talking,' observed Bobby.

'Now Daddy is God, is he there or is he in his coffin in the graveyard?' asked Francesca sensibly. Then, answering her own question, 'He's there, isn't he?'

'As far as I can tell he's in heaven and in the graveyard, sweetheart,' replied Bobby, 'but there are so many mysteries.'

'I hope Daddy-God is going to tell God-God off some more,' I said, hopefully.

'Maybe you are right,' said Bobby. 'I'm glad I didn't switch the television off.'

'Well, God-God told you not to switch it off,' I said.

'Yes, but that was for a different reason, if you had been attending. Anyway, shush now, both of you, let's watch to see what happens now that God and Daddy are one and the same,' commanded Bobby.

'In the physical state my reasoning was always straightforward and simple,' said Father-God, composed and reconciled to his new role, 'commensurate with a limited education and an ingrained peasant complexion. Culpability for the former was entirely mine but the latter was borne of inheritance. I held no shibboleths. I used to say, "this is as good as it gets".'

'Yes,' said Bobby excitedly, 'one of Daddy-God's favourite sayings: "This is as good as it gets", he often said, especially on a sunny morning in May.'

'May was his favourite month,' I said.

'That's because his birthday is in May,' chimed the little one.

'Prescient,' said God-God, 'but I would question the motive.'

'It is your energy so to do,' Father-God said gently. 'I believe the simple answers can be split apart to create more complex networks,' he continued, 'just as all the forces were unified at the moment of the Big Bang but as the universe cooled so they individually froze and decoupled to become complexities in their own right. No matter how complex the networks are, the complexity does not contaminate the simplicity of the original concept. The concept of creation is uniquely uncomplicated, based on a simple quantum algorithm. Why did you structure it thus?'

'You are now in a condition to discover for yourself,' smiled God-God.

'Let me see,' said Father-God. 'Upon discovering the more complex laws within, one could never appreciate the answer as being consummately simple. So the answer, although remaining precisely the same, changes in one's perceptions. Splitting answers apart does not make them simpler, neither does it make them more difficult. Paradoxically, if one searched—'

'What is Daddy talking about?' Francesca interrupted.

'I don't know, sweetheart,' Bobby replied, 'I honestly don't know. But remember, he has become Daddy-God, so he can say anything he likes now.'

'Oh! I understand,' she said.

'So do I,' I added.

'As they are both in the God role, I wonder if God-God is understanding Daddy-God,' Bobby said.

'God-God has got to because he's the original God. He's only letting Daddy think he's Daddy-God. He'll bowl a googly sooner or later,' I said.

'Ho ho! A Godly-Godly googly,' said Bobby, and we laughed heartily.

'—for an answer and it was ultimately forthcoming, the real miracle is that there was no question there in the first place,' Father-God concluded, as soon as we had ceased deviating from the lesson.

'Good, you are getting there. But how do you posit a question for an answer that exists before it is posed?' God-God asked.

'I bet God-God knows the answer to his own question,' Bobby reasoned.

'From the perspective of an atom,' continued Father-God, 'these questions are transient and superficial, disinclined to probe the greater truth of the universe. From the perspective of the universe, these questions are equally transient and superficial, disinclined to probe the greater truth of the atom. Both perspectives are without meaning, as they do not alter the original truth of the universe.'

'I have already pondered these superficialities aeons ago,' said God-God soothingly, gently shaking his head.

'In which case, time enough for some of the quantum anomalies to have been smoothed out,' reasoned Father-God graciously.

'The anomalies create a purpose by existing, sufficient purpose for creating the anomalies in the first instance. I have billions of enrolments pontificating on that matter in various classrooms,' smiled God-God, 'and besides, regardless of the superficiality of the discussion, I wonder if your children understand what is being said?'

Father-God nodded sagely. He ignored the correction with the steadiness of his familiar prejudice, but after some hesitation said, 'Yes, you are quite right. I am taking some time to settle into my new role.'

'Everyone does,' God-God smiled, 'though it is exceptional that your children are observing the process and have already reasoned its outcome. Did you not notice? They are already referring to you as Daddy-God and me as God-God' – whereupon both roared with happy laughter, the laughter of contentment and fulfilment and confidence. They laughed and laughed.

'They are laughing their heads off!' Bobby chuckled.

'I suggest we detain them a little longer: they will not come to any harm except for a little confusion,' God-God giggled.

'Ieuan is always in that state,' Father-God shook with laughter.

God-God and Father-God continued laughing together, enjoying the circumstance.

'Carry on, Ifan,' God-God said after a while of laughing.

'Ifan! Crumbs, God-God is on very familiar terms suddenly,' Bobby exclaimed.

'I have always believed one cannot ask questions any more than give answers,' Father-God continued, 'as all answers exist already. Any disparity occurs in the mind only, not in the physical world. I knelt at no shrine to substantiate or paradoxically to insure against my beliefs. I always held some other entity accountable because my simple mind could not envisage any other order.'

'Daddy-God is off on one of his preaching tours,' said Bobby, 'but he hasn't got a simple mind. He is just saying that because he is now Daddy-God.'

'You are so right. Your simple mind is incapable of envisaging any other order,' said God-God. 'Even when endowed with my spirit your thoughts succeed only in going round in little circles.' He laughed uncontrollably.

'Huh?' blurted Bobby.

'Try this then: we have the seventh draft of an accidental strategy,' continued Father-God, ignoring God-God's laughter, 'for which you will be assessed when all your various drafts, singularities, irregularities and failures will be placed before you. Regardless of the numbers – as most of them are all the product of a mechanism set in progress long before you came along – do you accept responsibility?'

'Hmm,' pondered God-God, fighting to compose himself. 'And how do you reconcile the postulation of that question with timelessness?'

'Set in progress in sentient perspectives, of course,' Father-God responded.

'Oh I see, the anthropomorphic view' – God-God giggled – 'from the gigantic visage of a molecule. You are learning, but slowly. You see, in your new role you are supposed to be omnipotent.'

'If those cases don't pertain, then your strategy is built from an accident, such as an accidental sneeze that sends the relatively contained universe into critical unbalance.'

'Oh, the sneeze hypothesis!' God-God again roared with uncontrollable laughter. 'It is amazing the billions of sentient beings processed through various classrooms who resort to the sneeze formula as the last resort of their God-transformation thinking.'

'Apart from fractals and other algorithms manifesting chaos, the sneeze draft contains mathematical unity,' continued Father-God, earnestly preventing God-God's laughter from deflecting his determination.

'Just like Daddy was,' said Bobby, 'never admitting he is wrong, even when he is Daddy-God and laughing.'

'Yes, "How dare facts get between me and my prejudice" was Daddy-God's middle name. Uncle Maldwyn's joke,' I said.

'Your prejudice, although masquerading as determination,' smiled God-God, 'never allows facts to deflect it.'

'I just said that!' I declared excitedly.

'So you did, Ieuan,' God-God said, 'but it was your uncle Maldwyn who said it originally.'

'Wow!' exclaimed Bobby, 'that's telling you,' and we laughed. We were becoming familiar with the magic show; even Francesca had relaxed into the magic show with God-God's laughter.

'The time thing does not require answering,' God-God continued, 'as there are an infinite number of correct answers. Ensuring the existence of sentient beings to be fleeting was my safeguard against them doing anything useful about time. There again, time does not exist for the point wave function of photons and such like; and the rest are not capable of witnessing it.'

'So being and becoming are unchanged by the magnitudes of time,' suggested Father-God. 'Accidental trials and development are compressed one and the same, and it would not matter if omega were critically balanced or not.'

'An absolute uttered through the towering intellect of a goldfish,' laughed God-God, 'and time turns into space, and matter is compressed into pure energy, no fingerprint left of previous editions – singularities could have been occurring for ever. The new universe has no recollection of its existence before the singularity.'

'Yes,' Father-God agreed.

'So singularities have occurred since ever, and there is nothing useful that can be said beyond that understanding. In human terms it can be proven mathematically, but it adds up to no more than figures on a page. Your older son Bobby will learn from this lesson, making use of it later in his fleeting nanowisp.' God-God smiled.

'Well, I never!' exclaimed Bobby.

'Well, I never, too!' echoed Francesca, quite at ease with the mysteries.

God-God and Father-God acted as one and the same. We did not understand the transference of roles in the first instance, nor the secondary unifying role. The whole magic show was fun to watch, although for me the subject was difficult to follow. The more complex the conversation became the more I lost the meaning, or it could have been the reverse. Francesca was still glued to the spot that God-God had commanded her to occupy.

'You realise your children are losing the meaning of our subject,' said God-God.

'Yes, I am aware.'

'I'm not losing interest. You just said I will learn from the lesson!' declared Bobby.

'I'm not losing interest either,' I declared, 'except I don't understand most.'

'I'm not losing interest,' declared Francesca bravely, 'except I don't understand.'

'The trouble is,' said Father-God, 'they have limited attention spans, especially Ieuan.'

'Oh, here we go!' I protested, 'I've been attending all the time.'

'That's rich coming from Daddy-God,' said Bobby. 'He could never listen more than three seconds to us before he lost interest. He's just saying that to impress God-God.'

'I'm listening even if I don't understand,' piped Francesca.

'Quite!' we all said.

'To elucidate,' said Father-God, 'the mystery—'

'There are no mysteries,' God-God interrupted with another burst of laughter.

'The mystery for me,' said Father-God, 'is not so much that a universe existed before the current Big Bang universe – before you interrupt again I now realise all the bangs regardless of their number occur instantaneously due to timelessness – containing energy and the laws, it is why you engage in communication with humans at their current level of technological comprehension, rather than in matters more advanced than their here and now. You never present the opportunity whereby they may attempt to grasp matters light years ahead of their picture plane. Today you trade in quantum dynamics and warped space, nano-systems, particle entanglement and the socio-political flavour of the month; at the time of Christ's birth you engaged their interest by discussing donkeys, metal coins and water wheels. Why do you never engage in topics that they have not hitherto uncovered for themselves? I believe that is the big question. It underlines your fallibilities and manifests recreation fields over which you have no choice.'

'The answer is simple,' replied God-God, smiling. 'I have presented the universe and its concomitant laws per se. What I say, regardless of its complexity, will only be understood within the parameters of their here and now experience; that should have been obvious. Why are humans so anthropocentric to assume they possess a right to advance beyond a current here and now into dialogue light years hence?'

'One last question,' said Father-God. 'Where were you before the Big Bang, any Big Bang, when the universe was unimaginably hot and compressed in a sphere no greater than a proton?'

'Caring over the universe, as always. Size is an illusion. Sentient beings will never liberate their minds from the constraints of size. I hope your children have benefited from this trivial conversation,' replied God, smiling the while.

'What are they talking about?' I asked.

'I think I know, but I'm not sure,' replied Bobby, 'because Daddy-God never discussed these matters with us.'

The three of us had undertaken a descent into bafflement in the order of our ages, but I was not too sure any more. All this had gone beyond the beyond point. I no longer grasped the significance of the magic television show, for it had metamorphosed from the simple fable of our recalcitrant father receiving a reprimand to role reversal, incantations of a heavy nature and portentous deliberations on timelessness. Then came God-God and the Father-God enigma. My simple mind of the day could grasp the individual implications but collectively they swamped me, as indeed they did little Francesca. Bobby retained as steady a nerve as his greater experience permitted, but clearly his balance had been under severe threat from time to time.

The door opened, and in walked Mother. Her eyes were still red from crying.

'Here you all are! What are you doing watching television now of all times? It's dark in here. You should be downstairs with our guests. They want to leave in case they get snowed in and are waiting to see you all.'

Francesca jumped up and embraced Mother.

'Daddy's on television, and he has become Daddy-God, look!' she gushed. 'We watched him enter the Kingdom of Heaven. God-God was angry with us and Daddy-God told him off. That's God-God talking to Daddy-God! They've been talking about everything. Everything!'

Mother looked at the television, then at Bobby and me, then back at Francesca. She looked again at the television standing there big and cold with Bobby's contraption balanced on its top, and nothing but snow all over the screen.

'Yes, sweetheart. Daddy-God talking to God-God. What will Bobby think of next?' Mother said with great satisfaction. 'Now let us go downstairs and meet the guests before they go. Come on, you two.'

The Mandelbrot Dilemma

All the ingredients to enable the artist's escape were present, but were confused in position and time. Although the broad brushstrokes of his painting were familiar, the details had assumed unintended characteristics. Trailing brushstrokes proliferated, fading into monochrome backgrounds, which he could no longer recall painting. The more urgently he sought escape from his painting, the more surreal became the environment. Fixing his gaze on one detail would result in the disappearance of others. Recognising a particular brushstroke lost him his direction; paradoxically, maintaining a fixed direction would lose the context. Each new action sent the artist deeper into the quagmire of his painting. The plot took a sinister turn when the painting invited him into an underground arcade, for original pointillist stipples had grown monstrously into the semblance of a city.

The arcade hung heavily with vapours of oil paint, and the artist was obliged to breathe the characteristic air of Old Holland medium; beautiful on canvas, stifling as environment. Searching for a way home he reached a stairway rising. It was a wide, dressed stone affair curving from a flourish at the bottom step in the fashion of Victorian elaboration. Dimly lit, rising into darkness, the whole apparition presented an incongruous image against the quaint higgledy-piggledy dashes of colour representing shops and crudely painted coffee stalls that adorned the atmospheric perspective of the arcade. Hopefully the stairway was an exit, so he began alighting.

At that moment a tiny shop nestling in the curve of the stairs suddenly presented itself, and the invitation of the stairway home lost its significance. It was the smallest shop ever seen yet its etched glass door possessed incongruously large proportions. The shop's interior appeared not much wider than its door; it was ill lit and gloomy, though something indefinable caught the artist's eye. He doubled back to appease the curiosity that led him from his intention.

As the rising stairway cut diagonally across the shop's glass side, its heavy banister conspired to block more of the already dismal light. Over the doorway a title, Heaven's Gate, carved in half-uncial script set in old gold on a faded black background, nostalgically paraded the shop's purpose. Cobwebs hung among the incised letters, betraying an indifference to attracting customers.

It was at this juncture that the painting's imagination further invoked an intangible atmosphere that became fatefully intriguing to the artist. Although he had previously resisted the temptation to visit brushstroke-cum-shops in his painting, and the discovery of the stairway meant an opportunity for escape, the surreal nature of Heaven's Gate nevertheless gripped his curiosity. He had not before seen the like in reality; perhaps a distantly remembered children's book containing Hogarth-style drawings of medieval constructions defying both logic and gravity resonated in his mind.

Certainly the artist could not remember painting this obscure composition, or for that matter contemplating its unique nature. His claustrophobic entanglement was manifestly exacerbated by the painting's independent tendency to produce detailed imagery of a built environment from brushstrokes hitherto intended to represent a bleak landscape in *The Endless March*, long after the incident. A parley of crudely painted people hobbling through the arcade added to his discomfort. Parts were missing – an arm, a leg, sometimes even the head. A leg alone walked past. None of this human presence was using the wide stairway.

The property next door was yet another *kaffee konditorei*, this one peddling the supposedly aromatic delicacies of Dasht-e-Kabir coffee. All pointillist marks seemingly turned into coffee shops. Once, during student days when he was obliged to be adventurous, the artist had sampled the Dasht-e-Kabir brand. To his horror he found it to be septically inedible, tasting so foul that thoughts of toxins, reconstituted camel dung and even survival sprang to mind. Contrarily, his colleagues gobbled the stuff down as if it were nectar from the gods. Alas, the days of youth when pretentiousness was the chief item of their frail inventories. He avoided the *kaffee konditorei*, satisfied there was no apparent connection with Heaven's Gate.

Some crudely painted oddities resembled troglodytes. They must have broken loose from the main composition of *The Endless March*, all dressed in pain, but the artist believed he was not guilty of painting parts.

'Old Holland with undertones of Lukas,' one of the characters said, pointing at her pained self. Not previously witness to such discomforting images of his handiwork hobbling about the painting's business, the artist failed to indict any genesis either here or there. It was a lightning stroke of imagination. Giving a shrug of resignation, he disclaimed ownership of details manifesting perpetual evolution. With ashen grey complexions befitting their indecorous attire, his palette had drained of colour. Each part was indistinguishable from one brushstroke to another.

Opposite Heaven's Gate a vibrating pavement washer was operating an old woman. The frenetic machine emitted clouds of turkey red noise, flooding the floor it was supposedly washing, revealing that the artist's synaesthesia was rampant inside the painting. Ignoring the floods of turkey red, the artist splashed across to her. In close-up her patchy clothing comprised flaking paint on a madder ground, exposing lines where the canvas had been prepared too often. He addressed the patchwork portrait. It was a long shot, but any port in a storm. From the opportunity of mounting the stairway home to Troed-yr-Henrhiw, his lack of focus had delivered him to making enquiry with unfinished characters.

'Excuse me, I am the artist. Do you by any chance know the destination of that stairway?' he asked, pointing to the culprit stairwell.

'I don't know,' she replied bluntly, hiding her face behind impressions of collar.

He tried another tack. 'Well, then, do you know what that little shop sells?' – this time pointing at Heaven's Gate.

She scowled, her glazed face cracking under the new arrangement. 'I don't know. You are the artist. You of all people should know. You got us into this. Go in and find out. I'm only the floor cleaner in this arcade.'

'What was your original character in my painting?'

She looked at him as if he were a patient escaped from St Elmo's asylum.

There being nothing else for it, he had to venture in and satisfy his curiosity. After all, it was his composition one way or another, but he had developed an innate reluctance to undertake simple processes of this kind following his traumatic experience. Being trapped in his painting obliged the artist to progress with caution.

The temperature in the vicinity of Heaven's Gate did not alleviate his feeling of deep foreboding, for it was cold and unwelcoming as an icy draught poured down the stairway: clammy, turpentine, unhealthy. He concluded that the physical ambience of the arcade had nothing to do with his psychological state, but he would need to think more constructively if he hoped to escape from his painting. His attraction to the little shop was a matter more of hope than solution.

Now was not the time for philosophy, yet he failed to grasp the ease with which he was able to inwardly justify pursuance of incautious diversions by the simple process of self-delusion. In this case the justification that readily stood to attention was a purpose that promised to be more beneficial to immediate objectives, but this hotchpotch principle could easily have lent itself to most of his diversions. The readiness to leap from a determined course had already compounded the complications of his artistic life, one of which underlined the reason he was lost in his painting in the first place. But who else would feather the canvas?

The huge door to Heaven's Gate invitingly possessed a push handle. It gave with a burst, emitting a monstrous booming clang similar to the bass bell of the St Stephen's Dom in Vienna, a sound to vibrate the organs. As he was a synaesthete all sounds triggered colours for the artist, of course, but no set-piece colour ever surprised him as much as the booming clang of the Heaven's

Gate door bell. The sound stimulated a riot of bright blue light that billowed everywhere as thick as fog, pouring throughout the confines of the little shop, into the arcade, bouncing off adjacent shops, off the pavement washer, vibrating in the spaces. Dry, dusty blue billowing along as sastrugi with a mind.

Blue noise cleared, revealing the exquisite interior of Heaven's Gate. The little shop was a wondrous sight, so small that if the artist had stretched out his arms he could have touched both sides simultaneously. Then, realising he had left the door open, he turned and closed it. To his horror a repeat performance of the huge chime once again stifled him in blue noise. His head buzzed with vibrant hues of forget-me-not, mouth full with the tincture of blue taste; hands became bluebells and the aroma of a blue palette pervaded – coeruleum, cobalt, Prussian and ultramarine carrying sound as four blue horsemen winged ahead. The proprietor must have been colour-sound blind.

A minuscule shelf, hardly big enough to hold a grail, projected from the right-hand wall of the tiny shop. Beside it stood two small wicker chairs. The wall had the appearance of being recently decorated white, but in patches, with passages missing to reveal age stains and remnants of Gothic graffiti. Faded plasterwork beneath the patchwork decoration showed a distinctly uneven surface that was neither here nor there. The opposite wall was constructed of sepia glass, revealing the external Victorian banister rising diagonally across it. The higher the solid stone stairway rose, so the greater was the darkness within Heaven's Gate. A bare electric light bulb attached to a fitting at the far end buzzed and crackled a feeble cadmium-yellow light.

Several small, framed pictures, just so little, arbitrarily speckled the wall as if hung by one of great inexperience in hanging matters, for they missed the horizontal intention. They depicted scenes and quotations from the Old Testament, and words that did not relate to anything previously witnessed. No other commodities were displayed in the shop, and it was difficult to ascertain its purpose, except the oblique picture references to the Bible. Certainly the artist did not recall painting such a strange composition. Then he saw the sight that transfixed him.

The sheer wonder of its strange imagery far exceeded the

mundane presbytery of his imagination. The ceiling comprised endless space filled with myriads of twinkling stars. The stars were not arbitrarily disposed, but rather organised in an intelligent design that plotted an awesomely beautiful pattern across the ceiling void, continually regressing higher and yet higher. As the ceiling replicated the confined lateral space of the floor, the apparition was obliged to take vertical liberties. In so doing it reached such heights that the points of light twinkled in the distant celestial space. Each point related one to another in spiralling groups; the groups related, but not to the individual points.

The artist was convinced this was uncertainty in visual form. All points constantly moved in scintillating orchestration. If he locked his sight on to one of them, so it would immediately freeze, as if the point knew it was being observed, while the others continued to move independently within their strict mathematical parameters. The moment the artist looked away from the frozen point of light, it would happily resume moving in accord with the greater order of the rest. He stared in astonishment as sections of the starry structure expanded again and yet again, rising and falling, freezing and flowing, animating without end. The spirals circled in endlessly regressing folds, mesmeric in their productivity. The artist was transfixed, having seen two-dimensional images of the like, but this was animation in three dimensions. He was baffled. How did it work?

The visual experience was a humbling mathematical art of immense complexity. It possessed cohesiveness of underlying order while simultaneously displaying arbitrarily changing imagery. A paradox of depth was contradicted by flimsy superficiality. The artist was at a loss; this extraordinarily complicated and awesomely beautiful structure was in no way the result of his hand. Nothing he had infused in his painting could remotely compare with its majesty. It inlaid a profound perspective on the artist's meagre dabbling. He could not recall ever contemplating such a unique invention, leave alone attempting to construct it.

He was glad he had ventured in, but how to understand it, how to grasp its message? The more he examined, the more obtuse became its meaning, as if the whole ceiling knew it was being analysed. He felt belittled, speechless, humiliated by its awesome beauty. How did it arrive in his painting if he were not its author? Profound answers remained untouched by trivial questions. Wait till he escaped home to tell Angharad.

The artist's bafflement was interrupted by the sound of unsteady footsteps descending a narrow ladder that reached up from the rear of the shop into the invisible perspective of the scintillating ceiling. Each rung scraped with a small cascade of colour falling ahead of the descending rung-steps. Eventually an old man alighted and swung round to confront the artist. The man was very, very old, far beyond the age for climbing ladders. He was bald in places and possessed an aura of tetchiness that herded around him like a flock of agitated sheep. His faded grey eyes flitted about the tiny shop as his bony fingers, possessing a separate mind, fidgeted with the enlarged sleeves of his cloak. Remaining droplets of the blue bell-noise trickled off his shoulders. He walked towards the artist with a pronounced stutter. His occasional straggly hair was long and theatrically unkempt.

The old man wore a frown that bore witness to too many sad episodes in a life compressed into a constant and forlorn piano chord. His lined face resembled a map of drainage channels curving off the Brahmaputra foothills; his faded hessian cloak reached to the floor and disappeared beyond. This old character framed the incongruity of the musty little shop, smelling of decaying scents and camphor caught in a late wind off the high shoulders of the Ahaggars. Even geometry could not define the mysteries that held this old man together. The artist's immediate response was to assume he would have been an appropriate portrait model for Leonardo da Vinci. After stuttering a few more steps forward the old man stopped, silhouetted against the cadmium light.

'This ceiling is amazing,' the artist blurted. 'Did you construct it, or has it come from my painting?'

'Oh, it's you!' exploded the old man. 'Of course it is my work! How could it be otherwise?' He was flustering to the best of his aged ability and was obviously pre-possessed of something.

'I'm glad you recognise me,' said the artist.

'The reason I descended the ladder was because I thought you were someone else,' the old man grumbled. 'If I had known it was you I would have remained up there.'

'Obviously you recognise me,' the artist repeated.

'Only inasmuch as you are not the Boss.'

'I am the Boss. I am the artist who painted this painting, and you said "Oh it's you" as if you recognised me,' replied the artist.

'If I had painted this nightmare the last thing I would do was to admit it. I recognise you only as not being the Boss.'

'How dare you be so rude! Then why are you in my painting? Admittedly the painting seems to have assumed details of its own, but I believe this is more to do with scale than anything else. As I am trapped in my painting I have no option at the moment but to follow my curiosity.'

'What are you talking about?' asked the old man incredulously. 'You are advanced.'

'What I am trying to say is I am the author of the painting, therefore I am the Boss.'

'And what I am trying to say is that you are not the Boss. The Boss is someone else completely different, someone else who matters.'

'I am someone else who matters, and I am completely different,' the artist insisted.

'You don't get it, do you? Of course you are someone else, and you may believe you are completely different. But to me you are not the Boss, and I suggest you pull yourself together before he arrives,' said the old man, becoming more insistent.

'I am the Boss and I have already arrived. You are here as a consequence of my painting. And if I may say so, you are a very tetchy old man,' piped the artist, also becoming insistent.

'Oh dear,' sighed the old man, 'please do not start all that again. Once more you seem to have forgotten your lines.'

'Lines? What lines am I supposed to have remembered? You talk in tongues. You refer to me specifically, yet you have not seen me before. Rambling.'

'Please stop. I suggest you settle before the Boss arrives.'

'I will leave before your Boss arriv—'

'No, you will not,' interrupted the old man.

The artist laughed. 'It is my painting, and I will come and go as I please.'

'You are most tiresome,' the old man sighed yet again. 'Little wonder your characters dislike you. Look at them, not a whole character among them. Look! There is a leg walking on its own over there! Sloppy artists.'

'You cannot realise how deeply embarrassing it is to see the unfinished nature of one's painting in close-up,' the artist muttered; then, changing the subject, 'Please tell me about this wonderful ceiling. I have never seen the like before. The best word I can use to describe it is magic, pure magic.'

'It is not magic. There is no such thing as magic,' the old man retorted.

'In that case what is it? I have never seen anything like it,' the artist said, persisting.

The old man sighed, looked hopefully in the direction of the door and beyond to the arcade, then sighed again. 'You would not understand,' he said dismissively, fearless of contradiction.

'Try me. What is it?'

'Oh dear,' sighed the old man again and yet again. 'Are you conversant with mathematics?'

'I'm afraid my grasp of mathematics is somewhat lim—'

'You will not understand,' the old man cut in.

'Please?'

'Regardless of whether I explain or not, you will not understand.'

'Then I shall not relent until you give me a chance to understand,' the artist threatened.

This threat configured the old man's attention, and he sprang a response.

'Before I attempt to explain that which I know you will not understand, allow me to reciprocate the threat. If you are here when the Boss arrives it is you who will experience the bigger regrets. Chances are you will never leave your painting, as the Boss will confirm your unsuitability for release.'

The old man awaited a response to this devastating prophecy. The artist pondered for a while, but considered the old man to be speaking lines captured from the history of Troed-yr-Henrhiw, so remained impassive.

'Very well, so be it,' said the old man impatiently. Have you studied the Sierpinski Gasket?'

'Er, let me think. Um, no,' the artist said, falling at the first hurdle.

'I thought so, you will not understand. I am wasting my time.'

'Is there anything other than a gasket?' asked the artist, hopefully.

'The Cantor Set.'

This time the artist's response was more honest and direct: 'No.'

'The Koch Curve?' The old man was launching on a parabola of complexity.

'Afraid not.'

'The Mandelbrot Set?'

'No. Are you inventing these commodities?'

'They are not commodities. They are entities. The collective noun you use proves you do not have a clue that these are fractals, rudimentary and otherwise,' the old man declared with a flourish of his bony hands.

'Fractals?'

'Fractals,' repeated the old man gruffly. 'To be crudely blunt, you artists are all self-opinionated boneheads. You scorn humility and thereby forgo the pleasures of learning the formal elements of science and mathematics by throwing them out of your so-called creative arena. Pah! More like your artistic playpen. You artists pretend these principles are of secondary importance to your monumentally self-centred so-called creativity. What an enormous blasphemy! Now it is all too late. Look at you – after all these years you end up trapped in your own painting, of all things. Look at your characters. Have some humility! I do not need to be more abject than I already am as you have obligingly proven ahead of me several points regarding your worthlessness.'

'How long were you in my painting?' asked the artist, switching tactics as an attempt at disguising truth flooding about the little shop. 'Do you think I haven't considered those issues since my unfortunate incident?'

'You may have addressed them, but it is too late – look at you,' the old man seethed.

'Who are you?' the artist asked.

'You may want to know who I am, but you do not need to know. As penance I shall state briefly what I am doing here.'

'Terrific!' the artist said.

'Of your own admission you say your grasp of mathematics is

somewhat limited. You flatter yourself. Your grasp of mathematics plunges to dismal depths. It fails to reach conversion of metric system into imperial as witnessed in the frame shop. I am sure you know nothing about algorithms, and especially the Mandelbrot Set—'

'Algorithms? That is yet another new term,' the artist wittered, taking no heed of the old man's words, 'and you know about the frame shop?'

'An algorithm is a set of steps designed to achieve a complex mathematical operation, each step carrying the operation forward by one small increment, and with perhaps a built-in repetition of a step or set of steps until certain conditions are reached. Are you following?'

'Umm—'

'Obviously not,' the old man grumbled, 'you artists! To continue. The formula for the Mandelbrot Set is very simple: the iteration in the complex plane of mapping a number, multiplying it by itself and then adding the original number. Or, in slightly different terminology, Z squared plus C, where Z is a variable complex number and C is a fixed complex number. Complex numbers are numbers involving the square root of minus one,' said the old man with embellished disdain.

'Is all this happening in my painting?'

'No. It is happening in your head. The Mandelbrot Set is the most complex object in mathematics and medicine. It would take an eternity to experience it all. But that is in two dimensions, which pales into insignificance compared to the three-dimensional Mandelbrot Set. Up there,' the old man pointed at the ceiling, 'is an experimental three-dimensional animated Mandelbrot Set. Each point of light is a fractal in its own right, as I am combining two and three dimensions in the expression. But that is easy. I have been instructed to introduce the inelasticity of dilated time within a Schwarzschild radius to control movement and devise an algorithm against which the Planck constant may postulate its large measure time superimposed on much shorter measurements. Ten to the power of minus forty-three seconds is an age compared to the divisions of time I am working with in the ceiling. Are you following?'

'No, I am simply astonished all of this is taking place inside my painting.'

'Too bad, because it now becomes somewhat more complicated.'

'More complicated! I am afraid I am not following without it becoming more complicated,' the artist spluttered.

'Uniquely it has a mathematical reality of its own,' continued the old man, who seemed to be rehearsing a lecture for another occasion, 'independent of other formulae. Consequently, when it is here the same entity is still over there; and when all of it is over there, the rest is still here. Two views of a different entity. As yet very little of the full set has been discovered by sentient beings because they persist in being satisfied by the superficial. Sentient beings need to learn a good deal more of the paradoxes and subtleties of mathematics before they are able to comprehend the total Mandelbrot infinity string set experience, which is another installation up there. Look out of the window. See the characters passing by? Follow one of them and they will freeze. The others continue to move. Do you know what controls that phenomenon?'

'Is it anything to do with movement being perceived against referential frames?' replied the artist, hesitantly.

'No,' said the old man. 'I asked what controls that phenomenon, not how movement is perceived. You artists, you don't even listen to the question. Yet society fawns around you as if the sun and wisdom flow out of every bodily orifice, and you start believing in your immortality. Pah!'

'I believe we artists have been illustrated in a bad press to you,' said the artist.

'Don't blame the press,' said the old man with a scowl, 'because you have adroitly presented your own press, such as your exhibitions, and press releases, and banging on about this and that. There! Now you have me talking in gutter language.'

The old man had become irate and impatient. The artist was already regretting his request for an explanation of the ceiling. He felt he had been much more content panicking about his entrapment. Now he was being harangued by an irate mathematician, which in no way alleviated his panic about entrapment.

'The phenomenon is controlled by particle wavefunction entanglement from initial conditions,' the old man continued in full flow, 'even for large objects like troglodyte characters, but the interaction between the myriads of particles is on such an immense scale that few sentient beings can grasp its complexity. The Boss asked me to take another look at the chaos aspect of his neurophysiology therapy but all I have arrived at so far is order. I shall report there is no such entity as chaos. The problem is that the two theories underlying the largest and smallest – general relativity that explains the expansion of the heavens and quantum mechanics that explains the fundamental structure of matter at the subatomic scale – are mutually incompatible, but you would not begin to understand the conflict either way, so it is best not entered into too deeply.'

'I now realise your identity,' the artist said smugly.

'Who do you think I am?' asked the old man, smiling.

'You are one of the characters I considered incorporating in *The Endless March*, and somehow my thoughts were frozen into the imagery of the initial composition,' responded the artist, boasting expansively.

'A fractal pretends to be complex but in reality is very simple,' replied the old man, and uttering an ironic laugh he added, 'which one could say is a mathematical metaphor for you.'

'I have received too many insults since entering Heaven's Gate,' said the artist, more cowed than when entering. 'I am neither complex nor simple.'

'Wrong,' retorted the old man, 'as it is your striving to be complex that makes you so simple. You are simplicity that masquerades as complexity. In your case simplicity means mundanely stupid, whereas simplicity in nature is the Boss's most profound achievement. The two are almost infinitely apart but of course connect eventually in the unifying clause.'

'Obviously, when I painted you – in whatever form – I erro-neously assumed misconceptions,' replied the artist, intent on bringing the old man back to his line of painterly thinking.

'Wrong, on at least two counts,' came the immediate response. 'First, you had nothing to do with it; second, they are not assumptions but certainties – you of all people should know that –

and third, they are not misconceptions, but clear concepts of the laws of physics.'

'That makes three counts.'

'Does it matter? You respond to the superficial, and miss the substance by a mile. One count is enough. Of course, you as an artist possess such limited capacity,' continued the old man, 'limitations that are not exclusively mathematical I fear, so seemingly there is little you are able to grasp. I will give you a few more hints, talking in language current to your time. Our appropriateness always adheres to the pertinent time for sentient beings. We are synonymous with your currency. We never go ahead of sentient beings.'

Whereupon the old man continued his fractal dissertation. 'The algorithm is perfectly legible and communicates a divine paradox in unfolding experiences, but from what I know of you, I seriously doubt you would be able to read it. We do not refer to the set in linguistic terms but simply as a universal experience. The incorporation of time is another instrument of mathematics. You seemed not to have grasped the implications in my reference to the Boss. Are you following?'

The artist had no answer to all this, stunned into silence. He was convinced he was in the company of someone possessing an immensely superior intellect in comparison to his own meagre eggcup. In order to avoid further manifestation of ignorance, he prudently changed the subject, a tactic that had never succeeded, even in less stressful circumstances.

'I take it you are expecting your Boss to arrive,' he said provocatively.

'Yes,' said the old man.

'This should be interesting,' the artist replied, and added: 'It is also interesting I painted you with an excellent brain and you are not disassembled like those in the arcade. Also, your cloak is altogether flowing and not stiff with paint, if I may say.'

'Of course it is altogether flowing spiritually, stupid. You seem incapable of grasping matters beyond the mundane. So much is wasted on you. Where is your humility? I am not allowing you to change the subject in order to avoid further manifestation of your ignorance until I am convinced you have grasped the greater artistic significance of the Mandelbrot Set.'

This last elicited a sighing resignation from the artist, for he anticipated the old man's lecture would next expose the sham of his art. The sigh was to no avail.

'Let me delve for a mere hop of time a little deeper into the Mandelbrot Set and the ceiling,' the old mathematician continued, unperturbed by the artist's demeanour.

'In the ceiling void above is a development of a celestial mathematical painting the vague beginnings of which Mandelbrot perfected. Here I have advanced it by the infusion of time, which places your dabbling into a proper perspective. The Mandelbrot Set possesses a simplifying mathematical property called self-similarity. Can you reflect that in your own painting? I have established that it is a fractal and is created from a simple algorithm. Does your artwork resonate with that? I have also established that these neat mathematical diversions are too difficult for you to comprehend. I have incorporated algorithmic compression in the grand design. Can artists incorporate algorithmic compression in their paintings?

'Now here is the most important aspect of the ceiling. The Mandelbrot Set reveals the hidden beauty of Nature for mere simpletons to appreciate. It remains a matter of great regret to the Boss and me that artists have turned their collective backs on the intricate mechanisms of Nature in favour of pondering their narcissistic self-imagery. Here is a perfect learning experience for you, yet in a miserable attempt to deflect the issue your acclamation plunges to the trivia of painted parts and cloaks altogether flowing. You failed to look quickly enough and consequently have missed the mistake for a lifetime. Call yourself an artist – pah!' declared the old man, momentarily forgetting his dignity. 'And I do not permit you may say. Rather, I suggest you consider your position,' he added.

The Mandelbrot ceiling had deep implications for the fatuousness of the artist's artwork. Being trapped he could not guarantee a release. Would that he could, for he would change his production forthwith, broadcasting the news afar. Angharad will be delighted. The old man possessed more information about the artist than the artist could reciprocate. The event driving the old man was the artist's crude attempt at changing the subject, of which there was justifiable criticism. He lacked humility, especially in the presence of such an awesomely beautiful ceiling.

'At last you appreciate your lack of humility,' said the old man sagely, intruding in the artist's thoughts.

'Yes,' murmured the artist, experiencing difficulty in admitting the obvious. Although inured to hostility, he was nonetheless taken aback by the old man's aggressive knowledge of mathematics and physics, ashamedly beyond his critical comprehension. Regardless, he believed that he alone had programmed everything – Heaven's Gate, the arcade, the Mandelbrot ceiling – into the painting in the first instance.

The artist was deeply impressed by the firmness of the old mathematician's responses. As logic stood, Heaven's Gate was a shop and the artist a potential customer. The old mathematician did not present a personality conducive to encouraging custom, but his enigmatic disposition and the shop's quaintness conspired to disguise purpose. The old man must have walked out of the galleries of Hieronymus Bosch and into *The Endless March*, having been clothed by Caspar David Friedrich.

'I'll have you know,' the old man said interrupting the artist's thoughts, 'I am not from the galleries of Hieronymus Bosch, nor have I been clothed by Caspar David Friedrich. Those artists learnt from me!'

Systematic detachment was eroding the artist's nerve and he was deeply confused. Obviously the old man was of an altogether intrusive form, but evaded identification. Clearly he was a mathematical physicist of immense gift, but whence he came and his telepathic abilities were mysteries. The artist was adrift; this was not an unfinished character; he did not belong to *The Endless March*. He had produced a three-dimensional mathematical artwork of indescribable beauty, yet was nonetheless existent before the artist's eyes. The painting invited him deeper into the mystery.

Although being repeatedly advised of his folly in entering Heaven's Gate, the artist was inclined to disagree due to the quantity of unanswered questions regarding status quo. The Boss was another unknown. Perhaps after all, the Boss might help the artist return to his studio; vague references to the Boss preventing release could be disregarded for already no worse predicament existed. The risk was worth taking, as no feasible alternative presented itself. Perhaps the canvas would fold back, revealing his studio; or perhaps the images would break up to reveal escape routes through the voids; perhaps a miracle would happen. It appears the artist had forgotten about the stairway home. The old man's disposition continually indicated the imminent arrival of the Boss. As a feint to delay accepting the inevitable, the artist enquired after the purpose of the shop and the identity of the Boss.

'What do you sell in your shop?'

'Sell in my shop? What are you talking about now? I have over-indulged you.'

'Well, it is set out as a shop from the arcade perspective – Heaven's Gate above the entrance and all that.'

The old man stared, displaying a combination of irritation and realisation. 'What is your name? You should not be here, obviously gone astray in the system. Can you remember your name?'

'Of course I can remember my name,' said the artist.

'Let us assume I cannot trawl your name from the galleries of our records. But you must have a name – what is it?'

'The artist.'

'The artist?' responded the old man incredulously.

'The artist is OK for me.'

'Peculiar,' said the old man, 'but to be expected given your condition.'

'Surely you mean circumstance.'

'No, when I say condition I mean condition.'

Unfazed, the artist pressed on with his line of questioning.

'Why is your shop called Heaven's Gate?'

'It is not a shop. It is a clinic called Heaven's Gate.'

'Seems like a tiny shop to me, although I admit your ceiling is heavenly; nevertheless, I cannot remember painting it,' said the artist.

The old man gazed at the artist and almost imperceptibly tossed his head at this arrival that had gone astray and was neither here nor there.

'That is because you did not paint it.'

For his part the artist was resigned to the characters in his painting taking hostile views, if they had heads to enable it, that is. It was fine for these to be an image in the form of a highly intelligent old man enabled to voice his view. A safe return to his studio and his girlfriend at Troed-yr-Henrhiw depended upon discovering the location of the exit from all of the confused ingredients surrounding him. Eliciting information from wherever was a matter of life or death. Not realising that he alone possessed the solution, he persisted in looking through the trees for the wood, which gave no alternative but to continue questioning the old man.

'If I may ask one other question: Who is your Boss?'

'The time has arrived when we should register your arrival, especially as you seem confused regarding your proper appellation. I have been very patient with you considering I hold no overall responsibility for you,' came the enigmatic response.

It seemed a fashion of the painting for its characters to communicate in convoluted riddles. The enigma was the artist's incompatibility with his painted symbols. How disappointing! Incompatibility with his own painted symbols. Bosch's *Ship of Fools*, yes; but Rembrandt's self-portraits? The answer as ever was elusive.

An order instructing him to register his arrival was incomprehensible. Each attempt took him further into a mysterious quagmire. As he had articulated the entity in which he was trapped, he was bemused by the characters expressing irritation. For his part the mysterious old mathematician was a refined form of character caught in *The Endless March*. The illusion prompted the artist to persist.

'You did not answer my question: who is your Boss?' he asked, unaware of the question's impertinence.

'I was coming to it,' came the patient reply, 'but your questions are so mundane. The Boss is the Boss of all you can perceive as this clinic, that you believe is within your painting and, for all I can divine, between the Rod of Nimbus and Galileo.'

'I don't follow. I included nothing like the Rod of Nimbus or Galileo in my painting. Are there more shops like yours in the arcade?'

At this the old man screwed up his face in exasperation. 'No wonder you are incarcerated in this asylum! If I were permitted I would sort you and your fellow artists out once for all. My Boss is Boss of here, Boss of this clinic. You are extraordinarily slow, but although you are most tiresome I suppose I should not blame you. I have attempted to provoke you into getting a grip on reality, but seemingly to no avail.'

'I am unsure which of us is the more clueless regarding the other's identity,' replied the artist. 'Incarcerated in this asylum! This asylum, as you demean it, is part of my painting. This clinic is part of my painting and either I am the Boss, or the Boss could be just another character in my painting.'

'I put the problem of your delusion down to overexcitement and fixation, due to sloppy artistic thinking, but my Boss may have a different diagnosis. The place has gone to pieces since I was given leave to formulate the three-dimensional Mandelbrot Set.'

'Who gave you leave to formulate the wonderful sculpture? The logical answer is that only I can conceivably be the Boss of all you perceive between the Rod of Nimbus and Galileo, or between the painting's original frames, wherever they are. But I cannot recall giving any of my characters leave, or even contemplating it.'

'With you everything is either a painting or a sculpture. Deluded artists!'

'What is it that so seriously upsets you? It is I who have the reason to be upset. Why do you persist in referring to the delusion theme? And what do you mean by "this clinic"? Why do you persist in referring to it as a clinic?'

'Because it is a clinic,' said the old man with great gravitas. 'This clinic is a variety of entities to its guests, including Heaven's Gate up here. My presence of mind must be slipping, because I assumed you had known all along, all along.'

'Up here? I thought we are down here, in an underground arcade. You characters are all over the place!'

'It is a blessing there are not too many artists. You are very slow at grasping the obvious. You had to stray into Heaven's Gate of all things. Now I am convinced the administrative processing has become sloppy since I took leave. Up here, here in heaven is a figure of speech.'

'Is this heaven?'

'Of course it is heaven if you wish it to be. Where did you think you were? Oh, this fixation that you are in your painting, yes, yes. Forget that, for you this is heaven – quite the normal heaven except the registration department appears to have gone to pieces. How did you think I could read your thoughts?'

'I deliberately avoided recognising your exceptional powers of telepathy in the hope they would go away.'

'Typical! And the Mandelbrot ceiling?'

'You are a very clever mathematical physicist, and I don't understand any of it.'

'I am inclined to send you up the ladder,' the old man snorted, 'but we will wait for the Boss.'

The artist mocked. 'Go on, tell me. If this is heaven then you are an angel.'

'Your remarks are due to your not being processed. I have been called an angel on several occasions by you unfortunate ones. More accurately, I should be an archangel. As you are too confused to recognise the circumstances unaided I need to tell you in order to bring this inconsequential banter to a close.' And with that the old man, taking a deep breath of forgiveness, continued: 'I am Archangel Gabriel, the Messenger for all spiritual events, for all celestial dimensions, for the narrowness of a rain's road, and more recently as the deliverer of Mandelbrot's ceiling.'

'I am still unconvinced,' replied the artist, indulging his ignorance, 'for I am the painter of this painting we are inhabiting, the creator of all the characters therein and the author of this arcade and your little shop.'

'Beware – you play with energies you can but dream of controlling. I am Archangel Gabriel and this is Heaven's Gate.'

'But a little shop like this carries no conviction of being Heaven's Gate,' the artist insisted.

From the moment of disclosing his identity Archangel Gabriel began expressing a marked impatience with the artist, now possessing a mandate to declare the upper limit of tolerance.

'You may deride,' said Archangel Gabriel, his voice assuming greater strength. 'You enjoyed your delusion of independence while it lasted. Now we must end your playtime. It has been a productive conversation, I must say. You do not require much provocation to reveal your problems. Looking out to the arcade, what do we see? Unfortunately, we see the sorry sight of unfinished images that represent your sloppy work. As for your superficial self-oriented thinking, you need a stark reminder of its consequences.' The archangel paused, scribbled some notes, and then said, 'Step outside. Go on, step outside Heaven's Gate.'

The artist hesitated. Archangel Gabriel was calling his bluff.

'Go on, step outside,' he commanded with great authority, 'step outside this instant!'

All the procrastinations of art gone, the artist had no option. Opening the door delivered a repeat performance of the booming bell, and clouds of thick blue fog momentarily enveloped everything. During his banter with Archangel Gabriel the artist had momentarily forgotten his synaesthetic malady. He cautiously stepped outside amidst the swirling density, expecting the arcade before him. But no. The clearing fog revealed that the arcade had disappeared.

Instead, he was met by bleak snow-swept steppes with a blizzard in full flight. The artist, dressed in his studio clothes, stood in deep snow. Ahead of him was a long line of prisoners – women, children and men alike – shuffling right to left, heads bent against the driving snow. Some helped others as best as conditions allowed. Standing off, armed guards, guns at the ready, herded them on. Some guards were close by, hitting the victims. Cries of pain arose above the buffeting wind. This was Armageddon's descent into hell. More to the artist's horror, this was his painting *The Endless March* precisely before matters took their sinister turn.

'*The Endless March!*' gasped the artist. 'My real painting, come to life! Down to the detailed brushstroke! Oh my God!'

Immediately picking up on Archangel Gabriel's message, he turned to make a quick exit back to the comfort of Heaven's Gate, but discovered it had gone, along with the arcade. Gone, of course. Now on all sides he was confronted by the same scene of horror. The one and the same horror he had painted back at his studio.

'Oh my God! A nightmare, oh my—'

A guard spotted him and came running over, shouting.

'What you doin' ourof line scum? Gerrin line!' and gave the artist a crushing blow with the butt of his rifle.

The artist cried out in pain. 'Stop! You've made a mistake! I'm the artist who painted this composition! I don't belong to them.'

'Painted?' the guard asked uncomprehendingly. 'Gerrin line prisoner, I'll shoot,' and he laughed.

'But you don't understand, I painted you as—'

Another blow, and penetrating cold was added to his confusion. Complying to avoid further pain, the artist staggered into line, a prisoner in his painting as a prisoner in line.

'You a fool getting out of line,' a young woman hissed. 'Lucky you not shot. They shot man back there stepped out of line, they laughed hollow, him dead in snow.'

'God! This is my nightmare come true! God, God! How do I get out of this?'

'How do us get out of it?'

'When the guards shoot, do people really die?' the artist asked.

'What?' another asked hopelessly.

'Oh heaven help us all, this is my nightmare come to life. Blast my arrogance with Archangel Gabriel! But that's too obvious, too copybook. There must be another answer.' The artist was muttering his thoughts. 'Far too Sunday School, too copybook – there must be another answer.'

'You are right about answer,' glowered a young man, his hand heavily bandaged. 'If guards don't get you, frost will.'

'Extraordinary!' exclaimed the artist, 'I remember painting that bandage on to your hand including the scarlet lake for blood. There is no wound beneath the bandage, believe me!'

'What you talking about? Hand pains, I saw blood coming out before bandage. I saw blood drop into snow.'

'Scarlet lake mixed with Old Holland vermilion tint,' replied the artist.

'But snow real.'

'Lukas Studio flake white. Look, I'm dressed only for my studio.'

'But cold real. You witness for self.'

'Watch out!'

'Walk on!' a guard roared.

'Help!' an old woman cried into her trailing headscarf. They stumbled out of earshot of a guard here, only to pass another one looming through the snow there.

'There another,' someone down the line hissed.

'How you fall behind? Not allowed.'

'I didn't,' replied the artist, 'I have just arrived from—' but he left it, as he was unsure himself where he had arrived from; besides, his characters would not understand. As the happy memories of his fun at Troed-yr-Henrhiw with Angharad faded, so he felt increasingly colder.

'In this place? Never!' groaned another prisoner.

They could not grasp the artist's circumstances, as the artist could not grasp Archangel Gabriel working on the Mandelbrot dilemma back in Heaven's Gate. The artist pulling strands of thoughts together... circumstances disallowed cohesive thought... concluded there must be a connection somewhere, somewhere in the painting. The prisoners were presented in the perfect detail that the artist had painted. Back in the sanctuary of his studio he had relished reproducing images that reflected pain and horror, detailed representations of suffering. All the minutiae of misery and deprivation conjured from the spectrum of his imagination. There were no sketchy spare parts as in the arcade. Here they were detailed, complete, all dressed in pain.

'Watch out!'

'Unfortunately I know everything that has happened and will happen. I am afraid you are characters in *The Endless March*, all destined to... destined... die,' said the artist, clumsily.

'And you. You die too,' they said, helpless.

'I painted this nightmare. I painted you – us – all walking around in a great circle until you – we – and I am probably destined as much as you to drop one by one through exhaustion and cold. That is why I titled it *The Endless March*. Gradually we all die in this big circle. This is very frightening. I should know, I painted the giant circle before I applied the blizzard,' he said, but still not really believing their same predetermined fortune would befall him. After all, he was their creator.

'What you talking about?'

'The front of this column is over there.' The artist pointed to his right into the snowstorm at right angles to the line. 'If you take right-angled coordinates. The reference frame is farther away. We will soon be passing fallen bodies in the snow.'

'Don't believe him!' someone shouted. 'We going camp. Soon there.'

'Believe me,' cried the artist, not relishing the realisation, 'I know because it was I who painted you all. We will never reach a camp. This is awful!'

'Believe he right,' said another man, 'because I saw guard two, three hours ago. We pass many our dead comrades.'

'Twice I pass same dead horse,' someone else added.

'There should be two dead horses,' the artist said, 'I painted two dead horses.'

A child cried distantly ahead.

'What him talking about? Him mad! Him not realise this real life and death nightmare. We did nothing for it – ripped away to here, prisoners.'

'Oh my God!' said the artist. 'An artist never considers living existences when he paints people, in whatever circumstances.'

The prisoners were becoming angry at the artist's trite comments. They clustered in a knot around him, wrath rising as a wave among the beleaguered people, their pain and sorrow welling.

'Push him out,' someone shouted. 'His talk get us shot.'

'Get out line, out line,' several chanted, 'get out line!'

'Get into line!' a guard shouted, raising his rifle to shoot.

'Get out line,' they chanted.

'Into line, last warning,' the guard yelled.

'I can't,' the artist squealed, 'my characters won't let me. Don't you understand?'

The guard advanced, pointing his gun. The artist shut his eyes and screamed. Out of the swirling blizzard something strongly gripped his arm and dragged him away from *The Endless March*. Amidst a whirl of snow and blue fog he was at once in the sanctuary of Heaven's Gate again. Tranquillity restored. Outside, the arcade was as before with the unfinished characters passing by as usual. Snow-melt dripped from the artist's clothing; he was shaking uncontrollably and glanced about nervously, seeking reassurance. His relief was monumental.

'How on earth did you manage that?'

'Manage what?' Archangel Gabriel asked quietly.

'That was amazing,' said the shivering artist, 'I stepped outside – you ordered me, and saw me step outside – straight into a nightmare. It was *The Endless March* for true, and I was being brutally hit into line by a guard, then pushed out of line by the characters I had painted. Then I was about to be shot by a guard. Up until then I thought I was inviolable but from that moment I truly believed I was going to die. Then you rescued me. How did you do it? Did you come out into the blizzard?'

'What blizzard?' asked Archangel Gabriel. 'I did not rescue you. Whatever you witnessed simply happened in your mind, and any rescuing was of your own doing. The reason you are here in Heaven's Gate is due to your painting such horrors. But the reason that drives you to paint these horrors is not so easy to explain. When dabbling to humour your cosy whims you pay no heed to the reality of forces beyond your comprehension. The rescue of your floundering mind may prove a little difficult. I am sure we can overcome such difficulties. We may begin to clear the backlog if I were to subject you to other scenarios of your mind on a graduated scale of terror to the power of squared pain. Each terror will be drawn from your portfolio of armchair Gothics.'

'Oh please don't,' wheedled the artist. 'Please believe me, I am already convinced. No more reality, please. I now believe you to be Archangel Gabriel.'

'Dear me, your believing me to be Archangel Gabriel is immaterial. You are so easily converted. Easy to convert, easy to lapse. We will need to make a determined effort to ensure the rescue of your floundering mind is a permanent feature. So far there has been no reality.'

'I can assure you,' replied the artist, the edge having been taken off his arrogance, 'it was reality out there and the proof is my mind is readily rescued.'

'And I can assure you, Mr Artist, your mind is not rescued,' replied Archangel Gabriel gravely, 'for your brief foray into *The*

Endless March has only succeeded in putting a temporary halt to your derision. Your artist's mindset cuts a lifelong depth of arrogance. You are still thinking entirely of yourself and have already forgotten the Mandelbrot ceiling. Too bad I have no mandate to administer punishment. But I can avail myself of your thoughtless compositions, and place you inside them.'

At which the artist quickly recollected various armchair compositions of horror he had concocted, and was overwhelmed by a sense of foreboding.

'I note your recollections,' said Archangel Gabriel. 'You have an abundant tapestry of horror from which I can choose. Good. So listen carefully. This is Heaven's Gate,' he continued, changing his tone to denote the commencement of a speech. 'Heaven's Gate has dimensions but little regard to position, either here in the arcade, or there next to your painted nightmare, everywhere and nowhere. It has position with little regard for dimension. It has position but no fixed point in space. It is a point in space with no fixed position. Simultaneously it is infinity contained in a single particle of paint – it is a particle of paint that reaches to infinity. Heaven's Gate is all the laws of nature that you know and many more yet to be demonstrated. It is an algorithmic compression containing such mundane trivia that artists will submit. Yet its awesome algorithmic beauty atones for the mediocrity of paintings. When you begin to accept these references you will start the journey home.'

Due to the events just past the artist was experiencing difficulty in listening carefully. Sufficient humility failed to prevent his mind from jiggling, or questions from making unhindered incursions. Questions regarding the position of Archangel Gabriel in his painting; the true horror of *The Endless March*; the malleable construct of Heaven's Gate and the arcade. He glanced nervously about, unable to place a fix on anything any more. He made a move for the door, which elicited a sigh from the observant archangel. Opening it just a little was sufficient to trigger a repeat performance of the noise and bell-fog. This time the artist did not venture out, but remained rooted in Heaven's Gate. Suddenly a scintillating flash zipped between the doorposts.

The artist was familiar with trick cinematography and computer-manufactured superimposed animation. These days it was difficult to tell the difference between representation and fabrication. Old-fashioned animation artists were redundant. But this was different. He jiggled the door. There it was again! Just there, he witnessed a shaft of parallel existences, in a glint, in a scintillating flash. There was his studio, in an algorithmically compressed electromagnetic beam. How was it done? How could he possibly read it? This was far beyond computer tricks, and unfortunately far beyond the artist's comprehension.

'Aha!' he exclaimed, 'the join. I have found the join!'

'Would that you had a clue of what you are experiencing,' sighed Archangel Gabriel, 'and perhaps we could all go home. You appear unable to pay heed to what I say. You are experiencing the join between this entity and the last, but do you know what to make of it? You have not forgotten the lesson so quickly, surely?'

'I'm sorry, I'll try to concentrate, honestly, but things are happening too fast.'

'Then listen carefully and try not to interrupt and maybe you will begin to comprehend your circumstances, and then maybe, a huge maybe, you can go home,' responded the patient Archangel Gabriel. 'If not, I shall begin my explanations all over again. Understand?'

'Yes.'

'Heaven's Gate is without gravity but possesses immense weight,' continued the archangel. 'It embraces the paradox of uncertainty with the certitude of assumption, the transience of time with the absolution of now. Its time is the speed of light that slows to a frozen hop to accommodate the individual soul and then blows the universe to particles just for the energy of it. Heaven's Gate is neither here nor there, but paradoxically is here, there and everywhere. Heaven's Gate is here for you: that is why it appeared as you walked along the arcade. If, in your travels, you reach there, Heaven's Gate will be there waiting for you.'

'I'm lost here, there and everywhere and in more ways than one,' interrupted the artist.

'I am aware,' continued Archangel Gabriel, ignoring his itinerant listener, 'you do not possess the capability to comprehend the existence of objects outside the limited confines of dimension, or the finite beauty of space. You have just witnessed the join between parallel studios but seem incapable of turning it to your advantage. If you possessed the capability, you would not be here, you would be there at Troed-yr-Henrhiw.

'You believe incomputable numbers belong to mystery; that omega has no conclusion; that mathematics is logical; that the universe is finite; that it all started with a demonstrable singularity. You steadfastly believe artists are able to render everything into representational imagery. How wrong! What about wavefunctions that operate in mathematical space? Or implausibly short-lived resonances? They did not accidentally fall off the Boss's workbench. And so on. They are all there for a purpose. All these and more turn themselves on their heads when you are not looking, – but why should I spoil your little daydreams? The solution lies with your technical indeterminacies, not the physical or metaphysical worlds. We have enjoyed many a laugh at the muddle the Boss made of previous editions, but we have reserved the biggest laugh for artists.'

'I don't know what to say.'

'Good,' replied Archangel Gabriel.

'I'm listening, but also I am still recovering from my ordeal.'

'Ordeal!' scoffed Archangel Gabriel. 'What about the ordeal you subjected your characters to endure in your nightmare painting?'

'Although I previously supposed a painting was a mere representation of images and that the symbols had no feelings, that a painting is just a two-dimensional rendition in colour and tone, I am now completely confused and have to admit *The Endless March* was extremely realistic.'

'Of course it is extremely realistic: it is real. For you, objects must have dimensions before you recognise their existence. You believe two-dimensional images do not possess living existence. You are so wrong!' declared Archangel Gabriel.

While Archangel Gabriel was talking, the artist once again failed to pay attention. The archangel's assessment of the artist's tendency to allow lessons to slide out of mind was once again demonstrated. On this occasion his proffered mentality determined an observation regarding the Mandelbrot ceiling.

'The ceiling, your Mandelbrot ceiling has changed. You have

modified it but it is just as beautiful,' the artist said, staring in amazement. 'Obviously you modified it when I was out – must have taken a considerable effort and time, surely?'

'No conscious time at all.'

'I was outside for more than five minutes.'

'You were outside for no conscious time at all, but if you insist on placing a scale on it, then billions of earth years, aeons even, will suffice,' the archangel replied.

'So no conscious time at all is equal to billions of earth years which in turn is equal to my five minutes here in Heaven's Gate?'

'Yes, I am saying billions of earth years are equal to no conscious time at all here in Heaven's Gate.'

'Good. That just about sums up you and Heaven's Gate,' said the artist, grasping the therapy the archangel was utilising.

'Listen,' declared Archangel Gabriel firmly, 'A may equal B but B refuses to equal A.'

'No doubt only here in Heaven's Gate,' the artist curtly responded.

'Everywhere.'

'Oh, sure,' said the artist with great dismay. 'Time has lost its currency, mathematics has lost its meaning, what next?'

'We await the Boss, that is what is next,' replied Archangel Gabriel, 'but you are at liberty to precipitate another lesson in the meanwhile. I attempted to resolve your problems but due to your obduracy have failed. You fail to grasp the elasticity of time. When the Boss arrives he can deal with you. Besides, I have disclosed my identity. A school of thought believes art should be constructed of materials. This is so wrong. As an artist you are ephemeral, existing so long, but ephemeral all the same. Apart from your personal ignorance, which under the circumstances is almost excusable, you need to be processed in order to be tuned to the reverential beauty of nature and to forget the delusion that artists contribute an important mantra to society. You need to learn from nature, and nature alone. You must discover art the way physicists learned the obscure mathematics of the universe. You have inverted natural logic, believing nature should learn from you. Pah! Like Heaven's Gate you have position but no dimension. Both you and Heaven's Gate are transient entities. The ingredients to enable your escape have been present all the time, but you confused them in position and muddled your grasp on time. The way to freedom is through becoming an artist of pure thought.'

The old mathematician had become unreachable in the realm of enigma. His modified ceiling was yet to be explored, his time dilation turned logical certainty into nebulous assumption, and the scintillating join between Heaven's Gate and the past was a lost key. Avenues of philosophical unreality were caught in the painting of which the brush had no say. The artist experienced great difficulty in reconciling hitherto assumptions on control with the archangel's games with time, cyberspace and mathematics, most of which had always been beyond the artist's comprehension, regardless. The notion that he occupied position having no dimension was going too far, offering a hook on which he could hang his ignorance. The extraordinary variegated characters in the arcade appeared no longer plausible in the light of the *Endless March* terror. He wondered what time it could be back at Troed-yr-Henrhiw.

'Twenty-five past eleven, your time,' said Archangel Gabriel without prompt, 'but you are wrong regarding your assumptions on control.'

'Thank you,' replied the artist, absent-mindedly. 'Is the Boss God?'

'If you wish him to be, but here he is the Boss,' replied Archangel Gabriel.

'So the visitor you are expecting is God, am I right?'

'The visitor I am expecting is the Boss. But in your condition you are free to think otherwise. It does not take Euclidian geometry to work it out. A kitten in a whirl of fur would know in which direction its milk lay.'

Only Archangel Gabriel could make connections between Euclidian geometry and kittens in a whirl of fur, although it had been commonplace during the artist's childhood for his father to make incongruous connections. The artist's difficulty in placing the archangel into a psychological perspective persisted. The explanation that most satisfied his scepticism was that a religious channel had been prattling on the radio in his studio as he painted *The Endless March*; probably the paint independently recorded the celestial imagery without a conscious effort from himself, or so he concluded.

'Utter nonsense!' barked Archangel Gabriel. 'All of your psychoanalysis is sloppy vacuity. Your thoughts open up vast fields of conceptual debris, but unfortunately I have neither mandate nor time to equivocate. It is sad you understand so little, though I am sure most of my suggestions are not beyond your intellectual capacity, which forces me to conclude artists cease exercising their brains once they have adopted the spurious mindset that they are creative. You possess sufficient conceit to flatter yourself without any inner justification, a flaw that should have been amended long before you were conceived. Fortunately you never procreated. As you are now in heaven, profanities you utter are meaningless.'

'I always thought my life as an artist was heavenly,' the artist reminisced magnanimously, 'but I never realised I was in heaven.'

'No one realises they are in heaven until it is demonstrated to them by the celestial bodies. As for you, well, you are here regardless of mal-administration and your folly. You would not be here if you were not in your heaven,' said the archangel.

'I didn't know I had died. The last thing I remember was climbing into my painting. My girlfriend Angharad was present and she believed it to be a party trick,' said the artist plaintively.

'*That was a mistake,*' hissed Inner Voice.

'Briefly explain how the party trick came about,' Archangel Gabriel commanded.

The artist was deeply troubled. His inner voice began chattering loudly, a sure sign of extreme stress. What started out as an adventure had quickly assumed the characteristics of a nightmare. Matters were out of his control. Would that he could go home.

'*Why did you have to tell him you climbed into your painting?*' Inner Voice asked: '*That makes you out to be a proper Charlie.*'

'I'll try,' the artist stammered.

'*Careful!*' Inner Voice said.

'The painting I was working on progressed so successfully that I began believing another hand was guiding mine, so expert were the brushstrokes, so well-organised were the colour and tonal relationships. Some passages were so far beyond my utmost ability that after a while I was obliged to assume the role of observer rather than producer. Then the inevitable happened – inevitable from my perspective. My painting developed a self-motivated animation that I was powerless to prevent.'

'For God's sake don't confess the naked women part, even if he is a character in your painting.'

'Why do you pause? Go on,' said the archangel.

'The... the... animation progressed to a degree where I was tempted to venture into it and join the events, for by now the sheer wonder of its imagery far exceeded the mere presbytery of my capacity.

'One morning, I decided to explore the amazing new world that had developed on my canvas seemingly of its own volition. Contrary to the advice of my girlfriend, who thought the joke had gone too far, I climbed in. Immediately, the nightmare began, for the painting was not as it had appeared from the perspective of my studio. I hastened to leave, but the painting gripped me in its maze, for the point where I had entered had disappeared and I was trapped inside my own brushwork. The heavy aroma of oil paint, linseed oil and turpentine spirit drenched the air, slowing my senses. All the ingredients to enable my escape were present, but my mind confused their position and I lost a grip on time.'

'Now he thinks you are a right twit.'

'I visited a frame shop some distance from here in the hope that *The Endless March* was there, but met with the Laughing Cavalier, an old girlfriend from art college days and deeper confusion. Then the painting invited me into this underground arcade. I arrived here in Heaven's Gate and matters seem to have taken a sinister turn where I am not in control of my destiny, and you insist I am dead.'

'What did you want to say the whole truth for?' Inner Voice was exasperated.

'Would that it were all as easy as that,' sighed Archangel Gabriel wistfully. 'We would be able to place your mind on the straight and narrow forthwith. Certainly your explanation conforms with our records, but you would not know.'

'Why not? People know when they die, when their lives end.'

'No, not that, but besides, they do not,' responded Archangel Gabriel, matter of fact. 'People are unaware of their own death:

Only those still living are aware of the death. When you die you do not even know you are dead. Often when you arrive here you think you are dreaming, or stuck in a lift, or are lost in a maze and are seeking a way out. Yet others – those in a special category – think they are trapped in their own productions such as memoirs, or dog kennels, or even their paintings, and are searching with no great urgency for a way back home. Anyway, we are straying from the subject.'

'Ask him does everyone search for a way home – keep straying from the subject.'

'Does everyone search for a way home?'

'Mostly, but it does not last,' came the reply.

'I always believed one would not be able to reflect if one were dead,' said the artist, still unconvinced by Archangel Gabriel's cleverness.

'The dead are quite able to reflect upon their lives,' the archangel replied, 'but logically the input of new data is truncated at death.'

'In that case, what is the difference between life and death? In life one is only able to reflect upon data readily available up to the event of now. What is the point of having both life and death, when one will suffice? Besides, I have learnt a good deal about your Mandelbrot ceiling which I never knew before I arrived here,' argued the artist.

'Clever – clever for you, that is,' the archangel smiled, 'but the answer has to be no difference whatever, but every difference as time goes on. Let us return to your antics with your painting.'

'Yes, I suppose so,' said the artist.

'Suppose so? Did we say that?'

'I have to conclude your digression,' said Archangel Gabriel. 'No more the riddle of life as it appears to a newborn child, the gradual process of comprehension through experience. But the Boss has deliberately designed chaos into the process. Could you imagine a universe structured in an orderly way? It would not work for the animate or the inanimate. Take for example the experience as witnessed by humans: only a few born at a given time would benefit from the order, the rest would be either too early or too late. This would cause enormous friction between sentient beings. The result? More ignorance than exists at present. So the grand design of seemingly chaotic order is in fact the best mathematics for order.'

'*Good, good. We are away from that climbing into your painting stuff,*' muttered Inner Voice.

'I believe I see a flaw in your argument,' said the artist. 'Sentient beings are a product of their environment through evolution, natural selection. All things – mountains, woodlice, rain, you, me – are constructed from stardust, the result of atoms being cooked inside stars. The life force utilises the matter that is at hand. That is, the natural laws determine the environment, which in turn determines the form of any sentient beings that may evolve. Symbiosis governed by natural laws possessing constructive as well as destructive powers. Sentient beings are not readily gifted with highly perceptive intellects at one and the same time as implied in your scenario,' the artist concluded with a flourish.

'I believe you might be recovering,' Archangel Gabriel responded. 'At this rate of improvement you will probably need only one more extramural experience to do the trick. Certainly we do not have to linger over your ridiculous posturing with your painting, although I would be interested to know what your girlfriend thinks of all this. We will find out in due course.'

'No, surely not! Leave her out of it! I promise I shall improve at a faster rate.'

'Promises, empty promises,' replied Archangel Gabriel blandly.

'I have that feeling that matter and events are structured in an orderly way with colours and shapes,' said the artist, attempting to improve on his recovery, 'as if the abstract creations are universally intelligible and have emerged, not through my brushwork, but due to an entirely different force. Of course it is all imagination.'

'That is as maybe,' replied Archangel Gabriel, 'but you are getting off the point of details, especially my modified Mandelbrot ceiling.'

'*Details are commonplace!*' nagged Inner Voice.

The artist imagined details were commonplace, but the circumstance and theatre of presentation created a radically new atmosphere that obliged his recognition of the small, self-centred world he had been playing in. The fleeting charade upside down inside his painting in an underground shopping arcade confronted the artist's pretentious life as a facade before reality, a fatuous assumption, a superficial construction masquerading as a self-important adjunct to society. Due to his condition the artist was unaware of the broader picture, of his tenuous grip on its delusive veneer.

'Thinking of delusive veneers,' continued Archangel Gabriel, 'brings to mind the order of experiencing. This benefits the individual who experiences the fact, sometimes not. More often the experience leads to greater confusion, and further quests, as in your case. But the greater confusion attendant upon the individual is inconsequential to human perception of the universal accident of things.'

'Accident?' queried the artist. 'Before this you stated it was deliberately designed.'

'Accident in the sense of when a sentient being experiences closure horizons of the whole set-up. They cannot return to talk about it.'

'Closure horizons ref event horizons?' the artist asked, signifying his having picked up the term without understanding its astrophysical implication.

'The Boss deliberately designed-in mathematical safeguards,' continued the archangel, oblivious to the question, 'against so-called intelligent minds grasping the direction of it all. Incidentally, can you give me a better description of a closure horizon?'

The artist thought about it. 'I cannot,' he admitted, 'but do designed-in mathematical safeguards exist in the universe or in one's mind?'

'Now don't overreach yourself in your delicate condition,' the archangel advised, 'but regardless, the answer is both – the mind is the universe and the universe the mind. This is one of the Boss's enigmas, but no more enigmatic than all his other enigmas.'

'You would not want clever people fiddling with the settings,' the artist suggested.

'The cleverest of people would not comprehend the settings

even if they had the opportunity to experience them, leave alone knowing how to fiddle with them. The Boss ensured the inclusion of a contingency that continuously conceals the assumed sequential stage of scientific exploration, although of course the stages are laid out arbitrarily, thus giving the illusion that the status as known by humans is all there is to know. The Boss has infinite thought. Neat, but no neater than the rest. You cannot comprehend these matters, but this discussion constitutes part of your therapy,' declared Archangel Gabriel, scribbling in a notepad that he had retrieved from his enlarged sleeve.

The artist was losing his grasp of Archangel Gabriel's line of conversation. He decided to ask a question of enormously mundane profundity, such as enquiring about God's favourite invention.

'What is God's favourite—' he began and,

'The woodlouse,' interrupted the archangel.

'The woodlouse? You must be joking!' the artist spluttered in disbelief. 'Douglas Adams said something like that, and we all laughed. You pinched that joke off Douglas Adams.'

'Although I am short of time, this is a scenario worth following. The woodlouse it is. Douglas Adams borrowed it from a Greater Organisation.'

'I cannot believe it is the woodlouse,' said the artist. 'There must be many cleverer and more intricate existences than the woodlouse, like for instance the immensely local environment of the strong nuclear force, or the conversion of energy into matter and back again. Come on, not the woodlouse. The woodlouse would not exist without the strong nuclear force, neither would anything else.'

'The woodlouse,' Archangel Gabriel repeated absent-mindedly.

'I've just thought of it – what about singularities?'

'Oh dear, too simple! Their quantum indeterminacy is a very short and simple fractal.'

'What about a beautiful woman?' asked the artist, introducing his favourite subject. 'My conviction is that God's best invention by far is a beautiful woman.'

'It appears you asked the question simply as a vehicle to introduce your favourite subject. I saw it coming hours ago. A beautiful woman is out of the question. Your choice is too specific, too personal and too individualised,' responded Archangel Gabriel disdainfully. 'There are ugly women, physically and mentally. Many humans, both female and male, vehemently dislike women. They see them as unnecessary competition. You hold perturbing fallacies regarding the attractiveness of women. On the other hand, the human response to the woodlouse is universal. It has to be the woodlouse because it is always determinate, along with the myriad artificers that guarantee replication.'

'The human response is immaterial,' said the artist. 'Simply because many humans, both female and male, vehemently dislike women does not negate a beautiful woman as being God's greatest creation. You speak as an old, miserable, woman-hating man, and the exercise says more about you than the merits of the categories.' The artist mocked, for the first time feeling a sense of superiority, at the same time forgetting he was debating with a character from his painting. 'To categorise the woodlouse as God's favourite invention and to dismiss beautiful women out of hand throws grave doubts on your grading methodology. Incidentally, in what category are artists placed?'

'Uncategorised,' replied Archangel Gabriel, evading elaboration of his shortcomings by pretending to write furiously on to his notepad.

'Uncategorised?'

'Uncategorised. Apart from their self-centred reflection, proving a point we celestial judges have repeatedly made, the Boss makes no claim on the creation of artists. He has always insisted they are the result of an accident, something to do with a sneeze on the Wednesday of the Seventh Edition. The offending program was retained as a concession to his wife—'

'Wife?' the artist interrupted. 'Are you saying God is married?'

'Of course, and what's more if it were not for his wife you would not ever have existed, for she persuaded him to retain the accidental artist program when he broke the news that Wednesday night. She laughed so heartily that the Boss agreed not to wipe the error off creation. You are so lucky. When we learnt about it we could not believe the Boss had allowed a woman to contribute to the Creative Process, but she is the Boss's wife after all, and we all have our little weaknesses. Going home to a wife, of all things! If the Boss were to die, heaven forbid, she would take over, and then what sort of a pudding would the universe be in? The only concession the Boss made to our protests was to place artists in "Uncategorised". No, definitely not artists or beautiful women; the woodlouse it is.'

'Perhaps if Mrs God took over then we might have a proper code of natural justice, not the arbitrary nonsense that affiliates to chaos and randomness, and perhaps we would enjoy equality regardless of gender, and perhaps we would hear less claptrap that we are all born sinners when we patently are not!'

'If I had a mandate to punish, I would certainly exercise it on you,' Archangel Gabriel growled.

'This chance encounter has been enormously enlightening. I can see the genesis of many of mankind's ills in your attitude,' said the artist, gaining in confidence.

'You still don't get it, do you? If you feel so superior, see if you can extricate yourself from Heaven's Gate and your painting,' the archangel mocked.

'Everything uttered within Heaven's Gate appears to be threats of retribution, some form of vengeful Armageddon, or oppression through the tools of entrapment. Where is the turn-the-other-cheek atonement, and the Father-forgive-them-for-they-know-not-what-they-do teaching we were subject to from the age of pushchair?'

'Up there,' said Archangel Gabriel, pointing at the Mandelbrot ceiling, 'lies the genesis of mankind's fortunes, the answer to your quest and the future of the universe. Don't come to me looking for sleep-inducing camphors laced with the lull of sweetness. Go on, extricate yourself from your painting.'

'That is precisely what I am trying to do. I am trapped somewhere in the psyche of my painting between the scintillation and the doorway and am looking for a lead as to the way back to my studio at Troed-yr-Henrhiw.'

'That which I set out to prove, you have proven for me,' responded the archangel.

'I am looking for help wherever.'

'As I explained, artists are reactionary accidents. Even when dead they claim to be passing by on the way to the Great Pyramids or to sketch some drains east of Andromeda, or trapped in their paintings but urgently seeking a way back to their studio at Troed-yr-Henrhiw. We pleaded with the Boss not to accede to his wife's frivolity, but ours not...'

'This is an elaborate joke the other characters set up. Having chosen the most intelligent of their number, presumably, they set you up in this little shop. The only flaw in my conjecture is this wonderful ceiling. I can't figure that out, and perhaps other matters, like telepathy,' muttered the artist who, in his infinite stupidity, had already forgotten his ordeal in the blizzard. The most important ingredient to enable his escape was part of him the while.

'Did I know you would enter Heaven's Gate of your own accord? Incidentally, Heaven's Gate set me up. See that washer woman yonder? The machine is managing her; that is the logic of your painting process. Pah!'

'But that does not prevent a sublime coincidence.'

'Was I expecting you?'

'No, you acted the impression you were expecting someone else.'

'Yes,' said an aloof Archangel Gabriel, 'someone else who matters. Everything you say is both contradictory and correct. I am expecting the Boss any second. You will regret coming here in the first instance, but you are not to blame. Remember, everything is both contradictory and correct.'

'*Everything is both contradictory and correct?*' squeaked Inner Voice. '*What does he mean by that?*'

Suddenly a storm of blue surged down the arcade, sucking up the body parts before it, clustering at the entrance to Heaven's Gate. Archangel Gabriel paled, and his demeanour altered markedly. His authoritative aplomb was abandoned in favour of an altogether more subservient disposition. The artist stared in wonder at the colossal clustering outside.

It was too late to leave, had the artist been able so to do. The door boomed open. An apparition the like of which the artist had never before experienced filled the aperture. Fogs of blues swirled frenetically as servants in a nest gone mad. The all-pervasive colour-sound obliterated the apparition, Archangel Gabriel, Heaven's Gate all no sooner seen than hidden. The bell-sound-colour varied its intensity according to the visitor's stature; here was the quintessence of colour and sound celebrating a most important visitor.

'*Uh-oh!*' chimed Inner Voice.

As thunderous booming rolled and echoed through the upper reaches of the Mandelbrot ceiling and the blues began to dissipate, the shimmering form of the new arrival became discernable. But this was no ordinary arrival. Amidst the colourful clamour Archangel Gabriel darted quicker than is respectable for an old man of his stature to a wicker chair beside the little shelf, sitting upright as a child behind the ordinance of good behaviour. The mode of gravitas and intelligent authority he had hitherto displayed for the artist had vanished, and was replaced by a countenance of awful subservience, as he busily wrote his notes.

The apparition was tall, lean and majestically dressed in blue-grey steel clothes, reaching from collar to the floor.

'*He resembles a stainless steel organ pipe,*' Inner Voice whispered timorously.

The new arrival beheld a presence of other-worldliness quite beyond the artist's imagination to comprehend. His hair and beard were long, true and grey and possessed an uncanny ability to disappear into the background as befitted undisciplined sounds dissipating among the levers of the Mandelbrot set reaching down in greeting from the ceiling. His semi-transparency beguiled a loosely sketched watercolour, dilute in quaver and form, but with no oil paint about him at all. The steel-grey uniform gave vent to scintillating colour-sounds of an ethereal variety that dropped to and through the floor as mirrored reflections of the Mandelbrot ceiling. Colours of B flat major emanated from the apparition as scents of stardust and tincture of great distance.

'*This is indeed The Boss. Notice Archangel Gabriel's pensive demeanour,*' Inner Voice whispered again.

The new arrival looked uncannily similar to the image the artist had expected, for since entrapment he had come to believe everything he saw was the true register of his subliminal imagination. Yet the characters had a high degree of independence, and he could not fathom *The Endless March* trick that Archangel Gabriel had played. Even so, the new arrival was an awesome image, but not beyond the wondrous Mandelbrot ceiling. Heaven's Gate had certainly got off to an amazing start.

Since the arrival of the Boss everything in Heaven's Gate appeared to shimmer.

'*This is to be expected*,' Inner Voice whispered. '*You should perceive precisely that which you strongly expect.*'

Objects hovering in the haze were tangible yet untouchable. Fixing his gaze on one detail of the Boss would cause the rest to fade into Heaven's Gate's background. Images were visibly tinted through other objects. The shimmering was beyond the artist's comprehension and, caught up in the changing events, he floated about in the storeroom of his memory, endeavouring to connect the sense with his memories of Troed-yr-Henrhiw.

Clearly, Archangel Gabriel was subservient to the new visitor. The artist was at a loss to identify the particular charade of his painting that encapsulated this scenario as, though all the clues were present, they were confused in position and time. Although the artist was ostensibly privy to the arrival of the Boss the lack of tangible connections left him resorting to guesswork, a science he had never really mastered.

Meanwhile, on entering Heaven's Gate, the new arrival passed by the artist without acknowledgement. No time of day or excuse me, just ghostly transfer, like neutrinos on their hurried way to eternity. Although the new arrival's surrounding aura of scintillation possessed poise, he nevertheless appeared in a hurry. The artist had been stoically receiving all the shocks his painting could muster—

'*More or less; certainly less outside during the blizzard episode*,' Inner Voice corrected. But the artist was nevertheless taken aback by the new arrival's lack of substance, his shadowy nature.

'*Obviously the Boss is God. Who else could treat you as a shadow in your own painting?*' the artist's Inner Voice declared.

The mechanics of his painting that called down God were beyond his palette. Glancing through the glass door, the artist saw characters from *The Endless March* pressing their faces against the glass, looking straight at him, silently mouthing,

'Help us, help us!'

Beyond were the guards in the blizzard keeping their respective distances in deference to God's attendance, but with their guns still at the menace. The artist felt utterly helpless.

'*Do you think it is all imagination?*' asked Inner Voice.

'Don't ask me. Ask God!' blurted the artist, pointing at the newcomer, and immediately regretted his presumptuousness. But his nervous outburst stirred neither God nor Archangel Gabriel.

If the apparition were God Proper then the artist could relax his concern that Heaven's Gate was within his painting; that the Mandelbrot ceiling reached up to eternity; that probably he had not invented them after all; whereupon the artist could seek help regarding his way back to Troed-yr-Henrhiw.

'*Think of it,*' Inner Voice prattled in swelling confidence, '*any moment now you shall step out of this nightmare back into your studio.*'

The Boss sat down in the vacant wicker chair and pressed a switch not previously noticed by the artist. Computer apparatus purred out of its home in the whitewashed wall, coming to rest above the shelf. He typed methodically on the keyboard, and then examined the information displayed on the screen. The while Archangel Gabriel was furiously filling in a sheath of documents. Neither the Boss nor Archangel Gabriel detracted to the Mandelbrot ceiling, which continued to scintillate in ever-changing effervescent colours. The artist wondered how they could possibly continue ignoring it, unless of course it was an everyday occurrence for these celestial spirits.

'Have you entered the chemical readings?' the Boss asked Archangel Gabriel. 'I cannot retrieve them here.'

'They are entered under the patient's pseudonym, sir, for security reasons,' replied Archangel Gabriel.

'*Sir?*' piped Inner Voice. '*Why does he address God as "sir"?*'

'What else—?' the artist began but aborted his sentence.

The Boss cast him a glance.

'Be with you in a while,' the Boss said.

'*Holy mackerel, now we are for it,*' squeaked Inner Voice. '*Things are going further downhill.*' But the artist was flattered the Boss was paying him attention, and modified his initial reaction.

'Now Gabriel, let me see your report,' the Boss demanded.

Archangel Gabriel handed him the bundle of documents upon which he had been scribbling.

'*Gabriel! God has dropped the Archangel part,*' squeaked Inner Voice excitedly.

'Let me see,' said the Boss, perusing the documents. 'Hmm... dear me... not looking... hmm...' and each time his voice trailed off at the point of vital information.

They looked in the direction of the artist.

'Have you had any trouble with him?'

'Quiet as a lamb. Insists I'm Archangel Gabriel – who am I to disabuse him of such delusions? Otherwise in the feeble amygdala stage, much reminiscing. Related a complex story regarding climbing into his painting and becoming trapped in it. Following the course of proven therapy I avoided discussing it. Trapped in his painting, would you believe? That's a new one.'

Both burst into suppressed giggles, the Boss squirming to manage his features in order to maintain the look of authority.

'Trapped in his painting, eh?' – more snuffles – 'please, no more like that, Gabe. Perhaps you should have pursued it further.'

'*Gabe?*' exploded Inner Voice. '*He thinks we call him Archangel, now God calls him Gabe!*'

'Sorry, sir.'

'Have you administered the fractal therapy?'

'Not as such. I have discussed your set and fractals with the patient, but his grasp is tenuous at best. Got very excited about its mathematical beauty. I ask you, mathematical beauty. See what we are up against? His mind inverts and blocks the process, probable neuro-synaesthetic collaboration, enhanced by immature colour-hearing that has never been positively addressed. Very akin to the Beelenfeld syndrome.'

'*The Beelenfeld syndrome? What is that? And why are they talking in this nonsensical terminology? It's more like a hospital than a little shop in Heaven,*' said a bewildered Inner Voice.

'I felt the physical therapy would produce a better response, so subjected him to the cold room, as per guidelines. But unfortunately the patient returned convinced he had been inside one of his oil paintings of a blizzard and had met its characters – a painting he was working on in his studio at the time of the incident. The physical therapy was a complete waste of time, except it elicited a deal of pleading from the patient for no repetition of it. The usual response.'

'I see.'

'I look forward to your administering the algorithmic therapy, sir.'

'Yes, it will have to be. Incidentally, I met the patient's father outside – what a character! Yet his son is as quiet as a lamb, you say. Talk about renting a storm to clear out the debris. Let loose for five minutes he would clear Swansea! Little wonder the patient is in here. With a father like that I wouldn't be at all surprised if his whole family were institutionalised. We would do society a favour by subjecting him to the full-frontal algorithmic therapy instead.'

'That bad, huh?'

'Worse. I will leave you to deal with him if he comes in.'

'Thank you very much, sir,' Archangel Gabriel said.

By now the artist was convinced he was quite confused. *'What are they talking about? Father? Renting a storm?'* Inner Voice asked. *'Swansea? I thought this was heaven. So many questions arising.'*

Suddenly, beyond the beyond happened. A door at the rear of Heaven's Gate opened, which the artist had previously failed to notice, probably due to the hubbub in his mind. In walked a beautiful blonde angel dressed in white. She was obviously a novice angel for her wings were still only buds on the scapulae beneath her whiteness, as if she were a magnificent Cabbage White about to be adorned. The little bumps became her and the artist could but stare.

'Sorry to interrupt, but Mr Pugh says he cannot wait any more and wishes to see his son now. He is becoming quite agitated,' she announced in a timid bleat.

'Mr Pugh? What in heaven's name is going on?' demanded an exasperated Inner Voice. The artist was plunged yet deeper into confusion. He could not remove his stare from the beautiful angel; inexplicably she was familiar to him, although their histories could not have overlapped from the relative perspectives of Heaven's Gate or Troed-yr-Henrhiw, certainly not in the artist's current state of entrapment. Her unexpected appearance in Heaven's Gate at once delighted, at twice bewitched him.

The artist recalled her name as Lois, and he fell to wondering what was she doing in his painting.

Lois wore her usual semi-detached look that she had perfected to a fine art, coyly glancing here and there for a mirror. Having been forewarned in a way unknown to the artist she effected a mere momentary recognition of him. To avoid eye contact she affected an intense interest in the floor. Truth was neither the artist nor Lois wished to be acknowledged by the other, although the former continued his imbecilic stare unabashed. What was she doing in Heaven's Gate and, more importantly, what was she doing in his painting?

'Thank you, Lois,' said the Boss, giving her a distinct wink.

'*A wink! Did you see that? God winked at her! What's becoming of heaven?*' Inner Voice gasped.

The artist was indeed taken aback. This was impossible to believe! The Boss would not, would never, wink at an angel. Probably the artist imagined it, and he sought other mitigating excuses, such as God's mind being preoccupied with something going awry in Andromeda or even further afield. The artist minded incongruously that distance and time did not exist for God, so it was immaterial where the subject of his preoccupation lay. But this was the Boss and Andromeda going awry would never enter the agenda of his theorems. Confusion abounded.

Alternatively, perhaps the Boss was testing Lois's readiness for the sprouting of wings. Unfortunately for the artist the horror of entrapment in his painting, the events at Heaven's Gate, the incomprehensible Mandelbrot set and the Boss winking at Lois all contributed to a general confusion far beyond his ability to cope. The artist prudently effected an ostrich strategy by dismissing his memory. But the strategy did not hold up.

'Thank you, Lois. Tell Mr Pugh he may join us shortly,' said the Boss, winking again.

At the sight of the Boss winking and the sound of Lois's name, Archangel Gabriel, who had had his back to her, swivelled round to face the new entrant. On recognising Angel Lois, his grumpy old face lit up.

'Ah, Lois, before you go – you remember those returns for ward visits and new admissions I needed by yesterday?' said Archangel Gabriel, smiling.

Angel Lois did not reply, but nodded sheepishly.

'I have not yet received them. Could you look smart and chase them up for me?' he asked, very administratively.

'Yes,' she bleated.

'Good, thank you, Lois. You deserve a reward. In fact, when I receive those returns I shall personally reward you,' he said, also winking at her as she turned to leave.

With her face bathed in a lascivious smile superimposed by a brushstroke of blush, Lois left and closed the door, but not before casting the artist one last little glance. Archangel Gabriel leaned towards the Boss and sniggered something surprisingly like: 'Poor thing, brain not in the right place, hidden somewhere between her beautiful thighs.' But this was obviously not what the archangel had said, as he was spiritually programmed not to even dream such carnal profanities, the celestial authorities having lobotomised that department of his brain in the very beginning. Proof was his determined denial that God's greatest invention was a beautiful woman.

'*Did you hear that?*' At all these unexpected developments Inner Voice began taking leave of its senses. '*Did you hear that? Did you hear that? Did you…?*'

The artist did most certainly hear something sounding atrociously like that and was attempting to adjust to a proper version that he should have heard, when to his horror the Boss whispered his reply to Archangel Gabriel: 'Well at least we cannot deny she uses her brain a good deal, and very efficiently too, so I hear' – at which they were both convulsed in spasms of inappropriate giggling. The Boss wiped away a tear of mirth with the back of his hand, and Archangel Gabriel snuffled in a handkerchief before blowing his nose into it.

'Oh dear, enough of all this, Gabe, all too much for us at our age!' – and they giggled yet more.

Meanwhile, the artist refused to believe what he was experiencing, and assumed it to be one of those time-warp phase conjunction scintillation things again, especially as the Boss and Archangel Gabriel were referring to Lois, with whom he alone believed he had discovered the pleasures of duplicity. Heaven's Gate was proving to be a Pandora's box sprung from many tubes of oil paint, and the artist had hopelessly lost his grip on the brush. He could but look up at the magnificent Mandelbrot ceiling and ponder.

'Do you like the ceiling, Ieuan?' Archangel Gabriel and the Boss were standing over him. Deep in daydreams Ieuan had not noticed their arrival at his bed.

'This is Mr Mandelbrot, Consultant Neurophysiologist, who is here to have a talk with you.'

'Mr Mandelbrot? Of the ceiling Mandelbrot?' Inner Voice asked.

'Hello again, Ieuan. Dr Archer tells me you have been as quiet as a lamb but that you are a little disoriented. He says you are enjoying a uniquely interesting relationship with your painting. Could you tell me about it?'

'Are you Mr Mandelbrot?'

'Yes, I'm the Consultant Neurophysiologist.'

'Dr Archer? He told me he was Archangel Gabriel,' said Ieuan with a hint of accusation.

'No, Ieuan. I told you my name was Gabriel Archer,' said Dr Archer, smiling, 'but it could have sounded like Archangel Gabriel to you.'

Ieuan was hardly listening. Among the clatter of revelations his Inner Voice was chattering indiscernibly about hocus-pocus, God reneging severally on agreements...

'Was that Angel Lois who came in just now?'

The two neuro-specialists burst into laughter. 'Well, she might think she is an angel, but Lois is a trainee nurse here. Where did you get that idea from? Wait until I tell her you think she is an angel, she will be all over you.'

Ieuan missed the point.

'Is it my father she was referring to?'

'Yes, he has travelled down from Aberystwyth to see you. Quite a character, your father. You must be very proud of him,' said Consultant Mandelbrot, testing.

'Down from Aberystwyth? In my painting? Archangel – I mean Dr Archer said this was Heaven and I had died. Besides, I'm in my painting. Where do you think I am?'

Consultant Mandelbrot cast Dr Archer a quick glance.

'Inverted contra therapy in conjunction with methyldimethyloxamine,' said Dr Archer to the consultant and, turning to Ieuan: 'You are in St Elmo's Hospital here in Swansea, Ieuan. You are safe here, so stop worrying about your predicament.'

'St Elmo's Hospital?'

'Yes, in Sketty.'

'What am I doing in hospital?'

'You have suffered a little setback, Ieuan, but we will soon put you right,' said Dr Archer.

'What sort of setback? Does it involve my painting?'

'In a way, yes, but in many other ways, no,' said Consultant Mandelbrot.

'What about the arcade and the Mandelbrot ceiling and the experience I had in the blizzard. They are real.'

'Sure, they are real. But some are more real than others. The Mandelbrot apparatus is real, the room you are in is real—'

'It said Heaven's Gate above the door,' Ieuan interrupted, 'and that was in the arcade, which is in my painting.'

'Some objects you observe maintain their original form due to their failure to stimulate associations of other experiences. Other objects are real but may be superimposed by your imagination. Remember, your imagination is fuelled by your memories. The superimposing memories can often obliterate the original object, as with this consultancy laboratory being perceived as Heaven's Gate, which in itself stimulated connotations of a biblical nature. Bear in mind, Ieuan, the experience you were most involved in during the past two or three months is your painting – so it is quite natural that most environments you experience will trigger one memory or another of that painting; so strong as it happens that you believe you are trapped inside it,' Consultant Mandelbrot said.

'If my imagination says I am trapped in my painting and I discover you are in it as well, why are you not concerned about the entrapment?'

'Because we are not trapped in your painting.'

'If I believe you are, you must be,' Ieuan obstinately insisted.

'Yes, Ieuan, we have a long way to go,' the consultant sighed.

'One minute I am trapped in my painting, the next I am in St

Elmo's Hospital. It is difficult to believe. I am very confused. Help me escape from my painting and everything will be OK.'

'Yes, methyldimethyloxamine of course,' replied Consultant Mandelbrot in lowered tones, taking Dr Archer aside. 'Any assessable effect?'

'Excitability suppression fairly rapid, but fixation consolidated.'

'Unusual. We will have to tackle the fixation before anything,' whispered Consultant Mandelbrot. 'Obsessive persecution... escape determination... release entrapment only to reintroduce persecution. Meanwhile' – he turned to Ieuan and spoke in a firmer voice – 'we have Mr Pugh to deal with. Your father has come down from Aberystwyth and wishes to see you.'

'Well, I don't wish him to see me here. How the devil did Aberystwyth get into it? My father is dead and long since gone to heaven. Let me escape from my painting first, then I'll see him.' Ieuan was talking gibberish. 'He won't understand or worse, he'll refuse to understand my entrapment. Will only blame me, as usual. Oh, my G—' Ieuan hesitated, double-checked that Consultant Mandelbrot was real, and proceeded with caution: 'Oh, my God! What a muddle.'

The consultant turned to Dr Archer on one side. 'Copybook case for the Mandelbrot Solution.'

'We have no option, sir,' replied Dr Archer enthusiastically.

'We will need to keep his father occupied for another half an hour. Ask Lois to take him to the restaurant and pour her charm down his throat and a coffee over him. That should keep him bemused the while. Next, we need to bolster the patient's confidence. Administer placebo X, simultaneously advising the miraculous effect the magic pill will have on – let me see – on helping him out of his painting.

'What about the methyldimethyloxamine compatibility, sir?'

'Works in accord with the Solution; ref my paper on the Saint Cross case.'

'Oh, of course. But Saint Cross had infantile delusions – believed his mistake was someone else's responsibility. Surely that case was different?'

'Vastly different, especially in personality and malintent. Saint

Cross was much more simple in all departments. This one's very complex, but the malady has a broad similarity: Saint Cross trapped in infancy with veneers of adulthood, this one trapped in his painting with veneers of logic,' replied Mr Mandelbrot.

'With respect, sir, I would beware assuming it to be just a veneer of logic.'

'Yes, you are right. Cannot be too careful with this form of complexity.'

'I agree this one is very complex,' said Dr Archer. 'You can see from my notes, I got nowhere. Nearly tied my reasoning in knots at times, his intelligence residing in an obtuse department of no avail to himself, science or society.'

'All the more reason we should apply my Solution.'

Dr Archer proceeded to administer placebo X to Ieuan, the while praising its propensities for expediting patients from predicaments of their own making, after which he disappeared in search of Student Nurse Lois.

Meanwhile, Consultant Mandelbrot organised a complicated set of electrodes and wired-up gadgets that were completely beyond Ieuan's comprehension. Indeed, the quizzical frown on Mandelbrot's face denoted a dubious level of comprehension by its originator. Ieuan gave up attempting to engage the thinking process, as he believed for a while medicine X was beginning to induce its relaxing effect. But soon he began doubting its efficacy and began to suspect the intent of the medicals.

'What is the function of all this paraphernalia and gadgetry?' he asked of Mandelbrot.

'They will record your brain patterns when you experience the Mandelbrot ceiling at close quarters. As your intelligence resides in an obtuse consciousness hitherto unmapped by electroencephalograms the exercise will be beneficial to neuro science and, through subsequent determinations, you. Upon experiencing the Mandelbrot solution no outward reactions of notable consequence will be manifest. The inner concatenations of your cerebral processes will however reflect the complex self-similarity of the fractal, effecting significant change to your mentality. Do you understand?'

'No, not a bit of it.'

'Good. Are you feeling drowsy?'

'No, not a bit.'

'Good.'

'Do I take it Angel Lois is to look after my father?' Ieuan enquired.

'Yes, Student Nurse Lois is to look after your father.'

'Ironic. My father will probably look after her.'

'Hopefully.'

Dr Archer returned muttering sullen oaths regarding recalcitrant Welshmen from Aberystwyth, their outlandishly argumentative behaviour, that he hadn't realised his contract included soothing the unsoothable and various other forget-me-nots, when he was interrupted by Consultant Mandelbrot.

'I should have warned you – took all my skill,' he remarked, still busy with the electrodes. 'Pass the monitor brace, please.'

'Doesn't seem drowsy in the least to me,' said Dr Archer, glowering at Ieuan.

'No, not a bit drowsy,' Mandelbrot replied. 'Impositional determinations.'

'Well, this should be entertaining, if nothing else,' said Dr Archer, obviously nursing a compound fracture of his pride following confrontation with the patient's father.

'Come along then, Ieuan. All we need you to do is take the lift up to the next floor where you will experience the Mandelbrot ceiling at first hand. Nothing to be concerned about, we will be with you all the way. Just don't tangle any of the trailing wires in the light show. Mind the step.'

'Looks more like Troed-yr-Henrhiw than a lift,' responded Ieuan.

'Good. Keep going.'

'Odd the placebo failed when he's so biddable in every other department,' muttered Archer.

The malady was akin to one of those meandering nightmares induced by fever. It was all too familiar. The cause as elusive as the cure, a blatant cunning where the fever takes over the levers of the mind, pulling there and pushing here, coercing a conviction that the mind is controlling the nightmare and all that needs to be done is to count backwards from infinity while head-standing in a bathtub half-full of warm linseed oil. Paradoxically, the cure added to the cause: the more Ieuan strove, the more discomfort he felt. Life's self-prescribed medicine exacerbated his condition by the second; each lift, each visitor, each consultant, each Heaven's Gate. It was unrelenting torture. Little wonder people handed over their ghosts without a by-your-leave for the life that had possessed them, reasoned the scattered remnants of Inner Voice. Ieuan shuddered violently.

'Feeling cold, Ieuan?'

He trembled a sweating nod. This was all too familiar. The demons in charge of the memory department took him back to the age of four when he was suffering a fever of particular note. His young mind had flown the scene in terror, leaving an unreliable brain to cope alone.

'One day you will regret deserting me,' it threatened.

It appears that that day had at last arrived in Heaven's Gate. But the ploy of fleeing the scene, borne of intuition rather than calculated expediency, had worked so well for his mind in the intervening period that it resorted to the antic on the most meagre of excuses. On this occasion the demons persisted in resuscitating the threat. Heaven's Gate expanded colossally, assuming *The Endless March* landscape with bleak snow-covered moors, where the leaden ceiling touched the stars. The shuddering assumed yet more violent proportions.

'Put another dressing gown over him – careful with the wires.' Mandelbrot's voice sounded distant, in another room.

'Can't figure out why he's shaking so violently' – Archer's voice, also in the other room.

'The Solution taking effect... past overwhelming... this is it...' voices became indiscernible to Ieuan as sounds merged with the tune of his nightmare as a life-sized four-engined Second World War bomber filled the skies of his bedroom, buzzing round in tight circles, lining up its target to bomb. Ieuan squirmed on his sweaty little pillow, which undulated on a heaving sea of woollen grass and blankets and the flotsam of yesterday's breakfast discarded hastily at the whim of nausea. His controlling subconscious heard Father and Uncle Maldwyn urgently radioing the pilot that the war was over and for God's sake don't start another world war, over. The bomber pilot radioed back a static-loaded message in a language Ieuan did not understand. One of the flowers on the wallpaper acted as translator, 'Freebooting, India-Papa – have target in sights, going for jugular, world war or not. Whole exercise will make the patient feel a lot worse, over and out' the petals prattled.

The bomber persisted in buzzing round and round ominously as Ieuan took over the radioing for help. Fortunately Mother heard the distress signals and entered the room.

This was good news; help had arrived. But alarmingly, as his attention had been occupied fighting the gremlins, she had grown to fit the immense proportions of the landscape.

'What is the matter? To whom are you talking?' she enquired in a booming voice.

'Bomber going to drop its bombs on me and I feel sick like the cat's dinner and I've got a headache and my back aches and my legs ache and my eyes hurt and why are you so big and I feel sick as the cat and why don't you stop that bomber thing?'

'There, there,' Mother boomed, and swatted the bomber down.

As soon as Mother had left the room however the confounded thing took off again and resumed its buzzing in threatening circles. Ieuan's controlling subconscious was obviously delighting in the hallucinations for the bombing runs mounted in fierceness. The demons delivered yet more harrowing images of future improbables, and once again Ieuan sent out distress signals, but to no avail. For the next three weeks he sent out calls for help, one for every wobbling star in the Mandelbrot ceiling, until he was overcome by nausea. He could take it no more and reacted by vomiting over the pillow and duvet and wires and electrodes and the floor. Consultant Mandelbrot came running in and, in a dreadfully miserable state, Ieuan complained that the pilot had ignored his messages that the war was over.

Mandelbrot swatted the offending bomber down amidst great pyrotechnics in the ceiling, after which Ieuan fell into a deep sleep. An engine far greater than the universe had been in operation, its mysterious elusiveness making the invisible neutrino a colourful crackerjack in comparison. What purpose it served in combating the fever is part of the mystery of *The Endless March*.

Ieuan awoke in another room letting two views of a different scene. He was alone. Consultant Mandelbrot and Dr Archer had gone; so had the wires and the fever. The Mandelbrot ceiling played hide and seek elsewhere for the ceiling of this room had been covered over. All signs of Heaven's Gate had disappeared. A door stood ajar at the far end, beyond which a courtyard and scullery familiar to him were partly visible. He arose and made his way through the door, finding himself at the rear of Troed-yr-Henrhiw. His heart raced at recognition of home.

The old grey stonework of the farmhouse, the overhanging trees and shade from the canopy of foliage, were a familiar sight. The little stone-walled vegetable garden was as before; nothing was any different. The water butt stood as solid as ever and the water level was where he had left it. His cat was sleeping in her usual place and ignored his familiarity. His clutch of hens in their run cooed their lazy, late-morning chitter; one informed Ieuan with her clucking that she had performed a miraculous feat by delivering an egg. The breeze through the foliage repeated its familiar, faded Saturday afternoon message. Beyond the oak trees the waterfall as ever sang its dancing game. Troed-yr-Henrhiw sat in God's little acre and everything appeared as before.

Ieuan hurried across the cobbled yard, through the back door and into the house, his footsteps ringing reassuringly on the familiar stone floor. He rushed with great excitement into the studio, ducking his head as usual to avoid the familiar low beams.

Angharad was standing near the studio chaise longue where he had left her sitting moments before. She was agitated and had been crying. She leapt at him with joy and flung her arms around him.

'Thank God you are all right,' she cried, 'it must have been a dream.'

'Sweetheart, what is it? Yes, I'm all right now, but you wouldn't believe!' he said.

He hugged her. It was heaven to see her and to hear her voice.

'You've been crying,' he observed. 'What's the matter?'

Not waiting for a reply, he glanced excitedly around the studio, at his painting, ran to the front window, drank in the view of the Rheidol valley. Then, returning to Angharad, he hugged her again. She was shaking.

'It's been awful, Ieuan,' she said. 'Where have you been so long? That painting is weird,' she added, pointing at *The Endless March*.

He stared at his painting. *The Endless March* was as before. Women, children and men bent against a driving blizzard being beaten on by armed guards. To the right, several figures and two horses lay dead in the driven snow.

'I'll have to destroy it. It's worse than weird, it's evil. In future I'm going to change the theme of my paintings to beautiful mathematical fractals. No more subjecting these poor victims to needless horror. Why have you been crying, sweetheart?'

'Destroy it, Ieuan, destroy it now.' Angharad had urgency in her voice. 'Your animation went too clever. I agree there is something evil about it. Very frightening.'

He held her and kissed her. 'Thank God you are real. Real, soft and warm. And you smell human, thank God.'

'Just a few moments ago,' said Angharad, pensively, 'something dreadful happened in that painting.'

'You wouldn't believe me if I told you,' Ieuan repeated.

'I know,' said Angharad, 'let me tell you. I know.'

Ieuan always indulged Angharad, but truly wished to give vent to his amazing experiences and, ignoring her tension launched into a tirade of disjointed explanations.

'After I climbed into my painting – this part you know – I became trapped in it, and the painting invited me down into an arcade and all the painted characters – you wouldn't believe – were walking about unfinished, headless people, even a leg walking past and everybody clothed in oil paint garments and—'

'Stop!' cried Angharad.

'—and there was an old Victorian staircase beneath which was tucked a little shop called Heaven's Gate—'

'STOP!' she screamed.

He stopped. She was crying again.

'What? What is it, sweetheart? Don't you want to hear about my adventures? Tell me what is on your mind.'

'I know your adventures. I saw them all in your painting.'

'WHAT?'

'I saw them in *The Endless March*. At first I thought it was some clever animation or back projection you had set up. So I looked around for the video. Nothing. The painting had come to life. I saw you being struck by the guard and alternately pushed into line, pushed out of line and then being shot by the guard. It was horrible.'

'What, shot dead by the guard? How do you know all this?'

'I SAW it happen! You lay in the snow, blood was coming from your head pouring into the snow. All the others shuffled on into the blizzard...'

'No, Archangel Gabriel saved me just before I was shot. He dragged me back into Heaven's Gate, I promise. How do you know all this?'

'You are not listening to me. I saw it happening in your painting.'

'Oh no.'

'I saw it all happening,' she repeated.

'Oh... no...'

'After you were shot, you lay dead in the snow,' she sobbed. 'Then, some of the peasants came right up to the front of the painting, large, looking at me, AT ME! Pressed against the front, they were mouthing, "Help us, help us." '

The Virtual School of Art Affair

'Something very odd about the building this morning,' said Johannes. 'Two main entrances again.'

'Two again,' confirmed his friend Rees.

'Real door not where it should be, did you notice?'

'Yes, found the right one second shot, walked into a door wall first time – whole building is bodily displaced, according to the avenue of limes.'

'Could be this time the limes are displaced,' suggested Johannes.

'No, no, otherwise the world would be displaced,' replied Rees. 'It's all relative of course, but the building is held in coordinates, nothing affected beyond the footprint.'

'Did you notice quanglement has tampered with our sign? The word "Virtual" has disappeared. We've reverted to our original centuries ago, except the "Swansea" hasn't come back.'

'Crikey, no! I didn't notice. What's in its place?'

'Nothing! We are simply blank School of Art. Virtual School of Art has disappeared, so to speak! Strange, really.'

'Very odd, almost as if entanglement is sentient and motivated,' muttered Rees.

'With a sinister eye on history,' added Johannes. 'Bet you didn't notice the grand staircase is wandering all over the place.'

'Didn't notice that either, came up by lift.'

'I guessed so,' said Johannes. 'The day Rees Bowen climbs the stairs God will stop unblocking those drains east of Andromeda, and nip over to watch the spectacle! Anyway, I must have climbed four storeys to get to the first floor.'

'God is on my side. Even when unblocking drains he still has time to watch over me – gave me the tip-off not to bother with the stairs this morning,' Rees quipped.

'God notwithstanding, nothing we can't handle at Virtual Download Centre,' Johannes said reassuringly.

Early birds Johannes Taliesin and Rees Bowen arrived every morning ahead of their colleagues. As usual a few numb virtuals were left parading up and down the building overnight, so accepted as part of the fabric that few acknowledged their presence. After a while, others began arriving.

'Hi Rees! Hi Yo-yo!' called a colleague.

'Morning,' the duo chimed.

'Did you notice we've got two main entrances again? I blame you two and your parallel virtuality research at Virtual Download Centre.'

'If you like.' Rees and Johannes turned their backs; it was too early in the morning to start protesting that their line of research was innocent of the quanglement problems that beset Virtual School of Art.

'What about all these old-fashioned virtual downloads wandering around with manual sketch pads and folios?' Johannes asked with an askance smile.

'Anyone would think we were a School of Art,' said Rees, catching on.

'Living up to the quantum entanglement adjustment! How quickly these downloads adjust,' quipped Johannes, and they burst into knowing laughter.

'Fortunately they are annihilated, otherwise we would be in deep trouble – overrun with art students of all things cluttering up our studio-labs, if Fermilab hadn't hit on the half-life footprint intersect limit,' Rees said.

'Ugh! Perish the thought! That would be worse than quanglement overspill. Only thing I regret is that some of these beautiful virtual girls from Swansea School of Art of yore are not real,' the ever-lecherous Johannes complained. 'Whose research is at fault this time, do you suppose?'

'Could be this iLupus-Planck lot preparing for the seminars,' Rees suggested.

'Could well be. Regardless, I'm looking forward to seeing their experimental seminars. Are you going along?'

'Oh, sure,' Rees replied, 'wouldn't miss them for a world of download.'

'Time do they start?'

'Ten.'

'In the meantime,' Rees continued, 'I've charged up a new board for you. I had to use your old one last night to alleviate the parallel interference when operating my latest Messalina download. Nearly got out of my depth last night!'

'Thank God Taliesin's board came to the rescue.' Johannes shook his head and smiled.

'True, it came in handy. But the new one is fully charged – your old one had .04 only.'

'Thanks for the thought, but I had set it at .04 in readiness for my Samuel Palmer downloads.'

'Honestly, Johannes Taliesin, you are a serial forger! I've done you a good turn, saved you from your criminal tendencies as well as the Duplication Police,' Rees said.

'Roll of drums... presenting the fortunate Rees Bowen,' Johannes responded with a flamboyant swish of the arm. 'His daddy pours the necessary into his Card Safe, no questions asked. Whereas on the other hand... another roll of drums... the impecunious Taliesin' – he continued the theatricals by enacting a grovelling limp across the vestibule – 'has to scrounge his wretched euros wherever he can, even if it means downloading Samuel Palmer forgeries.' They laughed as passers-by applauded mockingly. 'Beside all that, Rees,' Johannes continued confidentially, 'Messalina was a serial poisoner.'

'This is true,' admitted the contrite Rees. 'I was in peril for a time as her uncontrollable propensity for poisoning people insisted on downloading with her. But one has to tolerate the triviality of poisoning if one's greater goal is her licentious behaviour!'

They laughed heartily.

'But Professor Wheeler warned you,' said Johannes, returning to the chiding. 'Poisoning is part of the Messalina download. You seem obsessed with her. One day the bitch will succeed in poisoning you.'

'I'll watch my step.'

'It could already be too late. We still don't fully understand the properties of these new V-tray three-dimensional virtualisers. I saw coordinates for the Queen of Sheba on your board last week. Why don't you download her?'

'I did.'

'And?'

'Messalina poisoned her,' Rees laughed, as if tampering with history did not matter.

The two set off for Corridor Escher. Many fellow students and their current virtuals were milling about. Edvard Munch and one of his models passed by, looking lost; Anselm Adams was accompanied by a gaggle of enthusiastic students poring over his perfectly preserved antique SLR film process Leica; Damien Hirst was as jocular as he was all that time ago. Many images were muddled, as the students had been sloppy in fixing the coordinates; nothing changes.

'Do you know, I still can't see the point of all these downloads,' Johannes said suddenly, 'what have they produced? Technological wizardry apart, nothing! They have failed to produce one jot more than their living state achievements, which goes to prove they are nothing more than illusions.'

'What about the marvel at the phenomenon of them being retrieved from history?' Rees countered.

'Once the novelty wears off, what next? They may appear to have the bodily functions of normals, but that is also an illusion, in my view. The new technology is being used as sloppily as oil paint was in the twentieth century.'

'Yes, I agree,' said Rees, 'that silly Lois from Virtual Painting Special sniffs that when she sleeps with her Modigliani download, she achieves a level of sexual gratification none of us chaps ever succeeded in giving her.'

'I don't believe that,' scoffed Johannes, tossing his head.

'I don't either. Her boyfriend says she masturbates at the same time as he is making love to her and thinks of Modigliani instead of him,' Rees said mockingly.

'I don't think I could tolerate that, but first let me have the opportunity with Lois to test my intolerance!' Johannes joked.

'So much for Lois and her illusory sex life – nothing but ostentatious swankery. Next thing we will have girls claiming to be pregnant by their downloads,' Rees said.

'Virtual birth.'

'Hmm, impossible,' replied Rees, 'but if they cannot get pregnant, perhaps I cannot be poisoned by Messalina – sauce for the goose and all that.'

'There is no logic in your argument,' Johannes said flatly.

'Look at those two over there,' said Rees, pointing at a Tracey Emin download and her student escort. 'Don't know which is more attractive, virtual Tracey or her living lookalike.'

'The living lookalike is Anne Joslin from Virtual Fashion. Wonder what she wants with Tracey Emin? Anyway, prefer Anne any day to Tracey Emin, as famous as she became.'

'Hello Johannes, you back?' someone called.

'No,' he replied informatively, virtual absence or presence inconclusive.

'Back?' asked Rees. 'Where have you been?'

'Obviously not here according to their mind,' Johannes replied.

During periods of high-energy experiment in the studio-labs, quanglement configured with the unique geometry of the building's main corridor giving an illusion of endlessness. Assuming the fabric of permanence, the phenomenon stubbornly refused to be erased. Although the students light-heartedly nicknamed it Corridor Escher, its phenomenon was a constant source of discussion.

'Interesting no one has succeeded in downloading MC Escher,' Johannes wondered aloud.

'You would think our army of Chinese consultants should have solved the corridor enigma by now,' Rees added, 'but the Germans gave up, and that's saying something.'

'Perhaps we are overlooking the obvious – that it has nothing to do with the corridor, much nearer home, as it were.' Johannes had posited the recurrent topic of conversation.

'Yes, I'm beginning to believe the illusion is all in our minds.'

'Could be. Why should Escher prove so elusive?'

Whenever virtual downloads proceeded beyond the corridor's event screen they walked out of the wave-function zone, never to return. Even the most powerful V-trays failed to recapture them. Gradually the Old Master bank for downloads diminished, so Virtual School of Art was issued with an advisory warning by the

International Virtual Image Licensing Executive that carelessness could not continue indefinitely.

'Know what I'm thinking?' said Johannes. 'Today, virtual Old Master downloads disappear when they pass through the event screen. At this rate IVILE will have no work. I cannot think of a government organisation allowing themselves to be conditioned out of existence. I read in the library that not a single government organisation had been disbanded in the past 120 years, regardless of their uselessness through the effluxion of time. I'm sure IVILE will come up with a new invention to maintain their existence, mark my words.'

'What is your anti-government agency logic getting at this time, Yo-yo?'

'One day normal people like you and me, straying too far beyond the event screen, will vanish. Then IVILE will license the demise of ordinary humans, you watch.'

'Steady on with the normal people like you and me bit, Mr Taliesin. You are certainly not normal, so you have two reasons to avoid straying beyond the event screen!'

'Thanks, pal.'

The architrave between the vestibule and Corridor Escher possessed an architectural quality of benign Victorian endurance. Behind the fluted sgraffito columns, an electronic entanglement connected powerful computers whose constant hum was their only evidence. Otherwise the antique planes exhibited a prevailing mediocrity. Virtual School of Art's function was to educate in the finesse and methodologies of three-dimensional downloading of classical artists and artefacts from deep history.

As history had been replaced at the pre-university level by phasing focus-group constructions, a major component of instruction was the eradication of the years of indoctrination by calling down virtual imagery from the various layers of human memory. Reading had also been phased out and the VSofA's current enrolments were third-generation screen iconographers. Only a few dedicated readers of written language still enjoyed the subject, although most students were obliged to learn the ancient scripts in order to attach detail to their claim, grievance and complaint site-forms.

By and large, students enjoyed the unique non-creative nature of the Institution and, although the technology was still a hit-and-miss affair due to quanglement interference, success brought the School good publicity and, most importantly, money.

'Have you completed your report-site for Professor Price?' asked Rees.

'Not quite. It's not needed until Friday – work on it tonight.'

'I don't know, since we won the research scholarships all we seem to do is fill in monitoring forms and stuff like that,' Rees complained.

'Yes, stuff like reports for the sponsors, reports for Price, reports for the Quality Control Agency, reports for Health and Safety,' agreed Johannes.

'Yes, that sort of stuff.'

'On the other hand, at least we can operate *ultra vires* to the rest of our colleagues in Virtual Download Centre,' said Johannes optimistically.

'I agree. We have privileged access to the latest technology,' said Rees, 'which enables us to research the most confounding problems, like me downloading Messalina and you producing forgeries. By the way, where do you sell them?'

'Airport fringe markets. They've mushroomed since the street gangs have won control of airport security.'

'They let you?' asked Rees, surprised.

'Backhanders and the occasional forgery.'

'Honestly, Johannes, you'll come awfully unstuck one of these days. Don't expect me to bail you out, if you are alive to be bailed out that is.'

Johannes's impoverished background obliged such activities. Since enrolling at VSofA he had cultivated an instinct for survival beyond his meagre needs. A lone wolf devoid of means but possessing a sharp and compulsive mentality, Johannes constantly fought back his innate trust of human nature. On the other hand, Rees demonstrated a more measured intelligence born of solid private education and secure background. He was gregarious and good-natured, and approached life in a confident manner. While Johannes buried his lack of confidence behind gestures of flamboyance and verbal aggression, Rees demonstrated his bourgeois orthodoxies with confidence and ease. As with all societies utilising flexible values as tools of management, VSofA staff identified Johannes as the gremlin in the works, and kept a wary eye open for his compulsive and nefarious activities. Both Johannes and Rees sought the big breakthrough in their parallel virtuality research; Rees for the fame it would deliver, Johannes the money.

The two walked through the architrave into Corridor Escher. The corridor doubled as a treffpunkt and freeway to all departments, to major lecture theatres, studio-laboratories; it was a buzzing platform of activity. Recent downloads were being conducted to the seminars, while others were hailing lost friends. George Stubbs carried a dead horse past the throng.

'Way, make way for George Stubbs, please!'

'God, that thing stinks.'

'What do you expect? It's been dead for hundreds of years.'

The novice at the V-tray had clumsily snatched George Stubbs in the act of carrying the rotting dead horse upstairs to his studio for anatomical analysis. Big error.

A temporary computer-printed sign on flimsy paper was blu tacked to the bulwark: 'Beware and Achtung! You Are Entering Virtual Corridor Escher.'

'I like that,' said Johannes, 'Virtual Escher. Poor old MC's getting the treatment now.'

'Beware his neverendings. Except Escher was Belgian, and the neverendings were invented by Penrose,' responded Rees.

'What's that to do with it?'

'Achtung is German,' said Rees flatly, avoiding the Penrose mathematics.

'Yes, but what's that to do with it?'

Far above, the high arch carried faded graffiti. 'Roy cant spel' was from an age of reality long ago, an inscription that had remained due to institutional penny-pinching together with its inaccessibility. More recently another message had been added beneath it in minuscule four-point lettering: 'Beware! Quanglement Research! Those of virtual nervous temperament should not proceed beyond this point' – too small for anyone claiming normal senses to read.

'That's new, the smudge, under Roy.'

'Odd, hadn't noticed that before. Who managed to put that there?'

Thinking no more of it, they walked past a studio door that had hitherto been familiar to them. The seminar organisers had painted the door a different print, or had superimposed a virtual, the cliché of the month at VSofA.

'That's our studio we've just passed,' Rees observed.

'Didn't recognise it,' Johannes replied. 'Changed radically since yesterday evening.'

'Changed out of recognition.'

'Two views of the same door.'

'Two views of a different door. Where is it?' asked Rees.

'That's odd. Must be ours. Let's try it, anyway.'

A small note pinned to the studio door read 'Seminar 3/1: On Art Being Far Weaker Than Necessity. Profbirtwhistle'.

'Could have told you that.'

'Cynic.'

'That's me.'

They entered, and the door closed gently behind them. The room was in darkness.

'The seminar with no light, the old cliché trick,' whispered Rees.

'One would think the old chestnut of seminars in the dark had been roasted enough,' said Johannes.

'Shhh!' someone scolded from the darkness.

'I am an heretic,' Voice said from the dark; how far, how near, no references told.

'I have hijacked some of the more precious sanctimonies of society,' Voice went on, disembodied yet somewhere in the dark, neither male nor female, perhaps not alive, 'and turned them back as emissaries that question the justification rather than justify the question. The question I asked: is it essential or merely desirable? Necessity is more than desirable. Often necessity is essential: if one falls into a swollen river it is essential one climbs out as quickly as possible. Having escaped a horrible death, it is not essential to dry one's clothes immediately, merely desirable. A measure of discomfort will ensue, but at least one is alive.'

A whisper rippled about in the darkness. The darkness cliché still possessed a certain disconcerting currency.

'Often people confuse the merely desirable with essential,' the Stephen Hawking voice-alike beeped on, 'confusing their wants as being more important than their needs.'

'Blimebury,' muttered Rees.

'Disconcertment,' responded Johannes.

'Shhh! SHHH!' chorused the different audience from unseen directions.

'The question is not a new one,' Voice continued in a metallic monotone. 'Aeschylus asked it in relation to art, and considered art to be far weaker than necessity because, of the two, only the force of necessity is irresistible. For your part, dear invisible but somewhat not silent members of the audience, you are financially dependent upon the successful promulgation of art's essentiality, or at least the agreed compliance of silence. Remove a profession's incentives and the profession withers. Seriously, ladies and gentlemen, what are the incentives of art?'

Voice paused. Silence.

'What purpose is served by the lecture being delivered in the dark?' Johannes whispered to his friend. 'It's been proven for decades that after the initial impact the effect is alienation of the audience.'

'An interesting question,' Voice responded, 'I have been waiting for someone to ask the obvious.'

Johannes gave a start.

Another silence followed and seemingly no answer was forthcoming. Johannes was again plunged into thought, as other concerns occupied his limited imagination: for instance, the speed at which the windows of the Antique Studio door had been blackened out, for when it closed behind them it shut out the remnants of light from Corridor Escher. The place was pitch dark, lamp black. Realising they had entered a different studio, erroneously believing it to be theirs because the door to the Antique Studio did not possess a spring-load…

'This is not our studio,' Johannes whispered, a touch of alarm in his voice, when…

'Does it matter if this is not your studio? Does it matter if I am delivering this lecture naked or otherwise?' Voice interrupted. 'If I had not mentioned it you would not have considered the fact. Would turning on the light alter the importance of what I am saying? Is it essential or merely desirable that you know such trivial details? Art is by far weaker than necessity.'

'This bloody Voice hears everything I whisper!' hissed Johannes.

'If you were to apply a desirable-essential assessment template to any of the virtual art colleges of Britain today,' Voice continued, 'you should not be surprised to discover that practically all of them labour under the delusion that both their provision and output are 100 per cent essential.'

Voice paused, waiting for a reaction to the profound solitude of the last sentence. But of course it did not penetrate the mindset certainties of the blacked-out audience who, to the last, accepted that Voice was stating the obvious.

'Essential!' Voice exclaimed, met by murmurs of approbation from the audience, who had long since passed through that elusive zone where assumptions metamorphose to certainty as thick bone grows over the listening department.

'Essential to what criteria I ask? To the criteria of industry and commerce? Is this so? If this is so should not the provision be robust enough to withstand a fair degree of objective analysis? Should not the system strip away protective practices whereby brethren determine the essential-desirable practices of the brotherhood? Whereby the brotherhood determines the outcome of assessments? What a nonsense whereby the system guarantees the perpetuation of practices which no outsider may challenge!' asserted a confident Voice, eliciting a stunned silence from the unseen audience.

'The application of an objective assessment by impartial outsiders is a long overdue exercise. It would reveal that the majority of providers fall into the category of mediocrity.'

'What is this heresy?' someone at last demanded from the dark. 'Provision has been systematically developed over a period of a century or more to reflect the needs and aspirations of industry, commerce and the students!'

'Reflect the needs, my motherboard,' mocked Voice, 'proper

checks and balances have never been applied. When we clandestinely undertook a rigorous analysis we found most provision fell into the category of "desirable", and even that stretched credibility in many cases.'

'Am I hearing this?' the same unseen character roared from the audience.

'It is not the purpose of this seminar to put forward alternatives that would satisfy the "essential" benchmark,' continued Voice, completely ignoring the outburst, 'although we must confess we are very tempted to deviate into that interesting field, if only to satisfy ourselves that the task is a productive one.'

'I'm not taking this any more,' yelled the irate one. 'Put on the light, I wish to see my adversary.'

'Yes,' another unseen added from the dark, 'this is a self-respecting virtual school of art that dynamically fulfils society's needs.'

'My voice synthesiser you are,' taunted Voice.

'Put the lights on, we've heard enough!'

'Yes,' added Johannes impulsively, 'put the lights on, I haven't heard enough!'

'We strongly advise Johannes Taliesin not to act the virtual bigwig behind the mask of darkness,' warned Voice.

'How did you know it was me?' retaliated Johannes.

'We all knew it was you, Johannes Taliesin!' the audience chimed in consort with Voice.

'The reason for this puerile digression is to underline the preposterously unrealistic programs being delivered at virtual art schools,' roared Voice, completely overwhelmed with anger, 'under the pretence of being robust educational preparation for the realities of a cut-throat market where the essential criterion is to sell your commodity or services regardless of their lack of intrinsic quality. Unfortunately, poorly designed commodities proliferate an already detritus-strewn environment where rubbish is competing for street space with heaps of Turner Prize entries queuing at the gates of a temple to delusion. It is impossible to separate virtual rubbish from designed rubbish as long as arts councils and lottery committees continue their profligacy. What a bloody waste of money!'

'Voice swore!' Rees blurted.

Loud booing and protestation from the partisan audience all but drowned Voice. In response Voice turned up its volume.

'Where is your intelligence?' Voice boomed, vibrating the place. 'What hokum blinds your awareness of matters more needy than your mindless production of *objets de refuse* in a social and physical environment already proliferating rubbish? Are there not better things to do with clean money?' Voice boomed on, drowning the booing, 'Obviously, the last remnant of social conscience has departed from your reasoning. More seriously, has the last remnant of social conscience departed from the tax payer?'

'I'm getting out of here,' someone yelled, and a deal of pushing and shoving ensued, followed by, 'if I can find the bloody door. Put on the lights!'

'You will not find the door,' Voice said very loudly, 'until we have delivered our introduction.'

Then, continuing its assault on the profligacy of unrealistic expenditure, Voice began ticking off a list of the country's more disrespected virtual art schools in a noise so loud as to drown all opposition.

'Firstly, top of my list of most disrespected virtual art schools is: School of Art is by far weaker than necessity; second, School of Art is by far weaker than necessity; third, School of Art is by far weaker than necessity; fourth, School of Art—'

'Put on the lights, for God's sake,' came a hysterical voice, 'we've had enough of this heretical nonsense.'

'It's been making sense to me,' Rees muttered.

Slam! The lights went on.

Standing around, the usual students with their downloads blinked and looked about. Picasso was among them with Dali's Gala. Diminutive Toulouse-Lautrec tottered, towered over by his model. Botticelli had been placed there with Prima Vera, wonderful in her naked finery. Zara accompanied her downloaded Augustus John, who was drawing something on her hand. The Laughing Cavalier stood grimacing with disapproval. Hieronymus Bosch had his Ship of Fools on tiny wheels in tow. In a corner stood the scruffiest Mondriaan one ever saw, measuring the right angle of the walls. Damien Hirst devised autogiros in the air as Tracey Emin smiled enigmatically.

Alfred Jarry was the centrepiece of this motley audience, together with his pompous invention Ubu. They were eating excrement from a pisspot with gluttonous zeal. Jarry was yelling, 'Put on the lights! Put on the lights!' long after light had shone, 'put on the lights, I can't see this shit I'm eating.'

'Aha,' said Rees, 'the founder of the art movement, "the science of imaginary solutions" is in our midst. Déjà vu. I wonder why he's talking in English?'

'Because we speak English,' retorted Johannes.

'What are you two talking about?' asked virtual Jarry.

Intermingling with these greats were many ordinary but bemused students.

'There he is!' a stranger yelled, 'Johannes Taliesin. Who let you into such eminent circles? Who's your good-looking friend? Why don't you introduce me?'

'Piss off,' snapped Rees Bowen. 'I'd prefer not to be introduced to dipsticks.'

'Wasn't going to introduce you, anyway,' added Johannes. 'Let's get out of here.'

Scurrying for the door, Rees muttered, 'Of all the rooms to go into in this virtual corridor we had to choose a depository for used virtuals, cherry cakes and loony lookalikes.'

'I read in the library there used to be a screening process at the door of seminars and lectures, in times the article referred to as the good old days,' said Johannes.

'In that case bully for the good old days.'

'Regardless of the audience, the seminar was meaningless to me,' Johannes said as they burst into Corridor Escher. 'Whoever would dare to think we were a waste of money?'

'Good God, Johannes, we *are* a waste of money! That electronic voice contraption in there was talking absolute sense,' said Rees.

'What? Come on, Rees, do you believe that garble?'

'Johannes, whatever made you believe we were the chosen few? Art schools are a bloody waste of money, virtual or otherwise! Voice is right. Jarry eating shit from a pisspot was set up to symbolise the sorry mess art has sunk into.'

'But art has always been a sorry mess, Rees,' Johannes protested.

'Oh, come on, Johannes! That pretends the logic that rubbish tolerated in perpetuity renders it acceptable,' Rees countered. 'For goodness's sake wake up.'

'I hadn't thought about it... too busy thinking about other things... took it for granted we were the chosen few,' replied Johannes, stumbling into new thoughts.

The original corridor possessed a comforting familiarity, an undemanding matter-of-factness that neither threatened nor allayed. Its sameness satisfied.

'Oh, it's you two again,' the corridor said. 'This is me again. Always at your service. Please take me for granted, that is what I'm here for. I cannot be partisan, and I treat everyone unequivocally. You could call me an unequivocal corridor, but I prefer to be known as Corridor Escher, because I go on and on and on and on and on and on and on – ahem, for ever. I am your spiritual nine-o-nine to nowhere. I provide benches at regular intervals for friends to rest awhile during their long journey to nowhere. I am a thin, flat straight line hat, really.'

Rees Bowen shook his head. 'I'm getting strange thoughts after that seminar, are you?'

'I get strange thoughts all the time,' replied Johannes, 'but as this corridor is virtual, it's not here so my thoughts must be there, which means there's nothing to stimulate strange thoughts.'

'What are you talking about, Johannes?'

'I'm thinking about Voice's lesson.'

'I'm glad, but what are you talking about?'

'Where do you think our studio-lab shifted to? This is most disconcerting,' Johannes replied.

'Don't know, except I would say it's more than disconcerting,' said Rees.

'If we cannot find our studio-lab, then presumably no one else can.'

'Now listen here, Taliesin – stop all this silly reasoning. Your theory might be virtually true, but we don't know, do we?'

'So things are only worse than they seem.'

'Taliesin the optimist. Much worse in my opinion,' replied

Rees. 'Let's try another seminar before we leap to any more illogical conclusions. What about this one?'

They stopped outside a door never before seen, which fact only mildly concerned them.

'What does the flimsy bit of blu tacked paper say?'

'It's scrawled in half-uncial script, with overtones of pre-war German Gothic—'

'For God's sake get on with it! I didn't ask what face it is written in. What does it say?' Rees snapped.

'It says: "Quanglement and the Uncertainty Principle: Herr Prof Werner Heisenberg" whatever that lot has to do with quanglement,' announced Johannes, unperturbed by his friend's outburst.

'Heavens, Johannes, didn't they teach you anything other than English at school? The uncertainty principle has everything to do with quanglement.'

'Welsh,' retorted Johannes unheeding. 'It goes on: "A lesson in theoretical uncertainty in relation to the velocity and position of academic staff of Virtual School of Art, their occupational fuzziness, priority entanglement and their ability to hide in two places at the same time".'

'Please tell me you're making that up.'

'That's what it says, no make up. In fact I wish I were able to make up such wondrous phrases: the ability to hide in two places at once, if you please,' said Johannes wistfully, 'they certainly didn't teach me that at school.'

'Here's hoping the message is as sensible as in the last seminar.'

They entered a door that had not been there previously. The room was square.

'This room's square in all directions,' whispered Rees.

'Shhh!' came from the audience.

The wizened speaker on the podium wore white hair, a natty black high-buttoned suit over white shirt, white tie, tall collar up to the chin, if not higher.

'Like Carl Lagerfeld, the high collar hides the join where his new head transplant has been stitched on,' asserted Johannes knowingly.

'SHHH!' came crosser from the audience.

'…have learnt during the past hour before the late entry of Johannes Taliesin and Rees Bowen how mysterious is the behaviour of Virtual School of Art academic staff, with or without spin, and how an administrative formula can be drawn up to cope with their strange behaviour,' said the speaker in clipped tones with a strong German accent. 'The formula describes for us the quantum behaviour of individual staff as isolated entities, but we are all too fully aware of their propensity to entangle with or without provocation, interacting with one another in various ways detrimental to their clients' education regardless of values, indifferent to market trends, contradictory to flow-modules, abusive of social mores, real when they should be virtual, virtual when they should be real, here when they should be there, there when they should be here and indifferent to the institution's teleological predestiny.'

'Can't follow,' whispered Johannes hopelessly. 'You?'

'Quantum school of art, any old fool—'

'SHHH!' again.

'Shhh is getting tiresome!' Johannes said.

Following a clipped pause that dared not take liberties the speaker began his Gothic Glottal afresh.

'Quanglement in staff behaviour is best understood through the path-integral, as mentioned earlier before the late arrival of Rees and his sidekick Johannes, based on a relativistic Langrangian rather than on a Hamiltonian formalism. In a spin network of original types, the staff should be utilised as quanglement links that determine the virtual pathways to set piece lectures before virtual oblivion ensues. Thank you, that concludes my clip-piece. I will now take virtual questions before a panel of judges determines my sentence,' he said, sneezing with refined dignity into a white handkerchief the size of a tablecloth.

'This is your opportunity to discover what he's been talking about: go for it, Rees.'

'No fear, Johannes. You are far better at irritating speakers than I am: you ask him questions, go on.'

Johannes Taliesin stood up and cleared his throat.

'As I see it, your thesis contradicts Yang's study of parity violation, where forces cause elementary staff to disintegrate in the weak interaction. Is this so?' Johannes had begun his questioning politely enough.

'Strewth, Johannes, where on earth did you—' began Rees.

'Negative,' the speaker responded brusquely, 'I know only of the work Yang did on charge conjugation symmetry.'

Johannes was momentarily taken aback. His question, based wholly on knowledge gained from reading a tome in the science section of the library, was treated as an irrelevance by the speaker. Too bad, for Johannes had harboured that question for the appropriate opportunity to floor someone with it. Johannes may have been deficient in most personality orders, but fortitude was not one of them.

'Perhaps the Rudolf Clausius law on thermodynamics?'

'That's entropy; this is tele-transportation of Virtual School of Art staff. You should have attended from the beginning, Taliesin. Does anyone have a realistic question based on the lecture? At least something that can mask these irrelevances being asked by Johannes Taliesin?' the speaker asked, a strong hint of irritation in his manner.

'How does he know our names?' hissed Rees.

'The crypto-identikit w-site, of course,' came the casual reply from the podium.

'What's that?' asked Johannes compulsively.

'The interactive vids retrieve the identification encryptions relayed to my lectern; thought you were aware of such basics. Come along, somebody, any realistic questions?'

No realistic questions were forthcoming. Johannes had not grasped the implication of the speaker's explanations.

'Have you considered the event horizon?' Johannes asked.

'Good God, Taliesin! What's got into you. Can't you take shut up for an answer?' hissed Rees, but to his surprise the speaker took the question seriously.

'The event horizon has everything to do with the Privy Council's model for the Instrument and Articles of Government which in their greater wisdom guide the butchers, bakers and candlestick makers, but although is nothing to do with my lecture is nevertheless interesting to talk about,' the speaker trilled. 'Nothing that passes through the event horizon returns. We like to think of it as the Schwarzschild singularity. Here at Virtual School of Art you have the event screen in Corridor Escher that no one of significance sees fit to investigate since the Germans lost interest. Your research takes you through parallel virtuality with such socio-political correctness as the number of wheels that perambulators shed on the streets of Swansea annually, but you all think of it as growing on trees, real trees. This is to be expected of those who expostulate a dependency culture.'

An almost imperceptible click of the heels disguised an upward jiggle of the collar. His neck was severely stretched and he must have been dangerously close to suffering vertebral displacement. His controlled irascibility was understandable, given the nature of his self-propelling collar.

'Are there any serious questions forthcoming? Otherwise I shall depart to receive my sentence,' the speaker croaked in obvious discomfort with his collar.

'Professor Heisenberg, could I please indulge your immense knowledge in the field of uncertainty?' began a serious questioner, who looked disconcertingly like Albert Einstein, but was probably a test model being undertaken by a research student.

'Heisenberg! Heisenberg's Uncertainty Principle,' Rees muttered to Johannes, 'I guessed it was that Heisenberg. You read it out so stupidly, Yo-yo.'

'But even I know he was a long time ago,' whispered Johannes.

'Johannes, everybody knows that this Heisenberg has got to be a virtual.'

'What about Einstein over there?'

'Virtual, hence of limited intellect. Look who's sitting next to him,' Rees said.

'No, don't recognise him.'

'Next to him – on his right. Planck, Max Planck. Surely you've heard of Planck?'

'Never heard of Max Planck. He wasn't mentioned in the scientific tome I read,' admitted Johannes.

'God, you are stupid, Johannes; I don't know why I tolerate you.'

'I don't, either.'

'If uncertainty operated on a much larger scale,' continued the questioner, 'would it affect the whole of Virtual School of Art?'

'Can't be Einstein proper,' said Rees. 'Einstein proper would have known the answer to that simple question.'

'Of course. Uncertainty already affects Virtual SofA every time the Director devolves responsibility to lower-level managers. Their sloppiness is such that the whole institution acts as a particle escaping the discipline of the wave function, and you all know what happens when a manager confronts two slits.'

Well, Johannes didn't know for a start. The ensuing silence from the audience denoted either sagacity or ignorance, certainly the latter for Johannes Taliesin, because the subject was clear out of the boxes of the scientific tome he had struggled through without understanding. To fill the void, Professor Heisenberg decided to labour an interpretation of his Uncertainty Principle, reference Virtual School of Art staff.

'They may be tele-transported to Bletchley and left there until they come up with a solution. Could still be there for all I know, too feeble to open the Queen's telegram. If one is aware of the speed a Departmental Head will undertake their task, one is clueless regarding the location at which the task is accomplished. So much energy is expended in chasing an excuse that they leap up to the next salary level without measurably altering Virtual School of Art's atomic weight.'

'I'm not sure I know what you are talking about,' Johannes blurted. 'For instance, what does happen when a manager confronts two slits?'

'You admit having doubt regarding your grasp of what I am talking about, Johannes Taliesin,' Professor Heisenberg croaked, 'but I am absolutely certain regarding your monumental ignorance of this subject, because you are in the wrong seminar. Am I making myself clear? I suggest you attend the seminar "Incidentals in Accordance" which should be much more suited to your puerile mentality.' His last croak indicated that clearly the self-raising collar was competing with Johannes's irrelevant questions for the accolade of what could be irritating Professor Heisenberg the more.

'Bit stupid of us. I should have known better,' grumbled Rees as they crept ignominiously from 'Quanglement and the Uncertainty Principle'.

'The only uncertainty principle turned out to be a certainty principle – like he was certain of my ignorance,' said Johannes.

'Well, why do you have to stand up and tell everyone you spend your Saturday evenings in the library?'

'More like unprincipled of the virtual,' continued Johannes, ignoring the question.

'Sometimes, Johannes, you are not aware of what you are saying.'

'What?'

'Unprincipled of the virtual.'

'Well, naming us in the seminar for a start.'

'No, forget it. Let's give "Incidence in Concordance" or whatever it is a whirl,' said Rees humourlessly, 'and please don't ask any more questions that have no relevance to the subject of the lecture.'

'Might be worth it,' replied Johannes, 'just to see if I can make a bigger fool of myself.'

'Now don't get carried away. It would be good to find a seminar that explained how a student could climb into his painting and not be seen ever again,' said Rees, still in sour humour.

'Why? Are you thinking of disappearing?'

'I wasn't exactly thinking of myself,' came the sardonic reply.

They continued up Corridor Escher in silence. Rees was ill humoured with Johannes Taliesin's empty-headed questions on a subject best left alone, but Johannes stoically refused to allow the penny to drop. They walked past doors.

'Have you noticed how empty Corridor Escher has become?' asked Johannes.

'That's because it seems more virtual than uncertain in today's Virtual School of Art,' replied Rees.

'Even the seminars appear virtual,' Johannes reasoned. 'Disappointing really, because I was looking forward to these seminars.'

'But the first one was interesting.'

Presently the corridor formulated an umpteenth door on which was pinned:

'Incidentals in Accordance: Professor Elisa Furryhough Dispostulates.'

'Here it is, at least virtual Heisenberg got something right,' said Johannes.

'Virtual Heisenberg got several things right,' replied Rees, 'except he joined the hideous National Socialists.'

'Organ-pipe collar Heisenberg working for Hitler during World War Two,' exclaimed Johannes, 'strove hard to build an atom bomb, and the sod nearly succeeded. I wish I had asked about that when we were in his seminar, talking of irrelevant questions, and I would have given the s-h-one-t a much harder time.'

'That would not have made a scrap of difference to history. They downloaded a young Hitler at V-Cambridge and promptly hacked the bugger to death – didn't you know? Made not a scrap of difference to history.'

'At times I wonder why we bother to download these virtuals,' Johannes pondered.

'We have to accept that they are downloaded into a parallel time, a delusion of the grand order,' Rees reminded his friend.

'Yes, you are right. Let's give "Incidentals in Accordance" a twirl.'

They entered yet another new room, crowded and sinisterly ill-lit. Elisa Furryhough, an elderly woman of about thirty-five, looking worn out and alcoholically haggard, was lecturing. She smiled lasciviously rather than professorially.

'She looks like Messalina,' whispered Rees knowingly.

'Now follows the crucial description,' she dispostulated. 'At two point four seconds in excess of c following singularity the universe of creation is already ancient—'

'Oh, God!' exclaimed Johannes, aghast, 'physics again.'

'—and the receptacle's angle of incidence to the horizontal axis of the support mechanism presents itself at the precise optimum for the contrary incidence of the intruder to the axis—'

'Are you sure?' questioned Rees.

'—of the intruder's horizontal platform.'

The two looked at each other and Rees shrugged.

'Heisenberg recommended it to us.'

'At last, after an age lasting all of two point five seconds, the two incidentals are in perfect accord, the success of the operation betraying a false symmetry that the receptacle's angle of incidence was predestined to be presentable to the intruder's angle of incidence.' Elisa Furryhough smiled lasciviously.

'I don't know what this old scroat is talking about,' Johannes whispered.

'Neither do I,' Rees whispered back. 'It's either the beginning of time at the moment of the Big Bang, or the action of some sort of piston.'

'Hisst!' came from the front.

The lights dimmed slightly, and Elisa Furryhough faded accordingly.

'The exact number of false starts,' she said, smiling, 'can only be guessed at but could well approach the astronomical figure of ten to the power of twenty eight reciprocal reactions.' She beamed and nodded vigorously at the audience, at the same time coming back into bright clarity. 'Time is virtually non-existent. So many variables need to be discounted on a trial and error basis—'

'Oh, I get it,' exclaimed Rees, 'Paul Davies's multi-universe Big Bangs.'

'What? The library doesn't have Paul Davies. Out of print.'

'—Never have two incidentals been in such accord. For fractional illustration of the whole, a minute dimension can be removed from its context for analysis of its organisational capacity.'

'Perhaps not multi-universe Big Bangs after all,' said Rees, updating his commentary.

'Sounds like concomitant exuberation to me,' said Johannes.

'What?'

'Mutual concomitant exuberantly concordatious, that sort of stuff.'

'What?' Rees repeated.

'Under exactly the right pressure the subsurface padding on the high profile podium, which is an essential aspect of the function, extends with an optimum tension to exert lateral torque on the gravitational hawsers housing the centre of epicurean governance, so that the tangential action creates an intense circumstance of conviviality for the valance, while simultaneously affording an elastic check and balance for the quantum intruder to be neither here nor there or preferably in two places at once as it performs its neutrino-like function in the interior subterranean regions of the solid matter.'

'No, I've changed my mind. More like Heisenberg's quanglement again,' Johannes blindly suggested.

'But that contradicts his suggesting we come to this seminar in favour of his own,' argued Rees.

Their chatter was drowned by a wave of appreciative gasps sweeping the audience.

'Huh?' Johannes muttered, 'We missed that.'

'Given the designed circumstances, however,' continued Professor Furryhough, glowing with pride following the burst of audience appreciation, 'never before has the appropriate working of a government revealed such rewards and produced such recurrent cornucopian harvests from a receptive mechanism.'

Her voice rose with intellectual tremor at the 'cornucopian harvests' phrase.

'It is only to be hoped that more effort is given to assuring the right conditions for incidental accordance to function more regularly in the future.'

At that Professor Furryhough's lecture was interrupted by a burst of appreciative applause from the knowing audience. Without a word, Rees Bowen rose and walked out. Johannes followed. Back in uncertain Corridor Escher they walked in silence. Presently, Johannes asked:

'What an earth do you think all that was about?'

'On the surface of it, I'm clueless,' Rees responded, 'but we have to remember this is quantum virtuality at work. First I thought it was physics and the Big Bang, then engineering, then administration, then politics. Now I think only God knows.'

'Concomitant exuberant Big Bangs – nothing to do with Virtual School of Art,' Johannes said.

'My view, don't be too sure. Perhaps everything to do with Virtual School of Art,' Rees said, and burst into laughter.

'You know,' said Johannes, 'we've been taking these seminars seriously when all the while they are just illusions.'

'You're right. What we should do is start again, but this time see the funny side of them.'

They turned to retrace their steps, but the recognisable points had gone; no door or notice resembled their previous experiences. 'Incidentals in Accordance' had disappeared, along with the other seminar doors.

'Are we retracing our steps or going further down Corridor Escher towards the event screen? This is alarming.'

'Going round in circles but in a straight line, I hope.'

'Half spin without turning at all.'

Suddenly a buzz of students appeared ahead in the corridor, jostling a clumsy queue waiting to gain access to an event. On closer inspection they were attempting to gain access through a two-dimensional door painted on the wall. One member of the queue was Michelle Hastings, student at Virtual Fashion, a department of less notoriety than Virtual Download Centre. Michelle and Rees were good friends, almost a unit.

'Hi Shell, what are you queuing for?' Rees asked her.

'For the private view.'

'What private view?'

'*The Red Noise* and Other Paintings.'

'Michelle sweetheart, you've been working too hard, if that's at all possible in your department of virtual leisure. The entrance is a download some twit left suspended in progress – now it's nothing more than a door painted on the wall,' said Rees.

'Yes, that's part of the exhibition,' said Michelle. 'We've been waiting hopefully for someone from Virtual Download Centre to come along and join the queue. As soon as that occurs the door should become reasonably less virtual, enough for us to gain access, that is.'

'Oh sure,' grumbled Johannes, 'and who might the someone from Virtual Download Centre happen to be?'

Rees Bowen was more obliging. He and Michelle were kindred spirits – intelligent, well educated, well spoken, but, most important, affluent and carefree. Michelle and Rees had a good deal of time for each other, as the School of Art rumour would say. However, Michelle invariably ignored Johannes on account of his dialect, among other idiosyncrasies she instinctively disliked.

'Have you been to any of the seminars?' asked Rees, obligingly joining the queue.

'What seminars?'

'In the rooms here off Corridor Escher.'

'Rooms off Corridor Escher? Have you been drinking?'

'No, we have not been imbibing,' Johannes said defensively.

'Hisst!' snapped Rees in a loud whisper, 'let her think we have. It'll enhance our reputations!'

'Enhance your reputations, indeed! What seminars?' queried Michelle.

'Believe me,' urged Rees, 'there are seminars: "Art Being Weaker Than Necessity", "Quanglement and the Uncertainty Principle" by Werner Heisenberg – virtual of course – and "Incidentals in Accordance" by a strange old scroat called Professor Eliza Furryhough, would you believe.'

'Oh, I would believe anything where you two are concerned. You let him' – Michelle thumbed at Johannes – 'lead you by the nose. I cannot imagine why.'

'Not true!' Johannes protested.

'Some of the world's better animals are led by the nose,' Rees retorted with enormous confidence. 'Some, as an antidote to cloning, allow themselves to be led by the nose to service the female.'

'How ridiculous!' Michelle responded, shutting her eyes and giving a dismissive shudder. 'Anyway,' she continued, ' "Incidentals in Accordance" is probably rude. I attended a lecture by Prof Furryhough about two weeks ago. I didn't understand the talk until some bright spark decoded the enigma and presto! She talks of nothing but shagging. Since then I've learnt she has written a doctoral thesis on the subject.'

'Johannes thought it was physics – complex phrases and indeterminate descriptors of the first two-and-a-half seconds of the Big Bang, then concomitant exuberation,' Rees said, unmoved by her description.

'Rees thought she was describing the piston of an old-fashioned threshing machine, which is pretty close to shagging in my book,' Johannes said, moved by her description.

'Nothing of what we have heard so far has anything remotely

to do with VSofA,' said Rees, at which Michelle beamed acknowledgement.

'But everything to do with VSofA staff, according to virtual Werner Heisenberg,' added Johannes, and Michelle rearranged her attractive features to form a scowl.

'Right,' said Johannes, 'I'll download leprosy; Rees can download Messalina, set her loose among this lot.'

'Jesus God, Taliesin! Don't joke these matters,' spluttered the uncomfortable Rees.

'Pah! OK: I'll download prejudice, and see who turns up on the floor of Corridor Escher.'

'No, be reasonable, Johannes,' squirmed Michelle, 'just download the door, there's a dear.'

'I've got a better idea,' exclaimed Johannes. 'Let's get back to Professor Furryhough's lecture, if we can find the room again.'

'Good idea,' teased Rees, 'lead me by the nose, I'm backward in the art of shagging' – and he cast Michelle a sly glance.

Both Johannes and Rees desired Michelle, but of the two Johannes made a clumsy display of it. A studied indifference to Rees was framed by Michelle's dislike for Johannes, in order to keep a distance. The cussed nature of reality attraction now that downloading had made coupling so easy, exposed the chasmic differences in the characters of the two friends, for in attitude they were poles apart. Rees Bowen, full of confidence, always had a pertinent retort regardless of people's reactions. The reasons for his popularity were obvious: postulating a lesser being exposed his confidence and authority. Johannes Taliesin, more intelligent and cleverer with the cynical repost, psychologically yearned approbation that never came; trying hard to impress everyone, he succeeded in pleasing no one. Johannes failed to grasp society's instinctive suspicion of those who try, preferring natural ne'er-do-wells. Johannes's poor social skills and lack of money were not helped by his profound lack of self-esteem due to an all-pervasive atmosphere of Quaker quilt in his early years of home life.

Students at Virtual School of Art were attracted to an exudation of confidence, the only tolerable perspiration of others; they naturally hoped to contract the infection. Rees's self-effacing postulations captivated the confident Michelle, for they were sparkly negative and unconstructive. Johannes's helpfulness and subservience were treated suspiciously by her kind for they manifested insecurity: mimicking spontaneity was to suffer yesterday's answer. Few students had time for Johannes, who alighted on the bright answer before the bandwagon had appeared. For him life was too short to give time for the penny to drop.

He was stirred from his thoughts by Michelle's firm admonishment.

'No you don't,' scolded Michelle, having nothing of the game, 'transmute this painting into an operable door first. These virtuals are about to disappear.'

'Dematerialise,' corrected Johannes.

'Come on Johannes, be a dear,' said Michelle, patronisingly, ignoring the correction, 'I need to see *"The Red Noise* and Other Paintings".'

'Haven't got my V-Tray with me.'

'He's got one,' said Michelle, pointing to a fuzzy nondescript, 'use his.' She was confident that a formal request to Fuzzy Nondescript was unnecessary.

But as events transpired the need to borrow Fuzzy Nondescript's V-tray did not arise for, at a signal from deep within the logic cube of Virtual School of Art the virtual door yielded, taking half the queue with it and causing the wall to adjust its nature.

'Wow!' came exclamations from neutral enrolments.

'At last,' said Michelle, 'you coming?'

'Why not? Can't be less helpful than the seminars we've attended,' said Rees hopefully.

Johannes tagged on, seemingly uninvited.

Above the remains of the doorway a notice floated in and out of focus:

'Room 909'.

'Didn't know there were so many rooms in Corridor Escher,' Johannes remarked.

'909 is the international code used when the actual number is in doubt,' said Rees, adding, 'Thought you knew that. Even fatuous Michelle must know that – don't you, fatuous Shelli?'

'No, I did not, much as I dislike being placed in the same category of ignorance as Johannes.'

The notice changed to '*The Red Noise* and Other Paintings.'

'Now 909 has metamorphosed into a sign. If it can do that, God knows what other tricks are in store,' muttered Johannes with heavy foreboding.

'Don't be ridiculous, it's a simple case of facets operating from different angles, no trick at all,' corrected Rees.

'We can always count on Rees to be logical,' said Michelle.

At first sight 909 appeared as a vast aperture, right angled to Corridor Escher, its projection implausible in relation to the geometry of VSofA.

'Notice our School appears to have developed a sideways movement,' said Johannes.

'Stranger still, the rooms regress like a three-dimensional Mandelbrot Set,' added Rees.

'What's a Mandelbrot Set?' asked Michelle.

They entered the dimly lit Mandelbrot Set. It was full of people who must have been there all the time.

'Airlifted.'

'Parachuted.'

'Slid down a moonbeam,' said Michelle, which was as good a theory as any.

'This is the first exhibition of paintings I've visited where there are no paintings,' grumbled Johannes.

'Ooh look! A donkey. I love donkeys,' said Michelle and, rushing over to the animal, she shrieked with delight, 'He's a boy donkey! Fabulous!'

The donkey had crapped everywhere. Considering the size of the animal an exceptional amount of crap lay about, reaching in waves from the anteroom to the main Mandelbrot chamber, each space piled high with the stuff, forming its own fractal.

'Impossible,' Johannes stated. 'According to my farm experience that animal would have taken approximately seven months to produce such a quantity and anyway, stages would evidently be drying off by now.'

'Thus spake Johannes, authority on donkey dung stage drying,' Rees chided.

'You never know that knowledge gained in awful circumstances can be useful in pleasant ones.'

As Michelle fondly nuzzled the donkey's ears, he looked content with his life and satisfied with his bowel movements.

'Oh dear,' Michelle abruptly exclaimed, 'how disappointing, he's a download. There's a join behind his ears.'

'Thought so, crap of that proportion can only come from a download,' Johannes stated with authority.

'A load downloaded to accompany a download,' tittered Rees.

'Rees, that was awful,' said Michelle and they both laughed.

'What the Final Year Painting Specials download these days is nobody's business,' said Rees in admiration. 'They'll download favourable examination bodies next.'

'That's already been done. In olden times the art education fraternity appointed external moderators from their own brotherhood to examine the brethren, no outsider involved,' said Johannes cynically. 'That is downloading favourable examination bodies in any language you care to gabble.'

'How do you know this stuff?'

'I read it in the old steam-driven library, where there are real books that smell of binding and gum Arabic, under Instrument and Articles of Government,' replied Johannes.

'What on earth are you reading about Instrument and Articles of Government for? You must stop visiting that library – it's filling your head with the most weird rubbish,' Rees advised.

'That is as may be, but it allows me to inform you on the downloading of favourable examination bodies at moments like this,' Johannes chirped.

Each new Mandelbrot space promulgating in real time was promptly filled with private viewers and the ubiquitous donkey dung. Some visitors discovered the dung adhering with glutinous authority to their shoes, which caused much surreptitious scraping and wiping of feet on the carpet, even as conversations wiggled around profound nonentities. But the dung refused to yield, as the download had accidentally combined with olive green oil paint, uniting their sticky properties. Unfortunately the stench of donkey dung completely masked the pleasant aroma of linseed and turpentine spirit, much to the delight of Painting Special anarchists.

Not a single painting was in attendance. Many circumstance

downloads vied for space with the donkey dung, whose voluminous proportions enlarged as the show slithered on. A Mandelbrot corner housed a large ticking bomb painted shocking red, to which a small note was blu tacked: 'Warning and Achtung! Perigl! This bomb is set to explode at 12.55 hours and contains sufficient critical plutonium to blow Virtual School of Art and all who sail in her, especially that pompous VSofA moderator Professor Price who awarded my painted bomb a Fail, to Kingdom Come'. Upon reading the scribbled note Private Viewers chuckled and commented on the laconic humour of Final Year Painting Specials, painting a bomb and pretending to have failed when everyone knew political correctness forbade failure. How laconic!

Rees Bowen was in his element, smiling and chatting with all and sundry, like one of a group of old friends meeting after a war. Generally, Johannes was unforthcoming, as he found small talk with these types about as heavy going as the multiplying donkey dung. People not possessing an iota of self-analysis prattling on clueless about superficial artefacts as if they were earth-shatteringly important irritated him beyond. He was born on a farm where the common state of life meant being half buried in pig dung, his father having volunteered him as the chief pigsty clearer at eight; as a result of this wonderful gift he experienced great difficulty in finding anything worthwhile to say about downloaded donkey dung with prissy metropolitan elites. Johannes had sunk into one of his negative humours.

The Mandelbrot Gallery was a concatenation of corridors and vestibules, a masterpiece in Nouveau Lottery Horizontal, obviously designed by a committee of mathematicians. Members of the design committee had jiggled themselves silly on their hobby horses, very reminiscent of Gombrich's *Meditations on a Hobby Horse*, for they jiggled regressively to infinity. From one of the numerous nodal areas a facsimile bridge built entirely of cartridge paper warily crossed a ditch along which flowed a liquid composed of pee and white wine.

An inebriated P-viewer had toppled off the bridge; his obese form adequately dammed the stream, which was obediently backing up floods to mix with donkey dung and sticky shoes. A final year Painting Special student readily leapt forward with a new label: 'Organically grown recycled cartridge environmentally friendly artform of validated peedam and drunk'. P-viewers were quick to recognise the intrinsic strength of the cartridge paper bridge, having held the weight of Fat Man before his comatose dive into the recycled drink.

Transparent lifts soared up to another floor downloaded for the occasion. Geographically this section of the exhibition should according to architectural right be two floors up halfway across the busy Swansea High Street, but no one seemed bothered that they were suspended on a virtual lattice for the duration. Lifts of such gross transparency would soon muster a hostile army of the feminist brigade, downloaded from the distant past for the bugger of it, but tonight they were beyond the bridge of Brahms to care.

The cavernous nature of the nodal area belied its nature as a downloaded jute warehouse cunningly disguised to distraction by a vanload of architects. Irredeemably charmless wastes surrounding the warehouse had been cobbled on to the act, redesignated to obediently concatenate as a Mandelbrot Set. The wastes would soon sprout apartment blocks, prompting the chatterers to murder for their possession. A new metro line, the nine-o-nine to nowhere, will be laid in a trounce. In days of Virtual Emptiness political ideology accuses glitz of completely outweighing substance in the peace of mind of all five parliamentary parties scrambling for the same centre-left pap. What grabs their transient shallows is how the pipes look, not what vitriol travels in them. Famous for five seconds.

Makeshift shadeless light bulbs glared, revealing here and perhaps there further afterthought exhibits. Downloaded bakelite dolls were programmed to dance wildly widdershins, clunking back to back, breaking brittle pieces off, gobbled up by the hungry donkey. Dark corners beckoned. Ruminating middle-aged women, curious in their adopted ignorance, wandered into the Mandelbrot equation. Squeals of shocked delight greeted their losing Armani garments in the magic, as days like this had long since been forbidden. The bakelite dolls, growing to life-size, sought to dance with the half-naked women, whose dimpled avoirdupois wobbled perilously beyond control straight off the canvas of Stanley Spencer's *Mutton Chop Nude*.

'What in God's name are their husbands thinking?' wondered Johannes. 'I'm at a loss as to whether these people are individual miscreants or units of Virtual Rent-a-Nauseating-Spectacle.'

No one replied to his question. Meanwhile, behind a concatenate, the Armani numbers were being sold at knock-down beer money.

Each corner contained either a string quartet or an individual pianist, playing classic Beethoven pieces. A downloaded Ronald Smith in another alcove was performing an exquisite rendition of Mussorgsky's *Pictures at an Exhibition*, his fish-eye lenses sparkling in the glaring lights. Olivier Messiaen nonchalantly conducted his *Turangalila Symphonie* amidst the palaver of birdsong and donkey braying. The exhibition possessed no cohesion, as sounds and people entangled, a cacophony of noises rising in a crescendo, seas of corn swelling, imaging the land of mahogany shadows, the red noise blaring everywhere.

Sounds assumed a new scintillation. A young woman, completely naked save for her bikini decommissioned limply around an ankle, hauntingly reminiscent of Edvard Munch's *Puberty*, sat in a large bath of molten chocolate, which liquid she alternately ate and smeared.

'Yummy,' smiled Rees, 'I like the chocolate-coated girl.'

'I know her from the past,' cautioned Johannes sourly. 'Her name is Sally Spencer. She's full of exhibitionistic tricks like that.'

'You don't seem impressed,' said Rees.

'I know what's underneath the chocolate.'

'Skin, I hope.'

'Well, little exhibit Sally probably did not require much persuasion to appear naked albeit beneath a veneer of chocolate, that's for sure,' averred Johannes sourly, finding difficulty in disguising old memories.

'God, Johannes, you are a sourpuss at times. You should be more aware of what is happening to you,' warned Rees.

Sally Spencer's bikini had escaped the erogenous zones the garment was designed to cover. She appeared cool and grown-up about the art piece, contriving an atmosphere of casual normality. A notice read: 'Chocolate girl; experiment in participative art.

Please feel free to eat the chocolate. My marks depend on your participation.'

'Think I'll do as the notice requests, all in a good cause for the student,' said Rees.

'Hello Sally,' said Johannes.

'Hello Johannes,' replied Sally. 'I didn't realise you would be coming to an exhibition of Virtual Painting Special – surely not your scene?'

'Bet if you had you would still have exhibited yourself' – and he uttered a false laugh.

'You bet. Introduce me to your good-looking friend,' she replied curtly.

'This is Rees Bowen. He'll do anything you command him, even if it's not good for his soul. You can lead this horse to chocolate, and you can also make him eat,' said Johannes, mockingly.

Rees Bowen did not hear the tone of caution, and was already chatting at the bath-side, eliciting giggles with his salacious chocolate-oriented comments.

'I have always loved chocolate small talk,' he said.

'A prerequisite demands you love chocolate as well,' Sally grinned.

'Agreed, enough to eat it, especially when it's presented on a female dish,' was the rejoinder.

'Go on, then,' she invited, 'this dish floweth over.'

Virtual-Rent-a-Nauseating-Spectacle quickly accumulated, in accord with their contractual predetermination.

Rees began licking the chocolate off Sally's naked parts, an exhibition of such monumental triviality causing a small gibbering audience of P-viewers and Virtual-Rent-a-Nauseating-Spectacle to mutter and chant. The overt sexuality of *Chocolate Girl* excited their starved imagination – this was real activity, downloading virtual sex shows into the living room was so passé – to the degree where dignity was thrown into the peedam. They began uttering exultations, implorations, vitiations in perversity, animal noises of encouragement. The show imposed psychological strain on their transplanted features, which grew Max Beckman-like into grotesque primordial configurations. The men's faces transformed lupine long, fangs dripping of pee-wine, howling, hairy. Women bloated their faces round pink and pig, blood pressure at an all-time high, grunting consummate satisfaction.

The crescendo of rutting sounds emboldened Sally to splash more molten stuff, while Rees casually threw the redundant bikini parts to the audience. Inflamed, their animal lust fought wolf-pack nature over bits of chocolate-soaked cloth, tearing and snarling for a lick and suck. Meanwhile Rees was gone, tossing off his clothes with due disregard to decorum, joining Sally in the chocolate quagmire. Johannes was observing in horror the speed at which a crowd can descend to the animal.

Michelle, having abandoned her false donkey, joined Johannes in the circle reserved for non-participants. Her features expressed a mixture of jealousy and lust. Shaking with a malady that had not hitherto possessed her, she clutched Johannes's arm for security.

'Do something,' she implored, 'you are supposed to be his friend – stop him.'

'Why should I stop him?' queried Johannes, resigned to the spectacle.

'He always does as you suggest, stop him,' she pleaded.

'No, he doesn't always do as I say. You believe I lead him by the nose, but not when it comes to shagging chocolate-coated girls as a public spectacle. There are rules between friends, you know,' Johannes declared.

'If you don't stop him, I'll join them!' she threatened.

Johannes laughed encouragingly, 'Now don't be silly, Michelle Hastings. You know very well a threat of that nature will have the opposite effect on me. I'll definitely not stop him! Go on – join them, this should make my day.'

Having lost the leverage battle Michelle promptly burst into tears, torn between desperate bravado and an inbred sense of decorum; sentiment towards Rees, dislike of Johannes. What a conundrum!

'Oh Michelle, no vapours in front of me please; remember, you invited Rees into this show in the first instance. Go on, join them – Rees Bowen will love you for ever,' Johannes goaded, but shaping an expression of concern that it might be the last act

Michelle would perform before committing suicide.

Meanwhile, as Michelle's crisis was gathering in a crescendo, Canis Lupus and his wife Omnivorous Ungulate were orchestrating a forest of noises, grunting, panting, barking, squealing as proxy means of encouraging the chocolate-coated pair to achieve their act of choculation. A Final Year Painting Special student bravely wove between the heated animals and affixed a sign:

'Chock-a-Block; Cadbury@VSofA.orgy.'

'Johannes Taliesin' a voice called distantly from somewhere.

Johannes turned and looked about, but could not see the caller, just a new concatenate with welcome sign to a seminar room. The sign read: 'Seminar 2/3: The Genesis of Corruption'.

'Johannes Taliesin,' the vaguely familiar voice insisted again.

Again Johannes swivelled about him. 'Who's calling me?' he called back.

There was no reply.

'Who's there?' he asked, talking to the empty doorway.

'What's wrong with you? Who are you talking to?' Michelle asked.

'Someone calling my name, didn't you hear them?' he said.

'No I didn't, but I have decided to take your advice and join Rees and the girl. No doubt you will watch, you horrid letch.'

'Michelle Hastings, everyone else will watch as well,' said Johannes, 'but no doubt you will spread it around the VSofA by tomorrow that Johannes Taliesin is a beastly voyeur. Anyway, you won't.'

'I will.'

'I wonder who is calling me?' Johannes asked absent-mindedly, yet convinced Michelle would not join the chocolate duo.

'I have no doubt you would love me to take my clothes off,' said Michelle.

'Michelle, much as I would love to see you naked, it is obvious you are not taking your clothes off for my benefit. If you were to do that my eyes would be on joysticks. For God's sake, go on and make Rees jealous, that's your simple intention.'

'Right, then,' she snorted, and stormed towards the chocolate bath.

Although Johannes Taliesin had mixed feelings he turned his

back, lack of confidence ensuring he could not tough out the gossip. Only one thing would have given him greater pleasure than seeing Michelle naked and that was being in a private place with Michelle when she was naked. But Michelle's threat was all a sham. He was pleased with his self-discipline. Reluctantly, he turned to Seminar 2/3, 'The Genesis of Corruption' and sought the mysterious caller.

Upon his entering the portico to Seminar 2/3, three unusual events occurred. First, the cacophony of red noise behind him ceased abruptly as if switched off, obviously due to his walking through a white noise screen that was more powerful than the red noise he had left behind. Second, an elderly lady stepped forward to greet him with an index finger pressed to her lips.

'Shh,' she whispered.

'I wasn't making a sound,' protested Johannes.

'SHH!' she scolded.

As he had already elected to forgo the pleasure of watching Michelle undress, it was an easy matter to ignore the elderly lady by walking past.

The seminar room was dimly lit. A pale blue light fanned the speaker, who was apparently in full lecture. Johannes was about to take a seat when the third unusual event occurred: Michelle's shivering hand clutched his arm.

'I chickened out,' she whispered. 'Nice and quiet in here, isn't it?'

She was shaking uncontrollably and Johannes was about to speak when, 'SHH!' the old lady again scolded.

'...and nineteenthly, beware the system. It is the system that accommodates the means by which corruption can be expedited, by which the tenets of corruption can take root. As in the game of rugby, when set pieces are made too complex they break down due to too many individual manoeuvres, so a complex, multifarious, multi-layered administrative system will contain vulnerable synapses readily susceptible to dysfunction, interference, mutation, hijacking. Only the system is vulnerable to corruption, not the administered materials as that would return small rewards before the interference was discovered. The conduits, either macro structures or micro systems, are taken over, not the material that flows through them. Rarely if ever is a new parallel system constructed in order to expedite an objective where the intention is to utilise the articles of the extant system. The instrument is the goal of corruption, because from then on the article is the faithful servant of the corruptors.'

'What's this to do with Virtual School of Art?' whispered Johannes.

'Everything, it's fascinating,' returned Michelle, calming down but still clutching his arm.

'Machinations will be found within the system, often masquerading as the process itself, that is, within the conduits. Plausibility is everything. Successful corruption wears the mask of everydayness. The common mask of everydayness can hoodwink small businesses, international conglomerates and even nations. Note how Hitler in twentieth century Germany gained the ultimate corruption of absolute power before the eyes of good men and true whose presence was removed under the pretext of an Enabling Act to safeguard the German people. By the time they realised that they were the victims of a scheme to gain world domination, it was too late!'

'Wow,' gushed Michelle, earnestly engaging with every word, 'this is magic! Wish I had been here from the start.'

'Of course the system or conduit is supposed to have been structured in a form that would prevent anything other than authorised – legitimately authorised – business to be processed. But what happens if inherent weaknesses allow the system to be hoodwinked?'

The speaker stopped as if awaiting an answer.

'Construct a watertight system,' Michelle spoke out, much to Johannes's amazement.

'No system exists that is impervious to infiltration,' the speaker continued by way of answering Michelle's point. 'Or, to extend the argument, suppose the conduit itself is hijacked?'

'Construct checks and balances within the system that would disallow takeover,' shouted Michelle authoritatively.

'Yes, you have made two interesting points, young lady, and I hope to reply to them in due course. Please be minded we are talking about the open access net system where information availability is universal. The genie of security is out of the bottle – perhaps you have a suggestion as to how we may get the genie back into the bottle?'

'Hmm,' pondered Michelle, revelling in the conundrum.

'Meanwhile, I shall continue the lecture. Certainly, authorised business passing innocently through the system would be unaware of the system's new owners—'

'Implement security firewalls that agitate a fail-safe security shutdown if arbitrary codes set on a daily basis are violated,' interrupted Michelle, in complete command of her knowledge.

'—if authorised business itself does not contain the requisite policing, by its very nature, in order to ascertain any change in the system…' the speaker trailed off. Then, in a slightly peeved voice he enquired of Michelle, 'How do you know so much about the subject of corruption, or rather, counter-corruption management?'

'My father is Chief Security Controller for Yahgoog Systems, and he talks about his stratagems now and again at dinner,' was Michelle's innocent reply.

'Well, I'm stunned,' responded the speaker. The audience buzzed.

'So am I stunned,' said Johannes.

'May I reserve the right to continue the lecture?' the speaker asked.

'So long as I can reserve the right to interrupt,' chirped Michelle, and the audience rippled with laughter.

'The article has no imposition on the instrument. A cog in a machine is not programmed to gain cognisance of the machine's purpose: that is the outcome. Or its engine: that is the driver. Both process and conduit are inanimate. Animation exists only at the point of construction of the system in the first place, or subsequent tampering, alteration, modification, reprogramming, reconfiguring, reanimating, recalling, reprocessing—'

'Come on,' said Michelle, 'it's time to go. I've been in here long enough.'

With the suddenness of an off switch, Michelle leapt up and headed for the exit, still clutching Johannes's arm, pulling him with her.

'I didn't know you had it in you,' said Johannes as they left.

'I didn't,' replied Michelle, 'I made it up.'

'My God, Michelle, no wonder everyone loves you in Virtual Fashion.'

She grinned a sly smile.

At the exit to Seminar 3/2 they were confronted by Rees, fully dressed and cleansed of chocolate.

'Gosh, you cleaned up quickly,' said Johannes.

Rees ignored Johannes, but smiled broadly at Michelle, who sustained the conspiracy.

'It worked!' he announced to Michelle.

'Yes, it worked a dream,' she said, releasing her clutch on Johannes's arm.

'What worked?' asked Johannes.

'Virtual Parallel Veridicality Downloading – an experiment we undertook with Professor Hendy, the Painting Special Research placement,' replied Rees.

'Yes, I know Professor Hendy, but he doesn't tutor us,' said Johannes. 'When did you undertake the experiment?'

'Now! Right now!' And both Rees and Michelle laughed at their accomplishment.

'What's so funny? I don't follow.'

'Come and meet the Prof – all will be revealed,' said Rees.

The exhibition hall was much the same except Sally Spencer and the chocolate bath had gone, together with the Max Beckman menagerie. The stream and its cartridge paper bridge were still there, but Fat Man Peedam had gone.

'Where has Sally gone? She and her chocolate bath have disappeared. Besides, you didn't answer my question – how did you clean up so quickly?' asked a confused Johannes.

'Come through into this lobby.'

'Hello, Johannes Taliesin, thanks for your unwitting cooperation in the experiment,' said Professor Hendy.

'When you were distracted by Mr Peedam, Prof Hendy activated his Virtual Parallel Veridicality Downloader apparatus,' said Rees, beaming with success.

'And next thing I saw Sally Spencer naked in a chocolate bath, and you insisting on joining her,' said Johannes.

'The identification of the girl is immaterial so long as it was someone from your memory who could retain your attention and credibility. The whole chocolate bath scene was a virtual download, but with actual persons participating, sort of living parallel time,' said Professor Hendy.

'That explains my hearing my name being called,' said Johannes, 'now I get it!'

'That was when we were discussing you, bits filtering through the Veridicality Scrambler. You probably heard other parts of our conversation too, but it was drowned by the general buzz of other words from the P-viewers and the Rent-a-Menagerie,' said Professor Hendy.

'Yes, the phenomenon of recognising one's name above a cacophony of other noises,' reasoned Johannes. 'The filtering ability of the human brain is boundlessly clever.'

'That's it, familiarity tuning, and perspicacious selection,' said the professor.

'And you were in on it,' said Johannes, turning to Michelle.

'Yes,' she said, 'was I convincing?'

'Very convincing, especially the bit where you were going to take off your clothes and join Rees in the chocolate bath,' said Johannes. 'Was that part of the scenario?'

'What?'

'When you became jealously upset and threatened to join Rees and Sally in the bath of chocolate,' said Johannes.

'What was I doing in a chocolate bath with Sally?' said Rees, 'although on second thoughts it's best you don't answer that question.' He laughed lasciviously.

'Seriously – I've just realised,' said Michelle, 'although I was participating in the experiment, I cannot remember what I did or said.'

'Me neither,' said Rees.

'There are many aspects to resolve, participant amnesia for the transposed participants being one of them. However, I'm confident there will be no psychological consequences,' said Professor Hendy, a little apprehensively.

'Now he tells us,' Michelle said seriously.

'What about the prole, *vis*, me?' asked Johannes. 'Does he get psychological side-effects as well?'

'Most unlikely,' said the professor unconvincingly. 'In your case there's not much psychology to be side effected! Only teasing, Johannes.'

All, except Johannes, burst into laughter.

'What did I say, do?' asked Michelle of Johannes.

'In the seminar?' asked Johannes, and without waiting for a reply, 'you interrupted the speaker brilliantly! Sharp comments – gave him a hard time. I am amazed at your knowledge of counter-corruption methodologies. You have gone up in my estimation. Though I didn't realise your father is the Chief Security Controller for Yahgoog Systems.'

'Did I say that? He isn't. Daddy is Chief Partner in Hastings Solicitors, the family firm.'

'You announced your alter-father's profession to the speaker and the whole audience,' insisted Johannes.

'This is fascinating!' said the professor. 'This is a new outlet to virtual telecommunication, although we must beware not to predicate certainties on assumptions. It is my father who happens to be the Chief Security Controller for Yahgoog Systems, though he is near retirement now. I transferred the information to you, Michelle, but how it's done still mystifies me. At the studio-lab we have succeeded in transferring information on several occasions, but as yet the physics baffles us. There is huge potential for marketing the creative potential, taking into account of course our partners at Fermilab and CERN, not to forget Kamiokande. They will be pleased.'

'What did you witness, Johannes?' asked Rees.

'I went into that seminar room over there—' He pointed. 'Uh-oh, it's disappeared. I could have guessed that. Par for the course for Virtual SofA, things disappearing here and reappearing there.'

'Go on,' the others prompted, 'tell us your story.'

'Initially I heard my name being spoken and, being curious, responded by heading towards the portico of another seminar room. It was a seminar on the genesis of corruption. I was about to take a seat when a shivering hand, Michelle's, gripped my arm. She said "I chickened", obviously referring to her abandoned mission to join you and Sally Spencer in the chocolate bath.'

'Most revealing,' said Professor Hendy, 'do go on, please.'

'We had obviously missed an enormous amount of the seminar because at our point of taking a seat the speaker said "and nineteenthly". My arm was held in a vice-like grip by Michelle, most unusual, which initially took my easily misled mind off the lecture.'

Rees and Prof Hendy laughed.

'Ugh! Can't remember anything of the sort,' said Michelle with a shudder.

'After a while of heavy lecturing about the system accommodating the means by which corruption can be expedited I asked Michelle her view as to what had the seminar to do with Virtual School of Art. "Everything" was her reply.'

'I cannot remember any of this,' said Michelle. 'You could have had your wicked country bumpkin way with me for all I can recollect.'

'Oh, I was coming to that,' Johannes joked.

More laughter from Professor Hendy and Rees.

'That's not funny,' Michelle snapped, glaring at Rees.

'Rees had his wicked way with the chocolate-coated Sally Spencer,' Johannes said.

'Did I indeed! I wish Professor Hendy had perfected his apparatus in time, then I could have remembered the experience. By the way, who is Sally Spencer?' asked Rees wistfully.

'A girl I know. Pity you can't recall your adventure because she has a beautiful body.'

'The outcome is obvious,' said Professor Hendy. 'The methodology has combined the old-fashioned concept of performance art with the current wave of virtual art and taken them to a new level. Now we are genuinely into the realm of uncertain parallel virtual art. What my experiment has proven so far is that both Rees Bowen and Michelle Hastings have performed outside their consciousness, while the control has witnessed both of them in their veridical state. This was first done with entangled photons by a physicist called Cramer at Fermilab way back in 1985.'

'Simple hypnotic hallucinatory construction,' said Johannes.

'*Au contraire!* You, Johannes, actually learnt something new on the genesis of corruption. We are into subliminal parallel learning.'

'That sounds like the answer to the problem of ignorance. We could dispense with teachers – they are useless, anyway,' said Johannes.

'Can you recall more of the seminar, Johannes, and less of your cynicism regarding the teaching profession?'

'Sure. I learnt that administrative systems are subject to hijack under our noses in order to expedite corrupt procedures. And a nice one where successful corruption wears the mask of every-dayness; and no system exists that is impervious to corruption. Michelle constantly interrupted. Then she came out with a beauty: "Implement security firewalls that agitate a fail-safe security shutdown if daily codes are violated" or something similar.'

'Shelli, I didn't know you had it in you,' said Rees.

'That's what this one said,' she remarked.

'She hasn't,' said Prof Hendy. 'I hesitate to disabuse you of the belief that Michelle possesses an intellect only veridicality liberates. She probably possesses a profound intellect, but on this occasion it was not veridicality or anything else that liberated it. You see, it was I who supplied the information for both the speaker in the seminar and Michelle's interruptions.'

'Fascinating,' marvelled Johannes. 'I shall have to revise my opinion of the teaching profession.'

'I propose the three of you attend my studio-lab next Monday morning,' said Professor Hendy, 'when I shall present each of you with an individual analysis of your creative-aberative performance curve, which you will be allowed to program into your profiling bank. Thank you all for your cooperation, and especially you, Johannes. If you have any untoward mental states please let me have details next Monday.

'One last suggestion: in order to clear your minds of the veridicality event, you should attend Seminar 3/3 "Hideous Bile", which,' and he looked at his watch, 'is just about to begin. Down that corridor, third on the left. See you on Monday. Bye.' And he was gone.

The three unlikely musketeers stood for a moment, lost; then Johannes said, 'Come on gang, "Hideous Bile" it shall be,' and led the way.

The title, scribbled on an old-fashioned memorandum sheet in the rounded half-uncial script beloved of graphic designers in art schools of old said: ' "Hideous Bile": seminar 3/3. 1st in a series of 274.'

' "Hideous Bile". Prof Hendy was right,' muttered Johannes.

'First in a series of 274! Crickey, that's a lot of bile,' said Rees.

'He said it would clear our minds, so we had better go in, but I have never known bile to clear my mind,' said Michelle.

'Exactly what I was pondering: whether bile can clear minds,' said Rees.

'You may clutch my arm again if you like,' said Johannes, hopefully.

'I'll clutch Rees Bowen's arm this time, now that Professor Hendy is not controlling my judgements,' she replied. 'Anyway, Johannes, Professor Hendy wasn't a hundred per cent sure the experience hadn't damaged you psychologically.'

'All the more reason I need you to clutch my arm again.'

They entered.

The room was dimly lit and empty of people. An unprepossessing, weedy-looking lecturer, not before seen in Virtual SofA, stood at a lectern, to which he was glued with both hands, white knuckles. In a dim corner, a girl stirred.

'Stone the crows walking home,' whispered Rees, 'look who is in the dim corner.'

'Gosh, who rattled her site?'

'Who is she?' asked Michelle.

'Just continue clutching my arm, and don't ask questions about her, Shelli. Believe me, you don't want to know,' said Rees gravely.

'I have been waiting for you three. Professor Hendy advised me about your disruptive attitudes in his last seminar. We will not tolerate similar behaviour here. Please be seated,' said the weedy lecturer.

'We weren't disruptive in Professor Hendy's seminar. Besides, it was not a seminar: it was a research experiment,' said Johannes defensively.

'Disruptive behaviour immediately! Sit down!' Weedy shouted.

The three obediently sat down, which prompted Girl to burst into mocking laughter.

'Disruptive behaviour immediately! Sit down!' she laughed.

'Not yet, sweetheart,' Weedy said quietly to Girl. 'I'll tell you when to speak.'

'…Whenever, therefore, a comfortable people are confronted by an external threat they invariably seek explanation in the realms of appeasement on behalf of the aggressor's actions, rather than to climb out of their cosy cradles, gird their loins and face the challenge. Pacifists and appeasers rent more wrath on their kinfolk for having the temerity to bombilate warnings on a drum than on the aggressor who is threatening to curtail or even terminate their accustomed lifestyle, if not their lives—'

'Excuse me,' Michelle interrupted, 'how do the pacifists and appeasers know which of their kinfolk have the temerity to bombilate on the drum? I mean, for instance, it could be someone else, unrelated.'

'If you had arrived punctually like everyone else,' snapped the lecturer, emboldened by the nine inches the rostrum gave him, 'you would have heard the preamble which set the scene.'

'Which set the scene,' snapped Girl.

'That's you in your place,' Johannes giggled.

Michelle was not amused. 'Everyone else? What do you mean by everyone else. Besides us there is only one other member in the audience,' she said.

'That's him in his place,' said Rees.

But the lecturer had already resumed.

'Where or when is the genesis of their appeasement?'

'Hello? Genesis again. I smell the apparatus of Prof Hendy at work here,' said Johannes.

'Often, as with grave malignancies, the early manifestations are difficult to detect but easy to cure.'

'Easy to cure,' echoed Girl.

Suddenly another lecturer appeared, facsimile download identical to Weedy, together with a rostrum and white knuckles, a few metres across the front.

The three musketeers triangulated their incredulity between themselves and double Weedy.

'Holy entanglement,' spluttered Rees, 'Hendy's up to more tricks.'

'Here we go again, more quanglement,' exclaimed Johannes.

'Just think through the situation, you two,' Michelle said with great authority.

Weedy One remained unaffected, and continued speaking as if his doppelganger were not there:

'…whereas in later advanced stages everyone is able to detect the malignancy but no one can effect a cure.'

'No one can effect a cure,' Girl echoed.

'Heavens, she's irritating,' Michelle muttered.

'The lesson here,' continued Weedy Two seamlessly and without a by-your-leave, 'is that a problem identified by a genius can be cured by a simpleton.'

'But when a problem is identifiable by a simpleton,' rhymed Weedy One, 'even a genius will encounter difficulty in curing it.'

'The two-slit trick,' said Rees.

'I'm thinking through it, but I still don't know what is going on,' said Johannes.

'It's the two-slit trick,' Rees repeated.

'I'm thinking through it – er them,' said Michelle.

'At least I get the metaphor they are using,' said Johannes. 'It's Spengler. They are referring to a metaphor from Oswald Spengler. I read Spengler's *The Decline of the West* in the library.'

'Will you three kindly shut up or get out,' a voice came from behind, prompting the three to swivel round in surprise.

'My God! The place is full! I didn't hear anyone coming in.'

'This place is giving me the creeps, thinking through or not. I believe I'm failing at my own advice,' squeaked Michelle. 'Let's go.'

Weedy One and Weedy Two simultaneously turned and glared at the three.

'You will not leave until Professor Hendy gives you permission. Remain seated and show some respect to other members of the audience, who have been handpicked by Professor Hendy because they display the whole human spectrum of hideous bile,' they recited in unison.

'There you are! The title had nothing to do with the lecture,' spluttered Johannes.

'I have thought through this and have decided I am now hating it,' whispered Michelle. 'Today is turning into a proper nightmare, one way and another. I'm going to ask Daddy to take legal steps against the management of Virtual SofA.'

'If your daddy can prove it is not a virtual educational experience, that is,' One&Two chimed. 'Both you and he have signed a contract that states you are agreed the educational experience you shall receive at VSofA shall, *inter alia*, be clear of external interference.'

'My God! He— They heard me and we're trapped. I regret asking Johannes to transmute the painting into an operable door,' whimpered Michelle.

'As it happens, I didn't transmute the operable door. But I knew it would be my fault in the end,' giggled Johannes.

'Well, it is, isn't it?' jested Rees.

'Thanks pal, but I am not yet strong enough to bear the blame for everybody's downloading blunders,' Johannes muttered, 'and this is a major download blunder.'

'Quiet!' One&Two bellowed in unison, their knuckles achieving an even whiter tone.

'Quiet!' Girl bellowed in mimetic accord as the switches were thrown.

'That does it,' whispered Michelle. 'I'm not having a clone doll tell me to be quiet.'

'She's not a clone doll, Shelli,' said Rees, 'believe me.'

'Projecting the hypothesis a little further along the long march of everyman,' One&Two continued, 'the unwillingness of the masses to accept the warnings of the inspired, blinding themselves to the obvious, clutching myopically to their lifestyles, ghoulishly praying before the altar of their PCs, is as wilful an act of capitulation as surrendering their weapons and bodies to an aggressor.'

'What has this to do with VSofA?' demanded Michelle.

'We are coming to that,' they said.

'We are coming to that,' echoed Girl.

'Could you please control your clone, as she is distracting my attention to your singularly enthralling lecture,' Michelle said, having no option but to attack again.

'Shhh! Please!' someone at the back politely requested.

'We will have you know Girl is not a clone,' they said in unison, 'believe us.'

'To continue: here is a conundrum that both answers your question and comes to the point,' they said, 'if you accept a conundrum can come to the point. Let us render this classical confrontation model a little more metaphorically in order that our three belligerent, Spam-loving visitors from VSofA are stimulated a little more intellectually, hopefully furnishing their knowledge-base with sufficient facts to diminish their singularly provocative and puerile outbursts.'

'Puerile outbursts,' echoed Girl.

'That's us they are talking about, I think,' said Johannes drolly.

'What does he – they – mean by visitors?' asked Michelle.

'In place of the aggressor, supplement the effect of unprofitability, or the outcomes of a manipulated management by a reactionary workforce, or plain incompetence and unmarketability. The cosy cradle to catch the baby's fall is the institutionalised financial support system where money grows on trees, and the tree shakers masquerading under the guise of managers marinaded in departmentalism quickly acquire adeptness at shaking the tree or procuring greater pay-offs for a chronically static circumstance. The pacifists and appeasers who crave maintaining the status quo, i.e., that the tree-shaking shall continue and the expenditure on salaries and waste shall proceed unhindered, fight for their assumed right to continue shaking that tree.'

'That's Spengler again,' Johannes whispered. 'They have been boning up on Spengler.'

'Yes, you are right, Johannes Taliesin,' One&Two responded, 'but he was not the first to translate industrial suicide into that metaphor. Milton Keynes said it about the window-dressers of Broadway.'

'Huh?' Rees woke up. 'Milton Keynes? You mean Milton Friedman, surely.'

'We said Milton Freedman, if you had been awake.'

'Even if I had been asleep, which I wasn't, Milton Friedman said nothing of the sort about window-dressers in Broadway,' Rees protested.

'To continue,' One&Two said, 'almost invariably, in organisations where money grows on trees, the workforce rarely has a good word for management.'

They paused and, for the first time evident to the assembled crowd, separately looked about the auditorium. One gesticulated a codified message to Girl.

'I am only too aware of the mindset condition here in Virtual School of Economics,' said Two alone.

'And I will need to hammer the message home in Virtual School of Art,' said One alone, 'for if ever the inmates at the nursery were unaware there is a wolf at the door, it is at VSofA.'

'...it is at VSofA,' echoed Girl.

'We are in VSofA,' exclaimed Michelle.

'No, you are not, so please be quiet,' came from the audience.

'I get it,' said Johannes, 'we were with One and his sidekick Girl in VSofA—'

'—and suddenly the two-slit trick took us to Virtual School of Economics with identical Two,' completed Rees.

'Except he does not have a lackey roadie,' said Johannes.

'Yes, I have,' said Two. 'Her name is Michelle Hastings and she is sitting between you two idiots.'

'Oh, my God!' squeaked Michelle, 'let's get out of here.'

'As I said earlier, you will not leave until Professor Hendy is satisfied.'

'Please, Rees, let's ignore them and leave,' pleaded Michelle.

'There is nothing to worry about, sweetheart, they are downloads which have simply become entangled,' said Rees.

'What are you two talking about, would somebody explain?' asked Michelle.

'Hush, Shelli sweetheart, just relax and listen,' said Rees. 'You are quite safe with us. This is getting very interesting now we know the two-slit game the virtual institutions are playing.'

'The clue to all this is hidden in the text of the lecture,' said Johannes.

'Almost invariably,' One&Two continued once again in unison, 'in organisations where money grows on trees—'

'such as VSofA,' said One,

'and VSE,' said Two,

'the workforce rarely has a good word for management. The hideous bile—'

'AHA!' exclaimed Johannes.

'—spewed at meetings and in the common rooms assumes that the ones of bilious disposition have a clearer world view than does management,' One&Two declared.

'When did this tradition of the negative view of management begin in British industrial relations?'

'Why is it continually promulgated generation to generation?'

'Who enacts the discrediting?' One asked.

'What objectives to they hope to gain?' Two asked.

'Are they aware of the corrosive affect this has on the efficacy, and thereby profitability, of the company? Gratitude is considered irksome,' they chimed.

'Tacitus,' said Johannes, ' "gratitude is considered irksome" comes from Cornelius Tacitus.'

'Go on, you read it in the steam-driven library,' said Rees.

'Answers to these questions are not as multifarious as the persons occupying posts in the tree-shaking organisations. That is because of a conformity, which accords with the dictat "insanity, rare in individuals, is common in crowds", and, before Johannes Taliesin shows off his knowledge of ancient works, Thucydides wrote that two-and-a-half millennia ago. In the tree-shaking organisations, is this connection ever made in unambiguous terms to the workforce? The answer of course is yes, but in the entrenched mindset of the workforce, to say the least of management and the companies, opposition is such that any education provided for by VSE, we regret to say, is too little too late.

'The following paradox is predicated on mankind's infinite capacity for self-delusion: the price of freedom is eternal vigilance. Eternal vigilance requires constant social commitment. Social commitment demands group participation. Group participation has to be total for it to be worthwhile. Total group participation necessarily excludes individual options. The exclusion of individual options requires self-effacing obedience. In order that obedience is infallible it has to be absolute. Absolute obedience results in individual subservience.

'Subservience is achieved through oppression of the subservient. Oppression is subjugation of society. The consequence of subjugation is loss of freedom. Loss of freedom is slavery. Slavery is a product of tyrannical oppression. Tyrannical oppression is the instrument of totalitarianism. Totalitarianism manifestly precludes freedom. Freedom is lost the moment the prerequisites of eternal vigilance are implemented. Loss of freedom has to be an acceptable necessity. The only tenable option being eternal vigilance, the articulation of vigilance delivers loss of individuality, self-effacing obedience, subservience and subjugation. Thus the price of freedom is eternal subjugation.

'Of course, subjugation by the state requires commitment of the instrument of state, but commitment of the state instrument demands participation. For the state's instrument to succeed it has to be total, but total participation necessarily excludes individual options...

'This circular backwards paradox is predicated on mankind's infinite capacity for self-delusion. Self-delusion turns on the simple wheel of deception, but deception is merely a small house in the mansion of hypocrisy. Self-delusion accommodates the notion that the act of vigilance is rewarded by freedom. The intrinsic hypocrisy of democracies cultivates this illusion. In order to survive the caprice of the vote, the peddlers of democracies require hypocrisy to function as an instrument of government—'

'Here, here!' shouted Johannes, not being able to contain his enthusiasm any longer, 'couldn't agree more!'

'I wondered how long it would take reconstructed Genghis Khan to erupt,' said Rees.

'Do I take it you believe governments are hypocritical?' asked Michelle.

'Of course, in this age all types of governance are corrupt. If you believe otherwise you must live on another planet,' Johannes replied.

Meanwhile, One&Two were still speaking. '...hypocrisy is the all-pervasive religion of Western democracies. It is the core belief of ecumenicists generally, of specific designer creationists, of anti-evolutionists, of secularists. It is worshipped as an absolute by all of society except those too young or too stupid to comprehend. It is knitted into the fabric of commerce, education, industry, justice, law, politics, religion and society. Daily, hourly – no, every minute – society obeys the intrinsic fabric of hypocrisy by kneeling at its altar.

'But the young are taught by a standard regression of lessons. Truth was long ago manipulated to become an instrument of hypocrisy. When the instrument of hypocrisy is repeatedly paraded, then infants grow up to believe the whole truth of that which they witness being strongly believed in.

'Hypocrisy is worshipped by innocent participants in the groves of academia; by those who tend the orchards of money trees to accordingly relieve the trees of their burdens of fruit; by those whose hands rock the cradles; by the thespian politicians who parade for votes; by butchers, bakers and candlestick makers; by murderers and their lawyers; by tyrants and teachers; by the fishers of mankind casting their nets from the ship of fools, trawling their votes from the seas of the innocent...'

The two-slit trick lecturers faded fast under dimming light. Two recorders clicked emptily toward the points of disappearance. In their brief download function their message had warped from appeasement in the face of an aggressor to an aggressive attack on mankind's readiness to manipulate the element of hypocrisy by denying society's frailties. The audience was stunned into silence. Girl, mouth wide open ready to scoff at whatever the audience was about to say, faded joylessly in frost, her emptiness filled by a rush for the door.

'Well,' said Johannes as they left the seminar room, 'that was the most interesting seminar of my day.'

'True to form, you have to say that. My view is it appears to have been delivered for students of Virtual School of Economics,' said Rees.

'But I enjoyed the donkey and the veridical experiment, and I'm glad to be away from those two creepy downloads,' said Michelle.

'You have a thing about donkeys. Obviously your pampered upbringing has deprived you of certain experiences. My view, the donkey crapped too much,' Johannes suggested.

'Yes, but only temporarily,' Michelle countered.

'What has transient politics to do with a donkey?'

'How did we get from a lecture in anthropological deviousness delivered for students of Virtual School of Economics to donkey crap in the lapse of two sentences?' asked an exasperated Rees.

'Question sustained,' said a disingenuous Johannes. 'But how come we end up in Virtual School of Economics, which is at least seven kilometres from VSofA, when all we did was stroll a few metres down Corridor Escher?'

'Amazing as it may be, best question of the day comes from Johannes,' said Rees. 'In fact, the question of the day: either we were tele-transported to that building by Professor Hendy playing more experiments, or VSE undertook a similar exercise and their lecture theatre plus complement ended up in our building. The evidence strongly suggests it's another Hendy experiment because he knew we would be in that "Hideous Bile" seminar at that time.'

'Good thinking, Watson,' chirped Michelle.

'I met a second year Invective student from VSE down the Cross Keys not too long ago and she freely admitted VSofA was more advanced than they in tele-transportation quanglement research, so maybe one of their experiments went awry,' reasoned Johannes.

'I have a friend at VSE who says their work and agenda are as inward-looking as they have ever been,' Michelle said.

'I believe they both inflict these quanglement experiments on us without a clear view of the consequences,' Rees said.

'They let politics get between them and their subject, otherwise Government research money would dry up,' said Johannes.

'Did you witness Johannes mounting his hobby horse in one deft leap, without even putting his foot in the stirrup?' Rees teased.

The three enjoyed the joke, believing they had regained their reality following the seminars.

'Anyway, I think I'll call it a day and go back to my studio laboratory,' said Johannes. 'I've got some reality that needs attention, as well as Samuel Palmers to download.'

Back in Corridor Escher the three were claiming their bearings.

'God! Escher's crowded. where did they all come from suddenly?'

'Painting Specials with their Rent-a-Throng company.'

'Must have been a talk in the lecture theatre.'

'Didn't know there was a talk in the lecture theatre,' said Rees.

'Anyway, I go this way, I think,' said Johannes, heading off.

'Me, too,' said Rees. 'Bye Shelli, see you down the Keys tonight.'

'Maybe, bye!' came her hanging invitation.

Michelle was about to depart in the opposite direction, when an enormous commotion cut a swathe through Rent-a-Throng and stormed towards them. A latter-day Hun descended like a wolf on the fold from the atmospheric perspective of Corridor Escher. A swathe was cut by the ample form of Professor Price, professor of Virtual Download Centre, Examiner for Virtual Painting Special, his black gown billowing behind him like a tethered whale. The gown resonated with the Victorian arches of Corridor Escher, a delightful reminder of antiquity. Although this was clattering in the rafters of the good old days, the urgency of today's commotion bore a gilt-edge certainty about it. Rees and Johannes froze.

'Uh-oh,' muttered Rees, 'it appears you are the target of the bull run again, Johannes.'

'Ye gods! How can you tell that? What have I done this time?' Johannes stifled a curse.

Price was always in black humour, especially whenever he found himself having to deal with Johannes Taliesin, which by virtue of their stand-off status was a regular occurrence. But today, as a variation, his visage was lamp black. Obviously Johannes had committed an unspeakable transgression.

'There you are! I've been looking for you, Taliesin. The Principal wants to see you forthwith. Hell's teeth, where have you been this last hour?'

Professor Price always addressed Johannes in the old-fashioned derisive mode on account of his chronic dyspepsia. Without awaiting an explanation, however, he turned on Michelle.

'Who are you? Are you one of Hendy's Rent-a-Throng?' and before an answer came, 'are you with these two?'

'Michelle Hastings, no and yes.'

Professor Price gave a start as he coordinated his questions asked against Michelle's reply.

'Do you belong to this Institution?'

'Yes.'

'Hell's teeth young woman, don't be so obdurate. What is your department?' roared Price.

'Virtual Fashion,' Michelle replied coldly, Professor Price's fluster and bullying making no impression on her.

'I suggest you return to VF forthwith and in future desist from hanging around with these two reprobates!'

'I am here attending the Private View and seminars on the express instruction of Professor Hilfiger,' replied Michelle calmly, 'and while I agree with you these two are reprobates, I take advice from no one concerning my choice of friends.'

Thrown by Michelle's polite form of insubordination, Professor Price momentarily wobbled while concocting a face-saving reply. But no concoction ensued and, as the uncontrollable rage desperately needed venting, he returned to his attack on the two reprobates.

'Who gave you permission to excuse yourselves from this morning's demonstration?' he demanded. Obviously something other than the two reprobates' presumed absence without leave had kindled his rage.

'What demonstration, Professor Price?' Johannes enquired.

'No one gave us permission,' Rees dutifully answered the professor. 'We assumed as the seminars were being sponsored by iLupus-Planck, that the occasion had been sanctioned by you at Virtual Download.'

Professor Price was not having a good morning. Obediently his mood assumed a complexion of explosive purple, which in no way supported his faculty for reason. The two reprobates had witnessed him in similar dyspepsia before and had discovered dumb politeness by far outweighed the professor's authority and superior experience.

'Hell's teeth!' he roared, scrambling mentally for yet another line of attack, 'we had this demonstration set up by Rosemarie Peabody regarding a downloaded basic Fine Art Painting student of many years ago, which we decided would be an interesting comparator to today's shower,' he ended with a flourish, having turned the conversation once again to an attack on his terms.

'Well, we were not informed, Professor Price, and with respect, sir, we believe we work a lot harder than the disparate art student of yesteryear. Secondly, sir, and with utmost deference, we object to being constantly referred to as a shower,' Johannes responded, picking up on Michelle's method.

'Perhaps you could stop behaving in a manner that calls down such description,' was Professor Price's curt reply.

Meanwhile, Michelle Hastings choosing caprice as an alternative to heeding Professor Price's suggestion, stood about aimlessly, enjoying the to and fro between an incandescent professor and her two reprobate friends. At the word 'shower' she had burst into laughter, which elicited a scowl from Rees, to no avail. But her laughter had the detrimental effect of attracting the angry professor's attention again.

'As you are following instructions from Professor Hilfiger,' he said, 'perhaps you would benefit from attending the download organised by Rosemarie Peabody. There is a second running starting at eleven.'

'Come on, Shelli,' said Rees. 'Where is the demonstration, Professor Price?'

'The Antique Laboratory,' he said; then returning to the missing time, he asked, 'What was the subject matter of these seminars that have so mysteriously eluded my administration?'

'*The Red Noise* and Other Paintings,' said Michelle.

'Yes, yes. I know about the exhibition organised by the Virtual Painting Special shower, but heaven forbid, that is no seminar,' retorted Professor Price. 'Only fools and donkeys attend such hokum. At times I wish I weren't an examiner of them.'

'Michelle's favourite exhibit,' said Rees, 'the donkey.'

'Oh, really?'

' "Hideous Bile",' said Johannes, 'which was interesting inasmuch as the VSE had entangled their downloads with VSofA, so we had two for the price of one.'

' "Hideous Bile"? Is this another of your fantasies, Taliesin? And what do you mean, two for the price of one? Hell's teeth! This is wasting my time.'

'Two identical lecturers,' replied Johannes. 'I enjoyed the talk. It ended up with a powerful indictment of hypocrisy.'

'The first seminar we attended was "On Art Being Far Weaker Than Necessity" and was conducted in the dark until the audience rebelled,' said Rees.

'Old hat, in the dark,' muttered Johannes.

'Effectively it was a depository for downloads that refuse to fade, so we saw Einstein in two places.'

'At the same time?' Professor Price seemed to be losing his anger.

'No, come to think of it, there was a time lapse of at least twenty minutes between the sightings.'

'Can't believe it!' the professor said dismissively.

'True, believe it or not,' the reprobates asserted.

'Extraordinary! You are hark-backs. Your imaginations belong to the bad old days,' declared Professor Price, 'seminars being organised under my nose and I know nothing of them.'

'Best seminar was by Werner Heisenberg who referred to VSofA staff hiding in two places at once.'

'I've heard enough!' the professor roared.

'Perhaps someone has been attempting to download you, Prof,' Johannes suggested.

'Nonsense, Taliesin! I carry a suppressor with me at all times.'

'It has been known, even with a suppressor, and the victim experiences delusion and disorientation. Remember Professor Charlton and the V-tray printer,' replied Johannes.

'Nonsense, someone had spiked his coffee with Kardomah. In that case, in all seriousness I am inclined to the notion that someone is attempting to download you on a permanent basis, Johannes Taliesin,' Professor Price declared.

This last elicited titters from Rees and Michelle.

'Uncalled for, Professor Price,' retorted a grinning Johannes. 'As you are well aware I have been a virtual since climbing into *The Endless March* last year, where I became trapped, but along with all other VSofA professors and the Principal you signed a charter of confidentiality. You know I am subject to constant wave-function reorientation.'

Michelle uttered a sharp gasp, and shuddered visibly.

Rees giggled. 'Take no notice, Professor, Johannes is invoking the Bostrom edict again.'

'Surely he is, Rees. What are you talking about, Taliesin?' Professor Price asked in tones of incredulity, deliberately missing Johannes's point.

'My condition,' said Johannes, deadpan.

The professor smacked a palm on his forehead in desperation.

'Hell's teeth! Another thirteen grey hairs trying to follow your nonsense.' Professor Price shook his head. 'I'm inclined to send you to the Principal right now and forget the demonstration, but Professor Hancock insisted you should see the download demonstration before visiting him. I hope it improves your sense of reality because, dare I say, it is in dire need of adjustment. I shall check with iLupus-Planck reference your attendance at what will no doubt prove to be imaginary seminars. Now off you go to the Antique Laboratory. You have five minutes before second download commences.'

'What's the title, Professor Price?'

' "Baggardly Pompolions".'

' "Baggardly Pompolions", what does that mean?'

'Get on with it! You will soon find out,' said Professor Price, and he tore off in the opposite direction.

'My God! Someone trod on his tail this morning,' Johannes said, breathing a sigh of relief.

'You coming with us, Shelli?' asked Rees.

'Yes,' she said, 'why not? Your company has been most entertaining so far this morning.'

'Price seems to have it in for you,' said Rees, on the way to the Antique Laboratory.

'To the hilt.'

'Mind, you do taunt him somewhat – a virtual after climbing into your painting! Ha! Where do you get these notions from?'

'Don't know,' replied Johannes, 'they just appear on strange mornings like this one, but especially when Price is nagging me. Must be a historical throwback.'

'I take it you are not a virtual, then?' asked Michelle, tentatively.

'I don't think so,' replied Johannes, 'I haven't found a join yet.' And they giggled.

'It's probably hidden under layers of pustulating dead skin and other detritus,' suggested Rees.

'Rees Bowen!' squealed Michelle.

'Sorry, associating with him too long,' Rees said, thumbing at Johannes and: 'Wonder what the Prink wants you for?'

'Don't know again, but probably Orleans contacted him regarding my downloading French Conté crayons.'

'Is it forbidden in the Creative Armistice?'

'Not really, but it's in the zone of infringement surrounding it,' replied Johannes.

'Have you been downloading illegally?' squeaked Michelle, suddenly filled with admiration for her bête noire.

'Shush!' responded Johannes, 'don't want everyone to know.'

'Wait until I tell Daddy!'

'Don't waste your time, I'm not important enough,' said jaundiced Johannes.

'Anyway, Antique Clodbin,' said Rees. 'Let's go in.'

' "Baggardly Pompolions",' said Michelle. 'My, my, downloading illegally – so the rumour is true.'

'Are you a unit?' a stranger asked at the door.

'No. Three units,' Michelle answered.

'No. Two units,' interjected Johannes.

'What do you mean, two units?' Michelle asked.

'You and Rees equals one unit, I am the second.'

'Negative delete,' she said and, turning to the door stranger, 'Three units.'

'Hi Rees,' a sarcastic voice called from nearby. 'What was Price going on about regarding you two reprobates? What you been up to?'

'Nothing,' Rees retorted blankly, 'suggest you mind your own business.'

'Ohhh!' Accuser mocked good-naturedly. 'Mind my own business, that's big talk from virtual researchers.'

'He was going on about the party he's throwing tonight for his favourite students, but he cannot get the franchise to deliver the alcohol, although he had saved up his coupons,' said Johannes.

Everyone laughed.

'That's about as likely as the Chinese getting our coordinates right.'

More laughter.

'Hi, Michelle!' someone else shouted, 'Virtual Fashion student in one of our demonstrations – you're a brave girl.'

'No, I am not,' Michelle said.

'Oh, yes you are!' they all shouted.

'I notice from the convivial chatter you two are very popular in your VDC,' Michelle said to Rees and Johannes.

The three took their seats, and the auditorium calmed from the banter mood.

'They are a good-natured crowd,' said Johannes, 'but Professor Price enrols anyone who can sign their name to make up numbers. They masquerade as tomorrow's artists. The professor believes if they are c-literate and can push buttons, they will be ace virtual artists and he gets them to sign the bottom line before another institution grabs the income.'

'Similar to Hilfiger in Virtual Fashion,' Michelle said.

'Professor Price doesn't seem to grasp that we constitute an elite set-up, and all these Cheerful Charlies seem to do is dilute the quality,' Johannes said. 'I don't understand the mentality of those who think more is better. More is a damned sight worse.'

'Thus spake the arch conservative,' Rees chided. 'You are an anomaly, Johannes, out of your time, an arch conservative from a background of rural poverty. Don't know whether you're before or after our time. Regardless of that, remember we are all a waste of money, out of our time or not.'

'It's OK for you people of independent means who can afford to be comfortable liberal lefties. Me? I can only afford conservatism.'

'The more I know of you, Johannes, the less I can make you out,' said Michelle.

'Don't try too hard to make anything of me,' said Johannes, caught off-guard. 'You lot practice in nomansland where the politics of appeasement meet the politics of spite.'

'Ouch! Don't say nice things to him Shelli, the prat will fall for you. Tee-hee, only teasing Johannes,' mocked Rees.

'Shh!' came from somewhere, and the three giggled.

Rosemarie Peabody stood alone on the rostrum.

'Colleagues, thank you for assembling,' she began. 'We have decided to hold a second standing of "Baggardly Pompolions" not least due to the unforeseen developments regarding Professor Price. The least I can do is apologise publicly to Professor Price for the gross humiliation following mistaken identification by the demonstration download art student. The scene was most extraordinary, and I shudder to give details here.' A buzz swept the audience.

'Aha! That explains Price's lousy temper with you, Yo-yo,' Rees whispered.

'Honestly, if Price has an argument with his cat, he takes it out on me!' said Johannes, and the three giggled again.

Ms Peabody's body language expressed unease. 'Even our enormously powerful computers can squilch a blip at times. Fortunately we were able to throw a disabling switch before Professor Price was embarrassed beyond – are you present, Professor Price?'

She shielded her eyes from the spots and earnestly examined the audience.

'No, he went in the opposite direction,' said Johannes, and then *sotto voce*, 'thank God.'

'I don't blame him,' Ms Peabody responded. 'Regarding repetition of the unfortunate incident, please be assured – a chip has now been inserted in the D-apparatus that negates the tendency for false identification. So colleagues, the demonstration. The virtual download is of a typical fine art student from around the middle of the last century. You will note the general scruffiness of this virtual, and of course the enormous changes that have occurred in art education since that time. As we have now mastered the technology necessary for downloading olfactory stimulation, we have taken the precaution of directing the extractor fans at the podium. Needless to say, you should be aware that a repeat download does not guarantee identical simulations – we have not attained the utopian matrix stability at VSofA yet.'

Laughter rippled through the audience.

'Time has been allotted at the end for a discussion and questions.'

The usual lights flickered, gizmos whirred, lenses purred. Ms Peabody vacated the rostrum. The virtual lensing sharpened, and a quintessentially scruffy individual came into focus. He was thin and tall, wearing a beige woollen sweater loosely hanging almost to the knee. The sleeve ends hung in tatters and a large hole exposed his right elbow. He wore tight, wrinkled, greasy trousers over shiny suede boots, flat at heel. His hair was a woolly mass of ginger curls and his thin, white, pimply face possessed a vague beard. The download was a most unprepossessing sight.

'Good God!' someone exclaimed in the audience, 'it's Johannes Taliesin, Virtual Download Centre.'

'So it is. Hi, Yo-yo.'

'He really does look like you, Johannes,' Michelle giggled.

'Can't be two of them,' said Rees. 'God doesn't make the same mistake twice.'

'As he's a download from the past, then it is I who am the mistake,' Johannes declared.

'In that case, Johannes, God doesn't play dice.'

'Shh!' came the customary scolding.

'Although I claim my lot is meagre and struggle, realistically as an art student I enjoy better circumstances than the great majority of my fellows,' Download Fine Art Student began.

'Even sounds like you,' Michelle whispered.

'Both sides are unaware of the delights and privations of the other,' Download FAS continued. 'Certainly there is an ever-present aggravation to spin the privations and bury the delights, but these acts are simply part of the intrinsic hypocrisy propagated by our gurus, which courses the veins and tickles the locks in looking for recognition. I am more the artist than the white van man and his washing machine servicing jobby.

'But why the big production? Who constitutes the gallery if it is not already in your heads? These questions are confined to the refuse bin, relegated to an overused cliché that has been readily but inappropriately utilised on countless other occasions.'

'Did they actually talk like that in art colleges long ago?' Michelle asked of Johannes, convinced of the connection.

'Don't ask me, Michelle, I'm not Download!' replied Johannes, a little surprised.

'The rewards have been limited,' Download FAS continued, 'for only the art student is wrong – a modern parable on the Law of Diminishing Returns.

'Apart from a slight tear in the wing of my prayer I celebrated reaching the peak of my magistery with a need for more oxygen. Who to feather the canvas? Why the investment in a one-sided display of sincerity the slant of my hill could readily do without? And who is it at the tiller of this strange land-boat that comes scudding down Llechwedd Mawr, spinnaker gritting in the teeth of the gale?'

Download FAS paused momentarily, looking around the audience. Then, pointing his finger at somebody, he shouted:

'AVAST THERE, YE BAGGARDLY POMPOLIONS! CLEAR THE WAY, SCUD THAT GORSE AND CHAMPION A CAUSE FOR TACKING MY OPPOSITE BACKWARDS WORDPIECE!'

A rustle of alarm fleeted the audience. Michelle stared at Johannes; Johannes shrugged.

'But who is it feathering the billowing canvas?' Download FAS continued, 'flapping the land-bags on faded Saturday afternoons, painting a picture of storm-strewn surrealism? Who to feather the canvas, I frequently asked?

'Today I am a fisherman in paint-strewn overalls, clutching my tiller, wind-blasted flames flirting continuously with the changing shape of the land-boat scapegoat scudding down the hill. What a horror! The awful village idiot became an art student. Who gave me a boat to play with? Why did they not advise me boats are best on water? Don't let the glitterati catch a glimpse of me, lest they make me a genius overnight. You all know' – Download FAS swept a pointing hand – 'what happens to village idiots. They become discovered geniuses. The foolish public believe the rubbish they see on television!'

'I'm an undiscovered genius,' said Rees with his usual confidence.

'I'm an undiscovered village idiot,' Johannes said.

'Would you two either shut up or get out!' Download FAS shouted. A ripple of surprise ran through the audience.

'I am an artist in the land of mahogany shadows, a hermetically sealed world redolent of the symbol and prop of unreality. The hermit within me stands on his head with an agility achieved after many years of conditioning. The conditioning is structured to run a nano-wisp alongside the real world, shadowing its selected instances, balancing my scripts in an empty hall. The hall is papered with mirrors. But they do not reflect the symbols and props scattered arbitrarily. Rather, the images jeer with enlarged jaws the monstrous effect of their apocryphal stories.'

Download FAS paused, looking about the audience, who met his theatrical examination with silence.

'Are there any questions at this intermediate stage?' he asked.

'Yes,' said Michelle, quick as lightning, 'what are you talking about?'

'My lot as an art student – I thought it was obvious.'

'Of course it's obvious,' said one of the numbskull enrolments. 'Please continue, as most of us are finding your talk fascinating.'

Michelle recoiled in amazement, which brought Rees into the attack.

'Clever boots over there might be fascinated on his superficial level, but my friend Michelle is asking for elucidation at a deeper philosophical level.'

'There is no deeper philosophical level,' Download FAS quickly responded.

'There's a deeper philosophical level to everything, you poser,' shouted Johannes, joining in the tussle, 'even to claiming your lot is meagre and struggle.'

'I thought that was a good opening sentence,' retorted Download FAS.

'You cannot utter sentences without accepting responsibility for their concomitant meaning,' Johannes retorted.

Download FAS looked alarmed: clearly he was out of his depth. Ms Peabody empathised by clearing her throat and motioning with her hands to the audience to ease off.

'Might I interrupt,' she said, acting the good referee, 'and ask you to keep comments and questions to the end. Perhaps it is not wise to invite questions at the halfway stage,' she added, smiling nervously at Download FAS. For his part, Download looked relieved to have been extricated from a predicament of his own making.

'Cats lick cream off the faces of cutout kings,' he continued.

'But this is nothing. Let us embark on my journey deep into the land of mahogany shadows, where daydreams come true and wishes are screwed backwards to the studios with their paint-strewn easels and naked models. If the daydreams fail to material-ise, then the rules are changed and everyone including the fools is expected to believe it. If all else fails, I can join the others by climbing into my painting. There is an inherent danger when playing this game. The artist can become trapped in his painting and there is no return, no return, no return.'

'Did you know Download was going to say this?' Rees asked Johannes. 'You know, the climbing into one's painting bit you prattled on to Price about?'

'No.'

'This is uncanny: not only does he look like you, is dressed like you, sounds like you, but he is coming up with your ideas as well,' said Rees.

'And smells like him,' added Michelle.

'What?' Johannes levelled his gaze on Michelle.

'Only joking,' she replied.

'This is no joking matter,' said Rees, 'too uncanny to be joke-worthy.'

Deep in conversation, they had not noticed Download FAS had left the rostrum, climbed over the rows of seats and was standing beside them, wild eyed, nostrils flaring, glaring murder-ous eyes.

'Did you deliberately dress like that to annoy me?' he said, addressing Johannes.

'Oh dear,' said Johannes, 'we are about to have an incident.'

'My God!' exclaimed Michelle, 'the bodily function aroma! Go away, please.'

'Ms Peabody, could you please control your download?' Rees shouted across, but Rosemarie Peabody had already triggered an alarm system and was centring the sensor arms to render the download harmless. Just as Download took a swing he began to fade and, although Johannes instinctively took evasive action, the virtual fists passed harmlessly through bodies and seats. Then he was gone. Just the smell remained.

'I'm dreadfully sorry,' said Ms Peabody, 'that's the last time I experiment with Fine Art Students of the past. On every occasion they turn out to be aggressive. Unfortunately we did not have the opportunity to ask questions.'

'Strange to be confronted by one's doppelganger from the past,' mused Johannes, 'except I'm not the pugilistic type.'

'Verbally pugilistic perhaps,' said Rees.

'Why do you think old download took such a dislike to you?' Michelle pondered.

'Good ponder,' said Johannes. 'Dogs take a dislike to certain other dogs, but there is no intellectual reasoning behind the reaction. Humans and virtual humans pretend they possess the capacity for balanced sagacity and reflection – maybe on the surface, but just beneath they act like dogs. We have never understood why Price dislikes me with an unhealthy passion.'

'You must have crossed him initially.'

'That is what everybody says.'

'Colleagues, may I have your attention,' called Rosemarie Peabody in an uncharacteristically loud voice. 'Before you go, Voiceover as an expert historical witness has an analysis of Download FAS, which you may find interesting as a counter-argument to his unusual presentation.'

Everyone obediently sat down again.

'I hope Voiceover explains the aggression towards me,' Johannes said.

'I trust all will be explained,' said Ms Peabody. 'Switching now.'

'That illusory Fine Art Student you have been subjected to' – Voiceover went straight into the theme – 'expressed a deliberate act of conformism to the environment he frequents, which can never be your environment by any stretch of the imagination or compacting of years. We marvel at the social distance you have travelled in the meantime. Generally we saw him as unkempt but specifically dirty, exuding that obnoxious sweet-stale stink that was a cross between last night's beer house, the overcrowded doss house where he lodges and old dog crap. He wore his *eau de toilette* with a swagger, having laboured for months to achieve it. In his era women were attracted to him—'

'What? Attracted to that heap?' Michelle was aghast; other

women in the audience uttered noises of concurrence.

'Believe it or not in his era women were attracted to him, to which he postured indifference. The cocoon of mirrors he referred to gave a disingenuous presentation of reality. The only mirrors he cocooned himself in were imaginary, where each facet watched industriously lest his flaws and imperfections slip out and publicise themselves. He pretends to be the artist with the flamboyance of ostrich feathers, pretentiousness spun through with naivety. His propensity for self-delusion assumed a dimension sufficient to eclipse the matters whose existence reinstates his naivety. In other words, Download Fine Art Student was a self-perpetuating myth.

'Although he claimed his lot to be meagre and struggle,' Voiceover continued against a background of avid attention punctuated by sounds of accord, 'circumstances were allowed to degrade only as far as his well-being comfort would allow, whereupon lines were firmly drawn. This was typical of the behavioural ethos of that time. Peer group pretensions inveigled this weak article to assume the pose before the conclusion of fresher term, the image adopted ahead of a steady grasp of the substantive elements. Peer group and crossover pressure rejoiced but momentarily, for now they had competition in their midst. Download Fine Art Student's compromised position was exacerbated by the dilemma in which his fear to resist lest he had to face the consequences was countered by his inability to resist regardless of the consequences.

'This conundrum of insecurity he burdened with an arrogance that vied with zealotry, for there was nothing that was not subject to an instantaneous paste and patch job if the occasion demanded. He gathered his conscience with such consummate ease that the casual observer, glancing inward, admired the style by which the mask assumed the youth.

'In those days being an art student was a public licence for self-indulgence. The art student enjoyed more advantages and better circumstances than the majority of his fellows. Both sides, however, were unaware of the delights and privations of the other. Certainly there existed an ever-present aggravation to spin the privations and bury the delights. The world of the art student contained many houses that were the result of overnight construction as an exigency for meeting the decaying fabric of the cocoon. Regrettably the houses were easier to construct than demolish, and daily they demanded maintenance against the eroding questions of the student's admirers. His assumptions turned to certainty in a half-life of three months that his *modus vivendi* was foolproof: but it was transient, illusory, the reality apparent yet not there. His was the exposition of an ideology of illusory promises that could not demonstrate an anchor. Call down scenario!'

On the rostrum appears a corridor, buzzing with people. Students of the art education world are seen inhabiting a make-believe Flann O'Brien's *The Third Policeman* story where anything may happen.

Suddenly the Principal jumps out from his office and nails a passing student.

'Is it about a bicycle?' he demands.

'No, sir – but if it is any help to you I saw one being peddled up Mayhill this morning.'

'No, it certainly is not any help. Besides, what were you doing on Mayhill this morning?'

'I live on Mayhill.'

'Oh, that Mayhill, why did you not say?'

'I didn't know there is more than one Mayhill, sir.'

'There are twenty-three, you fool, and still counting.'

Scenario fades.

'What was that meant to illustrate?' Johannes asked amid concurring mutters from the audience.

'We will proceed,' Voiceover said in a firm electronic noise. 'In art education academic staff and students were never wrong and never made mistakes however accidental. If an error of judgement by some uncomprehendingly freak occurrence was ever made, or gross acts of negligence came about, or incompetence was bounding abroad, it was always someone else at fault. Accepting blame was off the agenda. A joint project with an art student resulting in success meant it was the art student's achievement; a joint project with an art student resulting in failure meant it was your fault. From the day of enrolment the art student was imbued with the mantra that it shall always be someone else's fault. Download Fine Art Student was no exception to this covenant.'

'Nothing historical in that – sounds like VSofA any day of the week,' said Johannes.

'We will proceed.' The electronic sound of Voiceover contained a hint of crackling. 'The art world pretended to be classless, shamelessly classless. The proletarians strove upwards, bourgeoisie strove downwards, both in the cosy knowledge that if matters became unmanageable they could flee to the cosy folds whence they came – the proletarian to the safety of poverty, the bourgeoisie to the comfort of mummy's purse. Both flights were taken under heavy disguise, lest their identities be blown by peer group all and Sunday best. And who is to feather the canvas—'

'That question again,' whispered Johannes.

'One conformist hailed from the salutary ranks of the bourgeoisie, the other the ranks of the proletariat. Yet they were so different. One sought the power of attention, the other sought the attention of power. Never count on the support of the powerless.'

'That's strong,' interrupted Johannes. 'Never count on the support of the powerless.'

'Hisst, Johannes Taliesin,' came from the audience.

'Both classes believed that through such striving they attained their objectives,' Voiceover went on, 'but each was as acceptable to the other as conflagration on the Mare Tranquillitatis. Whenever they collided in the middle, each viewed the other with deep disdain.'

'The age from which Download Fine Art Student came was fatuous, as opposed to the present time, which is more fatuous.'

A burst of jeering and cheering laughter thronged the lecture theatre.

'Strange places, art schools, real or virtual. A manager is trapped by class. The manager from proletarian ranks will eventually be nailed by the bourgeoisie for not holding enough dinner parties, wearing the occasional dinner jacket, genuflecting to the Fabians or skewing his old money to social causes. The manager from the bourgeoisie will eventually be nailed for trivia by a consortium of fascist unions. There were always exploitable loopholes in favour of hoi polloi, the flavour of the media minorities and fashionable perverts, but never management. It was odd how a hitherto watertight contract would contain potential leaks according to the miscreant's origins. Odd places, art schools, pretending they were training artists! Long since their ideologies had blinded them to their original mission.

'Strange essence was the law of nature that ensured the bindings of contracts would unravel the moment someone other than management committed the offence. Download Fine Art Student lived in a dream world! In the art school society of flexible values the same misdemeanour was considered harmless in some, a capital offence in others. Is it any different today?'

Voiceover paused.

'Is it any different today?' it repeated.

'Yes,' said Johannes, always ready to rise to the bait, 'the society we live in today has no values at all, leave alone flexible values.'

Silence. Johannes, unable to cope with silence following one of his statements, spoke on.

'In fact, art has no values any more, the only value if any being that which one can extort for an artefact or download. I had confirmation of that earlier this morning in the "On Art Being Far Weaker Than Necessity" seminar.'

'Shut up, Johannes Taliesin, your divulgences are embarrassing,' came from the back.

All the cameras turned and focused on Johannes.

'Cynicism from one so young attains a new order,' Voiceover commented. 'Remember, cynics are manufactured by life, they are not born with the medal pinned on them.'

'Agreed,' said Johannes.

'I hesitate to interrupt this cosy tête-à-tête with the malcontent who has furnished us with regular interruptions throughout this session,' a voice of authority said from the back, 'but I am concerned at the lack of reference to designer substance. Practically all that has been analysed to date relates to psycho-sociological trivia regarding the aimless wanderings of airheads. Hardly anything Voiceover has so far said has referred to the main mission of art schools, *vis*, the education and training of young people to grasp the physical aspects, the mental faculties to think through in advance the evolvement of certain options, and then judiciously selecting the optimum to proceed to production; and to acquire the practical skills and craftsmanship to execute that production.'

'Who is he?' whispered Johannes.

'Don't know,' said Rees.

'I know him,' whispered Michelle, 'he is Professor Barcode Cardigan – Professor Hilfiger commissions him from time to time to discuss intrinsic design tensions in clothing. Now he's the type of bloke I'd go to bed with.'

'I'll tell your daddy.'

'Daddy knows. Daddy is his legal adviser,' she said knowingly.

'Well, well, well!' said Johannes.

'We agree with Professor Barcode Cardigan,' said Voiceover, 'and as a consequence we will proceed with a new slant. Managers clandestinely tested natural law, but the chains followed them around like shadows. The insecurity of the persecuted could be realised in futile gestures of bonhomie, or seen masquerading as intense preoccupation with one's craft, or as indifference to slings and arrows, or in the loneliness of sitting at a single table. The most readily purchasable commodity in the senior common rooms of art schools was treachery.'

'When left to their own devices Download Fine Art Student and his erstwhile colleagues became repetitive and uninspiring. The more they assumed attitude, the less vitality their work possessed. Anyone venturing constructive advice was accused of breaking ranks and was peremptorily voiced down. They were dealt a latter-day fate similar to the justice administered by the Egyptians upon Hittite messengers who had the temerity to deliver unwelcome messages. King Suppiluliumas's son never reached Egypt during the siege of Carchemish. The scheming attackers never heeded the truth. So similarly the work in art schools rotted in stillbirth, the crossbar being systematically lowered to accommodate diminishing skills. But they could not see it coming, siege of this or that regardless.'

'Good stuff! Sounds as if it's an analysis of today's VSofA,' Johannes declared cynically.

'I wouldn't go as far as that, Johannes,' muttered Rees, ever the diplomat.

Johannes's declaration of on-side support for Voiceover

implemented an unplanned hesitation in the mechanisms of its predetermined discourse. A few glicks and scratches followed. The hesitation had turned into a pause.

'That's torn the fabric of its logic cube!' Rees tut-tutted.

'I was only agreeing with what was said,' Johannes said with a sniff.

Cameras scanned the audience, and once again all came to a halt focusing on Johannes. There they held a detached study of him for some embarrassing seconds.

'Uh-oh,' muttered Michelle, 'it's you they are scanning, Johannes.

A large image of Johannes appeared on the monitor showing him shrinking into his seat. A buzz of disapproval swept the audience.

'We thought Download Fine Art Student had been dematerialised,' Voiceover declared after a long while of whirring, purring examination, 'yet there he is sitting as smug as yesterday's transcript in the audience. How dare this happen when I have been programmed to assassinate the historical character? What sort of game is VSofA playing? How dare it come to pass, Ms Peabody?'

Johannes looked dead shifty. Subtle noises of enjoyment slipped from the audience.

'Er, the student in the audience you are examining is not the Download FAS you have been programmed to character assassinate,' Rosemarie Peabody said uncomfortably. 'He is Johannes Taliesin, current research student and bane of all academics at Virtual Download Centre. I can assure you any resemblance to Download FAS is purely coincidental.'

'This is worse! Bane of all academics?' muttered Johannes. 'What's with everyone this morning?'

'We are not convinced.' Voiceover was adamant. 'The scan discloses an infrared photon print match identification. We cannot continue while he is present. Fade him, and fade him properly this time.'

'This is silly,' protested Johannes. 'I am not the Download FAS.'

'Silly,' echoed Rees. 'He's not Download FAS, he's Johannes Taliesin, bane of all academics in Virtual Download Centre.'

'Infinitely worse than a Doppelganger!' shouted Voiceover, distorting the speakers. 'You are the real Download FAS. You must fade forthwith!'

'But we cannot fade realities, as your programming is aware,' protested Ms Peabody hopelessly.

'The infrared photon match would explain a lot of things about you, Johannes,' said Rees, not taking the situation as seriously as the commotion demanded.

'FADE!' Voiceover's distorted tones blared out.

'He is Johannes Taliesin, bane of all academics in Virtual Download Centre, and to prove it he downloads forgeries!' shouted Michelle.

'Thanks, Michelle, that helps my case majestically,' grumbled Johannes.

'This is serious,' Barcode Cardigan joined in, 'if we have an alien virtual in our midst, then we have a right to know, for all sorts of reasons.'

'Give me a good reason why you have a right to know,' shouted Johannes.

'That does not merit discussion,' Barcode Cardigan snorted contemptuously. 'We do not have to justify our right to know.'

'FADE!' Voiceover again crackled.

'Off you fade, Yo-yo. We always suspected something unusual,' a Virtual Download Centre colleague mocked.

Johannes the mistaken alien reflected on events as he walked alone up Corridor Escher. Many people and events passed him by. After several hundred metres it was apparent he was experiencing great difficulty in holding a reference against the chameleon tendencies of doors, bulwarks and corridor as they performed their fan dance with reality. Rees and Michelle had intended catching up with him but, hiding beneath spurious excuses, had not yet appeared. His predicament was alarming: a simple case of mistaken identity was a manageable concept, but for the infrared photon identification to place him as belonging to a different age was deeply threatening. But there again, why had his alien profile not shown up previously? Any number of stations in VSofA existed where infrared identification was utilised. This last nugget of reasoning convinced Johannes there had been an electronic malfunction in the workings of the Antique Laboratory; anyway, Ms Peabody had a reputation for muddling her programming.

Where once the Principal's office had been, now a brightly lit entrance beckoned to a zone not otherwise registered on the layout map. The usual habit of virtuals vanishing through walls and his walking through visiting downloads gave him a sense of reassurance and stability. But now shapes crept out of dark alcoves unformed and uncontrolled, as if drunk; his trip to gather materials for Samuel Palmer downloads had consumed his last beer euro, so no fear of that. Most disconcerting of all were the uncontrollable throwbacks. Either he was losing his grip on reality or the seminar organisers had lost control of their games. Voiceover must have been part of the muddle.

Johannes had been thrown out of lectures and demonstrations before through his natural argumentativeness fuelled by a narrow intellect. But on this occasion he had not earned expulsion; being thrown out through mistaken identity was deeply traumatic for one convinced he was unique. Ms Peabody should have defended him more strongly; her failure to do so added to his conspiracy mindset. How simple and straightforward Download Fine Art Student's life seemed to be compared with the multifaceted directionless phenomenon that was today's School of Art. Johannes longed to know, even experience, more of the old art schools; in many ways he envied Download Fine Art Student his pretentious but simple lifestyle.

Due to the iLupus-Planck high-energy seminars in the studio-labs, quanglement configuration was occurring throughout the old Victorian edifice. The effects were especially seen in Corridor Escher, where endlessness had become the dominant geometry of the day. The sponsors, in their zealous pursuit of commercial gain, had ignored warnings against commissioning sensitive equipment in the old buildings, and had overridden the scientific sobriety of the experts. Nevertheless, quanglement had happened frequently before, hence the appellation Corridor Escher. Countless virtuals had disappeared never again to be recalled. Neither staff nor students seemed to care. At this particular moment in the corridor's history Johannes was lost in its endless regression. Many events and people passed back.

Then he encountered the door he had been seeking. It was an imposing structure, in its usual livery of dark winsor blue, the name printed gold fading in Roman capitals: Principal. Professor KW Hancock, Rome Scholar. Professor Price had omitted to indicate the Principal's reason for summoning Johannes. Baggardly Pompolions, rather than delivering elucidation, had further fogged Johannes's already confused view. He glanced around to check whether Rees and Michelle were to be seen, but apart from a throng and buzz of strangers, there was no one he knew. He knocked.

Johannes waited for permission to enter. The noise of the throng masked any signal from within. He knocked harder.

'Min,' he heard distantly, which could have originated in the gaggle and giggle of Corridor Escher, but Johannes convinced himself the invitation had originated from within the Principal's office, so he opened the huge door and entered.

Principal Hancock was not there. Instead an old-fashioned Life Class of the previous century was in full operation, with about a dozen students busily drawing from the naked female model. Some students were standing at easels while others were seated on donkeys, all arranged in a semicircle around the rostrum. Everyone – students, model, tutor – turned and stared at the interloper. Johannes gasped. He looked about the life class, completely lost.

'Sorry,' he muttered, 'The Principal wished to see me… it said Principal on the door.' He motioned with his hand, backing out the while.

'No, don't apologise,' a tutor called quickly stepping forward, 'we have been expecting you. Do come in and join the class.'

'But I'm awaited by the Principal—' Johannes mumbled.

'That is correct. You have found the right place,' the tutor said cheerfully. 'Please join us.'

'The Principal wishes to see me,' he said, squirming.

'Yes, we know, and you have come to the right place. Please join the class,' chirped the tutor merrily.

'I have no equipment to join your class,' Johannes said as he wriggled uncomfortably.

'We have ample equipment,' the tutor responded.

'But life class and drawing the nude is not on my curriculum.'

'Please, stop procrastinating and join the class. We have ample equipment for drawing the nude. Please be assured that in reporting to the Principal you have come to the right place.'

'Is he here?' Johannes was far from convinced. Finding no Principal in his office and instead being confronted by an ancient life class in a much larger studio was most unexpected.

'In spirit, yes. Come along, close the door and join us.'

Johannes had never seen this particular room or a room of this nature before. The room contained a high ceiling; silken drapes in pale blue and rose hung on three of its walls. The fourth wall constituted an enormous window. Plaster casts of ancient classical sculpture littered the corners; the floor was of wooden boards, stained dark oak. The room was warm, presumably the normal temperature for a life studio when the model was wearing no clothes. An atmosphere reeking of ancient linseed oil and spirits pervaded, and the studio was similar to ancient life studios he had seen on image in the library.

The large window afforded a view out over the roofs of what he presumed to be old Swansea, but he did not recognise any of the buildings. A hill covered in terrace houses stood in the middle distance. In the foreground a church spire and its clock face were clearly visible. At a glance he noted the time.

Johannes looked back to the students, who had resumed paying attention to the model and were drawing manually on their papers. They were all relics of the past, feverishly grappling with the challenges of line form proportion that the naked model presented. Many of them resembled Download Fine Art Student, in their hairstyles, clothes and general demeanour. Neither males nor females were as well dressed as Johannes's peer group at Virtual Download Centre, but Johannes's scruffiness was not out of place.

Johannes could not prevent himself from staring at the model. She was exquisite and beautiful; being deprived of contact with the opposite sex obliged Johannes to continue staring at her, against his better judgement. Blonde with an almond complexion, she was precisely the image of his fantasies. Her stunning proportions and her features reminded Johannes of someone he had either met or seen on video, hence his recurring fantasy. His heart pounded; it was all too much to bear. The model, oblivious to the turmoil in Johannes's head, was relaxing languidly on a chaise longue.

In a matter of seconds the tutor had produced drawing board, paper and a variety of pencils. The board was heavy, factored from wood; the hand-made white paper possessed a hard surface to the touch; and the pencils were the old-fashioned graphite of differing tonal consistency and density. These were implements for manual drawing and Johannes was meant to use them. The tutor manoeuvred an easel into a gap between two students and his apparatus was set up on it. The other students smiled and nodded welcomingly. The model momentarily broke her head pose and smiled at him. He felt trapped.

Although the whole atmosphere was friendly and warm, Johannes was gripped by a violent spasm of panic. Here was a moment of stark surrealism: one minute walking the Escher Corridor on his way to keep an appointment with the Principal of the Virtual School of Art, the next in an ancient life class being expected to draw the model. He had never drawn anything before, leave alone a naked woman. He did not have a clue where to start. Glancing nervously about at other drawings to garner clues he was alarmed to note the masterly quality consistently attained by each student. Their confident dexterity was confirmation to him that he had walked into a downloaded life class from an antique School of Art of long ago. This greatly assuaged his panic, as obviously he was in the wrong place and was yet again the subject of mistaken identity.

'I'm quite sure I am in the wrong class,' he suddenly blurted, turning to the tutor.

'And I'm quite sure you are not, Mr Taliesin,' replied the tutor cheerfully.

'You know my name!' He felt a spasm of panic.

'Of course we do, Mr Taliesin.'

'But this class is a download. I don't belong here.' His confidence was encountering difficulty in returning. Johannes added, 'I wish I could draw to the standard of your download students, but unfortunately you and they are of another time. Besides, I can't draw.'

'On the contrary, Mr Taliesin, it is you who are the download, if you mean what I presume. We refer to the likes of you as visitors. You are an awkward reverse backward visitor from another school of art. If you were not, then you would be invisible and the group here would not recognise you, you understand? We have been expecting you.'

'How do you know my name?'

'Professor William Price telephoned me. He assured me he would persuade you to make yourself available, although he was obliged to use a little subterfuge, as he put it, otherwise you could prove obdurate. His description of you as a throwback to the good old days was highly accurate, so it was easy to recognise you. I set up an old door on which "Principal" was printed. All that was needed was for Professor Price to instruct you to report to the Principal. Simple and effective because, I am pleased to confirm, you are here.'

'It was Professor Price who give you my name, I take it?' Johannes enquired, deeply suspicious.

'Yes, of course. Professor Price commissioned me to undertake the exercise of adopting a student from Virtual School of Art to teach the formal elements of traditional life drawing.'

'Why did he choose me to be the control?'

'I requested a change to the tradition of nominating an outstanding student in favour of a recalcitrant loony who kicks the traces at every turn. He roared with laughter, saying without hesitation "Johannes Taliesin has to be my nominee". He added wishfully that the experiment should not go according to plan – that you be left stranded with us in "nomansland". I believe he was jesting.'

'That comment sounds like Price,' grumbled Johannes, 'but I don't think he was jesting although I have never witnessed him roaring with laughter.'

'Well, to be honest with you Mr Taliesin, it was more of a snigger than a laugh,' the tutor said.

'I can't draw,' said Johannes.

'So you insist in repeating, but please don't fret about it. The magic of this backwards time-shift experiment is that we will teach you how to draw during your stay here.'

'How long am I to stay for?'

'Only as long as it takes the tutorial group and me to teach you the rudiments of drawing.'

'How long do you think that will take?'

'As long as is necessary,' said the tutor patiently.

'I have just walked in here off Corridor Esher, VSofA – so I am still in VSofA, aren't I?' Johannes asked uncomfortably.

'Good Heavens, no! This is not VSofA, but the building is the same. For us the corridor is short and sweet, hung with chandeliers. Professor Price has told me that the corridor is now endless due to some strange configuration I don't begin to understand. It not only travels through space but through time. I believe Professor Price. If you, Johannes, pass through that door' – the tutor gestured towards the door through which Johannes had entered – 'you will experience an endless corridor. When any of us goes through it we enter the short and sweet corridor, as normal.'

'Are you implying our technology allows telephone calls to travel back in time? I have never heard of that.'

'Must do, otherwise Professor Price could not have arranged your visit with us,' the tutor said with a smile.

'I know VSofA uses virtual downloads, but I didn't know we simultaneously traversed time,' said Johannes.

'Obviously you do, otherwise you would not be here,' the tutor said.

'What if I make a dash for the door and escape?'

'Try if you like, but you know full well you will remain in this time zone until we see fit to break it.'

'It's going to be a long time, because I can't draw,' Johannes said, returning to his negative slant.

'Oh, for goodness's sake, Johannes Taliesin, stop grumbling and get on with it,' said a female member of the group. 'We are all becoming tired of your whingeing.'

'Yes,' said another, 'does everyone bellyache like you back in your time zone?'

'Bellyache?' retorted Johannes. 'Is that what you call astute questioning?'

These remarks from the students of the life class of long ago stung Johannes deeply. Severely chastened, he set about tackling his difficult task.

The clock on the tower struck the quarter hour. Johannes's drawing had developed dramatically from a small smudge to a large smudge. He was grappling with the graphite that had a constitution of its own; each additional mark compounded the statement of his incompetence. Johannes genuinely tackled the problem, within the parameters of his limited ability to persevere, that is; but the reality was that he had never been taught any formal approach to the methodology of drawing. His newly constituted fellow students took furtive glances at his work, looked at each other, stifling their giggles. Johannes's greatest challenge was sustaining his attention beyond the few-second threshold of interest that was his norm at VSofA. Major deficiencies in his attitude permeated the modules of his work. No thing in his production profile had hitherto highlighted his superficial approach to the learning programme. Apart from wrestling with his incompetence and lack of technical experience, he had the additional problem of wrestling with his lust for the model, a real naked woman reclining before him.

The tutor approached. 'Initially I left you to your own devices,' he said in good-natured tone, 'so that I and the tutor group can identify a reference point for us to undertake constructive criticism before the commencement of some systematic teaching.'

The students gathered round and gloated at his grotesque smudge. The model tip-toed over and peered; she stifled a giggle and her breasts shook; then she slipped back to her chaise longue. The students equally contained themselves in refined dignity, but nonetheless the management of their faces denoted judgemental attitudes.

'Putting it kindly,' the tutor began, 'this is what we would refer to as an attempt that has returned an impoverished alternative. Could I have constructive comments from members of the group, please?'

'No explicit delineation – in fact, cannot identify individual linear statements.'

'Proportional measurement non-existent.'

'Positioning on paper poor.'

'No reference to an initial marker.'

'Details have been tackled before the large areas, such as obsession with genitals to the detriment of body mass control.'

'Lack of mapping resulting in a sense of incoherence.'

'Inconsistency of pencil pressure, heavy when it should be light, and delicate in passages where it should be heavy.'

'Foreshortening haywire – cannot see evidence of fore-shortening.'

'Fingers have interfered with the drawing process, hence the smudging.'

'The language of the line seems to be *ultra vires* to the visitor's vocabulary.'

'Tonal gradation bears no reference to the light and tone on the model.'

'Any more?' the tutor asked.

'Isn't that enough?' asked Johannes in total alarm, whereupon the group, believing this to be wry humour, collapsed in laughter.

Johannes was in deep trouble; it had never occurred to him to attend to his lack of drawing skills, as his arrogant assumption was that modern art and design education did not use them. To be fair, life drawing was confined to the shelves of history at VSofA and the library. To that end, all of the formal elements of drawing and design were relegated to the waste bin; the only skills necessary for survival at VSofA were keyboard, a comprehensive working knowledge of available programs and the ability to avoid offending the professors. These skills failed to stand him in good stead in his present life-drawing predicament.

'It is clear that either you are wasting your school's time or your school is wasting your time.' The tutor's demeanour continued to be reasonable. 'In either case I regret to say the standard of your outcome is abysmal. What do you spend your time studying at your school of art?'

'Surely Professor Price should have told you. I study at the Virtual Download Centre in Virtual School of Art. Currently I am working on a research project to download Samuel Palmers on to genuine materials,' replied Johannes with a flourish.

This was met by stifled giggles and snuffles of incredulity

from the student group, causing the tutor to caste a glance disapprovingly.

'Yes, by download I understand you to mean offload a burden, or copy Samuel Palmer's work. But what I mean is – what are you studying?'

'I'm studying the skills of downloading successfully.'

'Obviously I am not making myself understood, Mr Taliesin, although I believe my questions are perfectly straightforward. Perhaps you have another language for it. Clearly, you can't draw and it is obvious you have never been in a Life Class before today. Yet you are a visitor from a school of art, so what art and craft skills are you actually studying?' The tutor spoke with great patient forbearing.

'I have explained,' said Johannes. 'With respect it appears you don't know what downloading means.'

'Well, in that case, perhaps you should explain this new method of study to us,' replied the tutor, becoming ever-so-slightly tetchy.

'We use three-dimensional computers combined with V-trays to download anything – people, places, works of art from the past. We play around with the quantum dynamics and accelerate out the quanglement to enforce the imagery through perspicacious venting of selected sub-atomic particles at the appropriate moment. Of course, the computer calculates the appropriate moment, as tolerances are so fine we could never hope to be accurate enough manually. We still encounter problems, such as the photon wave-function being too large and occluding the sub-atomic particle imagery, and quanglement dissipates the two-slit imagery, but most times we succeed.'

Johannes's newly accustomed fellow students were stunned. Obviously they did not have a clue what he was talking about. Even the model had the sense to stop giggling.

'And how, pray God, does art come into this?' asked the tutor with great deliberation.

'We download all things and people artistic, that is why we are called the Virtual School of Art. A few kilometres from us is an institution that concerns itself wholly with matters financial: their title is the Virtual School of Economics. Now and again our wave-functions become entangled because of the huge power inputs to generate the imagery, which causes interesting problems.'

'Which old masters do you reproduce?' a student asked.

'We don't reproduce them, we download the real thing.'

'I'm beginning to understand why you can't draw, Mr Taliesin,' said the tutor, 'but are there schools of art where drawing is still taught?'

'Not in the UK, but there is one at Delft,' replied Johannes, as helpful as possible.

'Did we hear you say not in the UK?'

'Yes.'

'Go on, tell us you are setting up a Virtual School of Art on the moon.'

'Not yet, but there are research stations on the moon funded by international syndicates.'

'Am I hearing this?'

'So far we have failed to prompt our downloads into creating anything other than that which they have already created. We frequently download Picasso because he is great entertainment.'

The old clock loudly chimed the half hour.

'Am I hearing this?' repeated one of the students.

'What in God's name has walked into our class?' another asked.

'Now give Mr Taliesin a fair hearing, please,' said the tutor and, turning to Johannes, asked, 'By downloading Pablo Picasso I take it you commission him to visit your school of art to give demonstrations?'

This struck Johannes as very funny. 'That would be too clever!' he laughed. 'No, as Picasso is dead we download him as a virtual image.'

They all roared with laughter. The model, having struggled throughout to contain herself, erupted in laughter. Johannes had never before seen a naked woman enjoying a good laugh, and he was entranced. The others took her laughter for granted.

'Picasso dead?' the tutor spluttered. 'Do you know something we don't know?' and they all began to wag and shake their heads in pity.

'Picasso has been dead for more than half a—'

'I've heard enough of this science fiction nonsense,' said a student irritably. 'Let us get back to drawing the model and ask this visitor to leave.'

'Picasso died in 1973,' insisted Johannes.

'Crystal ball stuff!'

'What year is this?' demanded Johannes unsubtly.

'The year, Mr Taliesin, is 1958, and Picasso is very much alive living in the South of France.'

'1958! My God, I've come back a long time.'

'I think I had better revisit Mr Taliesin's smudge,' said a wit, 'it is probably a highly coded download of the model.'

'As smudges go.' And they enjoyed the joke at Johannes's expense.

'I would like to go home,' Johannes said rather sadly.

'You are free to go, Mr Taliesin.' The tutor's voice contained a note of relief. 'But I must say Professor Price was fairly spot-on in nominating you. You are a recalcitrant loony, but with a strong undertone of enigma, which he failed to mention. Please go – you have given us much to think about.'

Without a word, Johannes took the opportunity to leave before anything else untoward arose. For a moment he thought of asking for his smudge as proof to show Rees and Michelle, but then thought better of it in case it heeded his progress back.

'Goodbye, Mr Download!' someone called.

'Bye.'

'I for one have enjoyed your visit,' said the model as a passing shot.

'And I have enjoyed looking at you,' returned Johannes with a smile.

'Goodbye, Mr Taliesin,' the tutor called.

Johannes was through the large door and out in the corridor in a matter of seconds.

Back in the illusive reality of Corridor Escher Johannes sat on a bench reflecting on his 1958 life class. The gaggling throng scuttled, but as before no temporaneous references were evident to indicate past, present or future. The endless corridor had the atmosphere of the 1958 life class, as he could not recognise any of the passing students; but the tutor had been convincing in explaining no endlessness existed in 1958. The cock-and-bull story spun by the tutor regarding Price telephoning him in 1958 was inexplicable. How could that be done without visiting the date? Johannes had learnt back in the First Year Introductory course that electrons cannot travel back in time, but there again, they cannot travel forward either. Why had no members of the life class given their names? What purpose was served in Price transporting him back to a life class in 1958? The events of the past few hours had conspired to rid Johannes of his optimism. He was overcome by a deep foreboding for the future.

He had been sitting on a corridor bench contemplating his predicament when:

'Hey, What did the Principal have to say to you?'

Johannes looked up to see the smiling faces of Rees and Michelle.

'Hi! Am I glad to see familiar faces.'

'What happened? What did the Principal say?' asked Rees.

'And what about that awful episode in the Antique Laboratory Lecture Theatre – is it true?' asked Michelle.

'Something much stranger has happened since the Antique Laboratory affair,' said Johannes. 'You see that door marked Principal?' He pointed excitedly. 'I presented myself through it but the Principal was not there. Rather, I walked straight into the middle of a life class in full process of all things, with a tutor and about a dozen students. An old-fashioned life class with a naked model and easels and manual drawing implements back in – guess what date. Guess how far back I have been reverse downloaded. Go on, guess.'

Corridor Escher buzzed more noisily than ever, almost drowning their talk.

'This is Johannes joking again. Could not be more than twenty years. Where was the Principal? What did he have to say?'

'Not there, I'm telling you. I'm aware of the technical limitations in time, but this was a hell of a lot more than twenty years,' Johannes insisted.

'Principal could have popped out and you had one of your Johannes unconnecting moments.'

'I don't get those moments these days, Rees.'

'But more than twenty is impossible – ghostly superposition of intrinsic uncertainty and all that, so the physicists say. Twenty years is the limit. It must have been twenty years ago.'

'No, it was much more. Besides, no one knows. Anyone who thinks they understand quanglement, doesn't. Same with retro downloading, I think – not making excuses for whoever initiated the experiment.'

'Can't be more than twenty,' Rees insisted.

'Well, they refute consciousness playing a direct role in the physical world at the quantum level but, as my expectations had been focused on meeting the Principal, my mind was not resistant to virtual downloading. You could say an unlimited length of time was unexpected, can't think of any other explanation.'

'I'm bored with this technical trivia.' Michelle's patience had burst. 'Tell us the date, for God's sake.'

'Believe it or not it was 1958!'

'1958? Don't believe it,' came the chorus.

'Truthfully, as I am sitting here.'

'You might believe you experienced it, but it would never have happened.'

'I'm telling you,' came the typically dogmatic Johannes reply.

'You could not be downloaded that number of years and come back with all your marbles in place, ref the Diderot case.'

'Johannes's marbles are never all in place even without downloading,' chirped Michelle.

'My marbles are in perfect order,' snapped Johannes.

'Oops,' Michelle giggled.

'I get it now,' Rees said, 'the Principal really is there but he gave you such a hard time that you temporarily lost the balance of your mind. You began believing you had been retrograde downloaded an absurd length of time into the past in order to psychologically block out his message. That pressure came on top of the incident in the Antique Laboratory Lecture Theatre – Johannes Taliesin the alien and all that. Sounds probable.'

'Sounds more like it, except the balance of Johannes's mind is permanently rather than temporarily lost,' Michelle teased.

'Rubbish! You two don't listen,' Johannes snapped. 'Twice I have told you the Principal is not in his room. In fact, there is nothing in his room. It is simply a portal to a 1958 life class. I was inveigled into going through that door because the tutor invited me in, saying they had been expecting me. He explained he had asked Price for a recalcitrant loony as a change to the top-rate adoptions previously, so Price—' Noisy laughter from the passing trade in the corridor interrupted the explanation. '—so Professor Price nominated me. Seriously.'

'Yes, yes, Yo-yo, now we are getting to the truth of it all,' said Michelle.

'Price nominated you?' queried Rees. 'Loony part is right but there's a flaw there somewhere.'

'I also believe there is a flaw there,' replied Johannes becoming irritated, 'but you try and find it. Price's order to report to the Principal was a ruse to get me to enter the Principal's door, that door, there.' He pointed.

'What about Price's bad mood?'

'Don't be silly, we know he was in a bad mood having been attacked by the Download FA Student. Even so, Price is always in a bad mood with me. This time especially I assume it was because he could not immediately locate me and his little project would be spoilt.'

'Yes, I'll buy that,' said Rees.

'I too was sceptical and asked a lot of questions to the extent that the students became upset with me – told me to stop bellyaching and get on with it.'

'Be fair, nothing new in Johannes bellyaching,' said Michelle.

'The tutor set up old-fashioned drawing equipment,' continued Johannes, ignoring Michelle, 'a wooden drawing board set up on a tripod easel, like the ones monitoring vids are set on, only made of wood. Then a large sheet of creamy-white cartridge paper with a peculiarly rough texture, and many graphite pencils of differing functions. All the materials and the studio itself possessed a peculiarly sweet smell of old paper, acetate and spirits. The students wore sweaters too big for them, even the girls, and their footwear was poor. They wore no perfume so strong body odours mixed with the acetate. The tutor told me to draw the model.'

'Draw the model?'

'Yes, draw the model. Shock horror, she was naked.'

'My God! Was she real-time naked or virtual?'

'Real-time naked.'

'How did you cope with that?' asked Michelle, her face glowing with interest.

'Badly, I'm afraid. She was blonde and beautiful – her skin was perfect considering history tells us 1958 was an austere time – but translating her body manually into meaningful lines on cartridge paper with old-fashioned pencils proved immensely difficult.'

'Joking!' Rees was incredulous.

'I struggled in vain and eventually returned a grotesque smudge! The other students produced superb master drawings à la Etty, Ingres and the like. They wouldn't believe I was studying at a school of art. I explained today's differences to theirs, but they couldn't understand, just kept staring at my smudge. The tutor described it as "an attempt at returning an impoverished alternative".'

Rees and Michelle burst into laughter.

'Nice one,' said Rees.

It was an embarrassing eye-opener. What we call art at VSofA is a sham,' said Johannes.

'Whatever experience you had it has made you grumpy,' said Michelle.

'What is grumpy about recognising the work we do here is a sham?' replied Johannes, 'In the school of art of their time they were producing superb drawings. I envy them their skill and togetherness. If I had possessed their drawing skill I would have been reluctant to return to this sham!'

'Was it *really* 1958?' asked referee Rees.

'Yes, the tutor assured me. The date came up during a discussion that referred to Picasso as if he were still alive. I advised them that from my perspective Picasso had died a long, long time ago, 1973 in fact, and they were convinced I was fantasising, as their date was 1958. Incidentally, what time is it now?'

'Eleven to one,' said Michelle, flashing her Ishihari.

'An old clock on a church tower was striking the quarter hours. Strange, but thinking about it the two times seem to tally – never known times to tally before. I've got a headache.'

'Understandable Price nominating you to represent the loony category,' Rees said with a shrug, 'but why set up a reverse download? What purpose would it serve? Got to be a flaw there somewhere.'

'Got to be a flaw,' Johannes agreed.

'Give us your view, Shelli.'

'They wanted to rid VSofA of Johannes,' she replied quick as a flash. 'Either that or Johannes is mistaken.'

'The reverse downloading must have been stressful,' Rees added.

'I've just had a thought – you two go visit the Principal, I'm sure you could invent a spurious reason for knocking on his door. Go on, witness for yourselves. If you have the courage,' Johannes said.

Suddenly Rees and Michelle were beset by their bravado. After a few moments, hesitancy, as the two looked furtively at each other, weighing their courage, Rees said, 'All right, we believe you, Johannes, but where does it get us?'

'It gets me back in Virtual Fashion,' said Michelle, her bluff called.

'Well, don't talk about it Michelle, do it,' said Johannes, greatly encouraged by his friend's submission.

'I'll just make it back in time – Nick's taking me out for lunch,' she said in an attempt to reclaim her pride.

Rees tossed his head in dissatisfaction; Johannes pulled a face.

She was about to depart yet again when an enormous commotion far down Corridor Escher cut a swathe through the throng. It was the ample form of Professor Price, his gown as usual billowing behind like a tethered whale.

'Uh-oh, checking up you've been to the Principal, no doubt. This should be worth watching,' said Rees, winking at Michelle.

'Can't wait, he set up the whole damn exercise. What's his complaint this time? No doubt it's about drawing smudges,' muttered Johannes aggressively.

'Ah! There you are Taliesin!' Professor Price shouted ahead. People stopped and stared. 'Why is it you cannot obey a simple instruction?'

'And what simple instruction have I not obeyed this time,

Professor Price?' Johannes asked in a tired as-if-I-didn't-know tone.

Professor Price reached the trio. Johannes remained seated as a mark of discourtesy. 'Professor Hancock has advised me he still awaits you. Why don't you go in, for God's sake, instead of gossiping here in the corridor with your fellow conspirators?'

The corridor traffic clustered, gaping at the unusual sight of a public reprimand.

'Be interesting to know when the Principal advised you,' retorted Johannes.

'Your obstreperousness compounds the problem, Mr Taliesin,' replied the professor angrily.

'Perhaps it would help if you had asked me before attacking. You see,' said Johannes in measured tone, 'I did, and he's not there.'

'What do you mean, you did?'

'I did. You should know, Professor Price. There's a 1958 life class in there instead, which I believe you are aware of. No sign of the Principal.' Johannes was exhibiting uncharacteristic signs of anger.

The impromptu audience gasped. Rees and Michelle glanced at each other nervously. This was a different Johannes: angry, assertive and implacably maintaining his line. They had doubted their friend and Price was getting the edge.

'*What*? What nonsense are you uttering this time?' Professor Price's voice assumed a falsetto.

'The life class. You know, the one you downloaded me to,' insisted Johannes, who then turned on the audience and, standing up, shouted angrily: 'What are you lot staring at? GO ON, GET ON WITH YOUR BUSINESS!'

Professor Price was taken aback. He stared wordless and open-mouthed at Johannes, at Rees and then at Michelle in turn. Swivelling briskly on a heel, he stormed to the Principal's door. Knocking just once and opening the door simultaneously, he peered around it. Johannes waited in angry silence.

'Taliesin here to see you, sir.'

What followed no one was able to retell. Price's head jerked back in surprise, his mop of dark hair swishing. A strange voice mumbled some indiscernible words from behind the half-open door.

'Good God!' boomed Professor Price loud and clear. 'Hard to believe! This is what Taliesin described – astonishing! Good God!'

Professor Price gingerly entered the Principal's office, with a precautionary hand still holding the door. More inaudible talking followed; the professor's questioning voice rang above the other. The atmosphere was tense. Johannes motioned to Rees and Michelle.

'Go look for yourselves,' he hissed. 'You doubted me long enough. Go on, take advantage of the safer situation, but don't enter the portal.'

His friends reluctantly crept up to the half-open door and peered around it. Immediately Michelle gave a start and as usual clutched the nearest arm, which fortunately belonged to Rees. After a period of mumbled conversation and indiscernible noises Professor Price abruptly retreated from the Principal's room, bumping into the peeping toms behind him. But their presence seemed not to register with him, such was his preoccupation with the event beyond.

"Stonishing!' he exclaimed, shaking his head.

He closed the door behind him with both hands firmly on the knob, as when shutting out something feared, unwelcome. Before letting go, the professor rattled the large door by its knob to ensure proper closure. He then walked slowly back to Johannes, who had remained rooted to his spot throughout, waiting for the doubting Thomases to witness for themselves.

'Well?' asked Johannes, 'am I right?'

'Yes, it's astonishing,' the professor said distantly, his face pale, expression glazed, voice mellow, anger gone.

'What did you see?'

'Incomprehensible.'

Rees and Michelle joined them. They stared at Johannes, Rees wearing a quizzical expression, blinking absent-mindedly, Michelle's features a mixture of alarm and panic as she clung like glue to Rees' arm. Professor Price continued shaking his head in disbelief, the while sneaking a glance at the door as if it were about to burst open again.

'How long were you in there?' he asked.

'Can't figure it out exactly,' replied Johannes, 'but it must have been the best part of half an hour.'

'HALF AN HOUR?'

'Thereabouts.'

'My God, Taliesin, we need to get you off to the Medical Centre pronto!' said the professor, suddenly displaying all sorts of care and welfare concerns for his student.

'What did you see?' Johannes asked Rees and Michelle, airily ignoring Professor Price's tone of panic.

They were deeply stunned; 'You were right,' Michelle muttered.

'In there,' Professor Price said, pointing towards the Principal's door, 'they confirm you had visited them. 'Xtrordinary!'

'Is there a Life Class?' quizzed Johannes assertively.

'Yes, a Life Class, in the Principal's office, expanded enormously,' he rambled. 'Obviously the main computer is double-phasing a quanglement transaction in accord with an event that occurred in that very room a long time ago. Let me make it clear, Taliesin, contrary to what you believe, I had nothing to do with it. God only knows what has happened to our Principal. I fear the worst. Incidentally, the tutor is not very flattering about your drawing skills. What beats me is how you managed to emerge in one—'

'Johannes?' Michelle interrupted.

'Taliesin? Are you listening to me? Taliesin!' Professor Price's voice registered alarm.

'Yo-yo! What's happening to you?' Rees called.

'Hell's teeth, we're losing him. Quick, Bowen, give me your suppressor. Quick!'

They scrambled in panic to unhook Rees's suppressor from his belt.

'Hold on, Taliesin!' Professor Price shouted, as he fumbled to activate it.

But it was too late.

'Johannnes!' Michelle yelled.

'Yo-yo?'

'Oh, my God, we've lost him!' said the professor despairingly.

'He's gone!' Michelle cried, 'he's GONE! DO something quick!'

But there was nothing they could do. Rees stared hopefully at the closed door of the Principal's office in stunned silence. They looked about despairingly, up Corridor Escher and down it. Johannes was nowhere to be seen. Michelle burst into tears. Johannes had gone.

IEUAN PUGH was born and grew up in rural mid-Wales. After attending Ardwyn Grammar School at Aberystwyth he trained at Swansea College of Art and Cardiff College of Art. He specialised in painting.

Pugh held many middle-management positions in art education before taking up the post of Principal at Bournville College of Art in 1981. He was a founder of the Birmingham Institute of Art and Design in 1987, and was appointed Principal of Loughborough College of Art and Design in 1989.Following the death of his partner, Gillian, he took early retirement in 1996.

He has mounted scores of one-man exhibitions of his oil paintings and drawings. Over one hundred of his works are in public and private collections. After mounting a major one-man show of paintings and drawings in the Gregynog Gallery at the National Library of Wales in 2004, Pugh focussed more on writing. *The Day God Met Father and Other Fables* is the first structured book to emerge from his many scripts. He is currently working on a second volume *Dead Man Airbrushed*.

Two elements of good fortune have influenced the author's creative work: he was born with a colour-hearing syndrome, known as synaesthesia; and his father, Evan, and uncle Maldwyn were enthrallingly idiosyncratic individuals who strongly influenced the patterns of his thinking. It was Maldwyn who first kindled and later nurtured Ieuan's interest in painting, and his father was an enthusiastic wordsmith of the genre of short sketch writing.

Although synaesthesia was a hindrance to Ieuan's early learning, the syndrome has nevertheless enriched the author's perception and imagination. For him words, especially names nouns and numerals, are perceived as possessing sound, meaning and colour simultaneously. The discrete colour-sounds appear set against a background tapestry. Often the author writes pieces that conform to a colour scheme, which are fun as creative writing but a little obtrusive when compiling an official report!

The eccentric natures of the author's father and uncle unwittingly injected colour and texture into everyday experiences. Their idiosyncrasies were prime instigators of creative thought. Both his father and uncle were naturally born eccentrics who spent their days striving to conform to the 'normality' of everyday life. Upon entering the art fraternity the author discovered the profound irony in this when he found himself surrounded by normal people striving to be 'eccentric' artists! The paradox has never gone away.

Printed in the United Kingdom
by Lightning Source UK Ltd.
126028UK00001B/16-48/A